TRAITORS' GATE

Anne Perry was born in London and lived abroad for some time before moving to her present home in the Scottish highlands. She has established a reputation for bestselling murder mysteries of the highest quality.

ANNE PERRY

Traitors' Gate

HarperCollins*Publishers*

This novel is entirely a work of fiction.
The names, characters and incidents portrayed in it
are the work of the author's imagination.
Any resemblance to actual persons, living or dead,
is entirely coincidental.

HarperCollins*Publishers*
77–85 Fulham Palace Road,
Hammersmith, London W6 8JB

This paperback edition 1997

1 3 5 7 9 8 6 4 2

First published in Great Britain by
HarperCollins*Publishers* 1996

Copyright © Anne Perry 1995

The Author asserts the moral right to
be identified as the author of this work

ISBN 0 00 649817 5

Set in Goudy

Printed and bound in Great Britain by
Caledonian International Book Manufacturing Ltd, Glasgow

To Donald Maass—with thanks

CHAPTER
ONE

Pitt sat back on the wooden seat and watched with profound pleasure as the sun faded on the old apple tree in the center of the lawn and for a few moments gilded the rough bark. They had only been in the new house a matter of weeks, but already it had a familiarity about it as if he were returning rather than moving in for the first time. It was many small things: the light on the patch of stone wall at the end of the garden, the bark of the trees, the smell of grass deep in the shade under the branches.

It was early evening and there were moths fluttering and drifting in the early May air, which was already cooler as twilight approached. Charlotte was inside somewhere, probably upstairs seeing the children to bed. He hoped she had also thought of supper. He was surprisingly hungry, considering he had done little all day but enjoy the rare full Saturday at home. That was one of the benefits of having been promoted to Superintendent when Micah Drummond had retired: he had more time. The disadvantages were that he carried far more responsibility and found himself, rather too often for his wishes, behind a desk in Bow Street instead of out investigating.

He settled a little lower in the seat and crossed his legs, smiling without being aware of it. He was dressed in old clothes, suitable for the gardening he had done through the day very casually, now and then.

There was a click as the French doors opened and closed behind him.

"Please sir . . ."

It was Gracie, the little waif of a maid they had brought with them, and who was now filled with importance and satisfaction because she had a woman in five days a week to do the heavy scrubbing and the laundry, and a gardener's boy three days. This fell under the heading of a considerable staff. Pitt's promotion had been hers as well, and she was immensely proud of it.

"Yes, Gracie," he said without getting up.

"There's a gentleman to see you, sir, a Mr. Matthew Desmond. . . ."

Pitt was stunned, motionless for a moment, then he shot to his feet and turned to face her.

"Matthew Desmond?" he repeated incredulously.

"Yes sir." She looked startled. "Shouldn't I 'ave let 'im in?"

"Yes! Yes, certainly you should. Where is he?"

"In the parlor, sir. I offered 'im a cup o' tea but 'e wouldn't 'ave it. 'E looks awful upset, sir."

"Right," he said absently, brushing past her and striding to the doors. He pulled them open and went into the sitting room. It was now filled with the last sunlight and looking oddly golden, in spite of its green and white furnishings. "Thank you," he added over his shoulder to Gracie. He went into the hall, his heart beating faster and his mouth suddenly dry with anticipation and something not unlike guilt.

He hesitated for a moment, a confusion of memories teeming through his mind and stretching as far back as consciousness would take him. He had grown up in the country, on the Desmond estate, where his father had been gamekeeper. He was an only child, as was Sir Arthur's son, a year younger than Pitt. And when Matthew Desmond had longed for someone to play with in the huge and beautiful grounds, Sir Arthur had found it natural enough to choose the gamekeeper's son. It had been an easy friendship from the beginning, and in time had extended to the schoolroom as well. Sir Arthur had been pleased enough to include a second child and watch his own son's application improve, with someone to share his lessons and to compete against him.

Even with Pitt's father's disgrace when he was unjustly accused of poaching (not on Sir Arthur's lands, but those of his nearest neighbor), the family were permitted to remain on the estate, with rooms in the servants' quarters, and Pitt himself had not been denied his continued education while his mother worked in the kitchens.

But it had been fifteen years now since Pitt had been back, and at least ten since he had had any contact with Sir Arthur or Matthew. As he stood in the hallway with his hand on the doorknob, it was not only guilt that stirred in his mind but a sense of foreboding.

He opened the door and went in.

Matthew turned from the mantelshelf, which he had been standing near. He had changed little: he was still tall, lean, almost narrow, with a long, erratic, humorous face, although all the laughter was bleached out of him now and he looked haggard and intensely serious.

"Hello, Thomas," he said quietly, coming forward and offering his hand.

Pitt took it and held it firmly, searching Matthew's face. The signs of grief were so obvious it would have been offensive and ridiculous to pretend not to have seen them.

"What is it?" he asked, sickeningly sure he already knew.

"Father," Matthew said simply. "He died yesterday."

Pitt was completely unprepared for the sense of loss which swept over him. He had not seen Arthur Desmond since before he had married and had children. He had only written letters to mark these events. Now he felt a loneliness, almost as if his roots had been torn away. A past he had taken for granted was suddenly no longer there. He had kept meaning to return. At first it had been a matter of pride which had kept him away. He would go back when he could show them all that the gamekeeper's son had achieved success, honor. Of course it had taken far longer than in his innocence he had supposed. As the years passed it had become harder, the distance too difficult to bridge. Now, without warning, it had become impossible.

"I ... I'm sorry," he said to Matthew.

Matthew tried to smile, at least in acknowledgment, but it was a poor effort. His face still looked haunted.

"Thank you for coming to tell me," Pitt went on. "That was ... very good of you." It was also far more than he deserved, and he knew it in a flush of shame.

Matthew dismissed it almost impatiently with a wave of his hand.

"He ..." He swallowed and took a deep breath, his eyes on Pitt's face. "He died at his club, here in London."

Pitt was going to say he was sorry again, but it was pointless, and he ended saying nothing.

"Of an overdose of laudanum," Matthew went on. His eyes searched Pitt's face, seeking understanding, assurance of some answer to pain.

"Laudanum?" Pitt repeated it to ascertain he had heard correctly. "Was ... was he ill? Suffering from—"

"No!" Matthew cut him off. "No, he was not ill. He was seventy, but he was in good health and good spirits. There was nothing wrong with him at all." He looked angry as he said it and there was a fierce defensiveness in his voice.

"Then why was he taking laudanum?" Pitt's policeman's mind pursued the details and the logic of it in spite of his emotions, or Matthew's.

"He wasn't," Matthew said desperately. "That's the point! They are saying he was old and losing his wits, and that he took an overdose because he no longer knew what he was doing." His eyes were blazing and he was poised ready to fly at Pitt if he even suspected him of agreeing.

Pitt remembered Arthur Desmond as he had known him: tall, ineffably elegant in the casual way of those who have both confidence and a natural grace, and yet at the same time almost always untidy. His clothes did not match each other. Even with a valet's best attention, he managed to select something other than whatever was put out for him. Yet such was his innate dignity, and the humor in his long, clever face, that no one even noticed, much less thought to criticize. He had been highly individual, at times eccentric, but always with such a basic sanity, and tolerance of human frailty, that he should have been the last man on earth to resort to laudanum at all. But if he had, then he was quite capable of absentmindedly dosing himself twice.

Except that surely once would have sent him to sleep anyway?

Pitt had vague memories of Sir Arthur's having long wakeful spells even thirty years ago, when Pitt had stayed overnight in the hall as a child. Then Sir Arthur had simply got up and wandered around the library until he found a book he fancied, and sat in one of the old leather chairs and gone to sleep with it open in his lap.

Matthew was waiting, staring at Pitt with mounting anger.

"Who is saying this?" Pitt asked.

Matthew was taken aback. It was not the question he was expecting.

"Uh—the doctor, the men at the club . . ."

"What club?"

"Oh—I am not being very clear, am I? He died at the Morton Club, in the late afternoon."

"In the afternoon? Not at night at all?" Pitt was genuinely surprised, he did not have to affect it.

"No! That's the point, Thomas," Matthew said impatiently. "They are saying he was demented, suffering from a sort of senile decay. It's not true, not even remotely! Father was one of the sanest men alive. And he didn't drink brandy either! At least, hardly ever."

"What has brandy to do with it?"

Matthew's shoulders sagged and he looked exhausted and utterly bewildered.

"Sit down," Pitt directed. "There is obviously more to this than you have told me so far. Have you eaten? You look terrible."

Matthew smiled wanly. "I really don't want to eat. Don't fuss over me, just listen."

Pitt conceded, and sat down opposite him.

Matthew sat on the edge of his chair, leaning forward, unable to relax.

"As I said, Father died yesterday. He was at his club. He had been there most of the afternoon. They found him in his chair when the steward went to tell him the time and ask if he wished for dinner. It was getting late." He winced. "They said he'd been drinking a lot of brandy, and they thought he'd had rather too much and fallen asleep. That's why nobody disturbed him before."

Pitt did not interrupt him but sat with an increasing weight of sadness for what he now knew would come.

"Of course when they did speak to him, they found he was dead," Matthew said bleakly. The effort of control in his voice was so naked that for anyone else Pitt would have been embarrassed; but now it was only an echo of what he himself was feeling. There were no questions to ask. It was not a crime, not even an event hard to understand. It was simply a bereavement, more sudden than most, and therefore carrying a kind of shock. But looked on with hindsight it would probably be a loss such as happens in most families sooner or later.

"I'm sorry," he said quietly.

"You don't understand!" All the rage built up in Matthew's face again. He looked at Pitt almost accusingly. Then he drew in a deep breath and let it out with a sigh. "You see, Father belonged to some sort of society—oh, it was benevolent, at least he used to think it was. They supported all sorts of charities. . . ." He waved his hand in the air to dismiss the matter. "I don't know what, precisely. He never told me."

Pitt felt cold, and unreasonably betrayed.

"The Inner Circle," he said, the words grating between his teeth.

Matthew was stunned. "You knew! How did you know, when I didn't?" He looked hurt, as if somehow Pitt had broken a trust. Upstairs there was a bang and the sound of running feet. Neither took notice.

"I'm guessing," Pitt replied with a smile that turned into a wince. "It is an organization I know a little about."

Matthew's expression hardened, almost as if some door had closed over his candor and now he was wary, no longer the friend, almost brother, that he had been.

"Are you a member? No, I am sorry. That's a stupid question, isn't it? Because you wouldn't tell me if you were. That's how you knew Father was. Did you join with him, all those years ago? He never invited me!"

"No I did not join," Pitt said tartly. "I never heard of it until recently, when I tangled with them in the course of my work. I've prosecuted a few of their members, and exposed several others for involvement in fraud, blackmail and murder. I probably know a great deal more about them than you do, and just how damnably dangerous they are."

Outside in the corridor Charlotte spoke to one of the children, and the footsteps died away.

Matthew sat silent for several moments, the emotions that churned through his mind reflecting in his eyes and the tired, vulnerable lines in his face. He was still suffering from shock; he had not accustomed himself to the knowledge that his father was dead. Grief was barely in check, the sudden loneliness, regret, a little guilt—even if he had no idea for what: simply chances missed, words unused. And he was terribly tired, wrung out additionally by the anger which consumed him. He had been disappointed in Pitt, perhaps even betrayed; and then immensely relieved, and again guilty, because he had accused him wrongly.

It was no time to require apologies. Matthew was near to breaking.

Pitt held out his hand.

Matthew clasped it so tightly his fingers bruised the flesh.

Pitt allowed him a moment or two of pure emotion, then recalled him to his story.

"Why did you mention the Inner Circle?"

Matthew made an effort, and began again in a more level voice, but still sitting far forward in his chair, his elbows on his knees and his hands under his chin.

"Father was always involved only with the strictly charitable side, until quite recently, the last year or two, when he rose higher in the organization. More by accident than design, I think. He began to learn a lot more about them, and what else they did, who some of the other members were." He frowned. "Particularly concerning Africa . . ."

"Africa?" Pitt was startled.

"Yes—Zambezia especially. There is a lot of exploration going on there at the moment. It's a very long story. Do you know anything about it?"

"No . . . nothing at all."

"Well naturally there's a great deal of money concerned, and the possibility of unimaginable wealth in the future. Gold, diamonds, and of course land. And there were all sorts of other questions as well, missionary work, trade, foreign policy."

"What has the Inner Circle to do with it?"

Matthew pulled a rueful face. "Power. It always has to do with power, and the sharing out of wealth. Anyway, Father began to appreciate just how the senior members of the Inner Circle were influencing policy in the government, and the South Africa Company, to their own advantage, regardless of the welfare of the

Africans, or of British interests, either, for that matter. He got very upset about it indeed, and started to say so."

"To the other members of his own ring?" Pitt asked, although he feared he knew what Matthew would reply.

"No . . . to anyone who would listen." Matthew looked up, his eyes questioning. He saw the answer in Pitt's face. "I think they murdered him," he said quietly.

The silence was so intense they could hear the ticking of the walnut clock on the mantelshelf. Outside in the street, beyond the closed windows, someone shouted and the answer came back from farther away, a garden somewhere in the blue twilight.

Pitt did not dismiss it. The Inner Circle would quite readily do such a thing, if it felt the need great enough. He doubted not its resolve or ability . . . simply need.

"What was he saying about them, exactly?"

"You don't disbelieve it?" Matthew asked. "You don't sound shocked that distinguished members of the British aristocracy, the ruling classes, the honorable gentlemen of the country, should indulge in the murder of someone who chose to criticize them in public."

"I went through all my emotions of shock and disbelief when I first learned about the Inner Circle and their purposes and codes of conduct," Pitt replied. "I expect I shall feel anger and outrage all over again sometime, but at the moment I am trying to understand the facts. What was Sir Arthur saying that would make it necessary for the Inner Circle to take the dangerous step of killing him?"

For the first time Matthew sat back in his chair, crossing his legs, his eyes still on Pitt's face. "He criticized their general morality," he said in a steadier voice. "The way they are sworn to favor each other secretly, and at the expense of those who are outside the Circle, which is most of us. They do it in business, banking, politics and socially if they can, although that is harder." His smile twisted. "There are still the unwritten laws that govern who is accepted and who is not. Nothing can force that. You may impel a gentleman to be civil to you, if he owes you money, but you can never force him to look on you as one of his own, whatever he owes you, up to and including his life." He did not find it curious, nor did he seek words for the indefinable quality of assurance which made a gentleman. It had nothing to do with intelligence, achievement, money or title. A man might have all these and yet still fail to meet the invisible criteria. Matthew had been born to it; he understood it as some men know how to ride a horse, or to sing in tune.

"It includes too many gentlemen," Pitt said sourly, memory returning of past cases and his bitter involvement with the Circle.

"That is more or less what Father said," Matthew agreed, his eyes on Pitt's face with a deepening intensity. "Then he went on quite specifically about Africa and the way they are controlling banking, whose interests control the funds for exploration and settlement. They are hand-and-hand with the politicians who will decide whether we try for a Cape-to-Cairo domination or concede to the Germans and concentrate on the south." He shrugged with a quick, angry gesture. "As always the Foreign Secretary is hovering around, saying one thing, and meaning another. I work in the Foreign Office, and I don't know myself what he really wants. There are missionaries, doctors, explorers, profiteers, big game hunters and Germans swarming all over the place." He bit his lip ruefully. "Not to mention the native kings and warrior princes whose land it is anyway ... until we wring treaties out of them for it. Or the Germans do."

"And the Inner Circle?" Pitt prompted.

"Manipulating behind the scenes," Matthew replied. "Calling in old loyalties secretly, investing quietly and reaping the reward. That's what Father was saying." He slid a little farther back in the seat and began to relax fractionally; or perhaps he was just so tired he could no longer sit upright. "What he objected to most intensely was the way the whole thing is secret. To give charity anonymously is fine and a perfectly honorable thing to do."

They were both oblivious of the sounds of movement in the passage beyond.

"That's what he originally thought the society was for," he went on. "A group of men banded together to have a better knowledge of where help was needed, and not to do it piecemeal, but with sufficient means to make a real difference. Orphanages, hospitals for the needy, and for research into specific illnesses, almshouses for old soldiers . . . that sort of thing. Then just recently he discovered the other side to it." He bit his lip, almost apologetically. "Father was a trifle naive, I think. You or I would have realized there was more to it a lot sooner. He thought the best of many people I would not have."

Pitt recalled what he knew of the Inner Circle.

"Didn't they warn him very quickly that they do not take criticism kindly, in fact they don't take it at all?"

"Yes! Yes they did. They warned him in gentlemanly and discreet terms, which he misread completely. It never occurred to him that they really meant it." Matthew's eyebrows rose and his hazel eyes looked at once amused and bitterly hurt. Pitt had a curious sensation of respect for him, and realized the depth of his resolve, not only to clear his father of any suggestion of weakness, but perhaps also to avenge him.

"Matthew," he began, leaning forward spontaneously.

"If you are going to warn me to leave it alone, you are wasting your time," Matthew said stubbornly.

"I . . ." That was precisely what Pitt had been going to do. It was disconcerting to be read so easily. "You don't even know who they are," he pointed out. "At least stop and think very hard before you do anything." It sounded feeble, desperately predictable.

Matthew smiled. "Poor Thomas, so much the elder brother. We are not children now, and one year doesn't make your seniority worth anything. It hasn't since we were ten! Of course I shall think carefully. That's why I've come to you. I know perfectly well I can't wound the Circle. It's a Hydra. Cut off one head and two more will grow." His face hardened again and all the light vanished out of it. "But I'm going to prove Father was not senile, or get killed in the attempt myself." He looked at Pitt very levelly, meeting his eyes without a flicker. "If we allow them to say such things about a man like Father, to silence him with murder, and then discredit him by saying he had lost his wits, then apart from anything else, what have we left? What have we made of ourselves? What honor can we claim?"

"None," Pitt said sadly. "But we need more than honor to win that battle; we need a great deal of tactical skill as well, and some sharp weapons." Pitt grimaced. "Or perhaps a long spoon will be more appropriate."

Matthew's eyebrows rose. "To sup with the devil? Yes, well put. Have you a long spoon, Thomas? Are you willing to join me in the battle?"

"Yes of course I am." He spoke without even thinking about it. Only the moment after did all the dangers and the responsibilities come closing in on his mind, but it was too late. And even if he had thought about it and weighed every one, he would still have made the same decision. The only difference would have been the sense of anguishing over it, the fear and the understanding of risk, and the margin of success that could be hoped for. Perhaps that would have been only so much time wasted anyway.

Matthew relaxed at last, allowing his head to rest against the antimacassar behind him. He smiled. Something of the tiredness and the look of defeat had been ironed out of his features. At a glance he almost resembled the youth Pitt had known so long ago, with whom he had shared adventures and dreams. They seemed both immensely wild, full of impossibilities—journeys up the Amazon, discoveries of the tombs of Pharaohs—and at the same time boyishly tame, still with the gentle, domestic ideas of right and wrong, children's notions of wickedness: theft of goods and simple violence the worst they knew. They had not imagined corruption, disillusion, manipulation and betrayal. It all seemed very innocent now, the boys they had been long ago.

"There were warnings," Matthew said suddenly. "I can see that now, although at the time I didn't. I was up here in London when they happened, and he made light of it each time."

"What were they?" Pitt asked.

Matthew screwed up his face. "Well, the first I cannot be sure about. As Father told it to me, he was traveling on the underground railway, at least he was intending to. He went down the steps to the platform and was waiting for the train—" He stopped abruptly and looked at Pitt. "Have you ever been on one of those things?"

"Yes, frequently." Pitt pictured the cavernous passages, the long stations where the tunnel widened to allow a platform alongside the train, the dark curved roof, the glaring gaslights, the incredible noise as the engine rattled and roared out of the black hole into the light and came to a halt. Doors flew open and people poured out. Others waiting took their opportunity and pressed in before the doors should close and the wormlike contraption be on its way back into the darkness again.

"Then I don't need to explain the noise and the crowds pushing and shoving each other," Matthew continued. "Well, Father was fairly well towards the front and just as he heard the train coming, he felt a violent weight in the middle of his back and was propelled forward almost over the edge of the platform onto the lines, where of course he would have been killed." Matthew's voice hardened and there was a harsh edge to it. "He was grasped and hauled back just as the train appeared and came hurtling in. He said he turned to thank whomever it was, but there was no longer any person there he could distinguish as his helper—or his assailant. Everyone seemed to be about the business of boarding the train, and no one took the least notice of him."

"But he was sure he was pushed?"

"Quite sure." Matthew waited for Pitt to express some skepticism.

Pitt nodded barely perceptibly. With someone else, someone he knew less closely, he might have doubted; but unless he had changed beyond recognition, Arthur Desmond was the last man on earth to believe he was being persecuted. He viewed all men as basically good until he was forced to do otherwise, and then it came to him as a shock and a sadness, and he was still ready to find himself mistaken, and delighted to be so.

"And the second?" Pitt asked.

"That was something to do with a horse," Matthew replied. "He never told me the details." He sat forward again, his brow creasing. "I only knew about it at all because the groom told me when I was home. It seems Father was riding down in the village when some unexpected idiot came down the road at a full gallop, completely out of control of his animal. He was careering all over the place, one side of the road to the other, arms flying, whip in his hand, and he just about drove Father into the stone wall alongside the vicarage. Caught his horse a terrible blow about the head with his whip. Terrified the poor beast, and of course Father was thrown." He let out his breath slowly, without moving his eyes from Pitt's face. "It could conceivably have been an accident; the man was either drunken out of his senses or a complete imbecile, but Father didn't think so, and I certainly don't."

"No," Pitt said grimly. "Neither do I. He was a damn good horseman, and not the sort of man to imagine things of anyone."

Suddenly Matthew smiled, a wide, generous smile that made him look years younger. "That's the best thing I have heard anyone say in weeks. Dear God, I wish his friends could hear you. Everyone is so afraid to praise him, even to acknowledge his sanity, never mind that he might have been right." There was sudden hurt in his voice. "Thomas, he was sane, wasn't he? The sanest and most honorable and innately decent man ever to walk the land."

"Yes he was," Pitt agreed quietly and with total honesty. "But apart from that, it doesn't rest on his sanity. I know the Inner Circle punishes those who betray it. I've seen it before. Sometimes it is social or financial ruin—not often death, but it is not unknown. If they couldn't frighten him, and they obviously couldn't, then there was nothing else for them to do. They couldn't ruin him financially because he didn't gamble or speculate. They couldn't socially because he didn't curry favor with anyone, or seek any office or alliances, and he couldn't have cared less about being accepted at court, or in the social circles of London. Where he lived his standing was unassailable, even by the Inner Circle. So there was only death left to them, to silence him permanently."

"And then to nullify all he said by dishonoring his memory." Matthew's voice was filled with anger, and pain flooded back into his face. "I can't bear that, Thomas. I won't!"

There was a knock on the parlor door. Pitt suddenly became aware again of where he was, and that it was nearly dark outside. He had not eaten, and Charlotte must be wondering who his visitor was and why he had gone into the parlor and closed the door without introducing her, or inviting the visitor to dine.

Matthew looked at him expectantly, and Pitt was surprised to see there was a flicker of nervousness across his face, as if he were uncertain how he should behave.

"Come in." Pitt rose to his feet and reached to open the door. Charlotte was standing outside looking curious and a little anxious. She had finished reading to the children and from the faint flush in her cheeks and the stray hair poked into a misplaced pin, he knew she had been in the kitchen. He had even forgotten he was hungry. "Charlotte, this is Matthew Desmond." It was ridiculous that they had never met before. Matthew had been closer to him than anyone else except his mother, at times closer than even she. And Charlotte was closer to him now than he had imagined anyone could be. And he had never taken her back to Brackley, never introduced her to his home, or to those who had been more than family to him before she was. His mother had died when he was eighteen, but that should not have cut the ties.

"How do you do, Mr. Desmond," Charlotte said with a calm and confidence Pitt knew was the product of her birth, not of any inner emotion. He saw the uncertainty in her eyes and knew why she moved a step closer to him.

"How do you do, Mrs. Pitt," Matthew replied, and his voice lifted very slightly with surprise because she answered his look squarely. In that brief second, with no more than a sentence and a meeting of glances, they had taken a certain measure of each other, understood the precise niche in society which they filled. "I am sorry to intrude, Mrs. Pitt," Matthew went on. "I am afraid it was most selfish of me. I came to tell Thomas of my father's death, and I regret that all consideration for anyone else went straight out of my head. I apologize."

Charlotte looked across at Pitt this time, her face full of shock and sympathy, then back to Matthew. "I am sorry, Mr. Desmond. You must be feeling quite terrible. Is there anything we can do to be of practical assistance? Would you like Thomas to go back to Brackley with you?"

Matthew smiled. "Actually, Mrs. Pitt, I wanted Thomas to find out precisely what happened, and that he has already promised to do."

Charlotte took breath to say something else, then realized perhaps it was inappropriate, and changed her mind.

"Would you like some supper, Mr. Desmond? I imagine you do not feel like eating, but you may feel worse if you leave it too long."

"You are quite right," he agreed. "On all counts."

She looked at him closely, at the distress and the weariness in his face. She hesitated on the edge of decision for a moment, then made her judgment.

"Would you like to stay here overnight, Mr. Desmond? It will be no inconvenience whatever. In fact you would be our first guest since moving here, and we should like that very much. If there is anything you need, and have not with you, Thomas could lend it to you."

He did not need to consider it. "Thank you," he said immediately. "I would far rather that than return to my rooms."

"Thomas will show you upstairs and have Gracie prepare the bedroom for you. Supper will be served in ten minutes." And she turned, with only a glance at Pitt, and retreated towards the kitchen.

Matthew stood for a moment in the hallway looking at Pitt. All sorts of half thoughts were plain in his face: surprise, understanding, memories of the past, of long talks and even longer dreams when they were boys, and some of all the distance between then and now. No explanations were necessary.

Supper was a light meal anyway: cold roast chicken and vegetables, and a fruit sorbet afterwards. It was hardly a time when it mattered, but Pitt was glad Matthew had come after his promotion, and it had not been during the time when mutton stew and potatoes, or whiting and bread and butter, were all they could have offered.

They spoke little, and that merely of unemotional subjects such as plans for the garden, what they hoped to grow in the future, whether all the fruit trees were likely to bear, or how badly they were in need of pruning. It was only to fill the silence, not any attempt to pretend that all was well. Charlotte knew as well as Pitt that grief must be allowed its time. To prevent it by constant diversion only increased the pain, like a denial of the importance of the event, as if the loss did not matter.

Matthew retired early, leaving Charlotte in the green-and-white sitting room with Pitt. To have called it a withdrawing room would have been pretentious, but it had all the charm and cool ease that would serve such a purpose.

"What did he mean?" she asked as soon as Matthew had had time to be up the stairs beyond hearing. "What was wrong with Sir Arthur's death?"

Slowly, finding words harder than he had expected to, he told her all that Matthew had said about Sir Arthur and the Inner Circle, the warnings he felt they had given him, and finally his death from laudanum at the Morton Club.

She listened without taking her eyes from his, and without interruption. He wondered if she could see in his face, as transparently as he felt them, both his grief and his sense of guilt. He was not even sure if he wanted her to know it. It was a bitterly lonely thing to hide, and yet he did not wish her to see him as the thoughtless man he felt, careless of so many years of past kindness that he had not been back, and now all he could do was repay a fraction of the debt by trying to redeem Sir Arthur's name from a dishonor he knew it did not deserve.

If she perceived it in him, she did not say so. Charlotte could be the most wildly tactless of people at times. And yet when she loved someone, her commitment was such that she could keep any secret, and refrain from judgment in a way few people matched.

"He is the last man to have taken laudanum at all," he said earnestly. "But even if he had, for some reason we know nothing of, I can't let them say he was senile. It's—it's an indignity."

"I know." She reached out her hand and took his. "You don't speak of him often, but I do know you feel very deeply for him. But regardless of that, it is an injustice one should not let by for anyone at all." Her eyes were troubled and for the first time since he had begun, she was uncertain of his reaction. "But Thomas . . ."

"What?"

"Don't let emotion . . ." She chose the word carefully, leaving the implication of guilt unsaid, although he was certain she knew that was what he felt. "Don't let emotion prompt you into rushing in without thought and preparation. They are not enemies you can afford to take lightly. They have no honor in the way they fight. They won't give you a second chance because you are bereaved, or rash, or motivated by loyalty. Once they realize you mean to fight them, they will try to provoke you into those very mistakes. I know you will remember Sir Arthur's death, and that will fire you to want to beat them: but also remember the way in which they killed him, how successful it was for their purposes, and how completely ruthless."

She shivered and looked increasingly unhappy, as if her own words had frightened her. "If they will do that to one of their own, imagine what they will do to an enemy, like you." She looked for a moment as if she were going to add something—perhaps a plea for him to think again, to weigh the chances of achieving anything—but she changed her mind. Probably she knew it would be pointless now, of all times. He did not suspect her of duplicity ever—she had not the heart for it, nor the temper—but possibly she was learning a little tact.

He answered the unspoken question. "I have to," he said gently. "The alternative is intolerable."

She did not say anything, but held his hand more tightly, and sat still beside him for a long time.

In the morning Matthew slept late and Charlotte and Pitt were already at breakfast when he came into the dining room. Jemima and Daniel were already dressed and had walked to school with Gracie. This was a new task in which she took great satisfaction, stretching up to every fraction of her four feet eleven inches and smiling graciously to people she either knew or considered she would like to know. Charlotte suspected she also had a brief word with the butcher's assistant on the corner on her return, but that was neither here nor there. He seemed quite a respectable youth. Charlotte had made a point of going in on one or two occasions herself, in order to have a good look at him and estimate his character.

Matthew looked rested, but there were still dark circles of shock under his eyes, and his thick brown hair with its fair streak across the brow looked tousled and ill cut, although it was probably only the result of having combed it with haste and inattention.

The usual courtesies were exchanged and Charlotte offered him bacon, eggs, kidneys, and toast and marmalade. Automatically she poured tea for him and he drank it while it was still too hot, burning his mouth.

After several minutes of companionable silence, Charlotte excused herself and withdrew to the kitchen about some domestic chore, and Matthew looked up at Pitt.

"There's something else I really ought to speak to you about," he said with his mouth full.

"Yes?"

"This is in your official capacity." He took another sip of the tea, this time more carefully. "And mine too."

"The Foreign Office?" Pitt was startled.

"Yes. It's Africa again." He frowned in concentration. "I don't know if you know anything about our treaties . . . no? Well it doesn't matter a lot for what I'm going to say. But we did make an agreement with Germany four years ago in 1886, and we are looking towards another this summer. Of course it's all been altered by Bismarck's losing power and the young Kaiser taking over everything. He's got this wretched fellow Carl Peters, who is as sharp as a knife and tricky as a load of monkeys. And Salisbury not making up his mind what he really wants doesn't make anything easier. Half of us suppose he is still looking for British domination of a corridor from the Cape to Cairo. The other half think he prefers to let that go as too costly and too difficult."

"Difficult?" Pitt questioned with puzzlement.

"Yes," Matthew said, taking another slice of toast. "For a start it's over three thousand miles between British South Africa and British-controlled Egypt. That means taking Sudan, Equatoria—currently held by a slippery customer called Emin Pasha—a corridor west of German East Africa: not so easy in the present climate." He regarded Pitt seriously to make sure he was following. Then to explain more clearly he started drawing on the kitchen table with his forefinger. "The whole area north of Transvaal, and that includes Zambezia and the territories between Angola and Mozambique, is still held by native chiefs."

"I see," Pitt said vaguely. "And the alternative you mentioned?"

"Cairo to Old Calabar," Matthew replied, biting into his toast. "Or Niger to the Nile, if you like. That's through Lake Chad, then westwards nearly to Senegal, taking Dahomey and the Ivory Coast from the French . . ."

"War?" Pitt was incredulous, and appalled.

"No, no, of course not," Matthew said hastily. "In exchange for the Gambia."

"Oh, I see."

"No you don't, not yet. There's also the question of German East Africa, where there's been a lot of trouble, uprisings and several killings, and Heligoland. . . ."

"I beg your pardon?" Now Pitt was totally confused.

"Heligoland," Matthew repeated with his mouth full.

"I thought Heligoland was in the North Sea. I can remember Mr. Tarbet saying it was. I'd no idea it was anywhere near Africa."

"It is in the North Sea, just as Tarbet said." Mr. Tarbet had been Matthew's tutor as a child, and thus also Pitt's. "Ideally placed for a naval base to blockade all the principal German ports on the Rhine," Matthew explained. "We could trade Heligoland to the Germans for some of their lands in Africa. And believe me, they would be glad enough to do that, if we managed it really well."

Pitt smiled wryly. "I can see that you have an extraordinary number of highly complex problems. But what exactly do you wish to consult the police over? We have no writ in Africa, or even in Heligoland."

"But you do in London. And London is where the Colonial Office is, and the German Embassy. . . ."

"Oh." In spite of himself, Pitt was beginning to see, or to fear that he did.

"And the British Imperial South Africa Company," Matthew went on. "And the various banks who fund explorers and missionaries, not to mention the adventurers, both literal and financial."

"Unarguable," Pitt conceded. "Why is that relevant?"

The faint flicker of amusement died out of Matthew's eyes and he became serious.

"Because there is information disappearing from the Colonial Office, Thomas, and turning up in the German Embassy. We know that because of the bargaining issues the Germans are aware of, and they shouldn't be. Sometimes they know things almost before we do in the Foreign Office. It hasn't done any great damage yet, as far as we know, but it could very seriously jeopardize our chances of a successful treaty if it goes on."

"So someone in the Colonial Office is passing information to the German Embassy?"

"I cannot see any alternative explanation."

"What sort of information? Could it not have come from some other source? Surely they have men in East Africa too?"

"If you knew a little more about African affairs you wouldn't ask that." Matthew shrugged. "Every report one gets is different from the last, and most accounts are open to a dozen interpretations, especially where the native chiefs and princes are concerned. It is our Colonial Office version the Germans are getting."

"Information about what sort of thing?"

Matthew drank the rest of his tea.

"So far as we know, at the moment it is mostly about mineral deposits and trading negotiations between various factions and the native chiefs. In particular one in Zambezia called Lobengula. We were very much hoping the Germans were unaware of the stage of negotiations we had reached in that matter."

"But they are not?"

"Difficult to say, but I fear not."

Pitt finished his own tea and poured more, helping himself to another slice of toast out of the rack. He had a deep liking for homemade marmalade. Charlotte had a way of doing it that was so pungent the flavor seemed to fill his whole head. He had observed that Matthew liked it as well.

"You have a traitor in the Colonial Office," he said slowly. "Who else is aware of what you have told me?"

"My immediate superior, and the Foreign Secretary, Lord Salisbury."

"That's all?"

Matthew's eyes widened. "Good heavens, yes. We don't want people all over the place to know we have a spy in the Colonial Office. Nor do we want the spy himself to know we are aware of him. We need to clear up the whole matter before it does any real damage, and then keep quiet about it."

"I can't work without authority," Pitt began.

Matthew frowned. "I will write you a letter of authority if you like. But I thought you were a superintendent now. What more authority do you need?"

"My assistant commissioner's, if I am to start questioning people in the Colonial Office," Pitt replied.

"Oh, well him of course."

"You don't believe this has any connection with the other matter, do you?"

Matthew frowned for a moment, then his face cleared as he understood.

"Good God, I hope not! The Inner Circle is pretty low, but I had not imagined it was involved in treason, which is what this amounts to. No. So far as I know, and from everything Father said, the Inner Circle interests are best served by Britain remaining as powerful and as rich as possible. Britain's loss in Africa would be theirs as well. Their robbing us is one thing; the Germans doing it is quite another." He smiled bitterly at the irony of it. "Why do you ask? Do you think there are Inner Circle members in the Colonial Office?"

"Probably, but I'm quite sure there are in the police. Of what rank I have no idea."

"As high as assistant commissioner?" Matthew asked.

Pitt ate the last of his toast and marmalade.

"Certainly, but I meant of what rank in the Inner Circle. The two have no connection, which is one of the things that makes it so appallingly dangerous."

"I don't understand you."

"You can find that someone in a position of great financial or political power," Pitt explained, "is quite junior in the Circle, and owes some kind of obedience to an Inner Circle member who appears to be nobody significant in the world. You don't ever know where the real power lies."

"But surely that . . ." Matthew began, then trailed off, his eyes puzzled. "That would account for some very strange discoveries. . . ." he started again. "A web of loyalties under the surface, conflicting with, and stronger than, all the ones you can see." His face was pale and tight. "God, that's very frightening. I hadn't perceived it quite like that. No wonder Father was so distressed. I knew well enough why he was angry, but not the helplessness, at least not the depth of it." He stopped and sat silent for several moments. Then he went on suddenly. "But even if it is all hopeless, I shall still try. I can't let it . . . just lie like this."

Pitt said nothing.

"I'm sorry." Matthew bit his lip. "You were not trying to dissuade me, were you? I'm a little frightened of it myself. But you will take up the matter of the information from the Colonial Office?"

"Of course. As soon as I go in to Bow Street. I assume you are making the official Foreign Office request? I may use your name?"

"Yes, certainly." He put his hand in his pocket and pulled out an envelope. He passed it to Pitt. "Here is a letter of authority. And Thomas . . . thank you."

Pitt did not know what to say. To brush it aside as a small matter also dismissed their friendship and reduced it to mere good manners.

"What are you going to do now?" he asked instead.

Matthew looked so inwardly weary, the night's sleep, if indeed he had slept, was merely a superficial relief. He set his napkin aside and stood up.

"There are arrangements to be made. They—" He took a deep breath. "They are having the inquest the day after tomorrow."

"I'll be there."

"Thank you."

"And . . . the funeral?"

"Two days after that, on the sixth. You'll be there, won't you? It's in Brackley, naturally. He'll be buried in the family vault."

"Of course I will." Pitt stood up also. "Where are you going now? Back to the Hall?"

"No. No, the inquest is here in London. I still have things to do."

"Is there anyone . . . if you want to come back here?"

Matthew smiled. "Thank you, but I really should go and see Harriet. I . . ." He looked faintly embarrassed.

Pitt waited.

"I recently became betrothed," Matthew went on with a faint color marking his cheeks.

"Congratulations!" Pitt meant it. He would have been delighted for him at any time, but now it seemed particularly fortunate that he had someone who could support him and share this time of loss. "Yes of course you should see her, tell her what has happened before she sees it in some newspaper, or hears it from someone else."

Matthew pulled a face. "She won't be reading newspapers, Thomas!"

Pitt realized with a jolt that he had committed a social gaffe. Ladies did not read newspapers, except for the court circulars or fashion columns. He had become accustomed to Charlotte and her sister, Emily, who, since leaving their father's home, accepted no restrictions whatever upon what they would read. Even Lord Ashworth, Emily's first husband, had allowed her that unusual latitude.

"Of course. I should have said until someone who has read a newspaper mentions it to her," he apologized. "That would seem a thoughtless way of allowing her to hear of it. I am sure she would wish to be every support to you that she can."

"Yes ... I ..." Matthew shrugged. "It seems so heartless to be happy in any respect now. ..."

"Nonsense!" Pitt said fervently. "Sir Arthur would be the first person to wish you any comfort you can find, and happiness too. You really don't need me to assure you of that. You must know it for yourself, unless you have forgotten completely what manner of man he was." It seemed strange and painful to speak of him in the past, and suddenly without warning he was caught by grief again.

Matthew must have felt something of the same emotion. His face was very pale.

"Of course. I ... can't ... just yet. But I will go and see her, of course. She is a very fine woman, Thomas. You will like her. She is the daughter of Ransley Soames, at the Treasury."

"Again, congratulations!" Pitt held out his hand; it was an automatic gesture.

Matthew took it, smiling briefly.

"Now we had both better go," Pitt said. "I to Bow Street, and then to the Colonial Office."

"Yes indeed. I must find Mrs. Pitt and thank her for her hospitality. I wish ... I wish you had brought her to meet Father, Thomas. He would have liked her. ..." He swallowed hard and turned away to hide his sudden loss of control.

"So do I," Pitt agreed intensely. "It is one of the many things I shall regret." He went out of the room tactfully, to permit Matthew the privacy in which to compose himself. And he went upstairs to look for Charlotte.

In the Bow Street police station he was fortunate to find Assistant Commissioner Giles Farnsworth present. He came only occasionally, being in command of a very considerable area, and this was an unusual time for him to visit. Pitt had expected to reach him only after a considerable effort.

"Ah, good morning, Pitt," Farnsworth said briskly. He was a handsome man in a smooth, well-bred manner, with sleek fair hair, clean-shaven face, and clear, very level blue-gray eyes. "Glad you are here in good time. Nasty robbery last night in Great Wild Street. Lady Warburton's diamonds stolen. Haven't got a full list yet, but Sir Robert will have it ready by midday. Most unpleasant. See to it personally, will you. I promised Sir Robert I'd have my best man on it." He did not bother to look at Pitt to receive his answer. It was an order, not a suggestion.

When Micah Drummond had retired he had recommended Pitt to take his place with such fervor that Farnsworth had accepted it, but with considerable reservations. Pitt was not a gentleman, as Drummond had been, nor had he any previous experience of commanding men, such as a commissioned rank in the army, again, as Drummond had had. Farnsworth was accustomed to working with men of Drummond's social rank in the position of superintendent. It made matters so much easier. They understood each other, they knew the rules as lesser men do not, and they were comfortable as something approaching equals.

Pitt would never be socially equal with Farnsworth, and there would never be friendship between them. The fact that Drummond had regarded Pitt as a friend was one of those inexplicable lapses that even gentlemen make from time to time. Although usually it was with people who had some particular skill or art to recommend them, such as the breeding of fine horses, or the design of a great garden with follies, parterres of box or lavender, or some brilliant new mechanical device for waterfalls and fountains. Pitt had never before encountered anyone who had such a lapse of judgment over a professional junior.

"Mr. Farnsworth," Pitt stopped him as he was about to leave.

"Yes?" Farnsworth was surprised.

"Naturally I will attend to Lady Warburton's diamonds if you wish me to, but I would rather put Tellman onto it and leave myself free to go to the Colonial Office, where I have been informed there is a leak of vital information about African affairs."

"What?" Farnsworth was appalled. He swung around, staring at Pitt. "I don't know anything about this! Why did you not report this immediately? I was available all yesterday, and the day before. You could perfectly easily have found me if you tried. You've got a telephone here. You should have one installed in your own home. You must keep up with the times, Pitt. Modern inventions are here for our use, not just to entertain those with more money and imagination than sense. What's the matter with you, man? You are too old-fashioned. Stuck in your ways!"

"I only heard of it half an hour ago," Pitt replied with satisfaction. "Immediately before leaving my home. And I don't think it is a suitable subject to discuss on the telephone, but I do have one."

"If it is not a suitable subject to discuss on the telephone, how did you hear about it?" Farnsworth demanded with a flash of humor and equal satisfaction. "If you wish to be discreet about it, you should have gone around to the Colonial Office to ascertain the situation before coming here. Are you really sure it is important information at all? Perhaps in your zeal to be discreet, you have insufficient knowledge to assume it is anything like as grave as you suggest. It is probably merely misplaced."

Pitt smiled and put his hands in his pockets. "A member of the Foreign Office visited me in person," he replied, "on the instructions of Lord Salisbury, and officially requested me to look into the matter. The information which we are speaking of has turned up in the German Embassy, which is how they know of the matter. It is not a few pieces of paper that no one can put his hand on."

Farnsworth was aghast, but Pitt did not allow him to speak.

"The Germans are aware of some of our negotiating positions with reference to possessions in East Africa, Zambezia, and the possibilities of a British corridor from Cairo to the Cape," he went on. "However, Lady Warburton's diamonds . . ."

"To hell with Lady Warburton and her diamonds," Farnsworth exploded. "Tellman can deal with that." A look of spite crossed his well-formed features. "I only said my best man, I did not name him. And that is not necessarily the most senior, by any means. You go to the Colonial Office immediately. Concentrate on it, Pitt. Leave everything else until you have that solved. Do you understand me? And for God's sake, man, be discreet!"

Pitt smiled. "Yes, Mr. Farnsworth. That is what I intended, before the matter of Lady Warburton came up."

Farnsworth glared at him, but said nothing further.

Pitt opened the door. Farnsworth went out. Pitt followed him, calling the desk sergeant to send for Inspector Tellman.

CHAPTER
TWO

Pitt walked down Bow Street to the Strand, where he found a hansom and gave the driver instructions to take him to the Colonial Office on the corner of Whitehall and Downing Street. The driver looked at him with slight surprise, but after only a moment's hesitation, urged the horse forward and joined the stream of traffic moving west.

Pitt spent the journey going over in his mind what Matthew had said, and formulating the way in which he would approach the subject when he reached Whitehall. He had read Matthew's letter of authority, and the brief instructions and details with it, but it gave him little feeling for the nature or degree of difficulty he would face in obtaining cooperation.

The cab progressed slowly, stopping for every tangle of coaches, carriages, drays and omnibuses from the Strand and Wellington Street where Pitt had hired it. They inched past Northampton Street, Bedford Street, King William Street, and Duncannon Street right to Charing Cross. Everyone was in a hurry and determined to have the right-of-way. Drivers were shouting at each other. A brougham and a hearse had apparently got their wheels locked and were causing a major obstruction. Two youths with a dray were calling out advice, and a costermonger was having a quarrel with a pie seller.

It was fifteen minutes before Pitt's cab finally turned left into Whitehall and made its way towards Downing Street, and when it stopped, the duty constable approached to see what they wanted.

"Superintendent Pitt, going to the Colonial Office," Pitt told him, producing his card.

The cabdriver opened his eyes with interest.

"Yes sir." The constable saluted smartly and stood rather more to attention. "Didn't recognize you, sir."

Pitt paid the driver and turned to go up the steps, aware that he was a good deal less than smart, and certainly not attired like one of the officials and diplomats. In their cutaway coats, winged collars, and striped trousers, they passed him on either side, carrying their furled umbrellas, although it was a fine May Day morning.

"Yes sir?" a young man enquired of him almost as soon as he came inside the building. "May I help you, sir?"

Pitt produced his card again as verification of his rank, which he admitted his appearance lacked. As always his hair was too long and curled untidily over his collar and from under his hat. His jacket was actually quite well cut, but his habit of poking all manner of things into the pockets had pushed it out of shape, and certainly his collar was not stiff, nor was it winged. His tie was something of an afterthought, and looked it.

"Yes, please," he replied immediately. "I have a confidential matter to discuss with the most senior official available."

"I'll make an appointment for you, sir," the young man replied smoothly. "Would the day after tomorrow be suitable to you? Mr. Aylmer should be available then, and I'm sure he will be happy to see you. He is Mr. Chancellor's immediate junior, and a very knowledgeable person."

Pitt knew the name of Linus Chancellor, Secretary of State for Colonial Affairs, as did every other man in London. He was one of the most brilliant of rising politicians, and it was held by many that one day he would lead the government.

"No, it would not," he said levelly, meeting the young man's eyes, and seeing a look of startled affront in them. "The matter is extremely urgent and must be attended to at the earliest moment possible. It is also confidential, so I cannot detail it to you. I have come at the request of the Foreign Office. If you wish to check with Lord Salisbury, you may do so. I shall wait for Mr. Chancellor."

The young man swallowed, uncertain now what he should do. He looked at Pitt with dislike.

"Yes sir, I shall inform Mr. Chancellor's office, and bring you his reply." He looked back at Pitt's card again, then disappeared upstairs.

It was nearly a quarter of an hour before he returned, and Pitt was beginning to find the waiting onerous.

"If you care to come this way, sir," the young man said coolly. He turned on his heel, leading the way back up again, knocking at the mahogany door and then standing aside to allow Pitt through.

Linus Chancellor was in his early forties, a dynamic man with a high forehead and dark hair which swept off his brow, showing a strong, jutting nose, wide mouth full of humor, volatility and a powerful will. He was a man to whom charm came easily, almost without conscious effort, and his natural fluency enabled him to say what other men struggled for and often missed. He was slender, of a good height, and immaculately dressed.

"Good morning, Superintendent Pitt." He rose from his seat behind a magnificent desk and offered his hand. When Pitt took it, his grip was firm and strong. "I am informed that your errand is both urgent and confidential." He waved to the chair opposite and resumed his own seat. "You had better explain it to me. I have some ten minutes before I have to be at my next appointment. I'm afraid I can spare you no longer than that. I am due at Number Ten."

That needed no explanation. If he were to see the Prime Minister, which was his implication, it was not something which could be delayed, whatever Pitt had to say. It was also a very forthright statement of the importance of his own time and position. He did not intend Pitt to underestimate him.

Pitt sat down in the large, carved and leather-padded seat indicated and began immediately.

"I have been informed this morning by Matthew Desmond of the Foreign Office that certain information regarding the Colonial Office's dealings with our current exploration and trading negotiations in Africa, specifically Zambezia, have fallen into the hands of the German Embassy. . . ."

He did not need to go any further. He had Chancellor's total attention.

"So far as I know, only Mr. Desmond, his immediate senior, and Lord Salisbury himself are aware of the loss," Pitt continued. "I require your permission, sir, in order to investigate from this office. . . ."

"Yes, of course. Immediately. This is extremely serious." The polite affectation of interest was gone, and in its place an earnestness which was unmistakable. "Can you tell me what manner of information you are speaking of? Did Mr. Desmond tell you, or indeed does he know?"

"Not in detail," Pitt replied. "I gather it is largely to do with mineral rights and treaties with local chieftains."

Chancellor looked very grave, his mouth pinched at the corners.

"That could be extremely serious. A great deal rests on it for the future settlement of Africa. I assume Mr. Desmond told you as much? Yes, naturally. Will you please keep me informed, Mr. Pitt? Personally. I imagine you have already investigated the possibility that whatever information it is could not simply have reached the Germans through their own people?" There was no real hope in his face; he asked as a matter of form. "They have a great many explorers, adventurers and soldiers in East Africa, particularly along the coast of Zanzibar. I will not bore you with the details of their treaties with the Sultan of Zanzibar, and the settlement uprisings and violence. Accept, for this matter, that they have a considerable presence in the area."

"I have not looked into it myself, but that was the first question I asked Mr. Desmond," Pitt replied. "He assured me it could not be so, because of the detail of the information and the fact that it corresponded precisely with our own version of events which are open to many interpretations."

"Yes—" Chancellor nodded. "You are supposing treason in our midst, Mr. Pitt. Probably of a very high order. Tell me what you propose to do about it."

"All I can do, sir, is investigate everyone who has access to all the information that has been passed on. I assume that will be a limited number of people?"

"Certainly. Mr. Thorne has charge of our African affairs. Begin with him. Now if you will excuse me, Superintendent, I shall call Fairbrass and have him take you through. I have a short space of time free at quarter past four this afternoon. I will be obliged if you will report to me then whatever progress you have made, impressions you have gained."

"Yes sir." Pitt stood up and Chancellor rose also. A young man, presumably Fairbrass, appeared in the doorway and after brief instructions from Chancellor, conducted Pitt through a number of handsome corridors to a further, spacious, well-furnished office not unlike the first. The plate on the door read JEREMIAH THORNE, and Fairbrass was apparently so in awe of Mr. Thorne he considered Pitt would need no information as to who he was. He knocked tentatively, and upon receiving an answer, turned the handle and put his head around.

"Mr. Thorne, sir, I have a Superintendent Pitt here, from Bow Street, I think. Mr. Chancellor asked me to bring him along." He stopped abruptly, realizing he knew no more. He withdrew and pushed the door wider for Pitt to go in.

Jeremiah Thorne was superficially not unlike his political master. There was a difference in his bearing which was immediate, but equally it was indefinable. He was seated behind his desk but he appeared also to be of a good height. He had widely spaced eyes, dark hair, thick and smooth, and a broad, generous mouth. But he was a civil servant, not a politician. The difference was too subtle to name. The assurance with which he bore himself was based on generations of certainty, of being the unseen power behind those who campaign for office, and whose position depends upon the good opinion of others.

"How do you do, Superintendent," he said with a lift of interest in his voice. "Come in. What may I do for you? Some colonial crime in which the metropolitan police is interested?" He smiled. "In Africa, I imagine, or you would not have been directed to me."

"No, Mr. Thorne." Pitt came into the room and sat down in the chair indicated. He waited until the door was closed and Fairbrass had had time to retrace his steps along the passage. "I am afraid the crime almost certainly began here in the Colonial Office," he answered the question. "If indeed there is a crime. Mr. Chancellor has given me authority to enquire into it. I need to ask you several questions, sir. I apologize for taking up your time, but it is essential."

Thorne sat back in his chair and folded his hands.

"Then you had better proceed, Superintendent. Can you tell me what this crime is?"

Pitt did not answer directly. Jeremiah Thorne was privy to most of the information in the Colonial Office. He was almost certainly in a position to be the traitor, however unlikely it was that so senior a person would do such a thing. The other possibility was that he might inadvertently either warn the traitor simply because he did not believe the person capable of such duplicity, or that he might do it through sheer inexperience in suspecting one of his own colleagues.

And yet if the man were naive enough not to understand the purpose of the questions, he was hardly competent to hold the position he did.

"I would prefer not to mention it until I am certain there has been a crime," Pitt hedged. "Would you tell me something about your principal staff, sir."

Thorne looked puzzled, but there was considerable humor in his dark eyes, masking any anxiety, if indeed he felt it.

"I report immediately regarding African affairs to Garston Aylmer, Mr. Chancellor's assistant," he said quietly. "He is an excellent man, very fine mind. A First at Cambridge, but I imagine it is not his academic qualifications you are interested in." He lifted one shoulder infinitesimally. "No, I thought not. He came straight to the Colonial Office from university. That would be some fourteen or fifteen years ago."

"Then he is close to forty?" Pitt interrupted.

"About thirty-six, I believe. He really is outstanding, Superintendent. He obtained his degree at twenty-three." He appeared about to add something else and then changed his mind. He waited patiently for Pitt to continue.

"What was his subject, sir?"

"Oh—classics."

"I see."

"I doubt you do." The smile was back in Thorne's eyes, bright like a hidden laughter. "He is an excellent all-round scholar, and a man with a profound knowledge of history. He lives in Newington, in a small house which he owns."

"Is he married?"

"No, he is not."

Then Newington was a curious place for him to live. It was south of the river, across the Westminster Bridge to the east of Lambeth. It was not far from Whitehall, but hardly fashionable for a man of such excellent position, and presumable ambition. Pitt would have expected him to have had rooms in Mayfair or Belgravia, or possibly Chelsea.

"What are his future prospects, Mr. Thorne?" he asked. "Can he look forward to further promotion?" Now there was a lift in Thomas's voice, but it was impossible to read his thoughts.

"I imagine so. He may in time take my position, or equally possibly he could head any of the other departments in the Colonial Office. I believe he has an interest in Indian affairs and the Far East. Superintendent, what has this to do with any possible crime that concerns you? Aylmer is an honorable man, about whom I have never heard the slightest suggestion of impropriety, let alone dishonesty. I don't believe the man even drinks."

There were many further questions, either of financial means or personal reputation, which Pitt could ask, but not of Thorne. This was going to be every bit as difficult as he had expected, and he had no liking for it at all. But Matthew Desmond would not have made the charge were he less than certain of it. Someone in the African section of the Colonial Office was passing information to the German Embassy.

"Who else, Mr. Thorne?" he asked aloud.

"Who else? Peter Arundell. He specializes in matters concerning Egypt and the Sudan," Thorne replied. He went on to describe him in some detail, and Pitt allowed him to finish. He did not yet wish to narrow down the area to Zambezia. He would like to have trusted Thorne, but he could not afford to.

"Yes," he prompted when Thorne hesitated.

Thorne frowned, but continued describing several other men with responsibility for other areas in the African continent, including Ian Hathaway, who was concerned with Mashonaland and Matabeleland, known together as Zambezia.

"He is one of our most experienced men, although very modest," Thorne said quietly, still sitting in the same easy position in his chair and regarding Pitt steadily. "He is perhaps fifty. And has been a widower for as long as I have known him. I believe his wife died quite young, and he has never remarried. He has one son who is in the Colonial Service, in the Sudan, and another who works in the missionary field, I am afraid I have forgotten where. Hathaway's father held quite a senior position in the church . . . an archdeacon, or something of the sort. He was from the West Country, Somerset or Dorset, I think. Hathaway himself lives in South Lambeth, just over the Vauxhall Bridge. I confess, I know nothing about his means. He is a very private person, very unassuming, but well liked, always a courteous word for everyone."

"I see. Thank you." It was not a promising beginning, but something decisive would have been too much to hope for at this stage. He hesitated, uncertain whether to ask Thorne now if he might trace the passage of information within the building, or if he should leave him unaware of the nature of the crime as yet, and pursue the personal lives of Aylmer, Hathaway and Thorne himself first, in hope of finding some weakness or deceit which might lead him eventually to his conclusion.

"That is all, Superintendent," Thorne cut across the silence. "Other than those I have mentioned, there are only clerks, messengers and assistants of junior rank. If you do not tell me what offense you are investigating, or at least its general nature, I do not know what further I can do to assist you." It was not a complaint, simply an observation, and there was still the mild, wry humor in Thorne's face as he made it.

Pitt equivocated. "Some information has found its way into the wrong hands. It is possible it has come from this office."

"I see." Thorne did not look horrified, as Chancellor had done. In fact he did not seem particularly surprised at all. "I presume it is financial information you are concerned with, or that which could be turned to financial advantage? I am afraid it is always a risk where great opportunities occur, such as those now in Africa. The Dark Continent"—his mouth curled at the corners at the expression—"has attracted its share of opportunists as well as those who wish to settle, to colonize, to explore, to hunt big game or to save the souls of the natives and spread Christianity over the face of the benighted lands and impose British law and civilization on the heathen races."

The assumption was wrong, but it suited Pitt very well to allow it to remain.

"Nevertheless, it must be stopped," he said seriously.

"Of course," Thorne agreed. "You are welcome to any assistance I can give you, but I am afraid I have no idea where to begin. It would be exceedingly hard to believe that any of the men I have mentioned would stoop to such a level, but they may be able to tell you something which will point to who is at fault. I shall instruct them accordingly." He sat forward in the chair again. "Thank you for coming to me first, Superintendent, it was most civil of you."

"Not at all," Pitt said easily. "I think I shall begin by tracing the course of the information in general, rather than specifically financial, and see exactly who is privy to what."

"Excellent." Thorne stood up, an indication that the interview was at an end. "Would you care to have someone conduct you through the convolutions of the system, or would you rather make your own way? I am afraid I have no knowledge of police procedure."

"If you could spare someone, it might save me a great deal of time."

"Certainly." He reached out and pulled the very handsome embroidered bell cord beside his desk and a moment later a young man appeared from the adjoining office. "Oh, Wainwright," Thorne said almost casually. "This is Superintendent Pitt from the Bow Street police, who has some enquiries to make. The matter is highly confidential at this point. Will you please take him everywhere he requires to go, and show him the passage of information we receive from Africa itself, and regarding Africa from any other source. There appears to have been an irregularity." He used the word delicately, and without further explanation. "So it would be much better at this point if you did not allow anyone else to be aware of exactly what you are doing, or who Mr. Pitt is."

"Yes sir." Wainwright sounded a trifle surprised, but like the good civil servant he aspired to be, he did not even suggest a comment in his expression, much less make a remark. He turned to Pitt. "How do you do, sir. If you care to come with me, I will show you the various types of communications we receive, and precisely what happens to each from its point of arrival onwards."

Pitt thanked Thorne again and then followed Wainwright. He spent the rest of the day learning precisely how all the information was received from its various sources, by whom, where it was stored, how passed on, and who was privy to it. By half past three he had satisfied himself that the specific details Matthew Desmond had given him could individually have been known to a number of people, but all of them together passed through the hands of only a few: Garston Aylmer, Ian Hathaway, Peter Arundell, a man named Robert Leicester, and Thorne himself.

However he did not report that to Chancellor when he went back to his office at quarter past four, and found him free as he had promised. He merely said that he had been given every assistance and had been able to rule out several possibilities.

"And what is there remaining?" Chancellor said quickly, his eyes keen, his face grave. "You still have no doubt that we have a traitor who is passing information to the Kaiser?"

"That is the Foreign Office's conclusion," Pitt replied. "But it does seem the only one to answer the facts."

"Extremely unpleasant." Chancellor looked beyond Pitt into the distance, his mouth pinched and his brows drawn down. "I don't mind what enemy I encounter face-to-face, but to be betrayed by one's own is the worst experience a man can endure. I hate a traitor more than anything else on earth." He looked at Pitt quickly, his blue eyes penetrating. "Are you a classicist, Mr. Pitt?"

It was an absurd question, but Pitt took it as a compliment that Chancellor obviously had no idea of his background. He could have been speaking to Micah Drummond, or even Farnsworth. It was a compliment to Arthur Desmond that he had helped his gamekeeper's son to the degree that such an error was possible.

"No sir. I am acquainted with Shakespeare, and the major poets, but not the Greeks," Pitt answered with a sober face.

"I was thinking more of Dante," Chancellor said. "He grades all the sins in his picture of the descent into Hell. He places traitors in the lowest circle of all, far beneath those who are guilty of violence, theft, lust, or any other depravity of mind or body. He holds it the worst sin which mankind can conceive, uniquely an abuse of our God-given gifts of reason and conscience. He places the betrayers eternally alone, held fast in everlasting ice. A very terrible punishment, Mr. Pitt, do you not think? But meet for the offense."

Pitt felt a moment of chill, and then a clarity that was almost uplifting.

"Yes . . ." he said. "Yes, perhaps it is the worst offense, the breaking of trust, and I suppose the eternal isolation is not so much a punishment as a natural conclusion which would be bound to follow such a nature. It is a self-chosen Hell, if you like."

"I see we have much in common, Mr. Pitt." Chancellor's smile was dazzling, a gesture of both warmth and intense, almost luminous, candor. "Perhaps there is nothing more important than that. We must get this abysmal affair dealt with. It darkens everything until we do." He bit his lip and shook his head fractionally. "The worst of it is that until it is exposed it poisons every other relationship. One quite unjustifiably suspects those who are perfectly innocent. Many a friendship has been broken for less. I admit, I should not look on a man the same if he had found it possible to suspect me of such treachery." He gazed at Pitt. "And yet since it is my duty, I cannot place any man beyond my suspicion. I dare not. What a filthy crime!" For a moment there was a bitter smile on his face. "You see what damage it has done already, by the mere fact of its existence?"

He leaned forward across the desk earnestly. "Look, Pitt, we can afford no niceties. I wish it were otherwise, but I know this office well enough to be perfectly aware, tragically, that it must be someone in considerable authority, which means probably Aylmer, Hathaway, Arundell, Leicester, or even, God forbid, Thorne himself. You will not be able to find which by chasing pieces of paper around here." Unconsciously he was drumming his fingers on the desk, almost without sound. "He will be cleverer than that. You will have to get to know the man himself, see a pattern, a flaw, and however small, a weakness. For that you need to know him in his personal life." He stopped, regarding Pitt with exasperation. "Come, man, don't show such surprise. I am not a fool!"

Pitt felt the color burn up his cheeks. He had not perceived Chancellor as a fool, or anything like it, but he had not expected such forthrightness either, nor such perception of what his investigation would entail.

Chancellor smiled quickly. "Forgive me. That was too frank. But nevertheless, what I say is true. You must meet them all socially. Can you come to the reception at the Duchess of Marlborough's this evening? I can obtain an invitation for you without any trouble at all."

Pitt hesitated only a moment.

"I realize it is absurdly short notice," Chancellor went on. "But history waits for no man, and our treaty with Germany is on the doorstep."

"Of course," Pitt accepted. What Chancellor had said was true. It would be an ideal situation in which to make some judgment of the men in a more personal capacity. "It is an excellent idea. Thank you for your assistance, sir."

"Yourself and your wife? You are married, I presume?"

"Yes indeed."

"Excellent. I shall have my footman deliver them by six. Your address?"

Pitt gave it, with pleasure that it was the new house, and after a moment or two, took his leave. If he were to attend a reception at Marlborough House in a few hours, he had a very great deal to attend to. And Charlotte would have even more. Her sister, Emily, from whom she usually borrowed gowns for the better social occasions, was currently abroad in Italy again. Her husband, Jack, was very newly a member of Parliament, and since Parliament was in recess for the summer, they had taken the opportunity to travel. Borrowing from her would not be possible. She would have to try Lady Vespasia Cumming-Gould, Emily's great-aunt by her first marriage, to Lord Ashworth.

"What?" Charlotte said in disbelief. "Tonight? That's impossible! It's nearly five o'clock now!" She was standing in the kitchen with plates in her hand.

"I do realize it is not much time. . . ." Pitt began. It was only now beginning to dawn upon him what an enormity he had committed.

"Not much time!" Her voice rose in something close to a squeal and she put the plates down with a clatter. "To prepare for something like this would take a week. Thomas, you do know who the Duchess of Marlborough is, I suppose? There could be royalty present! There could be everybody who is anyone at all—there almost certainly will be." Suddenly the outrage vanished from her face and was replaced by an overwhelming curiosity. "How in Heaven's name did you get an invitation to the Duchess of Marlborough's reception? There are people in London who would commit crimes to get such a thing." Amusement tugged at the corners of her mouth. "Don't tell me someone has?"

He felt laughter at the absurdity of it well up inside him too. It was such a wild contrast with the truth. Perhaps he ought not to mention it to her. It was a highly confidential matter, but he had always trusted her in the past, although of course no previous case had involved matters of state.

She saw his hesitation. "They have!" Her eyes were wide, and she was uncertain whether to laugh or not.

"No—no," he said hastily. "The matter is very much more serious than that."

"Are you not working on Sir Arthur's death?" she said quickly. "That can't have anything to do with the Duchess of Marlborough. And even if it had, you wouldn't just get an invitation because you wanted one. I don't think even Aunt Vespasia could do that." That was the height of social power.

Vespasia had been the foremost beauty of her day, not only for her classic features and exquisite coloring, but for her grace, wit and extraordinary panache. Now in her eighties, she was still beautiful. Her wit had sharpened because she was assured in her position, and no longer cared in the slightest what anyone thought of her, as long as she rested easily in her own conscience. She espoused causes few others dared to, liked and disliked whom and what she pleased, and enjoyed pastimes of which many a younger and more cautious woman would have been afraid. But she still could not command an invitation to the Duchess of Marlborough's receptions at short notice, and for someone else.

"Yes, I am working on Sir Arthur's death," Pitt answered with some stretching of the truth. He followed her as she whirled into sudden activity, turning to go into the passage and up the stairs.

"But I am also working on another matter Matthew left with me this morning, and it is in connection with that," Pitt said from behind her, "that we are going to the Duchess of Marlborough's this evening. The invitations came through Mr. Linus Chancellor, of the Colonial Office."

She stopped on the landing. "Linus Chancellor. I've heard of him. He's very charming, and extremely clever, so they say. He may even be Prime Minister one day."

He smiled, and then hid it almost immediately as he followed her into the bedroom. Charlotte no longer moved in the social circles where people discussed serious politicians, as she had done before she had shocked her friends by marrying a policeman, a dramatic reduction of both her financial and social circumstances.

Her face fell. "Is that mistaken? Is he not charming at all?"

"Yes, he is most charming, and I should judge also very clever. Who told you about him?"

"Emily," she answered, throwing open the wardrobe door. "Jack has met him several times. But also Mama." She realized what he had meant. "All right, only two people. You actually met him today? Why?"

He was undecided for only a moment.

"It is highly confidential. It is a matter of state. I am not revealing the whole business even to those I question. Certain information is being passed from the Colonial Office to other people who should not know it."

She swung around to stare at him. "You mean there is a traitor in the Colonial Office? That's terrible! Why couldn't you just say that, instead of hemming and hawing? Thomas, you are becoming pompous."

"Well—I . . ." He was horrified. He loathed pomposity. He swallowed. "Can you find something to wear and get ready, or not?"

"Yes of course I can," she said instantly, eyes wide, as if the answer were the only one possible.

"How?"

She shut the wardrobe door. "I don't know yet. Give me a moment to think. Emily is away, but Aunt Vespasia is not. She has a telephone. Perhaps I can reach her and ask her advice. Yes. I'll do that immediately." And without waiting for comment from him, she brushed past him and went across the landing and down the stairs to the hallway where the new telephone was situated. She picked up the receiver. She was extremely unfamiliar with the instrument, and it took her several minutes before she was successful. She was naturally answered by the maid, and was obliged to wait for several moments.

"Aunt Vespasia." Her voice was unusually breathless when she heard Vespasia at last. "Thomas has just been put onto a most important case, which I cannot discuss, because I know very little about it, except that he has been invited immediately, this evening, to attend the reception at the Duchess of Marlborough's."

There was a very slight hesitation of surprise at the other end of the line, but Vespasia was too well bred to allow herself anything more.

"Indeed? It must be of the utmost gravity for Her Grace of Marlborough to allow the slightest alteration to her plans. How may I be of assistance, my dear? I imagine that is why you have called?"

"Yes." From anyone else such candor would have been disconcerting, but Vespasia had never been anything but frank with Charlotte, nor Charlotte with her. "I am not quite sure what to wear to such a function," Charlotte confessed. "I have never been to anything quite so—so very formal. And of course I do not own such a thing anyway."

Vespasia was thinner than Charlotte, but of a similar height, and it would not be the first occasion for which she had lent her a gown. Policemen of Pitt's previous rank did not earn the kind of salary to afford their wives attire for the London Season, and indeed none of them would have been invited.

"I shall find something suitable and have my footman bring it over," Vespasia said generously. "And don't worry about the time. It is not done to arrive early. About half past ten would be excellent. They will serve supper at around midnight. One should be there between thirty and ninety minutes of the hour mentioned on the invitation, which if I recollect, is eleven o'clock. It is a formal occasion." She did not add that more intimate receptions might well begin an hour earlier. She expected Charlotte to know that.

"Thank you very much," Charlotte said with real gratitude. It was only after she had put the receiver back on its hook that she realized if Vespasia knew the time on the invitation, she must have one herself.

The dress, when it arrived, was quite the loveliest she had ever seen. It was of a deep blue-green shade, cut high at the front, and with a sheer sleeve, and decorated with a delicate beading at throat and shoulder. The bustle was narrow and heavily draped, caught up in a bow of gold and a shade of the gown itself, but so dark as to appear almost black. Included with it was a most elegant pair of slippers to match. The whole effect made her think of deep water, exotic seas and wild dawns over the sand. If she looked even half as wonderful as she felt, she would be the envy of every woman in the place.

Actually as she sailed down the stairs, several minutes later than she had said she would (having mislaid a packet of hairpins which were vital to the whole effect), Gracie was awestruck. Her eyes were enormous, and both children crouched, wide-eyed, on the landing. Even Pitt was a little startled. He had been pacing the hall with impatience, and when he had heard her step, he swung around, then saw her.

"Oh," he said, uncharacteristically lost for words. He had forgotten what a very handsome woman she was with her rich dark auburn hair and warm, honey skin. Tonight the excitement had given her a color and a brilliance to her eyes that made her close to truly beautiful. "That . . ." Then he became self-conscious, and changed his mind. This was not the time to indulge in compliments, however merited. "It becomes you very well," he finished. It was immeasurably less than he meant. Actually it awoke in him an awareness of her physical presence, and a strangeness, a frisson of excitement as if she had been someone he had newly met.

She looked at him a trifle uncertainly, and said nothing.

He had hired a carriage for the evening. It was not an event for which one could arrive in a hansom cab. For one thing, its cramped space would have crushed Charlotte's dress, or more accurately Vespasia's dress, and for another, and more importantly, it would mark him out as different, and inferior.

There was a considerable jostle of carriages in the driveway, and indeed in the street beyond, as dozens of people arrived at what Vespasia had said would be the optimum time. They were almost swept along up the stairs and into the great foyer and the hall beyond. On all sides they were surrounded by swirling skirts, nervous laughter, just a little loud, and voices high-pitched, too obviously intent upon immediate companions and affecting to ignore everyone else. The lights of the chandeliers were thrown back in tiaras, brooches, necklaces, earrings, bracelets and rings. The men were girded by scarlet and purple sashes of orders of merit, and chests gleamed with medals against the sober black and stark white of formal dress.

Up the great staircase and into the reception rooms they were announced by a majordomo whose face remained entirely expressionless, regardless of the name or rank of the personage he introduced. If he had never heard of Mr. and Mrs. Thomas Pitt, there was nothing in his features to register it, not a flicker of his eyes or intonation of his voice.

Pitt was far more nervous than Charlotte. She was bred to conduct herself at social events of this nature, even if not of this status. Pitt felt suddenly as if his stiff collar were cutting into his chin and he hardly dared turn his head. Charlotte had insisted on cutting his hair, and he was self-consciously aware now that he had not seen a respectable barber in years. His evening boots were excellent, a gift from Jack, but his black suit was of nothing like the quality of those around him, and he was certain they would be as aware of it as he was the first time they looked closely enough at him to conduct any sort of a conversation.

For the first fifteen minutes they drifted from one group to another, making the most superficial remarks, and feeling increasingly ridiculous and as if they were wasting time which could easily be better spent, even if only in bed asleep, ready for the next day and its duties.

Then at last Pitt saw Linus Chancellor, and beside him a uniquely striking woman. She was unusually tall, very nearly of a height with Chancellor himself. She was slender but well proportioned with handsome shoulders and arms, and awareness of her height had not made her stoop or try to hide it. She stood with head high and back straight. Her gown was palest oyster shading to pink and it flattered her dusky coloring and rather long, wide-eyed face.

"Who is she?" Charlotte whispered quickly. "Isn't she interesting, quite unlike most of the women here. There is nothing predictable about her at all!"

"I don't know, but perhaps she is Chancellor's wife," he replied under his breath, conscious of those close to him and possibly overhearing.

"Oh! Is that Linus Chancellor beside her? He's rather handsome, isn't he!"

Pitt looked at her with interest. He had not considered whether Chancellor was handsome or not, or indeed whether his looks might be appealing to women. He had only seen the strength and the imagination in his face, the unusual angle of nose and jaw and the power of will it suggested, the fine eyes and the total confidence of his bearing. He had seen him as a politician, and tried to estimate his skill and his ability to judge men.

"Yes, I suppose he is," he said with growing conviction.

Charlotte looked at the woman again, and at that moment saw her place her hand on Chancellor's arm, not obtrusively—it was not a statement of ownership—but discreetly, a gesture of pride and affection. She was moving herself closer to him, not drawing him to her.

"If he is married, then she must be his wife," Charlotte said with absolute certainty. "She would never do that in public were she not now, or about to become so."

"Do what?"

Charlotte smiled and did exactly the same, slipping her hand through Pitt's arm and moving half a step closer.

"She is still in love with him," she said a little above a whisper.

Pitt knew he had missed something, but also that it had been in some way a compliment.

Further discussion of the subject was circumvented by the approach of one of the most homely men Charlotte had ever seen. The most charitable description of him possible could only have said there was no malice in his face, and no ill temper. He was barely Charlotte's height, although she was admittedly rather tall for a woman. He was very heavily set, with plump arms and shoulders and a massive series of chins which gave his face a most odd shape, as if it were dominated by the excellent hair and brown eyes under inadequate brows, and then it all faded away into his shoulders. Nevertheless, it was not in the least displeasing, and when he spoke his voice was beautiful and quite individual.

"Good evening, Mr. Pitt. How pleasant to see you at such a gathering." He waited politely to be introduced to Charlotte.

"Good evening, Mr. Aylmer," Pitt responded, and turned to Charlotte. "May I present Mr. Garston Aylmer, of the Colonial Office?" He completed the introduction.

"How do you do, Mrs. Pitt." Aylmer bowed very slightly, an elegant gesture which seemed to come to him quite naturally. He regarded her with interest. "I hope you will enjoy yourself, although these functions can become tedious if one remains too long. Everybody says the same thing each time, and seldom means it anyway." He smiled suddenly and it illuminated his face. "But since we have not met before, perhaps we shall have something new and quite different to say, and be enthralled."

"I should love to be enthralled," Charlotte answered instantly. "I am not in the slightest interested in the weather, or in gossip as to who has dined with whom, or been seen in whose company."

"Nor I," Aylmer agreed. "It will all be different next week anyway, and then no doubt back to the same the week after. What shall we discuss?"

Pitt was more than happy to be ignored. He took a step backwards, excusing himself inaudibly, and drifted towards Linus Chancellor and the woman at his side.

Charlotte thought hastily. It was an opportunity too precious to miss.

"Something I know nothing about," she said with a smile. "Then you can tell me whatever you please, and I shall not find fault with any of it, because I shall have no idea if you are right or wrong."

"What an original and superb idea," he agreed, entering the spirit of it with enthusiasm. "What do you know nothing about, Mrs. Pitt?" He offered her his arm.

"Oh, countless things," she said, taking it. "But many of them are of no interest anyway, which is why I have not bothered with them. But some must be engrossing," she added as they walked up towards the steps to the terrace. "What about Africa? If you are in the Colonial Office, you must know immeasurably more than I do about it."

"Oh certainly," he agreed with a broad smile. "Although I warn you, a great deal of it is either violent or tragic, or of course both."

"But everything that people fight over is worth something," she reasoned. "Or they wouldn't be fighting. I expect it is terribly different from England, isn't it? I have seen pictures, engravings and so on, of jungles, and endless plains with every kind of animal imaginable. And curious trees that look as if they have all been sawn off at the top, sort of . . . level."

"Acacias," he replied. "Yes, undoubtedly it is different from England. I hate to confess it, Mrs. Pitt, because probably it robs me instantly of all real interest, but I have never been there. I know an enormous amount of facts about it, but I have them all second-hand. Isn't it a shame?"

She looked at him for only an instant before being perfectly certain he had no sense of loss whatever, and was still enjoying the conversation. It would be an overstatement to say he was flirting, but he was quite at ease with women, and obviously found their company pleasing.

"Perhaps there isn't any appreciable difference between second-hand and thirdhand," she responded as they made their way past a group of men in earnest conversation. "And it will be only a matter of description to me, because I shall never know if you are right or not. So please tell me, and make it very vivid, even if you have to invent it. And full of facts, of course," she plunged on. "Tell me about Zambezia, and gold and diamonds, and Doctor Livingstone and Mr. Stanley, and the Germans."

"Good heavens," he said in much alarm. "All of them?"

"As many as you can," she returned.

A footman offered them a silver tray with glasses of champagne.

"Well to begin with, the diamonds we know about are all in South Africa," Aylmer answered, taking a glass and giving it to her, then one for himself. "But there is a possibility of enormous amounts of gold in Zambezia. There are massive ruins of a civilization, a city called Zimbabwe, and we are only beginning to estimate the fortune that could be there. Which, quite naturally, is also what the Germans are interested in. And possibly everyone else as well." He was watching her face with wide brown eyes, and she had no idea how serious he was, or whether it was at least partially invention, to amuse her.

"Does Britain own it now?" she asked, taking a sip from her glass.

"No," Aylmer replied, moving a step away from the footman. "Not yet."

"But we will?"

"Ah—that is a very important question, to which I do not have the answer." He led the way on up the steps.

"And if you did, no doubt it would be highly secret," she added.

"But of course." He smiled and went on to tell her about Cecil Rhodes and his adventures and exploits in South Africa, the Rand

and Johannesburg, and the discovery of the Kimberley diamond mine, until they were interrupted by a young man with a long nose and a hearty manner who swept Aylmer away with apologies, and obviously to his annoyance. Charlotte was left momentarily alone.

She looked around her to see whom she might recognize from photographs in the *London Illustrated News.* She saw a most imposing man with lush side-whiskers and curling beard, the light of the chandeliers gleaming on the bald dome of his head, his sad, bloodhound eyes gazing around the room. She thought he might be Lord Salisbury, the Foreign Secretary, but she was not certain. A photograph with only shades of gray was not like a living person.

Linus Chancellor was talking to a man superficially not unlike himself, but without the ambition in his face, or the mercurial temperament. They were deep in conversation, almost as if oblivious of the whirl of silks and glitter of lights, or the buzz of chatter all around them. Beside the second man, but facing the other way, apparently waiting for him, was a most unusual woman. She was of arresting appearance because of her supreme confidence and the intelligence which seemed to radiate from her. But she was also quite unusually plain. Her nose was so high at the bridge, in profile it was almost a continuation of the line of her forehead. Her chin was a little too short, and her eyes were wide set, tilted down at the corners, and too large. It was an extraordinary face, compelling and even a trifle frightening. She was dressed extremely well, but one was so startled by her countenance it was of no importance whatever.

Charlotte exchanged a few polite and meaningless words with a couple who made it their duty to speak to everyone. A man with light auburn hair addressed her with effusive admiration, then once again she found herself alone. She did not mind in the least. She knew Pitt was here to pursue a specific case.

A delicately pale woman of about her own age was standing a few yards away, her fair hair elaborately coiffed, her pastel gown stitched with pearls and beads. She glanced discreetly at Charlotte over her fan and turned to the good-looking young man next to her.

"She must be from the country, poor creature."

"Must she?" the young man said with surprise. "Do you know her?" He made a move as if to approach Charlotte, his face alight with anticipation.

The woman's eyes widened dramatically. "Of course not. Really, Gerald! How would I know such a person? I merely remarked that she must have come up from the country because of her unfortunate coloring." She grasped Gerald's arm firmly, restraining him.

"I thought it was rather pleasing." He stopped short. "Sort of like well-polished mahogany."

"Not her hair. Her complexion. Obviously she cannot be a milkmaid, or she would not be here, but she looks as if she could have been. I daresay it is riding to hounds, or some such thing." She wrinkled her nose very slightly. "She looks positively robust. Most unbecoming. But I daresay she is unaware of it, poor creature. Just as well."

Gerald pulled his mouth down at the corner. "How typical of you to feel such compassion for her, my dear. That is one of your most charming traits, your sensitivity to the feelings of others."

She glanced at him very quickly, some inkling in the back of her mind that there was an element in him she had missed, then chose to ignore it and swept forward to speak to a viscountess she knew.

Gerald shot a look of undisguised admiration at Charlotte, then followed obediently.

Charlotte smiled to herself and went to look for Pitt.

She glimpsed Great-Aunt Vespasia across the room, looking quite magnificent in a gown of steel-gray satin, her heavy-lidded silver eyes brilliant, her white hair a more gracious ornament to her head than many of the tiaras glistening around her.

As Charlotte looked at her, Vespasia quite slowly and deliberately winked, then resumed her conversation.

It took Charlotte several minutes to find Pitt. He had moved from the main reception room with its blazing chandeliers up a shallow flight of steps into a quieter room where he was deep in conversation with the man who resembled Linus Chancellor, and the extraordinary woman who was with him.

Charlotte hesitated, uncertain whether if she approached, she might be interrupting, but the woman glanced up and their eyes met with a jolt of interest that was almost a familiarity.

The man followed her line of sight, and Pitt also turned.

Charlotte went forward and was introduced.

"Mr. Jeremiah Thorne of the Colonial Office," Pitt said quietly. "And Mrs. Thorne. May I present my wife."

"How do you do, Mrs. Pitt," Mrs. Thorne said immediately. "Are you interested in Africa? I do hope not. I am bored to weeping with it. Please come and talk to me about something else. Almost anything would do, except India, which from this distance is much the same."

"Christabel . . ." Thorne said with alarm, but Charlotte could see that it was largely assumed, and he was possibly quite used to her manner, and in no way truly disturbed.

"Yes my dear," she said absently. "I am going to speak with Mrs. Pitt. We shall find something to entertain us, either something profoundly serious and worthy, like saving souls or bodies; or else totally trivial, like criticizing the fashions of everyone else we can see, and speculating on which respectable lady of uncertain years is seeking which wretched young man to marry her daughter."

Thorne smiled and groaned at the same time, but there was quite obviously profound affection in it; then he turned back to Pitt.

Charlotte followed Christabel Thorne with considerable interest; the conversation promised to be different and lively.

"If you come to these sort of things as often as I do, you must find them desperately tedious by now," Christabel said with a smile. Her large eyes were very penetrating, and Charlotte could imagine she would paralyze many a timid soul into silence, or stuttering and incoherent sentences.

"I have never been to one before." Charlotte decided to be just as frank. It was the only defense against pretentiousness, and being caught at it. "Since my marriage I have been out socially only on certain specific occasions that have called for . . ." She stopped. To have admitted they were when she was involving herself in Pitt's investigations was perhaps a little too candid even for this occasion.

Christabel's high eyebrows rose even higher, her face full of interest. "Yes?"

Charlotte still hesitated.

"You were going to say?" Christabel prompted. There was nothing unfriendly in her stare, simply a consuming interest.

Charlotte gave up. She knew already Christabel would not forgive a lie, or even half of one, and naturally since Thorne knew Pitt's profession, she assumed Christabel did too. "A little meddling in my husband's cases," she finished with a slight smile. "There are sometimes places which as a member of the police—"

"How perfectly marvelous!" Christabel interrupted her. "But of course. You have no need to explain, my dear. It is all quite clear, and completely justified. This time you are here because he has been invited on this wretched business of African information going missing." A look of contempt crossed her face. "Greed can make people do the grubbiest of things . . . at least some people." She caught sight of Charlotte's face. "Don't look so upset, my dear. I overheard my husband speaking about it just now. One was always aware of the possibility. Wherever there is a fortune to be made, there will be those who cheat to get advantage. It is simply unusual that they have had the courage and openness to bring in the police. I applaud it. But you will still find this evening growing dull, because very few people say anything they really mean."

A footman stopped by them with another tray of champagne glasses. Christabel declined with a wave of her hand, and Charlotte followed suit.

"If you wish to meet someone interesting," Christabel went on, "and I cannot think what she is doing here, of all places—come and meet Nobby Gunne." She turned as if to lead the way, assuming assent. "She's a marvelous woman. Been up the Congo River in a canoe, or something equally unlikely. Maybe it was the Niger, or the Limpopo. Somewhere in Africa where nobody had ever been before."

"Did you say Nobby Gunne?" Charlotte asked with surprise.

"Yes—extraordinary name, isn't it? I believe it is actually short for Zenobia . . . which is even more odd."

"I know her!" Charlotte said quickly. "She's about fifty or so, isn't she? Dark hair and a most unusual face, not at all conventionally pretty, but full of character, and not in the least displeasing."

A group of young women passed them, giggling and looking over their fans.

"Yes, that's right! What a generous description of her." Christabel's face was filled with amusement. "You must have liked her."

"I did."

"If it is not an impertinent question, how did a policeman's wife come to meet an African explorer like Nobby Gunne?"

"She is a friend of my sister's great-aunt by marriage," Charlotte began, then was obliged to smile at the convolution of it. "I am also very fond indeed of Great-Aunt Vespasia, and see her whenever I am able."

They were at the foot of the stair and brushed by an urn filled with flowers. Christabel whisked her skirt out of the way absentmindedly.

"Vespasia?" she said with interest. "Now there is another remarkable name. Your aunt could not by any chance be Lady Vespasia Cumming-Gould?"

"Yes, she is. You know her also?"

"Only by repute, unfortunately. But that has been sufficient for me to form a great respect for her." The banter and air of mockery drained out of her face. "She has been concerned in some very fine work to bring about social reform, most particularly the poor laws, and those regarding education."

"Yes, I remember. My sister did what she could to assist. We tried our hardest."

"Don't tell me you gave up!" It was more of a challenge than a question.

"We gave up on that approach." Charlotte met her gaze squarely. "Now Emily's husband has just become a member of Parliament. I am concerned with my husband's cases which fight injustice of various sorts, which I am not at liberty to discuss." She knew enough not to mention the Inner Circle, no matter how she might be drawn to anyone. "And Aunt Vespasia is still fighting one thing and another, but I do not know precisely what at the moment."

"I didn't mean to insult you," Christabel apologized warmly.

Charlotte smiled. "Yes you did. You thought I might simply have been playing at it, to give myself something to do, and to feel good about, and then given it up at the first failure."

"You're right, of course." Christabel smiled dazzlingly. "Jeremiah tells me I am far too obsessed with causes, and that I lose all sense of proportion. Would you care to meet Zenobia Gunne again? I see her just at the top of the stairs."

"I should indeed," Charlotte accepted, and followed Christabel's glance to where a very dark woman in green stood staring across the room from the balcony, her eyes wandering from one person to another, her face only mildly interested. Charlotte recognized her with a jolt of memory. They had met during the murders on Westminster Bridge, when Florence Ivory was fighting so hard for women to have the right to vote. Of course there was no conceivable chance of her succeeding, but Charlotte could understand the cause well enough, more particularly when she had seen the results of some of the worst inequities under present law. "We were concerned for women's franchise," she added as she followed Christabel up the stairs.

"Good heavens!" Christabel stopped and turned; her face was full of curiosity. "How very forward thinking of you!" she said with admiration. "And completely unrealistic."

"And what are you concerned with?" Charlotte challenged.

Christabel laughed, but there was intense emotion in her face. "Oh, something equally unrealistic," she answered quickly. "Do you know what an 'odd woman' is, in modern parlance?"

"Not 'peculiar'?" Charlotte had not heard the term.

"Not in the least, and becoming more common all the time . . ." Christabel ignored the fact that they were on the stairs and people were obliged to brush past them. "She is a woman who is not paired up with some man, and therefore surplus, in a sense, unprovided for, without her accepted role of caring for a man. I would like to see 'odd women' able to educate themselves and take up professions, just as men do, provide for themselves, and have a place of honor and fulfillment in society."

"Good heavens." Charlotte was genuinely amazed at her courage. But it was a wonderful idea. "You are right."

A flash of temper darkened Christabel's face. "The average man is not a whit cleverer or stronger than the average woman, and certainly no braver." A look of total disgust filled her. "You are not going to quote that belief that women cannot use both their brains and their wombs, are you? That is an idea put about by men who are afraid that we may challenge them in their jobs, and sometimes win. It is a total canard. Rubbish! Nonsense!"

Charlotte was half amused, half awed, and certainly the idea was exciting.

"And how are you going to do it?" she asked, squeezing sideways a trifle to allow a large lady to pass.

"Education," Christabel replied, and there was a note of defiance underneath the assurance Charlotte felt was paper thin. In that instant she admired her courage intensely, and felt fiercely protective of the vulnerability and the hopeless cause she saw behind it. "For women, so they have the skills and the belief in themselves," Christabel went on. "And for men, to give them the opportunity to use them. That is the hardest part."

"That must need a lot of money. . . ." Charlotte said.

She was prevented from replying by the fact that they were almost level with Zenobia Gunne, and she had seen their approach. Her face lit with pleasure as she recognized Christabel Thorne, and then after only a moment's hesitation, she remembered Charlotte also. Then quite comically she also remembered that Charlotte was not always strictly honest about her identity. In the past, for purposes of assisting Pitt, she had affected to have nothing to do with the police, even assuming her maiden name.

Nobby turned to Christabel.

"How very nice to see you, Mrs. Thorne. I am sure I know your companion, but it is some little while since we met, and I am embarrassed to say I do not recollect her name. I do apologize."

Charlotte smiled, both with genuine friendship—she had liked Nobby Gunne greatly—and with amusement at her tact.

"Charlotte Pitt," she replied graciously. "How do you do, Miss Gunne. You seem in excellent health."

"I am indeed," Nobby answered, and she looked happier, and not a day older, than when Charlotte had seen her several years earlier.

They chatted for a few moments about various subjects, touching on the political and social events of interest. They were interrupted when a tall, lithe man with a heavily tanned complexion accidentally backed into Nobby in his effort to avoid a giggling young woman. He turned to apologize for his clumsiness. He had an unusual face, far from handsome: his nose was crooked, his mouth a little large and his fair hair was receding very considerably, and yet his presence was commanding, his intelligence apparent.

"I am sorry, ma'am," he said stiffly, the color spreading up his bony cheeks. "I hope I have not hurt you?"

"Not in the least," Nobby said with mild amusement. "And considering the encounter you were avoiding, your haste is understandable."

The color in his cheeks became even deeper. "Oh . . . was I so obvious?"

"Only to one who would have done the same," she replied, meeting his eyes squarely.

"Then we have something in common," he acknowledged, but with no indication in his voice that he wished to continue further or to make her acquaintance.

"I am Zenobia Gunne," she introduced herself.

His eyes widened; his attention became suddenly real.

"Not Nobby Gunne?"

"My friends call me Nobby." Her tone of voice made it apparent he was not yet included in that number.

"Peter Kreisler." He stood very upright, as if it were a military announcement. "I also have spent much time in Africa and learned to love it."

Now her interest was quickened also. She introduced Charlotte and Christabel only as a matter of form, then continued the conversation. "Have you? In what part of Africa?"

"Zanzibar, Mashonaland, Matabeleland," he answered.

"I was in the west," she responded. "Mostly up the Congo and that region. Although I did also travel up the Niger."

"Then you will have dealt with King Leopold of the Belgians." His face was expressionless.

Nobby schooled her features just as carefully. "Only in the very slightest," she replied. "He does not regard me in the same light as he would were I a man; for example, Mr. Stanley."

Even Charlotte had heard of Henry Mirton Stanley's triumphant progress through London only a week or so since, when on April 26 he had ridden from Charing Cross Station to Piccadilly Circus. The crowds had cheered him to the echo. He was the most admired explorer of the age, a double gold medalist of the Royal

Geographical Society, a friend of the Prince of Wales and a guest of the Queen herself.

"There is some good fortune in that," Kreisler said with a bitter smile. "At least he will not ask you to lead an army of twenty thousand Congolese cannibals up to defeat the 'Mad Mahdi' and conquer the Sudan for Belgium!"

Nobby was incredulous. Her face was comical with disbelief.

Christabel looked shocked. Charlotte for once was speechless.

"You cannot be serious!" Nobby cried, her voice rising to a squeak.

"Oh, I am not." Kreisler's mouth was touched with humor. "But apparently Leopold was. He had heard that the Congo cannibals are excellent warriors. He wanted to do something to make the whole world sit up and take notice."

"Well that would certainly achieve it," Nobby agreed. "I can scarcely imagine what a war that would be! Twenty thousand cannibals against the hordes of the 'Mad Mahdi.' Oh, my God—poor Africa." Her face was touched with genuine pity beneath the wry amusement and the bantering tone. One could not mistake that she was conscious of the human misery it would involve.

Beyond their introduction, Kreisler had so far practically ignored both Christabel and Charlotte. He glanced at them to avoid rudeness, but all his interest was with Nobby, and the sense of her emotion had quickened it further.

"That is not Africa's real tragedy," he said with bitterness. "Leopold is a visionary, and frankly something of a lunatic. He poses very little real danger. For a start he is extremely unlikely to persuade any cannibals at all into leaving their own jungles. And for another, I would not be surprised if Stanley remains here in Europe anyway."

"Stanley not go back to Africa?" Nobby was amazed. "I know he has been there for the last three years, and then in Cairo for about three weeks, I hear. But surely after a rest he will return? Africa is his life! And I believe King Leopold treated him like a brother when he went back to Brussels this time. Is that not so?"

"Oh yes," Kreisler said quickly. "It is almost an understatement. Originally the king was lukewarm, and treated Stanley very offhandedly, but now he is the hero of the hour, studded with medals like a porcupine with quills, and feted like visiting royalty. Everyone is buzzing with excitement over news from Central Africa, and Stanley has but to turn up and he is cheered till people are hoarse. The king enjoys the reflected glory." There was light in Kreisler's blue eyes, laughter and pain at the same time.

Nobby asked the necessary question.

"Then why would he not return to Africa? He has left Belgium, so it cannot be that which is holding him."

"Not at all," Kreisler agreed. "He has fallen in love with Dolly Tennant."

"Dolly Tennant! Did you say Dolly Tennant?" Nobby could scarcely believe her ears. "The society hostess? The painter?"

"The same." Kreisler nodded. "And there has been a great change in her. She no longer laughs at him. It even seems she returns at least a good part of his regard. Times and fortunes have altered."

"My goodness, haven't they indeed," she agreed.

That particular speculation continued no further because they were joined by Linus Chancellor and the tall woman Charlotte had remarked upon earlier. Closer to, she was even more unusual. Her face was curiously vulnerable and full of emotion, which did not detract in the slightest from the strength in it. It was not a weakness, but an ability to feel pain with more intensity than was common. It was the face of a person who would launch herself wholeheartedly into whatever she undertook. There was no caution in it, no withholding for the sake of safety.

Introductions were performed for everyone, and she was indeed Chancellor's wife, as Charlotte had supposed.

Chancellor and Kreisler appeared to know each other, at least by repute.

"Recently back from Africa?" Chancellor asked politely.

"Two months ago," Kreisler replied. "More recently than that, from Brussels and Antwerp."

"Oh." Chancellor's face relaxed in a smile. "In the wake of the good Mr. Stanley?"

"By accident, yes."

Chancellor was obviously amused. Probably he had also heard of King Leopold's plans to conquer the Sudan. No doubt he had his sources of information every bit as immediate as Kreisler's. Perhaps it was Kreisler himself. It occurred to Charlotte that it was more than likely.

Christabel Thorne took up the subject, looking first at Kreisler, then at Chancellor.

"Mr. Kreisler tells us he is more acquainted with the east of Africa and the new lands of Zambezia. He was about to tell us that the real tragedy of Africa does not lie in the west, nor in the Sudan, but he was prevented from elaborating by some turn of the conversation. I think to do with Mr. Stanley's personal hopes."

"For Africa?" Susannah Chancellor asked quickly. "I thought the king of the Belgians was building a railway."

"I daresay he is," Christabel returned. "But we were referring to his amorous intentions."

"Oh! Dolly Tennant!"

"So we hear."

"Hardly a tragedy for Africa," Chancellor murmured. "Possibly even a relief."

Charlotte was now quite sure he knew about Leopold and the cannibals.

But Susannah was genuinely interested. She looked at Kreisler seriously.

"What do you believe is Africa's tragedy, Mr. Kreisler? You have not told us. If your regard is as deep as Miss Gunne indicates, you must care about it very much."

"I do, Mrs. Chancellor," he agreed. "But unfortunately that does not give me any power to affect it. It will happen regardless of anything I can do."

"What will happen?" she persisted.

"Cecil Rhodes and his wagons of settlers will press further up from the Cape into Zambezia," he answered, looking at her with intensity. "And one by one the native princes will make treaties they don't understand and don't intend to keep. We will settle the land, kill those who rebel, and there will be slaughter and subjection of God knows how many people. Unless, of course, the Germans beat us to it, driving westward from Zanzibar, in which case they will do the same, only worse—if past history is anything to judge from."

"Rubbish!" Chancellor said with good humor. "If we settle Mashonaland and Matabeleland we can develop the natural resources there for everyone's good, African and white alike. We can bring them proper medicine, education, trade, civilized laws and a code of society which protects the weak as well as the strong. Far from being Africa's tragedy, it would be the making of it."

Kreisler's eyes were hard and bright, but he looked only momentarily at Chancellor, then turned to Susannah. She had been listening to him with rapt attention, not with agreement, but rather with growing anxiety.

"That's not what you used to say." She looked at Chancellor with a crease between her brows.

His smile had only the barest shadow behind the obvious affection. "Perceptions change, my dear. One becomes wiser." He shrugged very slightly. "I now know a great deal that I did not two or three years ago. The rest of Europe is going to colonize Africa, whether we do or not. France, Belgium, Germany at least. And the Sultan of Turkey is nominally overlord of the Khedive of Egypt, with all that means to the Nile, and thus to the Sudan and Equatoria."

"It means nothing at all," Kreisler said abruptly. "The Nile flows northward. I'd be surprised if anyone in Equatoria had even heard of Egypt."

"I am thinking of the future, Mr. Kreisler, not the past." Chancellor was not in the least perturbed. "When the great rivers of Africa are among the world's highways of trade. The time will come when we will ship the gold and diamonds, exotic woods, ivory and skins of Africa along those great waterways as easily as we now ship coal and grain along the Manchester ship canal."

"Or the Rhine," Susannah said thoughtfully.

"If you like," Chancellor agreed. "Or the Danube, or any other great river you can think of."

"But Europe is so often at war," Susannah went on. "Over land, or religion, or any of a dozen other things."

He looked at her, smiling. "My dear, so is Africa. The tribal chieftains are always fighting one another. That is one of the reasons why all our attempts to wipe out slavery kept on failing. Really, the benefits are immense, and the costs relatively minor."

"To us, possibly," Kreisler said sourly. "What about to the Africans?"

"To the Africans as well," Chancellor answered him. "We shall bring them out of the pages of history and into the nineteenth century."

"That is exactly what I was thinking." Susannah was not convinced. "Transitions as sudden as that are not made without a terrible wrench. Maybe they don't want our ways? We are forcing them upon a whole nation without taking their opinions into account at all."

A spark of intense interest, even excitement, lit for a moment in Kreisler's eyes, and then as quickly was masked, as if deliberately.

"Since they cannot conceive what we are talking about," Chancellor said wryly, "they can hardly have an opinion!"

"Then we are deciding for them," she pointed out.

"Naturally."

"I am not certain we have the right to do that."

Chancellor looked surprised, and somewhat derisive, but he held his tongue tactfully. Apparently no matter how eccentric his wife's opinions, he did not wish to embarrass her publicly.

Beneath the surface argument he seemed to feel a confidence in her that overrode such things.

Nobby Gunne was looking at Kreisler. Christabel Thorne was watching everyone, each in turn.

"I was listening to Sir Arthur Desmond the other day," Susannah continued with a slight shake of her head.

Charlotte grasped her empty champagne glass so tightly it nearly shot out of her fingers.

"Desmond?" Chancellor frowned.

"From the Foreign Office," Susannah elaborated. "At least he used to be. I am not sure if he is there anymore. But he was most concerned about the subject of exploitation of Africa. He did not believe we would do it honorably at all. . . ."

Chancellor put his hand over hers very gently.

"My dear, I am grieved to have to tell you, but Sir Arthur Desmond died about two days ago, apparently by his own hand. He is not a source to be quoted with any authority." He looked suitably sad.

"No he didn't kill himself!" Charlotte burst out before thinking whether it was in the least wise, or would serve her purposes. All she could think of was Matthew's weary face and his distress, and Pitt's love for a man who had befriended him. "It was an accident!" she added in defense.

"I apologize," Chancellor said quickly. "I meant that he brought about the situation himself, whether by carelessness or design. Unfortunately it seems he was losing the clarity of mind he used to have." He turned back to his wife. "Thinking of Africans as noble savages, and wishing that they should remain so, is a sentimentality history does not allow. Sir Arthur was a fine man, but naive. Africa is going to be opened up by us or by others. Best for Britain and for Africa that it should be us."

"Would it not be better for Africa if we made treaties to protect them and keep Africa as it is?" Kreisler asked with apparent innocence which was belied by both his expression and the hard, thin edge to his voice.

"For adventurers and hunters like yourself?" Chancellor asked with raised eyebrows. "A sort of endless playground for explorers, with no civilized law to dictate anything at all."

"I am not a hunter, Mr. Chancellor, nor am I a scout for others," Kreisler rejoined. "An explorer, I accept. And I leave both the land and the people as I found them. Mrs. Chancellor has an excellent moral point. Have we the right to make decisions for other people?"

"Not only the right, Mr. Kreisler," Chancellor replied with absolute conviction. "Also the obligation when the others concerned have neither the knowledge nor the power to do it for themselves."

Kreisler said nothing. He had already registered his feelings. He looked instead at Susannah, his face thoughtful.

"I don't know about anyone else, but I am ready for supper," Christabel said in the momentary silence which followed. She turned to Kreisler. "Mr. Kreisler, since we outnumber you two to one, I am obliged to ask you to offer us an arm each to conduct us down the stairs. Miss Gunne, do you mind sharing Mr. Kreisler with me?"

There was only one possible answer, and Nobby gave it with a charming smile.

"Of course not. I shall be only too pleased. Mr. Kreisler?"

Kreisler offered his arms, and escorted Christabel and Nobby to supper.

Linus Chancellor did the same for Charlotte and Susannah, and together they swept down the great staircase, where at the bottom Charlotte recognized Pitt, who had been speaking to a very quiet, self-possessed man, quite bald, whom she judged to be nearer fifty than forty. He had round, pale blue eyes, a rather long nose, and a sense of calm about him, as if he knew some inner secret which was infinitely satisfying.

Pitt introduced him as Ian Hathaway, also of the Colonial Office, and when he spoke, Hathaway had the kind of voice, and perfect diction, that she felt she must have known him before, or at least met him.

She thanked Linus Chancellor and Susannah, and then found herself accompanied by two men as she approached the supper table, which held every kind of cold delicacy: pies, cold meats, fish, game, preserves in aspic, pastries of all sorts, and a multitude of ices, sherberts, jellies and creams amid crystal, flowers, candles and silver. The conversation at once became more sporadic, and largely meaningless.

Vespasia woke late the following morning, but with a considerable feeling of pleasure. She had enjoyed the reception more than usual. It had been a very grand affair and its splendor had brought back pleasant memories of her prime when she had commanded the admiration of every man who saw her, when she had danced the nights away and still risen early to ride in Rotten Row and return home with the blood pounding in her veins and ready to face a day of involvement in a dozen causes and intrigues.

She was still sitting in bed lazily eating her breakfast, smiling to herself, when her ladies' maid came to say that Mr. Eustace March had called to see her.

"Good gracious! What time is it?" she asked.

"Quarter past ten, m'lady."

"Whatever brings Eustace here at this time of the morning? Has he lost his pocket watch?"

Eustace March was her son-in-law, the widower of her late daughter, Olivia, who had borne him a large number of children and died comparatively young. Her marriage had been her own choice, but one Vespasia had never understood; nor had she found it easy to like Eustace. He was in every way her opposite. But it was Olivia who had married him, and as far as it was possible to judge from exteriors, he had made her happy.

"Shall I tell him to wait, m'lady? Or should I say you are unavailable today and he should come back another time?"

"Oh no. If he can wait, tell him I shall be down in half an hour."

"Yes m'lady." She withdrew obediently to deliver the message to the parlormaid to give to Eustace.

Vespasia finished her tea and set the tray aside. It would take her half an hour at least to prepare for the day satisfactorily. Her maid had returned and was waiting to assist her, and she rose and began with a wash in hot water and scented soap.

She entered the cool, classically spacious withdrawing room and saw Eustace standing by the window looking into the garden. He was a very solid man, very robust. He believed intensely in good health as a fundamental Christian virtue, to be coupled with sanity of mind, and thus a proper balance in all things. He approved of plenty of long walks in fresh air, open windows regardless of the weather, a fine appetite, cold baths and good sportsmanship as an ideal of manhood.

He turned around with a smile as he heard Vespasia come in. His rather grizzled hair was grayer than last time she had seen him, and definitely receding a little at the front, but as always he had a good color and a clear eye.

"Good morning, Mama-in-law, how are you? Well, I hope?" He seemed in particularly fine spirits, and obviously had something he wished to say to her. His enthusiasm was bursting from him and she was afraid he was going to grip her hand and wring it.

"Good morning, Eustace. Yes, I am very well, thank you."

"You are quite sure? You are up a little late. Early is best, you know. Good for the circulation. A good walk would make you feel fit for anything."

"For my bed again," she said dryly. "I did not get home until three in the morning. I attended the reception at the Duchess of Marlborough's. It was most enjoyable." She sat down in her favorite chair. "To what do I owe the pleasure of your visit, Eustace? You have not come simply to enquire after my health. You could have done that with a letter. Please do sit down. You look so restless standing there, bristling with energy; as if you were about to leave even as you tell me what is on your mind."

Eustace obeyed, but perched on the edge of his chair, as if relaxing would put a strain on him more than he could bear.

"I have not been to call on you for some time, Mama-in-law. I came principally to rectify that omission and to see how you are. I am delighted to find you so well."

"Rubbish," she said with a smile. "You have something to tell me. It is on the tip of your tongue. What is it?"

"Nothing specific, I assure you," he reiterated. "Are you still engaged in fighting for social reforms?" He leaned back in the chair at last and crossed his hands over his stomach.

She found his manner irritating, but perhaps that was more due to memory than anything in the present. It had been his intolerable bullying and insensitivity which had at least in part precipitated the tragedy which had overtaken the whole family in Cardington Crescent. Only afterwards had he been even touched with the slightest perception of his own part in it. For a brief period he had been bewildered and ashamed. It had passed rapidly, and now he was fully back to his original ebullience and the total conviction that he was right in all his major beliefs and opinions. Like many people of intense physical energy and good health, he had an ability to forget the past and proceed with the present.

Nevertheless, she found his attitude patronizing, like that of a benevolent schoolmaster.

"Now and then," she replied coolly. "I have also entertained myself with renewing some old acquaintances." She did not tell him that the principal among these was Thelonius Quade, a high court judge some twenty years her junior, who had in the past been an ardent admirer, deeply in love with her. The friendship, reawoken, was increasingly precious to her. That was something she did not wish to share with Eustace. "And also there are Thomas Pitt's cases," she added truthfully, although she knew Eustace would not like it. Apart from its being socially unacceptable to involve oneself with the police, it would far more piquantly bring back his own memories, griefs, and probably even guilt.

"I think that is rather unsuitable, Mama-in-law," he said with a frown. "Especially when there is so much that is worthy to be done. I have never minded your eccentricities now and then, but . . ." He stopped. Vespasia's eyes froze him and the rest of his sentence died on his lips.

"How generous of you," she said icily.

"What I mean is—"

"I know what you mean, Eustace. This whole conversation is unnecessary. I know what you wish to say, and you know what my reply will be. You do not approve of my friendship with Thomas and Charlotte, still less of my assisting them now and again. I have every intention of continuing, and do not consider it to be any of your concern." She smiled at him very slightly. "Shall we proceed from there? Do you have some particular worthy cause in mind in which you think I should be involved?"

"Now that you mention it . . .". He recovered his composure almost immediately. It was a quality in him she both admired and found intensely irritating. He was like one of those toys with a round, weighted base which one cannot knock over because automatically it rights itself the moment you let go of it.

"Yes?"

His face lit with enthusiasm again. "I have recently been permitted to join a most exclusive organization," he said eagerly. "I say 'permitted' because members are accepted only when proposed by another member and closely examined by a selection committee. It is entirely charitable of course, with the highest possible aims."

She waited, trying to keep her mind open to hear all he said. There were, after all, a legion of societies in London, most of them excellent in their purposes.

He crossed his legs, his face supremely satisfied. He had rather round, hazel-gray eyes, and they were shining with enthusiasm.

"Because all the members are men of means and in many cases considerable power in the community, in the world of finance or government, a great deal can be accomplished. Even laws changed, if it is desirable." His voice rose with the vigor of his feelings. "Enormous amounts of money can be raised to aid the poor, the disadvantaged, those suffering from injustices, disease or other misfortune. It is really very exciting, Mama-in-law. I feel highly privileged to be a member."

"Congratulations."

"Thank you."

"It sounds most praiseworthy. Perhaps I should join? Could you propose me?"

She watched his face with amusement. His mouth fell open, and his eyes reflected utter confusion. He was not even sure whether she was indulging in some distasteful joke. He had never been entirely certain of her sense of humor.

She waited, regarding him without a flicker.

"Mama-in-law, no serious society I know of accepts women! You must surely be aware of that?"

"Why not?" she asked. "I have money, no husband I am obliged to obey, and I am as capable of doing good as anyone else."

"That is not the point!" he protested.

"Oh. What is the point?"

"I beg your pardon?"

"What is the point?" she repeated.

Eustace was saved from justifying what to him was an assumption about the nature of the universe which was as beyond questioning as it was beyond explanation. The parlormaid came in to say that Mrs. Pitt had arrived.

"Oh, good gracious. Thank you, Effie," Vespasia said, acknowledging her. "I had not realized it was so late. Please ask her to come in." She turned back to Eustace. "Charlotte will accompany me while we take our cards to the Duchess of Marlborough."

"Charlotte will?" Eustace was dumbfounded. "To the Duchess of Marlborough? Really, this is preposterous, Mama-in-law! She is utterly unsuitable. Heaven knows what she might say or do. Surely you're not serious."

"I am perfectly serious. Thomas has been promoted since you last saw him. He is now a superintendent."

"I don't care if he is commissioner of Scotland Yard!" Eustace said. "You still cannot have Charlotte call upon the Duchess of Marlborough!"

"We are not going to call upon her," Vespasia said patiently. "We are simply going to leave our cards, which, as you know as well as I do, is customary after attending a function. It is the accepted way of expressing our appreciation."

" 'Our appreciation'! Charlotte was there?" He was still completely nonplussed.

"She was."

The door opened and Charlotte was shown in. As soon as she saw Eustace March her face registered a conflicting mixture of emotions—surprise, anger, self-consciousness—all overridden by curiosity.

Eustace's feelings were much plainer. There was nothing in his face but a pure and simple embarrassment. He rose to his feet, his cheeks flaming.

"What a pleasure to see you again, Mrs. Pitt, how are you?"

"Good afternoon, Mr. March." She swallowed hard and came forward.

Vespasia could guess what manner of event she was remembering, most probably the ridiculous episode under the bed. No doubt, from the scarlet in Eustace's cheeks, so was he.

"I am in excellent health, thank you," she added. "I am sure that you are also." That may have been a memory of his ever open windows in Cardington Crescent, even on cloudy mornings when the wind blew the breakfast room to almost intolerable temperatures, and everyone except Eustace was shivering over the porridge.

"Always, Mrs. Pitt," Eustace said briskly. "I am blessed in that manner."

"Eustace has been telling me about an excellent society he has been privileged to join," Vespasia said, indicating a chair for Charlotte.

"Ah—yes," Eustace agreed. "Dedicated to works of charity, and to influencing society for good."

"Congratulations," Charlotte said wholeheartedly. "You must feel a great sense of achievement. It is certainly sorely needed."

"Oh indeed." He resumed his own seat, sounding far more relaxed. He was back to discussing a subject which obviously pleased him enormously. "Indeed, Mrs. Pitt. It is most gratifying to feel that one can join with other men of like mind and dedication to the same purposes, and together we can be a real force in the land."

"What is the name of this society?" Charlotte asked innocently.

"Ah, you must not ask further, my dear lady." He shook his head a fraction, smiling as he did so. "Our aims and purposes are public and open to everyone, but our society itself is anonymous."

"You mean secret?" Charlotte asked boldly.

"Ah well." He looked taken aback. "I would not have chosen that word; it has a ring about it which gives quite the wrong idea, but it is anonymous. After all, is that not the way Our Lord commanded us we should do good?" His smile returned. " 'Let not your left hand know what your right hand doeth'?"

"Do you think a secret society was what He had in mind?" Charlotte asked with absolute seriousness, staring at him as she awaited his answer.

Eustace stared back at her as if he had been stung. His brain knew she was tactless, but he had almost forgotten the manner and the reality of it. It was ill-mannered to embarrass anyone, and she consistently embarrassed him; he thought, deliberately. No woman could be quite as unintelligent as she sometimes appeared.

"Perhaps 'discreet' would be a better word," he said finally. "I see nothing questionable in men helping each other to meet the needs of the less fortunate. In fact it seems like excellent sense. The Lord never extolled inefficiency, Mrs. Pitt."

Charlotte smiled suddenly and disarmingly. "I am sure you are right, Mr. March. And to claim public admiration for every act of charity is to rob it of any virtue at all. It is possibly even a fine thing that you yourselves will know only a few other members, simply those of your own ring. Then it is doubly discreet, is it not?"

"Ring?" All color had gone from his face now, leaving it oddly pale under the sun and windburn of his complexion, assiduously earned in good outdoor exercise.

"Is that not an appropriate term?" Charlotte asked, wide-eyed.

"I—well . . ."

"Never mind." Charlotte waved it away. She had no need to press it; the answer was obvious. Eustace had joined the Inner Circle, in innocence, even naïveté, as had so many before him—Micah Drummond and Sir Arthur Desmond, to name only two. Micah Drummond had broken from it and survived, at least so far. Arthur Desmond had not been so fortunate.

She turned to look at Vespasia.

Vespasia was very grave. She held out her hand to him.

"I hope you will be a powerful influence for good, Eustace," she said without pretense. "Thank you for coming to tell us your news. Would you care to stay to luncheon? Charlotte and I will not be long."

"Thank you, Mama-in-law, but I have other calls to make," he declined rapidly, rising to his feet and bowing very slightly, then similarly to Charlotte. "Charming to meet with you again, Mrs. Pitt. Good day to you both." And without waiting for anything further he left the room.

Charlotte looked at Vespasia and neither of them spoke.

CHAPTER
THREE

The inquest on Arthur Desmond was held in London since that was where he had died. Sitting in the gallery of the court, Pitt was grimly sure that it was also so that members of the Inner Circle could keep a greater command of the proceedings. Had it been in Brackley, where he and his family had been known and revered for three centuries, the personal regard in which he was held might have overridden even their power.

As it was he sat beside Matthew, who this morning looked almost haggard, and together they waited while the formal opening of the inquest took place amid a hush of anticipation. The room was full. People bumped and jostled each other making their way through the narrow doorway and under the beamed arch into the main area. The buzz of noise died away as people took their seats, facing the single bench at the front, the table to one side where an official in a black gown took notes, his pen at the ready, and the other side, where there was a stand for witnesses.

Pitt felt a strange sense of unreality. He was too filled with emotion to allow his mind to function with the clarity it usually had on such occasions. He had lost count of the number of inquests he had attended before this.

He looked towards the front. He could see at least fifteen or twenty men of sober bearing, dressed in full or half mourning, sitting shoulder to shoulder ready to give testimony as they were called. Most of them had the solid, confident look of wealth and assured position. He assumed they were either professional experts of some sort or else the members of the club who had been present on the afternoon of Sir Arthur's death. A nervous man, a few years younger, dressed less expensively, was probably one of the club stewards who had served the brandy.

The coroner was ill-suited by appearance for his task. Anyone more robust and full of the vigor of life would be hard to imagine. He was large with red-gold hair and a highly florid complexion, features broad and full of enthusiasm.

"Well now," he said heartily, as soon as the preliminaries were completed. "Wretched business. Very sorry. Let us get it over with as soon as we may, with diligence and dispatch. Diligence and dispatch, best way to deal with the trappings of loss. Condolences to the family." He looked around the room and saw Matthew. Pitt wondered whether he had already met him, or if he were simply skilled enough to recognize bereavement at a glance. "Shall we proceed? Good, good. Let us hear the first witness to this sorry event. Mr. Usher, send for him, if you please."

The usher obediently called for the club steward, who was, as Pitt had surmised, the man with the less expensive coat, and whose general embarrassment was now acute. He was overwhelmed, afraid of making a mistake. His manners were self-conscious, as were his clothes and his voice. He was awed by all the majesty of the law, even at this level, and by the finality of death. He mounted the witness stand with his eyes wide and his face pale.

"No need to be afraid, my man," the coroner said benignly. "No need at all. You didn't do anything wrong, did you? Didn't kill the poor creature?" He smiled.

The steward was appalled. For half a second, a blood-chilling second, he thought the coroner was serious.

"N-no sir!"

"Good," the coroner said with satisfaction. "Then compose your-self, tell us the truth, and all will be well. Who are you and what do you do? What have you to tell us about all this. Speak up!"

"M-my name is Horace Guyler, my lord. I am a steward at the Morton Club for Gentlemen. It was me as found poor Sir Arthur. I mean, o'course we all knew where 'e was, but . . ."

"I take your meaning perfectly," the coroner encouraged. "It was you who discovered he was dead. And I am not a 'my lord.' That is for the judges. I am merely a coroner. 'Sir' will do very well when you address me. Proceed. Perhaps you had better begin with Sir Arthur's arrival at the club. What time was that? When did you first see him? What was his appearance, his manner? Answer one at a time."

Horace Guyler was confused. He had already forgotten the first question, and the second.

"Sir Arthur's arrival," the coroner prompted.

"Ah. Yes sir. Well, 'e came in just after luncheon, which would be about quarter past three, sir, or thereabouts. 'E looked perfectly well to me at the time, which of course I realize now, but 'e must a' bin awful poorly. I mean, awful distressed in 'isself, about summink."

"You must not tell us what you realize now, Mr. Guyler, only what you observed at the time. What did Sir Arthur say to you? What did he do? What was his manner? Can you recall? It is only five days ago."

"As far as I remember, sir, 'e simply wished me a good day, same as always. 'E were always a very courteous gentleman. Not like some. And then he went through to the green room, sat down and read a newspaper to 'isself. *The Times*, I think it were."

There was a vague stirring in the room, murmurs of approval.

"Did he order anything to drink, Mr. Guyler?"

"Not straightaway, sir. About 'alf an hour later 'e ordered a large brandy. Best Napoleon brandy, 'e wanted."

"So you took it to him?"

"Oh yes sir, o' course I did," Guyler admitted unhappily. "O' course, I didn't know that then 'e was real upset and not 'isself. 'E seemed perfectly 'isself to me. Didn't seem upset at all. Just sat there reading 'is paper and muttering to 'isself now and then at pieces as 'e didn't agree with."

"Was he angry or depressed about it?"

"No sir." Guyler shook his head. "Just reading, like a lot o' gentlemen. 'E took it serious, o' course. But then gentlemen does. The more important the gentleman, the more serious 'e takes it. And Sir Arthur used to be in the Foreign Office."

The coroner looked grave. "Any subject in particular that you are aware of?"

"No sir. I weren't that close to 'im. I had a lot of other gentlemen to serve, sir."

"Naturally. And Sir Arthur had only the one brandy?"

Guyler looked unhappy. "No sir. I'm afraid 'e had a considerable number. I can't recall ezzac'ly 'ow many, but at least six or seven. Best part of one o' them 'alf bottles. I didn't know 'e weren't 'isself, or I'd never 'ave sent them!" He looked wretched, as if it really were somehow his responsibility, even though he was a club employee and might well have jeopardized his position had he refused to serve a member as he wished.

"And Sir Arthur remained in his usual spirits the whole time?" the coroner asked with a tiny frown.

"Yes sir, far as I could tell."

"Indeed. And what time did you serve the last brandy, do you recall?"

" 'Alf past six, sir."

"You are very precise."

"Yes sir. On account of a gentleman that asked me to call 'im to remind 'im of a dinner engagement 'e 'ad, so I knew ezzact."

There was no sound in the room.

"And the next time you saw Sir Arthur?"

"Well, I passed by 'im a few times, on me other errands like, but I took no notice 'cause 'e looked like 'e were asleep. O' course I wish now I'd a' done summink. . . ." He looked wretched, eyes downcast, face flushed.

"You are not responsible," the coroner said gently, the bonhomie gone from his expression. "Even had you known he was unwell and called a doctor, by the time anyone arrived there was probably little he could have done to save him."

This time there was a stirring in the room. Beside Pitt, Matthew shifted in his seat.

The steward looked at the coroner with a lift of hope.

" 'E were one of the nicest gentlemen," he said dolefully.

"I'm sure." The coroner was noncommittal. "What time was it when you spoke to Sir Arthur, Mr. Guyler, and realized that he was dead?"

Guyler drew a deep breath. "Well first I passed him an' thought 'e were asleep, like I said. Gentlemen who 'as drunk a lot o' brandy of an afternoon does fall asleep sometimes, an' is quite 'ard to rouse."

"I'm sure. What time, Mr. Guyler?"

"About 'alf past seven. I thought as if 'e wanted dinner it were time I booked a place for 'im."

"And what did you do?"

For a quarter of an hour no one in the court had moved or made any but the slightest of noises, merely a squeak of benches as the weight altered, or a creak and rustle of skirts from one of the two or three women present. Now there was a slow sighing of breath.

"I spoke to 'im, and 'e didn't answer," Guyler replied, staring straight ahead, painfully conscious of all eyes upon him. The court official at the table was taking rapid notes of everything he said. "So I spoke again, louder. 'E still didn't move, and I realized . . ." He took a deep breath and let it out slowly. He looked very nervous as the memory of death became sharper to him. He was frightened of it. It was something he chose never to think of in the normal course of things.

The coroner waited patiently. He had watched emotions like Guyler's chase across thousands of faces.

Pitt watched with a continuing sense of remoteness. Grief boiled up inside him; grief, a sudden overwhelming isolation as if he had been cut adrift from a safety he had been familiar with all his life. It was Arthur Desmond they were discussing so dispassionately. It was ridiculous to feel that they should have cared, should have spoken in hushed or tearful voices as if they understood the love, and yet he did feel it, even while his mind knew the absurdity.

He did not dare look at Matthew. He wanted to be done, to walk as quickly as he could, with the clear wind in his face, and the rain. The elements would keep him company as people could not.

But he must remain. Both duty and compassion required it.

"In the end I shook 'im." Guyler lifted his chin. "Just gentle like. 'E looked a terrible color, and I couldn't 'ear 'im at all. Gentlemen who is fallen asleep after the brandy very often breathe 'ard and deep. . . ."

"You mean they snore?"

"Well—yes sir."

There was a titter of laughter somewhere on the public benches, immediately suppressed.

"Why doesn't he get to what matters?" Matthew said fiercely beside Pitt.

"He will do," Pitt answered in a whisper.

"It was then I knew something was wrong," Guyler went on. He stared around the courtroom, not out of vanity but to remind himself where he was and dispel any memory of the club drawing room and what had happened there.

"You realized he was either ill or dead?" the coroner pressed.

"Yes sir. I sent for the manager, sir, and he sent for the doctor."

"Thank you, Mr. Guyler. That's all. Thank you for coming."

Guyler departed with relief, and the club manager took his place. He was a large, solid man with an agreeable face and a walleye which was most disconcerting. It was never possible to be certain whether he was looking at one or not. He testified to having been called by the steward and finding that Sir Arthur was indeed dead. He had sent for the doctor who was usually called upon if any of the gentlemen were taken unwell, which regrettably did happen from time to time. The average age of the membership was at least fifty-five, and many were a great deal older. The doctor had confirmed death without hesitation.

The coroner thanked the manager and permitted him to depart.

"This is pointless!" Matthew said between his teeth. He leaned forward and put his head in his hands. "It's all perfectly predictable and meaningless. They're going to get away with it, Thomas! Death by accidental overdose of an old man who didn't know what he was doing or saying!"

"Did you expect anything different here?" Pitt asked as quietly as he could.

"No." There was defeat in Matthew's voice.

Pitt had known it would hurt, but he was unprepared for how hard he found it to watch Matthew's distress. He wanted to comfort him, but there was nothing he could say.

The next witness was the doctor, who was professional and matter-of-fact. Possibly it was his way of dealing with the shock and finality of death. Pitt saw the dislike on Matthew's face, but it was born of emotion rather than reason, and this was not the time for an explanation which was irrelevant. It had nothing to do with what he was feeling.

The coroner thanked the doctor, dismissed him and then called the first of the members of the club who had been in the room during that afternoon. He was an elderly man with enormous white side-whiskers and a polished dome of a head.

"General Anstruther," the coroner said earnestly, "would you be good enough, sir, to tell us what you observed on that particular occasion, and if you consider it relevant, anything that you were aware of regarding Sir Arthur's health and state of mind."

Matthew looked up sharply. The coroner glanced at him. Matthew's face tightened but he said nothing.

General Anstruther cleared his throat loudly and began.

"Decent chap, Arthur Desmond. Always thought so. Getting older, of course, like the rest of us. Forgetting things. Happens."

"That afternoon, General," the coroner prompted. "How was his demeanor? Was he . . ." He hesitated. "Distrait?"

"Ah . . ." Anstruther hesitated, looking deeply uncomfortable.

Matthew sat rigid, his eyes unwaveringly on Anstruther's face.

"Is this really necessary?" Anstruther demanded, glaring at the coroner. "The fellow's dead, damn it! What more do we need? Bury him and remember him kindly. He was a good man."

"No doubt, sir," the coroner said quietly. "That is not in any sense in question. But we do need to ascertain exactly how he died. The law requires that of us. The circumstances are unusual. The Morton Club wishes to clear its name of any question of carelessness or impropriety."

"Good God!" Anstruther blew through his nose. "Who's suggesting such a thing? Absolute nonsense. Poor Desmond was not well and a trifle confused. He took too much laudanum along with brandy. Simple accident. No more to be said."

Matthew jerked up. "He was not confused!" he said aloud.

Everyone in the room turned towards him, surprised and more than a little embarrassed. One did not show emotion of such a sort, especially not here. It was not done.

"We sympathize with you, Sir Matthew," the coroner said clearly. "But please contain yourself, sir. I shall not allow any statements to pass without requiring they be substantiated." He turned back to the witness stand. "Now, General Anstruther, what causes you to say that Sir Arthur was confused? Please be specific."

Anstruther pursed his lips and looked annoyed. He was obviously very loath to accede. He glanced once at the front bench. "He . . . er . . . he forgot what he had said," he replied. "Repeated himself, don't you know? Got his facts muddled now and then. Talked a lot of nonsense about Africa. Didn't seem to understand."

Matthew rose to his feet before Pitt could restrain him.

"You mean he disagreed with you?" he challenged.

"Sir Matthew!" the coroner warned. "I will not tolerate repeated interruption, sir. We are aware of your very natural grief, but there are limits to our patience. This inquest will be conducted in proper order and decorum, with respect both for the truth and for the dignity of the occasion. I am sure you would wish that as much as anyone."

Matthew drew in his breath, possibly to apologize, but the coroner held up his hand to silence him.

Matthew sat back down again, to Pitt's relief.

"General, please be good enough to elaborate upon what you mean." The coroner turned to General Anstruther. "Did Sir Arthur merely disagree with you upon some matters? What precisely causes you to believe his reasoning was confused?"

The dark color washed up Anstruther's cheeks, making his white whiskers seem even more pronounced.

"Talked a lot of nonsense about secret combinations of people plotting together to conquer Equatoria, or some such thing." He glanced again at the front row, and then away. "Made a lot of wild accusations. Absolute nonsense of course. Contradicted himself half the time, poor devil. Terrible thing, to start losing your sense of . . . of . . . God knows, all your old loyalties, where your trust and decency lie, who your own people are, and what the values are you believed all your life."

"You mean Sir Arthur had substantially changed from the man he had been in the recent past?"

"I wish you wouldn't force me to say this!" Anstruther persisted angrily. "Let us bury him in peace, and his latter misfortunes with him. Let us forget this nonsense and remember him as he was a year or so ago."

Matthew groaned so audibly that not only did Pitt hear him,

the man on the far side of him heard as well. He looked around sharply, then flushed with discomfort at Matthew's obvious emotion, and looked away again.

"Thank you, General," the coroner said quietly. "I think you have told us enough for us to have some idea. You are excused."

Anstruther took out a white handkerchief and blew his nose savagely, then left, looking to neither side of him.

The Honorable William Osborne was called next, who said much the same as Anstruther had, adding one or two instances of Arthur Desmond's strange and irrational opinions, but he did not mention Africa. He was altogether a smoother and more assured man, and while he expressed regret in words, his manner did not suggest any emotion at all, except a slight impatience.

Matthew stared at him with implacable dislike, a growing bewilderment in his pain. It was more than possible that both Anstruther and Osborne were members of the Inner Circle. Pitt loathed to admit it, but it was also possible that Arthur Desmond had been somewhat irrational in his opinions, and that they were borne more of emotion than a knowledge of fact. He had always been highly individual, even eccentric. It was possible that in old age he had become detached from reality.

Another regular club member was called, a thin man with a sallow face and a gold watch with which his fingers were constantly fiddling as if it gave him some kind of comfort. He repeated what Osborne had said, occasionally using the same phrases to describe what he apparently viewed as the disintegration of Arthur Desmond's faculties of reason and judgment.

The coroner listened without interruption, and then adjourned the sitting until after luncheon. They had not begun until ten o'clock, and it was already well past midday.

Pitt and Matthew walked out into the brilliant sunlight side by side. Matthew was silent for several yards along the pavement, sunk in gloom. A passerby jostled him, and he seemed almost unaware of it.

"I suppose I should have expected this," he said at last as they turned the corner. He was about to walk on and Pitt caught him by the arm. "What?" he asked.

"Opposite." Pitt indicated a public house sign for the Bull Inn.

"I'm not hungry," Matthew said impatiently.

"Eat anyway," Pitt instructed, stepping off the curb and avoiding a pile of horse droppings. Matthew trod in it and swore.

At another time Pitt might have laughed at the sight of Matthew's face, but he knew this was not the occasion. They hurried to the far side, and Matthew scraped his feet angrily against the curb. "Don't they have any crossing sweepers anymore?" he demanded. "I can't go inside like this."

"Yes you can. They'll have a proper boot scraper at the door. Come on."

Reluctantly Matthew followed Pitt to the entrance, used the iron scraper meticulously, as if the state of his boots were of the utmost importance, and then they went in side by side. Pitt ordered for both of them and they sat down in the crowded, noisy room. Tankards gleamed on pegs above the bar, polished wood shone darkly, there was sawdust on the floor and the smell of ale, heat and bodies.

"What can we do?" Matthew said finally when their meal was served: thick bread with sharp crusts, butter, crumbling cheese, dark aromatic pickles and fresh cider.

Pitt made his sandwich and bit into it.

"Did you ever mean that we could achieve anything?" Matthew went on, his plate untouched. "Or were you just trying to comfort me?"

"Of course I meant it," Pitt replied with his mouth full. He was also angry and distressed, but he knew the importance of keeping up their strength if they were to fight. "But we cannot prove them liars until we know what they've said."

"And then?" Matthew asked with disbelief in his voice.

"And then we try," Pitt finished.

Matthew smiled. "How very literal of you. Absolutely exact. You haven't changed, have you, Thomas?"

Pitt thought of apologizing, and then realized there was no need.

Matthew appeared to be on the point of asking him something further, but decided against it and bit into his own sandwich. He ate it with surprising appetite, and did not speak again until it was time to leave.

The first witness of the afternoon was the medical examiner, who gave his evidence in detail, but he was very practiced at this unhappy task and avoided scientific terms. Quite simply, Arthur Desmond had died of an overdose of laudanum, administered within the hour. It was sufficiently large to have killed anyone, but there was a certain amount of brandy in his stomach, and that might well have masked the flavor. Personally he thought the laudanum would have tainted the brandy. He favored a very good cognac himself, but that was a matter of taste.

"Did you find any other signs of illness or deterioration?" the coroner asked.

The medical examiner pulled a long face. "Of course there was deterioration. The man was seventy! But that taken into account, he was in excellent health. I'll be happy to be as fit if I reach that age. And no, there was no other sign of illness whatever."

"Thank you, Doctor. That is all."

The medical examiner gave a little grunt and left the stand.

Pitt would have wagered that he was not a member of the Inner Circle. Not that he could think how that fact would be of any use.

The next witness was also a doctor, but an utterly different man. He was serious, attentive, polite, but he knew himself to be of great importance. He acknowledged his name and his qualifications and addressed himself to the matter in hand.

"Dr. Murray," the coroner began, "I believe you were Sir Arthur's physician; is that correct?"

"I was indeed."

"For some time."

"The last fourteen years, sir."

"Then you were very familiar with the state of his health, both in mind and body?"

Beside Pitt, Matthew was sitting forward, his hands clenched, his face tense. Pitt found himself also straining to hear.

"Naturally," Murray agreed. "Although I must confess I had no idea the deterioration had gone so far, or I should not have prescribed laudanum for him. I am speaking of the deterioration in his mood, his frame of mind."

"Perhaps you would explain further, Dr. Murray. What precisely are you referring to? Was Sir Arthur depressed, worried over some matter, or anxious?"

Now there was a breathless silence in the room. Journalists sat with pencils poised.

"Not in the sense you mean, sir," Murray replied with confidence. "He had bad dreams, nightmares, if you will. At least that is what he told me when he came to see me. Quite appalling dreams, you understand? I do not mean simply the usual unpleasant imaginings we all suffer from after a heavy meal, or some disagreeable experience." He shifted his position slightly. "He seemed to be increasingly disoriented in his manner, and had developed suspicions of people he had trusted all his life. I admit, I assume that he was suffering some senile decay of his faculties. Regrettably, it can happen to even the most worthy people."

"Very sad indeed," the coroner said gravely.

Matthew could bear it no longer. He shot to his feet.

"That's absolute nonsense! He was as lucid and in command of his mind as any man I know!"

A flash of anger crossed Murray's face. He was not accustomed to being contradicted.

The coroner spoke quite quietly, but his voice carried across the entire room, and everyone turned to stare.

"Sir Matthew, we all understand your grief and the very natural distress you feel at the loss of your father, and especially at the manner of it, but I will not tolerate your interruptions. I will question Dr. Murray as to his evidence." He turned to look at Murray again. "Can you give any instance of this behavior, Doctor? Were it as strange as you suggest, I am surprised you gave him laudanum in sufficient quantities to allow the event which brings us here."

Murray did not seem in the least contrite, and certainly not guilty. His words, like Osborne's, were full of apology, but his face remained perfectly composed. There were the marks of neither pain nor humor in it.

"I regret this profoundly, sir," he said smoothly, and without looking towards Matthew. "It is a sad thing to have to make public the frailties of a good man, especially when we are met to ascertain the causes of his death. But I understand the necessity, and the reason for your pressing the point. Actually I was not aware of all these things myself at the time I prescribed the laudanum, otherwise, as you say, it would have been a questionable act."

He smiled very faintly. One of the men in the front now nodded.

"Sir Arthur told me of his nightmares and his difficulty in sleeping," Murray resumed. "The dreams concerned wild animals, jungles, cannibals and similar frightening images. He seemed to have an inner fear of being overwhelmed by such things. I was quite unaware of his obsession with Africa at that time." He shook his head. "I prescribed laudanum for him, believing that if he would sleep more easily, and deeply, these thoughts would trouble him less. I only learned afterwards from some of his friends how far his rational thoughts and memory had left him."

"He's lying!" Matthew hissed, not looking at Pitt, but the words were directed to him. "The swine is lying to protect himself! The coroner caught him out so he twisted immediately to excuse himself."

"Yes, I think he is," Pitt said under his breath. "But keep your counsel. You'll never prove it here."

"They murdered him! Look at them! Sitting together, come to blacken his name and try to make everyone believe he was a senile old man who had so lost his wits he accidentally killed himself."

Matthew's voice was cracking with the bitterness which overwhelmed him.

The man on the far side of him looked uncomfortable. Pitt had the distinct impression he would have moved away were it not that it would have drawn such attention to him.

"You won't succeed by attacking him face-to-face," Pitt said harshly between his teeth, aware—with a chill in his stomach—of a new fear: that they had no way of knowing who was involved, who was friend and who enemy. "Keep your powder dry!"

"What?" Matthew swung around, incomprehension in his eyes. Then he understood the words, if not the weight of all that was behind them. "Oh. Yes, I'm sorry. I suppose that's exactly what they'd expect, isn't it? Me to get so angry I lose my sense of tactics."

"Yes," Pitt said bluntly.

Matthew lapsed into silence.

Dr. Murray had been excused and the coroner had called a man named Danforth who was a neighbor of Arthur Desmond's in the country, and he was saying, with some sadness, that indeed Sir Arthur had been extraordinarily absentminded lately, quite unlike his old self. Yes, unfortunately, he seemed to have lost his grasp on matters.

"Could you be more specific, sir?" the coroner suggested.

Danforth looked straight ahead of him, studiously avoiding the public benches where he might have met Matthew's eyes. "Well sir, an instance that comes to mind was approximately three months ago," he replied quietly. "Sir Arthur's best bitch had whelped, and he had promised me the pick of the litter. I had been over to look at them, and fine animals they were, excellent. I chose the two I wanted and he agreed, approved of it in fact." He bit his lip doubtfully for a moment before continuing, his eyes downcast. "We shook hands on it. Then when they were weaned I went over to collect them, only to find Arthur had gone up to London on some errand. I said I'd come back in a week, which I did, and he was off somewhere else, and all the pups had been sold to Major Bridges over in

Highfield. I was very put out." He looked at the coroner, frowning. There was a slight movement in the room, a shifting of position.

"When Sir Arthur finally came back I tackled him on the matter." The umbrage was still apparent in his voice and in the set of his shoulders as he gripped the edge of the box. "I'd set my heart on those pups," he went on. "But Arthur looked completely confused and told me some cock-and-bull story about having heard from me that I didn't want them anymore, which was the exact opposite of the case. And then he went on with a lot of nonsense about Africa." He shook his head and his lips tightened. "The terrible thing was, he obviously believed what he was saying. I'm afraid he had what I can only call an obsession. He imagined he was being persecuted by some secret society. Look, I say, sir . . . this is all very embarrassing."

Danforth shifted awkwardly, clearing his throat. Two or three men in the front now nodded sympathetically.

"Arthur Desmond was a damn decent man," Danforth said loudly. "Do we have to rake up all this unfortunate business? The poor devil accidentally took his sleeping medicine twice over, and I daresay his heart was not as strong as he thought. Can't we call an end to this?"

The coroner hesitated only a moment, then acquiesced.

"Yes, I believe we can, Mr. Danforth. Thank you for your evidence, sir, in what must have been a painful matter for you. Indeed, for all of us." He looked around the room as Danforth left the stand. "Are there any more witnesses? Anyone who has anything relevant to say in this matter?"

A short, broad man stood up in the front row.

"Sir, if you please, so this tragedy can be laid to rest, I and my colleagues"—he indicated the men on either side of him—"the full extent of the front row were in the Morton Club on the afternoon of Sir Arthur's death. We can confirm everything that the steward has said, indeed everything that we have heard here today. We would like to take this opportunity to extend our deepest sympathies to Sir

Matthew Desmond." He glanced around in the general direction of the bench where Matthew sat hunched forward, his face white. "And to everyone else who held Sir Arthur in esteem, as we did ourselves. Thank you, sir." He sat down amid murmurs of agreement. The man immediately to his right touched him on the shoulder in a gesture of approval. The one on the left nodded vigorously.

"Very well." The coroner folded his hands. "I have heard sufficient evidence to make my verdict sad, but not in doubt. This court finds that Sir Arthur Desmond died as the result of an overdose of laudanum, administered by himself in a moment of absentmindedness. Possibly he took the laudanum in mistake for a headache powder, or a remedy for indigestion. We shall never know. Death by misadventure." He looked up at Matthew very steadily, something of a warning in his expression.

The court erupted in excitement. Newspaper reporters made a dash for the doors. People in the public benches turned to one another, bursting with comment and speculation; several rose to their feet as a relief from sitting.

Matthew's face was ashen, his lips parted as if he were about to speak.

"Be quiet!" Pitt whispered fiercely.

"It is not a misadventure!" Matthew retorted between his teeth. "It was cold-blooded murder! Do you believe those—"

"No I don't! But on the evidence, we are damned lucky they didn't bring in a verdict of suicide."

The last traces of color drained out of Matthew's face. He turned to look at Pitt. They both knew what suicide meant: it was not merely dishonor, it was a crime against both the church and the state. He would not be given a Christian burial. He would die a criminal.

The coroner adjourned the court. The people rose and filed out into the sunshine, still talking busily, full of doubts, theories, explanations.

Matthew walked beside Pitt in the dusty street, and it was several minutes before he spoke again. When he did his voice was husky, almost paralyzed in the savaging of his pain and confusion.

"I've never felt like this in my life. I didn't think it was possible to hate anyone so much."

Pitt said nothing. He did not trust his own emotions.

Vespasia spent the afternoon in what had once been a very usual pursuit but was now one she practiced less and less often. She sent for her carriage at five minutes before three o'clock, and dressed in ecru-colored lace and a highly fashionable hat with a turned-up brim and trimmed with a huge white cabbage rose. And then, carrying an ivory-handled parasol, she came down the front steps and was assisted up into her carriage.

She instructed the coachman to take her first to Lady Brabazon's house in Park Lane, where she stayed for exactly fifteen minutes, which was the appropriate duration for an afternoon call. Less would have been too brief for courtesy, more would risk outstaying one's welcome. It was even more important to know when to leave than it was to know when to arrive.

Next she drove to Mrs. Kitchener's in Grosvenor Square, arriving a little before half past three, still well within the hour allotted for ceremonious calls. From four until five was for those less formal. From five until six was for those with whom one was on terms of friendship. Vespasia adhered to the convention. There were rules of society one might disobey, and there were those where it would be pointless and unacceptable. The timing of afternoon calls was among the latter.

What she was hoping to learn was a little more about the various members of the Colonial Office from a social point of view. For this it was necessary she begin to circulate again, in order that she might hear the appropriate gossip.

From Mrs. Kitchener's she proceeded north to Portman Square, and then to George Street, and Mrs. Dolly Wentworth's house, where she presented her card and was immediately invited in. It was now just past four o'clock, and an hour when tea might be offered and a call might last a little over the usual fifteen minutes.

"How charming of you to visit, Lady Cumming-Gould," Dolly Wentworth said with a smile. There were already two other ladies sitting perched on the edges of their chairs, backs ruler straight, parasols propped beside them. One was elderly with a handsome nose and imperious manner, the other at least twenty-five years younger, and from the resemblance in brow and coloring, presumably her daughter. Dolly Wentworth had a son, as yet unmarried. Vespasia drew her own conclusions as to their purpose, and was very soon proved correct. They were introduced as the Honorable Mrs. Reginald Saxby and Miss Violet Saxby.

Mrs. Saxby rose to her feet. It was customary for one party to leave as another arrived, and in no way a discourtesy. Miss Violet Saxby followed suit reluctantly.

"So unfortunate George should have been at his club," Mrs. Saxby said critically.

"I am sure he will be devastated to have missed you," Dolly murmured. "I often wonder why men go to their clubs so very often. It seems to me that some of them spend every afternoon there, or else at the races, or cricket, or some such thing."

"I don't know why they have clubs at all," Violet said petulantly. "There are hundreds of clubs for men, and barely half a dozen for women."

"The reason for that is perfectly obvious," her mother retorted. "Men have clubs in which to meet each other, talk a lot of nonsense about politics and sport and the like, and occasionally a little gossip, or business. It is where their social life is largely conducted."

"Then why not for women?" Violet persisted.

"Don't be absurd, child. Women have withdrawing rooms for such things."

"Then why do they have clubs for women at all?"

"For those who don't have their own withdrawing rooms, of course," Mrs. Saxby said impatiently.

"I don't know any ladies who don't have their own withdrawing rooms."

"Of course you don't. Any lady who does not have her own withdrawing room is not fit to be in Society, and consequently, she is not," Mrs. Saxby rejoined.

And with that Miss Saxby had to be content.

"Oh dear," Dolly said when they were gone. "Poor George is finding being single something of a trial." Further explanation was unnecessary.

"I think it is being so very eligible that is the trial," Vespasia said with a smile.

"Of course you are perfectly right. Please do sit down." Dolly waved vaguely at one of the pale blue chairs. "It seems like simply ages since I have seen you anywhere where it was possible to have a sensible conversation."

"That is because I have been to far too few such places." Vespasia accepted the invitation. "Although I did enjoy the Duchess of Marlborough's reception this week. I saw you in the distance, but of course one can never reach people at these affairs, except by accident. I did meet Susannah Chancellor. What an interesting creature. She reminded me of Beatrice Darnay. She isn't one of the Worstershire Darnays, is she?"

"No! Not at all. I don't know where her family comes from originally, but her father was William Dowling, of Coutts Bank."

"Indeed. I don't think I know him."

"Oh, you wouldn't, my dear. He's been gone several years now. Left a very considerable fortune. Susannah and Maude inherited it all, equally, I believe. No sons. Now Maude is dead, poor child, and her husband inherited it, along with the principal interest in the family banking business. Francis Standish. Do you know him?"

"I believe I have met him," Vespasia replied. "A distinguished-looking man, if I recall correctly. Very fine hair."

"That's right. Merchant banker. That sort of power always gives men an air of confidence, which has its own attractions." She settled a little more comfortably in her seat. "Of course his mother was related to the Salisburys, but I don't know how, precisely."

"And a woman of the most unusual appearance, named Christabel Thorne . . ." Vespasia continued.

"Ah, my dear!" Dolly laughed. "I think she is what is known as a 'new woman'! Quite outrageous, of course, but most entertaining. I don't approve. How could I? How could anyone with the least sense? It is really rather frightening."

"A new woman?" Vespasia said with interest. "Do you think so?"

Dolly's eyebrows rose. "Don't you? If women start wanting to leave their homes and families, and carve out a totally new role for themselves, whatever is going to happen to society in general? No one can simply please themselves all the time. It is completely irresponsible. Did you see that fearful play of Mr. Ibsen's? *A Doll's House*, or some such thing. The woman simply walked out, leaving her husband and children, for no reason at all."

"I think she felt she had reason." Vespasia was too old to care about being contentious. "He was excessively patronizing and treated her as a child, with no power or right to make her own decisions."

Dolly laughed.

"For heaven's sake, my dear, most men are like that. One simply finds one's own way 'round it. A little flattery, a little charm, and a great deal of tact to his face, and disobedience once his attention is elsewhere and most things can be achieved."

"She did not want to have to work for what she felt was every woman's right."

"You are sounding like a 'new woman' yourself!"

"Certainly not. I am a very old woman." Vespasia changed the subject. "What does this Christabel Thorne do that is so radical? She has not left her home, I'm sure."

"Far worse than that." Now there was real disapproval in Dolly's face; the laughter had gone entirely. "She has some sort of an establishment which prints and distributes the most detailed literature encouraging women to educate themselves and attempt to enter the professions. I ask you! Who on earth is going to employ a woman lawyer, or architect, or judge, or a woman physician? And it is all quite pointless. Men will never tolerate it anyway. But of course she will not listen."

"Extraordinary," Vespasia said with as little expression in her voice as she could manage. "Quite extraordinary."

They got no further with the subject because another caller arrived, and although it was well past four o'clock, it was apparent that Vespasia should take her leave.

The last person she visited was Nobby Gunne. She found her in her garden staring at the flag irises, a distracted expression on her face. Curiously, she looked anxious and yet inwardly she had a kind of happiness which lent her skin a glow.

"How nice to see you," she said, turning from the iris bed and coming forward. "I am sure it must be teatime. May I send for some for you? You will stay?"

"Of course," Vespasia accepted.

They walked side by side across the wide sunny sweep of the lawn, the occasional longer spikes of the uncut edges catching their skirts. A bumblebee flew lazily from one early pink rose to another.

"There is something about an English summer garden," Nobby said quietly. "And yet I find myself thinking more and more often of Africa."

"Surely you don't wish to go back there now, do you?" Vespasia was surprised. Nobby was past the age when such an enterprise would be either easy to arrange or comfortable in execution. What was an adventure at thirty could be an ordeal at fifty-five.

"Oh no! Not in the slightest." Nobby smiled. "Except in the occasional daydream. Memory can be misleadingly sweet. No, I worry about it, most particularly after the conversation we had the other evening. There is so much money involved in it now, so much profit to be made from settlement and trade. The days of exploration to discover a place, simply because no white man had seen it before, are all past. Now it is a matter of treaties, mineral rights and soldiers. There's been so much blood already." She looked sad, gazing at the honeysuckle spilling over the low wall they were passing.

"Nobody talks about missionaries anymore. I haven't heard anyone even mention Moffatt or Livingstone in a couple of years. It is all Stanley and Cecil Rhodes now, and money." She stared up at the elm trees shining and whispering in the sun, and below them the climbing white roses beginning to open. It was all intensely English. Africa with its burning heat and sun and dust seemed like a fairy story not real enough to matter.

But looking at Nobby's face, Vespasia could see the depth of her emotion, and how deeply she still cared.

"Times do change," she said aloud. "I am afraid that after the idealists come the realists, the practical profiteers. It has always been so. Perhaps it is inevitable." She walked quietly beside Nobby and stopped in front of a massive lupine whose dozen spikes were already showing pink. "Be grateful that you were privileged to see the best days and be part of them."

"If that were all"—Nobby frowned—"if it were only a matter of personal regret, I would let it go. But it really does matter, Vespasia." She looked around, her eyes dark. "If settlement of Africa is done badly, if we sow the wind, we will reap the whirlwind for centuries to come, I promise you." Her face was so grim, so full of undisguised fear, that Vespasia felt a chill in the summer garden and the cascades of blossoms seemed bright and far away, and even the warmth on her skin lacked a sense of reality.

"What exactly is it you think will happen?" she asked.

Nobby stared into the distance. She was not marshalling her thoughts; that had obviously already happened. She was seeing some inner vision, and the sight appalled her.

"If some of Linus Chancellor's plans go forward, and the men he is allied with, who are putting up enormous sums of money to colonize the interior ... I'm speaking about Mashonaland, Matabeleland, the shores of Lake Nyasa, or on towards Equatoria ... as they plan to, because they believe there is unlimited gold there," she replied, "then hordes of people will follow who are not in the least interested in Africa or its peoples, or in developing the land for themselves, or their children, but simply to rape it of its minerals." A butterfly drifted past them and settled on an open flower.

"There'll be profiteers of every kind, swindlers and cheats will be the least of them; there'll be violent men with their own private armies, and one by one they will draw in the native tribal chiefs. The internal wars are bad enough now, but they are only armed with spears. Think of it when some have guns and others don't."

She turned to face Vespasia. "And don't underestimate the Germans. They have a very powerful presence in Zanzibar, and are keen to press inland. There's been fearful bloodshed there already. And that may not be the worst of it. The Arab slavers will protect their interests by force, if they can. They have risen against the Germans once already."

"Surely the government is aware of all this?" Vespasia asked dubiously.

Nobby turned back to the garden, shrugging her shoulders very slightly. "I don't know if they believe it. It all seems different when you talk about it in England, so many names on paper, secondhand accounts, and all very far away. It's different when you've been there, and loved it, when you've known the people. They are not all noble savages with clear eyes and simple hearts."

They were walking again very slowly over the soft grass. She laughed jerkily. "They can be as devious and exploitative as any white man, and just as despotic. They can sell their enemies into slavery to any Arab who will buy them. It is the customary way to deal with prisoners of war. I don't think it's the morality that's the difference; it's the degree of power." She blinked hard. "It's our modern inventions, gunpowder, steel, our massive organization ...

we can do so much more evil, or good, with it. And I am so afraid with the greed for profit, the hunger for empire, it will be mostly evil we do."

"Is there anything to be done to prevent it?" Vespasia asked her. "Or at least to moderate it?"

"That is what troubles me," Nobby replied, starting to walk away from the border back across the lawn towards the shade of the cedar tree. They both sat down on the white bench.

"I am uncertain, and confused at present, but I feel that there is. I have spoken a little lately to Mr. Kreisler. He is very recently returned, and I respect his opinions." There was a very faint trace of color in her cheeks, and she did not look at Vespasia. "He was familiar with Abushiri, the leader of the rebellion against the Germans in Zanzibar. I gather it was principally a group of ivory and slave traders, who were beginning to feel restricted in their activities, but it was put down very messily. I confess, I know very little. Mr. Kreisler only mentioned it in passing, but it left me with an increasing anxiety."

Vespasia felt it too, but for different reasons. She was aware of the fall of Otto von Bismarck, the brilliant chancellor of Germany, the virtual creator of the new unified country. His nominal master, the old Kaiser, had been ill at the time, and died very shortly afterwards, of cancer of the throat. Now the sole ruler of the young and enormously vigorous state was the youthful, headstrong, supremely confident Kaiser Wilhelm the Second. German ambitions would know no cautious or restraining hand.

"I remember Livingstone's early years," Nobby said with a self-conscious smile. "That makes me sound old, doesn't it? How excited everyone was then. Nobody said anything about gold or ivory. It was all a matter of discovering people, finding new and wonderful sights, great cataracts like the Victoria Falls." She stared up through the dark green boughs of the cedar at the brilliance of the sky. "I met someone who had seen it once, just a few months earlier. I was standing outside in the evening. It was still hot, really hot. England is never close to the skin like that, touching, breathing heat.

"All the acacia trees were flat-topped against a sky burning with stars, and I could smell the dust and the dry grass. It was full of insects singing, and half a mile away at the water hole, I heard a lioness roar. It was so still, I felt as if I could have reached out and touched her."

There was a sadness close to tears in Nobby's face. Vespasia did not interrupt her.

"The man was an explorer who had set out with a party. A white man," Nobby went on quietly, almost as if to herself. "He was ill with a fever when he reached us. He staggered into our camp so exhausted he could barely stand. He was wasted until he was skin and bone, but his face lit up when he spoke and his eyes were like a child's. He had seen it some three months before . . . the greatest cataract in the world, he said . . . as if the ocean itself poured off the cliffs of the sky in an endless torrent, leaping and roaring into a chasm of which one could not see the bottom for the white spume flying and the endless rainbows. The river had a dozen arms, and every one of them flung itself into that gorge and the jungle clung to the sides and leaned over the brink in a hundred different places." She fell silent.

"What happened to him?" Vespasia asked.

Somewhere above them a bird was singing in the cedar tree.

"He died of fever two years later," Nobby answered. "But please God the falls will be there till the end of time." She stood up again and began to walk back across the grass towards the house, Vespasia behind her. "I'm sure tea must be ready. Would you care for some now?"

"Yes please." Vespasia caught up with her.

"Mr. Kreisler hunted with Selous, you know," Nobby continued.

"Who is Selous?"

"Oh! Frederick Courtney Selous, a marvelous hunter and

scout," Nobby replied. "Mr. Kreisler told me Mr. Selous is the one leading the Rhodes column north to settle Zambezia." The shadow was back in her face, and yet there was a lift in her voice, a subtle alteration when she spoke Kreisler's name. "I know Mr. Chancellor is backing Rhodes. And of course Francis Standish's bank."

"And Mr. Kreisler disapproves," Vespasia said. It was not really a question.

"I fear he has reason," Nobby answered, looking across at Vespasia suddenly. "I think he loves Africa genuinely, not for what he hopes to gain, but for itself, because it is wild and strange, beautiful and terrible and very, very old." There was no need to say how much she admired him for it; it shone in her face and whispered in the gentleness of her voice.

Vespasia smiled and said nothing. They continued side by side across the lawn, their skirts brushing the grass, and went up the steps and in through the French window to take tea.

There was a charity bazaar the day after which Vespasia had promised to attend. It was being conducted by an old friend, and in spite of disliking such events, she felt obliged in kindness to support her efforts, although she would far rather simply have donated the money. However she thought Charlotte might find it entertaining, so she dispatched her carriage to fetch her if she wished.

As it turned out, it was not at all as she had expected, and the moment she and Charlotte had arrived, she knew it would at least be entertaining, at best possibly informative. Her friend, Mrs. Penelope Kennard, had omitted to tell her that it was a Shakespearean bazaar, where everyone who had any official part in the proceedings dressed as a character from a Shakespearean play. As a result they were greeted at the garden gate by a very handsome Henry V, who bade them welcome in ringing tones. And almost immediately they left him, they were assaulted by a villainous Shylock demanding money or a pound of flesh.

Startled only for a moment, Vespasia good-naturedly handed him a handsome entry fee for herself and Charlotte.

"Good gracious, whatever next?" she murmured as they passed out of earshot and towards a stall where a young society matron was attired as Titania, Queen of the Fairies from *A Midsummer Night's Dream*, and looking very fetching indeed. A great deal more of her was visible than even the most daring evening gown would have displayed. Lengths of gauze were swathed around her, leaving arms, shoulders and waist bare, and much more could be guessed at beneath its diaphanous folds. There were two young gentlemen bickering over the price of a lavender pomander, and several more waited eagerly to take their turn.

"Effective!" Charlotte said with reluctant admiration.

"Oh very," Vespasia agreed, smiling to herself. "The last time Penelope did one of these bazaars it was all characters from Mr. Dickens, and not nearly so much fun. They all looked rather alike to me. Look! There! Do you see Cleopatra selling pincushions?"

Charlotte followed Vespasia's indication and saw a remarkably handsome young woman with dark hair and eyes, a rather Grecian nose, perhaps a trifle high at the bridge for beauty, and a willful, highly individual mouth. It was a countenance that could indeed have belonged to a woman used to power and an extraordinary mixture of self-discipline and self-indulgence. She was at that moment offering a small, embroidered, lace-edged pincushion to a gentleman in an immaculate frock coat and striped trousers. He looked like a city banker or a dealer in stocks and securities.

A bishop in traditional gaiters walked by slowly, smiling in the sun and nodding first to one side then the other. His eyes lingered for several moments upon Cleopatra, and he very nearly stopped and bought a pincushion, before judicious caution prevailed and he continued on his way towards Titania, still smiling.

Vespasia glanced at Charlotte; words were unnecessary.

They walked gently on between the stalls where imaginatively dressed young women were selling sweetmeats, flowers, ornaments, ribbons, cakes and pictures, and yet others were offering games to play for various prizes. She saw one booth decked out in curtains of shadowy material with silver stars pinned to them, and letters proclaiming that for a sixpence the witches of Macbeth would tell your fortune and recite to you all the great achievements which lay in your future. There was a queue of giggling girls waiting their turn to go in, and even a couple of young men, pretending they were there simply to accompany them, and yet with a spark of interest in their faces.

Just past them Charlotte saw the sturdy figure of Eustace March, standing very upright, talking intently to a broad man with flowing white hair and a booming voice. They both laughed heartily, and Eustace bade him farewell and turned towards Charlotte. He saw her with a look of alarm, but it was too late for him to pretend he had not. He straightened his shoulders and came forward.

"Good afternoon, Mrs. Pitt. How pleasant to see you. Supporting a worthy cause, I see!" He laughed jerkily. "Excellent." Vespasia had stopped to speak to an acquaintance, and he had not seen her. He hesitated, searching for something to say, undecided whether he had satisfied good manners sufficiently to leave yet. "Lovely day. A joy to be out in it. Fine garden, don't you think?"

"Delightful," Charlotte agreed. "Most kind of Mrs. Kennard to lend it for the bazaar. I think there will be a great deal to clear up after all these people."

He winced very slightly at her candor in mentioning such a thing.

"All in a good cause, my dear lady. These small sacrifices are necessary if we are to be of service. Nothing without effort, you know!" He smiled, showing his teeth.

"Of course," she agreed. "I imagine you know a great many of the people here?"

"Oh no, hardly any. I have little time to mix in Society as I used to. There are too many important things to be done." He looked poised to depart and set about them immediately.

"You interest me greatly, Mr. March," she said, meeting his eyes.

He was horrified. It was the last thing he had intended. She always made him uncomfortable. The conversation so seldom went as he had wished.

"Well, my dear lady, I assure you ... I ..." He stopped.

"How modest of you, Mr. March." She smiled winningly.

He blushed. It was not modesty but an urgent desire to escape.

"But I have thought a great deal about what you said only yesterday concerning organizing together to do good," she said eagerly. "I am sure in many ways you are right. When we cooperate, we can achieve so much more. Knowledge is power, is it not? How can we be effective if we do not know where the greatest need lies? We might even end up doing more harm, don't you think?"

"Yes, I imagine that is true," he said reluctantly. "I am so glad you have realized that hasty judgment is very often mistaken. I assure you, the organization to which I belong is most worthy. Most worthy."

"And modest," she added with a perfectly straight face. "It must have been so distressing for you that Sir Arthur Desmond was saying such disagreeable things about it, before the poor man died."

Eustace looked pale, and acutely uncomfortable.

"Er ... most," he agreed. "Poor man. Senile, of course. Very sad." He shook his head. "Brandy," he added, pushing out his lower lip. "Everything in moderation, I always say. A healthy mind in a healthy body. Makes for both virtue and happiness." He took a deep breath. "Of course I don't hold with laudanum and the like at all. Fresh air, cold baths, brisk exercise and an easy conscience. No reason why a man shouldn't sleep every night of his life. Never think of powders and potions." He lifted his chin a little and smiled again.

A menacing Richard III walked crabwise past them, and two young women laughed happily. He shook a fist and they entered into the spirit of it by pretending to be frightened.

"An easy conscience requires a life of extraordinary virtue, frequent and profound repentance, or absolute insensitivity," Charlotte said with a slight edge to her voice, and only turning to look at Eustace at the last moment.

He blushed very pink, and said nothing.

"Unfortunately I did not know Sir Arthur," she went on. "But I have heard he was one of the kindest and most honorable of men. Perhaps he had pain, and that was what caused him to be wakeful? Or anxieties? If one is responsible for others, it can cause a great deal of worry."

"Yes—yes, of course," Eustace said unhappily. She knew memory was awakening in him, with all its discomforts. If he slept well every night, she felt he had no right to.

"Did you know him?" she pressed.

"Uh—Desmond? Oh . . . well . . . yes, I met him a few times. Not to say I knew him, you understand?" He did not look at her.

She wondered if he and Sir Arthur could conceivably have been in the same ring of the Inner Circle, but she had no idea even how many people were in a ring. She thought she recalled from something Pitt had said that it was no more than half a dozen or so, but she was unclear. For it to be effective, the groups would surely have to be larger than that in some way? Perhaps each ring had a leader, and they knew the others, and so on.

"You mean socially?" she asked with as much naïveté as she could manage. She found it was not very much. "At hunt balls and so on? Or to do with his work?"

Eustace looked somewhere over his left shoulder, his cheeks pink. "His work?" he said with alarm. "I . . . I am not sure what you mean. Certainly not."

It was sufficient. He had taken her to be referring to the Inner Circle. Had it been a social acquaintance he would have admitted it without embarrassment, but she had been almost sure Eustace March did not move in the higher regions of old society, landed gentry, the true aristocracy where Arthur Desmond lived because he was born to it.

"I meant the Foreign Office." She smiled sweetly. "But of course I knew it was unlikely."

"Quite. Quite so." His answering smile was sickly. "Now, my dear lady, if you will excuse me, I must be about my duty. There is so much to do. One must show one's presence, you know? Buy a little here and there, give encouragement and set the example." And without allowing her a chance to argue he hastened away, nodding to either side as he saw acquaintances present or wished for.

Charlotte stood thoughtfully for a few moments, then turned and went back the way Vespasia had gone. Within a few moments she was near Cleopatra's pincushions again, and found herself interested to observe the interplay of an elderly matron, torn between envy and disapproval, and a young lady fast approaching an unmarriageable age, unless she were an heiress. With them was a gentleman Charlotte's practiced eye recognized as having had his collars and cuffs turned, to make them wear another six months or so. She had turned enough of Pitt's to know them when she saw them.

It was after a few moments she realized she had heard Cleopatra addressed as Miss Soames. Could she be Harriet Soames, to whom Matthew Desmond was betrothed?

When the purchase was made and the three people moved away, Charlotte went up to the counter of the stall.

"Excuse me?"

Cleopatra looked at her helpfully, but without interest. Closer to she was even more unusual. Her dark eyes were very level, her mouth not voluptuous, her upper lip unfashionably straight, and yet her face was full of deep inner emotion.

"May I show you something?" she asked. "Is it for yourself, or a gift?"

"Actually I overheard the previous purchaser address you as Miss Soames. Are you by any chance Miss Harriet Soames?"

She looked puzzled. "Yes. I am. But I am afraid I cannot recall our having met."

It was a polite and predictable reply from a well-bred young woman who did not wish to be rushed into an acquaintance with a person she knew nothing about, and to whom she had not been introduced.

"My name is Charlotte Pitt." Charlotte smiled. "My husband has been a lifelong friend of Sir Matthew Desmond. May I offer you my felicitations on your betrothal, and my sympathies for the death of Sir Arthur. My husband feels his loss so deeply, I know he must have been a most unusual man."

"Oh—" Having received a satisfactory explanation, Harriet Soames was perfectly prepared to be friendly. Her face softened into a charming smile. "How kind of you, Mrs. Pitt. Yes indeed, Sir Arthur was one of the nicest people I ever knew. I expected to be in awe of him, as one usually is of a prospective father-in-law, but from the moment I met him, I felt completely at ease." Memory in her face was touched at once with pleasure and pain.

Charlotte wished even more sharply that she had met Sir Arthur. She would have felt his death more keenly herself, but she would have been better able to share Pitt's emotion. She knew that his grief bit very deep and was mixed with guilt, and at the moment she was outside it. It was beyond either of them to alter that.

"Sir Matthew came to visit us the other evening," Charlotte continued, largely for something to say. "I had not met him before, but I found I liked him immediately. I do wish you every happiness."

"Thank you, that is most kind." Harriet seemed about to add something further, but was prevented by the arrival of a young woman whose face grew more and more appealing the longer one looked at it. At a glance one would have said she was ordinarily pretty with regular features and typically pleasing English fair coloring, not flaxen, but the warm deep tone of honey, and her complexion was unfashionably glowing with natural color. But with further regard there was an intelligence and humor in her face which made her anything but ordinary.

Not realizing Charlotte and Harriet were speaking as friends, rather than vendor and purchaser, she did not hesitate to interrupt, and then hastily apologized when Harriet introduced them. The newcomer's name was Miss Amanda Pennecuick.

"Oh, I am so sorry," Amanda said quickly. "How appallingly rude of me. Forgive me, Mrs. Pitt. I have nothing of the least importance to say."

"Nor I," Charlotte confessed. "I was merely introducing myself, since my husband is a very old friend of Sir Matthew Desmond's." She assumed Amanda knew of Harriet's betrothal, and her face made it immediately plain that she did.

"I am so cross," Amanda confided. "Gwendoline Otway is doing those fearful astrology readings again, and she promised she wouldn't. You know there are times when I feel I could slap her! And she has dressed herself as Anne Boleyn."

"With or without her head?" Harriet asked with a sudden giggle.

"With it . . . for the moment," Amanda replied grimly.

"I didn't know Anne Boleyn was Shakespearean." Harriet screwed up her brow.

"Farewell. . . . 'A long farewell to all my greatness,' " a beautifully modulated masculine voice said from just behind Amanda's shoulder, and they turned to see the bright, homely face of Garston Aylmer. "Cardinal Wolsey," he said cheerfully, looking at Amanda. "*Henry the Eighth*," he added.

"Oh, yes of course. Good afternoon, Mr. Aylmer," she replied, regarding him levelly, and almost without expression in her face, which was difficult because it was a countenance naturally given to emotion.

"Why does it displease you so much that she should pretend a little astrology?" Charlotte asked. "Is it not a fairly harmless way of entertaining people and raising money for the bazaar?"

"Amanda disapproves of astrology," Harriet said with a smile. "Even as a game."

"The stars are not in the least magical," Amanda said quickly.

"At least not in that sense. The truth of them is far more wonderful than a lot of silly names and ideas about classical heroes and imaginary beasts. If you had any idea of the real magnitude . . ." She stopped, aware that Garston Aylmer was staring at her with intensity, and an admiration in his face so plain no one watching him could have been unaware of it.

"Forgive me," she said to Charlotte. "I really should not allow myself to get so upset over something so silly. No doubt she is amusing people who would never look through a telescope even if you placed one into their hands." She laughed self-consciously. "Perhaps I had better buy a pincushion. Please let me see that one with the white lace on it."

Harriet passed it across.

"Perhaps you would allow me to escort you to tea, Miss Pennecuick? And you, Mrs. Pitt?" Aylmer offered.

Charlotte knew well enough when not to intrude. She had no idea what Amanda felt, but Aylmer's feelings were apparent, and she rather liked him.

"Thank you, but I have come with my great-aunt, and I should find her again before too long," she declined.

Amanda hesitated, apparently considering the matter, then coolly accepted, excusing herself to both Charlotte and Harriet. She made her purchase and left, walking beside Aylmer, but not taking his proffered arm. They looked unsuited together; she was so slender and elegant, and he was quite unusually plain, short legged, and definitely too plump.

"You should have gone," Harriet said under her breath. "Poor Amanda."

"I really did come with my great-aunt," Charlotte replied with a wide smile. "Honestly."

"Oh!" Harriet blushed. "I'm so sorry! I thought you were . . ." She started to laugh, and a moment later Charlotte joined in.

Fifteen minutes later she found Vespasia and together they

went to the tent where afternoon tea was being served. They saw Aylmer and Amanda Pennecuick just leaving, apparently still in conversation.

"An unexpected couple," Vespasia observed.

"His design, not hers," Charlotte replied.

"Indeed." Vespasia looked at the young girl who had come to offer them sandwiches and little cakes decorated and iced in a variety of designs. They made their choice, and Vespasia poured the tea. It was still too hot to sip when Charlotte noticed Susannah Chancellor at the next table, which was rather more behind them so it was half hidden by a samovar on a stand and a large potted plant with a price ticket poking out of it. However, when for a moment neither she nor Vespasia were speaking, Susannah's voice was just audible. It sounded polite and curious, but there were the beginnings of anxiety in it.

"I think you are leaping to conclusions without knowing all the facts, Mr. Kreisler. The plans have been very thoroughly thought through, and a great many people consulted who have traveled in Africa and know the natives."

"Such as Mr. Rhodes?" Kreisler's voice was still on the borders of courtesy, but he was not concealing his disbelief, nor the dislike he felt for Cecil Rhodes and his works.

"Of course he is one of them," Susannah agreed. "But certainly not the only one. Mr. MacKinnon—"

"Is an honorable man," he finished for her. His voice was still light, almost bantering in tone, but there was an intensity beneath which was unmistakable to the ear. Charlotte could not see him, but she could imagine the unwavering look in his eyes, even if he were pretending to smile. "But he has to make a profit. That is his business, and his honor depends upon it, even his survival."

"Mr. Rhodes has a great deal of his own money invested in this venture," Susannah went on. "Neither my husband nor my brother-in-law would have backed him as they have were he simply an adventurer with no stake in it himself."

"He is an adventurer with a very great stake in it himself," Kreisler said with a slight laugh. "He is an empire builder of the highest order!"

"You sound as if you disapprove of that, Mr. Kreisler. Why? If we do not, then others will, and we shall have lost Africa, perhaps to Germany. You can't approve of that, can you? Or of the slavery that goes on now?"

"No, of course not, Mrs. Chancellor. But the evil there now is centuries old, and part of their way of life. The changes we will bring about will not necessarily get rid of them, only produce war with the Arabs, who are the largest slavers, with the ivory traders and with the Portuguese, and undoubtedly with the Germans and the Sultan of Zanzibar. And most of all, it will set up our own empire in Equatoria, which will eventually overtake Emin Pasha, Lobengula, and the Kabaka of Buganda and everyone else. White settlers with guns will drive out the old ways, and in half a century the Africans will be a subject people in their own land. . . ."

"You're exaggerating!" There was laughter and disbelief on the surface of her voice, but underneath a beginning of worry, a sharp note of doubt. "There are millions of Africans, and only a handful of us . . . a few hundred."

"Today," he said harshly. "And tomorrow, when there's gold— and land? When the wars have been fought and there is adventure and profit to offer all the younger sons with no lands here? For those who've made a mess in Europe, or whose families won't support them or protect them anymore?"

"It won't be like that," she said urgently. "It will be like India. There will be a proper standing army, and a civil service to administer it and keep the law and . . ." She stopped.

"Is that what you believe?" he said so softly Charlotte had to strain to catch his words.

"Well . . ." Susannah hesitated. "Not exactly, of course. It will take time. But yes, eventually it will."

"India is a culture and a civilization thousands of years older than ours. They were reading and writing, building cities and painting great art, dreaming philosophy, when we were running around painting ourselves blue and wearing animal skins!" he said with his contempt barely hidden.

"We still brought them the benefits of our laws," she said. "We settled their internal quarrels and united them as a great country. We may be upstarts in some ways, but we brought them peace. We'll do it in Africa too."

Kreisler said nothing. It was impossible to imagine what expression was in his face. Neither Charlotte nor Vespasia had said a word since they had both recognized Susannah Chancellor's voice. Their eyes had met a dozen times with thoughts that needed no speech.

"Did you know Sir Arthur Desmond?" Susannah said after a moment or two.

"No. Why?"

"No reason, except that he would have agreed with you. He seemed to be worried about Africa too."

"Then I should like to know him."

"I am afraid that is not possible. He died last week."

Kreisler said nothing, and a moment later they were apparently joined by Christabel Thorne, and the conversation became quite general, and to do with the bazaar.

"A man of great passions, Mr. Kreisler," Vespasia said, sipping the last of her tea. "An interesting man, but I fear a dangerous one."

"Do you think he is right . . . about Africa?" Charlotte asked.

"I have no idea. Perhaps, at least in part, he is. But I am quite sure he has no doubts at all. I wish Nobby were not so fond of him. Come, my dear, we have done our duty now. We may feel free to leave."

CHAPTER
FOUR

Charlotte and Pitt arrived early at the village of Brackley for the funeral of Arthur Desmond. They alighted from the train into brilliant sunshine; the small station had only a single platform stretching a hundred yards or so with the building in the center containing the waiting room, ticket office and stationmaster's house. The rest bordered on fields already deep in corn, and the heavy trees beyond were towering vivid green with new leaf. Wild roses in bud were hanging sprays out of the hedgerows and the may blossom, with its sweet perfume, was starting to open.

Pitt had not been back to Brackley for fifteen years, and now suddenly it enveloped him in familiarity as if he had left only last night. Everything was exactly the same, the angle of the station roof against the sky, the curve of the lines as the track swerved away towards Tolworth, the huge coal bunkers for refueling. He even found he stepped automatically to avoid the bad patch of platform where it had become worn immediately before the doorway. Only it all looked just a little smaller than he had recalled, and perhaps a little shabbier.

The stationmaster's hair had turned gray. Last time he had seen him it had been brown. And he wore a black band of mourning on his arm.

He was about to speak some automatic word of greeting, then he stopped and looked again. "Young Thomas? It is young Thomas, isn't it? 'Course it is! I told old Abe as you'd come. A sad day for Brackley, an' no mistake."

"Good morning, Mr. Wilkie," Pitt replied. He added the "Mr." intentionally. He was a superintendent of police in London, but this was his home; here he was the gamekeeper's son from the Hall. The stationmaster was his equal. "Yes, very sad." He wanted to add something else about why he had not been back in so long, but excuses were empty, and today no one would care. Their hearts were full; they had no room left for anything but the sense of loss which united them. He introduced Charlotte and Wilkie's face lit up. Clearly it was a courtesy he had not fully expected, but one that pleased him greatly.

They were no farther than the door onto the road when another three people came in from the platform. Apparently they had been farther along in the train. They were all gentlemen of middle or later years and, to judge from their dress, of substantial means. With a cold jolt of memory Pitt recognized at least one of them from the inquest, and felt a rush of hatred so powerful he stood motionless on the step in the sunlight and Charlotte went on without him. Had it not been so ridiculous, he would have liked to have gone back and accused the man. There was nothing remotely useful he could say, simply relieve himself of some of the anger and pain he felt, and the outrage that the man could say such things publicly, regardless of what he may have suspected in private. It was a kind of betrayal of whatever friendship he and Arthur Desmond had shared.

Perhaps it was the sheer indignity of it which stopped him, and the knowledge that it would embarrass Charlotte—although she would understand—and even more, Wilkie, the stationmaster. But it was also his own sense of guilt. Had he been back here more often he would have been in a position to deny the slanders from knowledge, not merely memory and love.

"Thomas?"

Charlotte's voice cut across his thoughts and he turned and followed her out onto the bright road, and they set out the half mile or so to the village street, and the church beyond.

"Who were they?" she asked.

"They came to the inquest." He did not add in what capacity and she did not ask. Almost certainly his tone of voice had told her.

It was a short walk and they did not speak again. There was no sound but that of their feet on the roadway and the faint whisper of breeze now and then in the hedges and trees, and birds calling. Far away a sheep bleated and a lamb replied, sharper, higher pitched, and a dog barked.

The village too was unusually silent. The grocer, the ironmonger and the baker were all closed for business, blinds drawn, and wreaths or black ribbons on the doors. Even the smithy's forge was cold and tidy, and deserted. A small child, perhaps four or five years old, stood in the doorway of one of the houses, its face solemn, wide-eyed. No one was playing outside. Even the ducks on the pond drifted idly.

Pitt glanced at Charlotte and saw the awe in her face, and the soft sadness, for a community in mourning, and for a man she had never known.

At the farther end of the main street there were half a dozen villagers dressed in black, and as Charlotte and Pitt approached them they turned. At first all they saw was Charlotte's black gown and Pitt's black armband and black tie, and they felt an immediate fellowship; then after a second look one of them spoke.

"Young Tom, is that you?"

"Zack, you didn't ought to speak like that!" his wife whispered quickly. "He's a gentleman now, look at him! I'm sorry, young Thomas, sir. He didn't mean no disrespect."

Pitt scrambled through memory to place the man whose dark hair was streaked with gray and whose face was burned by weather and lined with screwing it up against the wind.

"That's all right, Mrs. Burns. 'Young Tom' is fine. How are you?"

"Oh, I be fine, sir, an' Mary and Lizzie too. Married and got children, they 'ave. O' course you knew as our Dick joined the army?"

"Yes, I heard." The lie was on Pitt's tongue before he had time to think. He did not wish her to know how completely he had lost touch. "It's a fine career," he added. He dared not say any more. Dick might have been maimed or even killed.

"Glad ye've come back for Sir Arthur," Zack said with a long sniff. "I s'ppose it's time we went. Bell's started."

And indeed the sound of the tolling of the church bell was carrying over the fields in a sonorous, mournful knell that must have reached the next village in the still air.

Farther back along the street a door closed and a figure in black emerged and started towards them. The smith came out of his house, a huge-chested, bowlegged man. He wore a rough jacket which barely fastened, but his black armband was new and neat and very plain to see.

Pitt offered Charlotte his arm, and they began to walk slowly away from the village along the road towards the church, which was still some quarter of a mile away. They were joined by more and more people: villagers, tenants and laborers from the local farms, the grocer and his wife, the baker and his two sisters, the ironmonger and his son and daughter-in-law, the cooper, the wheelwright, even the innkeeper had closed for the day and turned out in solemn black with his wife and daughters beside him.

From the other direction came the hearse drawn by four black horses with black plumes over head and shoulders, and a driver with black cloak and top hat. Behind it Matthew walked bareheaded, his hat in his hand, his face pale, Harriet Soames by his side. After them were at least eighty or ninety people, all the servants from the Hall both indoor and outdoor, all the tenant farmers from the estate with their families, and after them the neighboring landowners from half a dozen miles around.

They filed into the church and those who could not find a seat stood at the back, heads bowed.

Matthew had saved a place in the family pew for Pitt and Charlotte, as if Pitt were a second son. Pitt found himself overcome with emotion, gratitude, guilt, a warmth of belonging that brought tears to his eyes and prevented him from speaking. He dared not look down in case they spilled over. And then as the bell ceased and the minister stepped forward it became purely grief and a profound sense of having lost something irretrievable.

The service itself was simple, all the old, familiar words which were both soothing and deeply moving as the mind repeated them over in silent poetry, the terms of brevity of life like a flower in its season. The season was over, and it was gathered into eternity.

What was special about this particular funeral was the number of people who were met, not because it was required of them, but because they wished to be there. The gentry, the men from London, Pitt ignored; it was the villagers and tenant farmers who held the meaning for him.

When it was over they went to the burial in the Desmond family vault, at the far side of the churchyard under the yew trees. It was silent in the shade, even though there were above a hundred people still there. Not one of them moved or spoke as the coffin was placed inside and the door closed again. One could hear the birds singing in the elms on the far side, in the sun.

Next came the long ritual of thanking people, the expressions of sorrow and condolences.

Pitt glanced at Matthew where he stood on the path back towards the lych-gate on the road. He looked very pale, the sun catching the fair streak across his hair. Harriet Soames was beside him, very close, her hand on his arm. She looked somber, as befitted the occasion, but there was also a gentleness in her when she looked up at Matthew, as if she had more than an ordinary understanding of his anger as well as his grief.

"Are you going to stand with him?" Charlotte whispered.

He had been undecided, but in that moment he knew. "No. Sir Arthur was a father to me, but I was not his son. This is Matthew's time. For me to go there would be intrusive and presumptuous."

Charlotte said nothing. He was afraid she knew that he also felt he had forfeited his right to do that by his long absence. It was not Matthew's resentment he feared but that of the villagers. And they would be right to resent him now. He had been gone too long.

He waited a little while, watching Matthew's face as he spoke to them with great familiarity, accepting halting and deeply felt words. Harriet stood beside him smiling and nodding.

One or two neighbors paid their respects, and Pitt recognized Danforth, who had given evidence so reluctantly. There was a strange play of emotions over Matthew's face: resentment, caution, embarrassment, pain, and resentment again. It was not possible from where Pitt stood to hear what each of them said before Danforth shook his head and walked away towards the lych-gate.

Others followed, and then the men from London. They looked oddly out of place. The difference was subtle, an unease in the wide spaces with the view of fields beyond the churchyard and giant trees in the sun, the sense of the seasons and the heavy physical labor of turning the earth, plowing and reaping, the comfortable familiarity with animals. It was nothing so obvious as a difference in clothes, but perhaps a more closely barbered head, thinner soles to the boots, a glance as if the road winding away towards the trees and boundaries of the Hall were an enemy and not a friend, a distance one was not happy to walk when one was more accustomed to carriages.

Matthew spoke to them with an effort. It would not have been apparent to any one of them, only to Pitt, who had known him from childhood and could see the boy in the man.

When the last of them had said what was expected, and Matthew had managed to reply, Pitt went over to him. The carriages had been dismissed. Together they walked the bright road back up towards the Hall, Matthew and Pitt in front, Charlotte and Harriet behind.

For the first hundred yards or so it was in agreeable silence, during which Charlotte gained the impression that Harriet would like to say something but could not find the words to broach the subject.

"I think it is the greatest tribute that all the village should come," Charlotte said as they passed the crossroads and turned into the narrower lane. She had never been here before, and had no idea how far it would be, but she could see huge stone gateposts about a quarter of a mile away, obviously the entrance to an estate of size. Presumably there would be a surrounding parkland, and also a drive of some length.

"He was deeply loved," Harriet replied. "He was the most charming man, and quite sincere. Anyone less hypocritical I could not imagine." She stopped, and Charlotte had the distinct impression she would have added "but," except that sensitivity prevented her.

"I never knew him," Charlotte answered. "But my husband loved him dearly. Of course it is some time since he saw him, and people do change in some ways. . . ."

"Oh, he was still as honest and generous as ever," Harriet said quickly.

Charlotte looked at her, and she colored and turned away.

They were almost at the gates.

"But absentminded?" Charlotte said it for her.

Harriet bit her lip. "Yes, I think so. Matthew won't have it, and I can understand that. I do sympathize, really . . . my mother died when I was quite young, and so I have grown very close to my father also. Neither Matthew nor I have siblings. That is one of the things that draws us together, an understanding of the loneliness, and the special closeness to a parent. I could not bear anyone to speak ill of my father. . . ."

They turned in at the gates and Charlotte saw with a gasp of pleasure the long curve of the drive between an avenue of elm trees, and another quarter of a mile away the great house standing on a slight rise. Long lawns fell away to the banks of a stream to the right, and to the left more trees, and the roofs of the coach houses and stables beyond. There was a grace in the proportions which was immensely pleasing to the eye. It sat naturally on the land, rising out of it amid the trees, nothing alien or awkward, nothing jarring the simplicity of it.

Harriet took no notice. Presumably she had been here before, and although she was soon to be mistress of it, at this moment such thoughts were far from her mind.

"I would protect him as fiercely as if he were my child, and I his parent," she said with a rueful smile. "That's absurd, I know, but emotions don't always have reasons we can see. I do understand how Matthew feels."

They walked several paces in silence. The great elms had closed over their heads and they were in a dappled shadow. "I am afraid that Matthew will be hurt in this crusade to prove that Sir Arthur was murdered. Of course he does not want to believe that his father could have been so ... so disturbed in his mind as to have had the thoughts he did about secret societies persecuting him, and to have taken an overdose by accident."

She stopped and faced Charlotte. "If he pursues this, he may very well have the truth forced upon him, and have to face it in the end, and it will be even harder than it is now. Added to which, he will make enemies. People will have some sympathy at first, but it will not last, not if he starts to make accusations as he is doing. Could you persuade your husband to speak to him? Prevail upon him to stop searching for something which really is ... I mean, will only hurt him more, and make him enemies no one can afford? Patience will turn into laughter, and then anger. That is the last thing Sir Arthur would have wanted."

Charlotte did not know immediately what to say. She should not have been surprised that Harriet did not know anything of the

Inner Circle or imagine that such a society could exist. Had she not known of it herself, the suggestion would have seemed absurd to her too, the delusion of someone whose fancy had become warped, and who imagined conspiracies where there were none.

What was harder to accept, and hurt the emotions as well as the reason, was that Harriet thought Sir Arthur had become senile, and had indeed been responsible for his own death. Of course it was good that her concern was born of her love for Matthew, but that would be of only marginal comfort to him if he realized what was in her mind. At the moment his grief for his father was much too raw to accept it.

"Don't speak of this to Matthew," she said urgently, taking Harriet's arm and beginning to walk forwards again in case their hesitation should be questioned. "I am afraid at this point he may feel your disbelief as another wound, if you like, another betrayal."

Harriet looked startled, then slowly realization came into her face.

They were still moving very slowly and Pitt and Matthew were drawing ahead of them, not noticing their absence.

Harriet increased her pace to keep their distance from those coming after them. She did not wish to be overheard, still less for Matthew to turn around and come back to them, fearing something amiss.

"Yes. Yes, perhaps you are right. It is not really sensible, but I think I might take a great deal of time to come to accept that my father was no longer the man I had known, no longer so ... so fine, so strong, so ... wise," she went on. "Perhaps we all tend to idealize those we love, and when we are forced to see them in truth, we hate those who have shown us. I could not bear Matthew to feel like that about me. And perhaps I am asking equally as much of your husband, if I am to request him to tell Matthew what he so much does not wish to hear."

"There is no point in asking Thomas," Charlotte said honestly, keeping pace beside her. "He thinks just as Matthew does."

"That Sir Arthur was murdered?" Harriet was amazed. "Really? But he is a policeman! How could he seriously believe . . . are you sure?"

"Yes. You see, there are such societies . . ."

"Oh, I know there are criminals. Everyone who is not totally sheltered from reality knows that," Harriet protested.

Charlotte remembered with a jolt that when she had been Harriet's age, before she met Pitt, she had been just as innocent about the world. Not only the criminal aspect of it was unknown to her, but perhaps more seriously, she had not had the least idea of what poverty meant, or ignorance, endemic disease, or the undernourishment which produced rickets, tuberculosis, scurvy and such things. She had imagined that crime was the province of those who were violent, deceitful and innately wicked. The world had been very black and white. She should not expect of Harriet Soames an understanding of the shades of gray which only experience could teach, or a knowledge outside the scope of her life and its confines. It was unfair.

"But you didn't hear what Sir Arthur was saying," Harriet went on. "Who it was he was accusing!"

"If it is quite untrue," Charlotte said carefully, choosing her words, "then Thomas will tell Matthew, however it hurts. But he will want to look into it himself first. And that way, I think Matthew will accept it, because there will be no alternative. Also, he will know that Thomas wants Sir Arthur to have been right, and sane, just as much as he does himself. I think it would be best if we said nothing, don't you?"

"Yes. Yes, you are right," Harriet said with relief. They were fast approaching the last section of the driveway to the house. The elms had fallen away behind them and they were in the open sunlight. There were several carriages standing on the gravel before the front doors, and the gentlemen ahead were going into the Hall for the funeral meats. It was time they joined them.

It was when he was almost ready to leave that Pitt was given the opportunity to speak to Danforth and ask him further about the episode of the dogs. Sir Arthur had always cared deeply about his animals. If he took the matter of finding homes for his favorite bitch's pups lightly, then he had changed almost beyond recognition. It was not as if he had forgotten the matter entirely; according to Danforth he had sold them to someone else.

He found Danforth in the hallway taking his leave. He still looked uncomfortable, not quite sure if he should be here or not. It must be his testimony at the inquest weighing on his mind. He had been a close neighbor and agreeable friend for years. There had never been bad blood between the estates, although Danforth's was much smaller.

"Good afternoon, Mr. Danforth." Pitt approached him as if by chance. "Good to see you looking so well, sir."

"Er—good afternoon," Danforth replied, squinting a little in an effort to place Pitt. He must have looked as if he came from London, and yet there was an air about him as if he belonged, and a vague familiarity.

"Thomas Pitt," Pitt assisted him.

"Pitt? Pitt—oh yes. Gamekeeper's son, I recall." A shadow crossed his face, and quite suddenly the past flooded back and Pitt could recall the disgrace, the fear, the shame of his father's being accused of poaching, as if it were yesterday. It had not been Danforth's estate, but that was irrelevant now. The man who had pressed the charge and seen him sent to prison, where he had died, had been one of Danforth's social class and background, one who owned land as he did; and poachers were a common enemy.

Pitt felt his face burn and all the old humiliation come back, the resentment and the feeling of being inferior, foolish, of not knowing the rules. It was absurd. He was a policeman now, a very senior policeman. He had arrested better men than Danforth, wiser, richer, and more powerful men, men of better blood and lineage.

"Superintendent Pitt, of Bow Street," Pitt said coldly, but the words fumbled on his tongue.

Danforth looked surprised.

"Good God! Not a police matter, for heaven's sake. Poor man died of . . ." He let out his breath with a sigh. "They don't send superintendents for—suicide. And you'll never prove it. Certainly not through me!" Now his face was equally cold, and there was a bitter affront in his eyes.

"I came to pay my respects to a man I loved deeply," Pitt said with a clenched jaw. "And to whom I owe almost all I have. My occupation has no more to do with my presence here than does yours."

"Then dammit, sir, why did you say you were from the police?" Danforth demanded. He had been made to look a fool, and he resented it.

Pitt had done it to show that he was no longer merely a gamekeeper's son, but he could hardly admit that.

"I was at the inquest." He evaded the subject. "I know what you said about the pups. Sir Arthur always cared very much about his dogs."

"And his horses," Danforth agreed with a frown. "That's how I know the poor fellow was really losing a grip on things. He not only promised me the pick of the litter, he actually came with me to choose. Then, dammit, he went and sold them to Bridges." He shook his head. "I could understand simple forgetfulness. We all forget the odd thing now and again as we get older. But he was convinced I'd said I didn't want them. Swore blind to it. That's what was so unlike the man. Terribly sad. Fearful way to go. But glad you came to pay your respects, Mr. er—Superintendent."

"Good day, sir," Pitt acknowledged him, and then without giving it conscious thought, turned and went back through the baize door into the kitchens. He knew precisely where he was going. The paneled walls were so familiar he could recognize every variation in the wood, every place worn smoother and darker by countless touches of the hand, or brushes of fabric from the shoulders of foot-men and butlers, and skirts of maids, housekeepers and cooks for generations past. He had added to the patina of it himself when his mother had worked here. In the history of the Hall, that must seem like only yesterday. He and Matthew had crept down here to beg biscuits and milk from the cook, and odd titbits of pastry. Matthew had teased the maids, and put a frog in the housekeeper's sitting room. Mrs. Thayer had hated frogs. Matthew and Pitt had laughed themselves nearly sick when they heard her scream. Tapioca pudding for a week had been a small price to pay for the savoring of such a delight.

The smell of furniture polish and heavy curtains and uncarpeted floors was indefinable, and yet so sharp he would hardly have been surprised to face the mirror and see himself reflected a twelve-year-old boy with lanky limbs, steady gray eyes and a shock of hair.

When he turned into the kitchen, the cook, still in her black bombazine with her apron over it, looked up sharply. She was new since Pitt's time, and to her he was a stranger. She was flustered as it was, with the loss of her master, being allowed to attend the service herself, while still being in charge of the funeral meats.

"You lost, sir? The reception rooms are back that way."

She pointed to the door through which he had come. " 'Ere, Lizzie, you show the gentleman—"

"Thank you, Cook, but I am looking for the gamekeeper. Is Mr. Sturges about? I need to speak to him about Sir Arthur's dogs."

"Well I don't know about that, sir. It isn't 'ardly the day for it. . . ."

"I'm Thomas Pitt. I used to live here."

"Oh! Young Tom. I mean . . ." She colored quickly. "I didn't mean no . . ."

"That's all right." He brushed it aside. "I'd still like to speak to Mr. Sturges. It's a matter Sir Matthew wished me to look into, and I need Sturges's help."

"Oh. Well 'e was 'ere about 'alf an 'our ago, an' 'e went out to the stables. Land needs to be cared for, funeral or no funeral. You might find 'im out there."

"Thank you." He walked past her, barely glancing at the rows of copper pans and kettles, or the great black cast-iron range still emanating heat, even with all its oven doors closed and its lids down. The dressers were filled with china, the larder door closed, the wooden bins for flour, sugar, oatmeal and lentils were tight. All the vegetables would be in racks outside in the scullery, and the meat, poultry and game would be hung in the cold house. The laundry and still room were along the corridor to the right.

He went out of the back door, down the steps and turned left without conscious thought. He would have known his way even in the dark.

He found Sturges just outside the door to the apple room, the ventilated place with shelf after shelf of wooden slats where all the apples were placed in the autumn, and as long as they did not touch each other, usually kept all through the winter and well into the late spring.

" 'Allo, young Tom," he said without surprise. "Glad as you made it for the funeral." He looked Pitt directly in the eye.

It was a difficult relationship and it had taken many years to reach this stage. Sturges had replaced Pitt's father, and to begin with Pitt had been unable to forgive him for that. He and his mother had had to leave the gamekeeper's cottage and all their furnishings which had gone with it, the things they had grown accustomed to: the kitchen table and dresser, the hearth, the comfortable chair, the tin bath. Pitt had had his own room with a small dormer window next to the apple tree. They had moved up into the servants' quarters in the Hall, but it was nothing like the same. What was a room, when you had had a house, with your own doorway and your own kitchen fire?

Of course he knew with his head how lucky they were that Sir Arthur either had believed Pitt's father innocent or had not cared, and had given his wife and child shelter and made them welcome.

Many a man would not have, and there were those in the county who thought him a fool for it, and said so. But that did not stop Pitt from hating Sturges and his wife for moving into the gamekeeper's cottage and being warm and comfortable there.

And Sturges had then walked the fields and woods that had been Pitt's father's work and his pleasure. He had changed a few things, and that also was a fault not easily forgiven, especially if in one or two instances it was for the worse. Where it was for the better, that was an even greater offense.

But gradually memory had softened at least a little, and Sturges was a quiet, patient man. He knew the habits and the rules of the country. He had not been above poaching on the odd occasion as a youth, and he also knew it was by the grace of God, and a landowner willing to look the other way, that he had never been caught himself. He made no judgment as to whether Pitt's father had been guilty or innocent, except to remark that if he were guilty, he was more of a fool than most men.

And he loved animals. At first tentatively, then as a matter of course, he had allowed young Thomas to help him. They had begun in suspicious silence, then as cooperation necessitated speed they had broken the ice between them. It had melted completely one early morning, about half past six when the light was spreading across the fields still heavy with dew. It had been spring and the wildflowers were thick in the hedges and under the trees, the new leaves opening on the chestnuts, and the later beeches and elms thick with bud. They had found a wounded owl, and Sturges had taken it home. Together they had cared for it until it mended and flew away. Several times all summer they had seen its silent form, broad winged and graceful, swooping in flight around the barn, diving on mice, crossing the lantern's ray like a ghost, and then gone again. From that year on there had been an understanding between them, but never any blunting of criticism.

"Of course I came," Pitt answered him, breathing in deeply. The apple room smelled sweet and dry, a little musty, full of

memories. "I know I should have come earlier. I'll say it before
you do."

"Aye, well, so long as you know," Sturges said without taking
his eyes off Pitt's face. "Look well, you do. And very fancy in your
city clothes. Superintendent now, eh? Arresting folk, no doubt."

"Murder and treason," Pitt replied. "You'd want them arrested,
wouldn't you?"

"Oh aye. No time for murdering people, at least not most people. Done well for yourself then?"

"Yes."

Sturges pursed his lips.

"Got a wife? Or too busy bettering yourself to go a-courting?"

"Yes, I have a wife and two children: a son and a daughter." He
could not keep the lift of pride out of his voice.

"Have you indeed?" Sturges looked him straight in the eye. He
tried to keep his dour manner, but the pleasure shone out of him
in spite of it. "Where are they then? Up London way?"

"No, Charlotte is here with me. I'll bring her to meet you."

"You do that, if you want." Sturges was damned if he was going
to appear as if he cared. He turned away and began absentmindedly
tidying some of the old straw.

"Before I do, can you tell me what happened about the dogs
and Mr. Danforth?" Pitt asked.

"No I can't, Tom, and that's a fact. Never took to Danforth a
lot, myself, but he was always fair, far as I knowed. And bright
enough, considering."

"He came over and chose two pups?"

"Aye, he did that." He heaped the straw in a pile. "Then a couple o' weeks later sent a note by one o' his men to say he didn't
want 'em anymore. And a couple o' weeks after that, came back to
collect 'em and was as put out as all hell that we hadn't still got
them. Said a few unkind things about Sir Arthur. I'd have liked to
'ave given 'im a piece of my mind, but Sir Arthur wouldn't 'ave
wanted me to."

"Did you see the note, or did Sir Arthur just tell you about it?"

He stared at Pitt, abandoning the straw.

" 'Course I saw the note! Were writ to me, me being the one as cares for the dogs, and Sir Arthur himself up in London at the time anyway."

"Very strange," Pitt agreed, thoughts racing in his head. "You are quite right. Someone is playing very odd games, and not in any good spirit, I think."

"Games? You mean it weren't Mr. Danforth going a bit gaga?"

"Not necessarily, although it does look like it. Do you still have the note?"

"Whatever for? Why should I keep a thing like that? No use to anyone."

"Just to prove it was Mr. Danforth who was in the wrong, not Sir Arthur," Pitt replied.

"And who needs proof o' that?" Sturges pulled a face. "Nobody else as knows Sir Arthur thought it was 'im!"

Pitt felt a sudden lift of happiness, and found himself smiling in spite of the occasion. Sturges was a loyal man, but he moderated the truth for no one.

"Sturges, do you know anything about the accident Sir Arthur had when the runaway horse came down the street and the rider caught him with his whip?"

"Some." Sturges looked unhappy, his face drawn into lines of doubt. He leaned against the apple racks. "Why are you asking, Tom? Who told you about it anyway? Mr. Matthew?" He had not as yet adjusted to the idea that Matthew was now the master, and heir of the title.

Somewhere outside a horse whinnied, and Pitt heard the familiar sound of hooves on the cobbled stableyard.

"Yes. He seemed to think it was not an accident." He did not want to put words into Sturges's mouth by saying it had been devised as a threat.

"Not an accident?" Sturges looked puzzled but not dismissive of the idea. "Well, in a manner o' speaking, o' course, it wasn't. Fool came down the road like Jehu. Man like that should never 'ave bin on a horse in the first place. I look on an accident as something as couldn't be helped, 'cept by the Almighty. Two ha'pence worth o' sense 'd helped this. Came galloping down the street like a clergy-man, by all accounts, whip flyin' all over the place. It was a mercy no one else was hurt but Sir Arthur, and the animal he was ridin' at the time. Caught the poor beast a fair lashin' 'round the head and shoulders. Took us weeks to get 'im right again. Still scared o' the whip, it is. Probably always will be."

"Who was the rider?"

"God knows," Sturges said with disgust. "Some idiot from the far aside of the country, seems like. No one 'round here knew him."

"Did anybody know who he was? Do you know now?" Pitt pressed.

The sunlight was warm through the apple room door. A yellow-haired retriever poked its head in and wagged its tail hopefully.

" 'Course I don't know," Sturges answered angrily. "If I knew who he was I'd have had him on a charge." It was a brave state-ment, more wish than actuality, but Pitt was quite sure he would have tried.

"Who else saw it happen?" Pitt asked him.

The dog came in and Sturges patted it automatically. "Nobody, far as I know. Wheelwright saw the man go past. So did the smith, but didn't see him hit Sir Arthur. Why? What are you saying? That it was Sir Arthur's fault? He got in the way?"

"No." Pitt did not resent his anger, or the defensiveness in his face. "No, I'm saying it may not have been an accident in any sense. The man may have spurred his horse to a gallop intention-ally, meaning to catch Sir Arthur with the whip. . . ."

Sturges's face was full of amazement and disbelief.

"Why would anybody want to do that? It don't make sense. Sir Arthur had no enemies."

Pitt was not sure how far he should go in telling Sturges the truth. Perhaps the Inner Circle would be straining his belief a little far.

"Who would it be then?"

"Sir Arthur had no enemies. Not around here." Sturges was watching him closely.

"Is that what he thought?"

Sturges stared at Pitt. "What have you heard, Tom? What are you trying to say?"

"That Sir Arthur was a danger to a certain group he had joined, and about whom he had discovered some very unpleasant truths, and was bent on exposing them. They caused this accident as a warning to him to keep his covenants of silence," Pitt answered him.

"Oh aye, this Circle he spoke about." Sturges blinked. "Pretty dangerous to go that far though. Could have killed him!"

"You know about the Circle?" Pitt said with surprise.

"Oh yes, he talked about it. Evil men, from what he said, but from up London." He hesitated, searching Pitt's face. "You mean what I think you mean, Tom?"

"Well, was he wandering in his mind, imagining things?"

"No he was not! Upset, maybe, pretty angry about some of the things he said was going to happen abroad, but as sane as you or me." There was no pretense in his voice, no effort to convince himself of something that in his heart he had doubted. It was the quality of his tone as much as any words that drove away Pitt's last reservations. He was filled with a sudden and intense gratitude, almost a kind of happiness. He found himself smiling at Sturges.

"Then, yes," he replied firmly, "I mean what you think I do. It was a warning, which he was too angry and too honest to heed, and so they murdered him. I don't know how it was done yet, or if there is any way I can prove it, but I shan't stop trying until I do."

"I'm glad of that, Tom. I'm right glad of that," Sturges said quietly, leaning a little to scratch the dog's head. "It grieves me sore that those who didn't know him should think what they do of him. I'm not a vicious man. There's too many die as shouldn't as it is, but whoever did that to him, I'd dearly like to see them hanged. The whole of Brackley will be grateful to you if you do that, an' I can speak for all." He did not add that he would even be forgiven for not having come back, but it was in his face. He would have held it crass to put such a delicate thing into words.

"I'll do everything I can," Pitt replied. To have made a promise he did not know if he could keep would be a second betrayal. Sturges was not a child to be given words of comfort instead of the truth.

"Aye. Well, if there's aught I can do, or anyone here, you know where we are. Now you'd best be getting back to the baked meats, or you'll be missed."

"I'll find Charlotte and bring her to meet you."

"Aye. You said you'd do that, so be about it then."

In the morning Pitt was back in his office at Bow Street. He was barely through the door when Inspector Tellman came in, his lantern face dour and resentful as always. He had been forced to respect Pitt, both superficially in his manner, and genuinely because of his ability. However he still felt affronted that Pitt, whom he viewed as socially little better than himself, and professionally no better at all, should have been promoted to the senior position when Micah Drummond resigned. Drummond had been a gentleman, and that made all the difference. He expected gentlemen to be given superior posts; it was no reflection of their ability. For Pitt to have been given it he took personally.

"Good morning, Mr. Pitt," he said sharply. "Missed you yesterday, sir. Quite a few things to report." He made it sound as if he had been waiting there all night.

"Good morning, Tellman. I was at a family funeral in Hampshire. What have you got?"

Tellman pursed his lips, but made no reference to the bereavement. That happened to everyone. It stirred emotions in him, but he was certainly not going to allow Pitt to know about them.

"Those people you had the men check up on," he replied. "Bit difficult when we don't know what we are looking for, or why. They're all very respectable seeming gentlemen. What are they supposed to have done?"

"That is what I need to find out," Pitt replied tersely. He disliked not being able to tell the man as much truth as he knew. His instinct was to trust Tellman, but he dare not take the chance. The Circle could be anywhere.

"Blackmail," Tellman said darkly. "Makes it hard. You can blackmail a man for dozens of different things, but I suppose mostly it's cheating, theft or fornicating with someone he shouldn't." His expression did not change, but his contempt seemed to fill the room. "Although with gentlemen, it's not easy for the likes of us to know who he shouldn't, and who doesn't matter a damn," he added. "Some gentlemen swap wives and mistresses around like lending a good book. It's all right, so long as nobody actually catches you reading it. Doesn't even matter if they know you got it. Everyone knows what the Prince of Wales does, and who cares?"

"You could keep a particular eye for debt," Pitt suggested, ignoring the social comment. He was already well familiar with Tellman's views. "Anyone with a style of living that his income doesn't seem to support."

"Embezzlement?" Tellman said with surprise. "What can you embezzle from the Colonial Office?" His voice became heavily sarcastic. "Sorry, Tailor, old boy, can't pay me bill the usual way this month, but have a couple of telegrams from Africa, that should see you right." Then quite suddenly his face changed and his eyes lit with knowledge. "Geez! That's it, isn't it? There's information gone missing! You're after a traitor! That's why you are not saying anything. . . ."

"I'm still not saying anything," Pitt said, masking his surprise at

Tellman's acuity and facing him with a long, level stare. "You must suppose what you will, and keep it to yourself. The assistant commissioner would be very angry if he thought we mentioned such a possibility, and I think the Prime Minister would be even angrier."

"Did you get called to see the Prime Minister?" Tellman was impressed, in spite of himself.

"No. I have never met the Prime Minister, and the only place I have been to in Downing Street is the Colonial Office. You still haven't told me what you have found out."

Tellman looked sour. "Nothing that seems of any relevance. Jeremiah Thorne is as virtuous as is possible. Seems to be devoted to his wife, who is exceedingly plain, and spends a lot of money on some teaching foundation to do with women. It is highly disapproved of, except by the very moderns, but that might be scandalous at the worst. It isn't illegal and she doesn't do it secretly. In fact she is quite brazen about it. No one could blackmail her over it; she'd probably thank them for the notoriety."

Pitt already knew that to be true.

"What else?"

"Mr. Hathaway seems to be a very proper gentleman who lives quietly, alone, taking his pleasures rather seriously. Reads a lot, goes to the theater now and then, takes long walks in the fine weather." Tellman recited it dryly, as if the man were as boring as the details. "He knows a lot of people, but does not seem to have more than a passing acquaintance with them. Dines out once a week at his club. He is a widower with two grown sons, also eminently respectable, one in the Colonial Service and the other in the church." Tellman's mouth curled down at the corners. "His tastes are good, he likes quality, but not excessively expensive. He seems to live well within his salary. No one has an ill word to say about him."

Pitt drew in a deep breath. "And Aylmer? Is he a paragon of virtue as well?"

"Not quite." There was a shadow of humor at the back of Tellman's bleak expression. "Face like a burst boot, but fancies the ladies all the same. Quite a charmer in a harmless sort of way." He shrugged. "At least it is harmless from all I have been able to find out so far. I'm still looking into Mr. Aylmer. Spends quite a lot of money—more than I can see the source of so far."

."More than his Colonial Office salary?" Pitt asked with a quickening interest, and at the same time a pang of regret.

"Looks like it," Tellman replied. "Of course he could have been saving up, or he might even have private means. Don't know yet."

"Any ladies in particular?"

"A Miss Amanda Pennecuick. Very nice-looking young lady indeed, and very well bred."

"Does she return his interest?"

"Apparently not. Although that has not yet deterred him." He looked at Pitt with amusement. "If you are thinking she is pursuing Mr. Aylmer in order to get information out of him, she's very clever at it. From all I could see, she is trying to avoid him, and not succeeding."

"She wouldn't wish actually to succeed, only to appear to try," Pitt pointed out, "if she were doing as you suggest. Find out about Miss Pennecuick. See who else her friends are, her other admirers, her background, any connection she might have with . . ." He stopped. Should he mention Germany?

Tellman waited. He was far too quick to be deceived. He knew the reason for Pitt's hesitation, and the resentment of it was plain in his eyes.

"Africa, Belgium or Germany," Pitt finished. "Or anything else that's unusual, for that matter."

Tellman put his hands in his pockets. It was not intended insolence as much as instinctive lack of respect.

"You missed out Peter Arundell and Robert Leicester," Pitt prompted.

"Nothing interesting," Tellman replied. "Arundell is a clever young man from a good family. Younger son. Oldest got the title, next one bought a commission in the army, third one went into the Colonial Office, that's him, youngest one got the family living somewhere in Wiltshire."

"Family living?" Pitt was momentarily confused.

"Church," Tellman said with satisfaction that he had left Pitt behind. "Well-to-do families often own the living and can give it to whoever they like. Bring in quite a lot, some of those country parishes. Lot of tithes. Where I grew up the priest had three livings, and hired a vicar or a curate for each one. Himself, he lived in Italy on the proceeds. They don't do that anymore, but they used to."

It was on the edge of Pitt's tongue to say he knew that, but he refrained. Tellman would probably not believe him anyway.

"What about Arundell?" he asked. "What sort of a man is he?" It did not matter. He had no access to the information on Zambezia.

"Just what you'd expect," Tellman replied. "Rooms in Belgravia, attends a lot of Society functions, dresses well, dines well, but a good deal of it at other people's expense. He is a bachelor and highly eligible. All the mothers with unmarried daughters are chasing after him, except those with something higher in their sights. He'll no doubt marry well in the next few years." Tellman finished with a slight downturn of his mouth. He despised what he knew of Society and never lost an opportunity to say so.

"And Leicester."

Tellman grunted. "Much the same."

"Then you'd better get on with Amanda Pennecuick," Pitt instructed. "And Tellman . . ."

"Yes sir?" It was still sarcasm underlying his voice, not respect, and his eyes were too direct.

"Be discreet." He met Tellman's look with equal candor and challenge. No further explanation was necessary. They were utterly different in background and values. Pitt was from the country with the innate respect, even love, for the landed gentry who had made and preserved his world, and who had personally given him so much. Tellman was from the city, surrounded by poverty, and hated those born to wealth, most of whom he considered idlers. They had created nothing, and now only consumed without returning. All he and Pitt had in common was a dedication to police work, but that was sufficient for a complete understanding, at least on that level.

"Yes, Mr. Pitt," he said with something close to a smile, and turned on his heel and left.

Just under half an hour later Assistant Commissioner Farnsworth sent for Pitt to come to his office. The note was written in such terms there was no question about obeying, and Pitt went from Bow Street and caught a hansom along the embankment to Scotland Yard to report.

"Ah." Farnsworth looked up from his desk when Pitt was shown in. He waited until Pitt had closed the door before he continued. "This matter at the Colonial Office. What have you found?"

Pitt was reluctant to tell him how very little it was.

"They are all outwardly without fault," he replied. "Except possibly Garston Aylmer." He saw Farnsworth's face quicken with interest, but took no notice. "He has something of a weakness in his regard for a Miss Amanda Pennicuick, which is apparently not returned. He is a remarkably plain man, and she is unusually handsome."

"Not an uncommon occurrence," Farnsworth said with obvious disappointment. "That's hardly suspicious, Pitt, simply one of life's many disappointments. Being plain, or even downright ugly, has never stopped anyone from falling in love with the beautiful. Very painful sometimes, but a tragedy, not a crime."

"A great deal of crime springs from tragedy," Pitt answered him. "People react differently to pain, especially the pain of wanting something out of reach."

Farnsworth looked at him with a mixture of impatience and contempt. "You can steal anything from a meat pie to a diamond necklace, Pitt, but you cannot steal a woman's affection. And we are not talking about a man who would descend to thieving."

"Of course you cannot steal it." Pitt was equally derisive. "But it is sometimes possible to buy it, or to buy a very good semblance of it. He wouldn't be the first plain man to do that."

Farnsworth disliked agreeing with him, but he was forced to do so. He had too much knowledge of life to argue the issue.

"Selling information to the Germans for money to get her gifts, or whatever she wants?" he said reluctantly. "All right. Look into it. But for God's sake be discreet, Pitt. He's probably a perfectly decent man simply in love with the wrong woman."

"I was thinking also of the possibility that Miss Pennecuick may have an interest in Germany, and rather than Aylmer selling information for money, she might be drawing it from him as the price of her favor. Unlikely, but we have nothing better yet."

Farnsworth chewed on his lower lip. "Find out all you can about her," he ordered. "Who she is, where she comes from, who else she associates with."

"I have Tellman on it."

"Never mind Tellman, get on it yourself." Farnsworth frowned. "Where were you yesterday, Pitt? No one saw you all day."

"I went to Hampshire to a family funeral."

"I thought your parents died a long time ago?" There was challenge in Farnsworth's voice as well as question.

"They did; this was a man who treated me like a son."

Farnsworth's eyes were very hard, clear blue.

"Indeed?" He did not ask who that man was, and Pitt could not read his face.

"I believe you went to the inquest on Sir Arthur Desmond," he went on. "Is that true?"

"Yes."

"Why?" Farnsworth's eyebrows rose. "There's no case there. Tragedy that a man of his standing should end that way, but illness and age are no respecters of persons. Leave it alone now, Pitt, or you'll only make it worse."

Pitt stared at him.

Farnsworth misunderstood his surprise and anger for incomprehension.

"The least that is said about it, the least will have to be known." He was irritated by Pitt's slow-wittedness. "Don't let the whole sorry matter drag out before his friends and associates, never mind the general public. Let it all be forgotten, then we can remember him as the man he used to be, before all this obsession began."

"Obsession?" Pitt said thinly. He knew he would achieve nothing by pursuing it with Farnsworth, and yet he could not help himself.

"With Africa," Farnsworth said impatiently. "Saying there were conspiracies and secret plots and so on. He thought he was being persecuted. It's quite a well-known delusion, but very distressing, very sad. For heaven's sake, Pitt, if you had any regard for him at all, don't make it public. For his family's sake, if nothing else, let it be buried with him."

Pitt met his eyes squarely and did not look away.

"Sir Matthew does not believe his father was mad, or so forgetful or careless as to have taken laudanum in the middle of the afternoon, and in such a quantity as to kill himself."

"Not unnatural," Farnsworth dismissed it with a slight movement of his well-manicured hand. "It is always hard to accept that those we love are mentally deranged. Wouldn't have cared to think it of my father. I have every sympathy with him, but it has nothing to do with the facts."

"He may be right," Pitt said stubbornly.

Farnsworth's lips thinned. "He's not right, Pitt. I know more about it than you do."

It was on the edge of Pitt's tongue to argue with him, then he realized that over the last ten years his knowledge of Sir Arthur was sporadic at best, although Farnsworth could not know that. Still, it left him in a fragile position to argue.

His thoughts would not have shown in his face, but something of his emotions must have. Farnsworth was watching him with growing certainty, and something like a bitter amusement.

"Just what is your personal knowledge of Sir Arthur, Pitt?"

"Very little . . . lately."

"Then believe me, I have seen him frequently and he was unquestionably suffering from delusions. He saw conspiracies and persecutions all over the place, even among men who had been his friends for years. He is a man for whom I had a high regard, but feelings, however deep or honorable, do not change the truth. For friendship's sake, Pitt, let him rest in peace, and his memory be as little damaged as possible. In kindness you must do that."

Still Pitt wanted to argue. Sturges's weatherbeaten face came sharply to his mind. Or was his judgment just loyalty, an inability to believe that his master could have lost touch with reality?

"Right," Farnsworth said briskly. "Now get on with the job in hand. Find out who is passing information from the Colonial Office. Give it your entire attention, Pitt, until it is finished. Do you understand me?"

"Yes, of course I understand," Pitt said, while still in his head determining not to leave the death of Arthur Desmond as it was, a quietly closed matter.

CHAPTER
FIVE

———————————

"What it affects mostly is treaties," Matthew said with a frown, regarding Pitt over his desk at the Foreign Office. He looked a little less harrowed than at the funeral in Brackley, but the shadow was still there at the back of his eyes and in the pallor of his skin. There was a tension in his body which Pitt knew too well to ignore or misread. The past was still intimate, for all that had happened since, and the experiences which separated them.

If anyone had asked him for dates, he could not have given them, nor even the events that one might have considered important. But the memories of emotion were as powerful as if they had happened yesterday: surprise, understanding, the desire to protect, the confusion and the learning of pain. He could recall vividly the death of a beloved animal, the first magic and surprise of love, the first disillusionment, the fear of change in people and places that framed one's life. These things he and Matthew had faced together, in some things at least, he a year the sooner, so when Matthew's turn came, he had already experienced them, and shared his emotions with an acuteness no one else could.

He knew now that Matthew was still just as deeply hurt over his father's death; only his outward command of himself was better, as the sense of shock wore away. They were sitting in his wide office with its polished oak furniture, pale green carpet, and deep windows overlooking St. James's Park.

"You mentioned the treaty with the Germans," he answered. "What I really need is to know what the information is, as far as you can tell me. That is the only way I am going to have a chance to trace where it came from, and through whose hands it passed."

Matthew's frown deepened. "It isn't quite as cut and dried as that. But I'll do what I can."

Pitt waited. Outside somewhere in the street a horse whinnied and a man shouted. The sun made bright patterns through the window and onto the floor.

"One of the things that stands out most is the agreement made with King Lobengula, late in the year before last," Matthew began thoughtfully. " 'Eighty-eight. In September Rhodes's delegation, led by a man called Charles Rudd, rode into the king's camp in Bulowayo—that's in Zambezia. They are the Ndebele tribe." His fingers drummed on the desk softly as he spoke. "Rudd was an expert in mining claims, and apparently quite ignorant about African rulers and their customs. For that purpose he had along a fellow called Thompson, who spoke some language understood by the king. The third member of the party was called Rochfort Maguire, a legal man from All Souls' College in Oxford."

Pitt listened patiently. So far this was of no help to him at all. He tried to imagine the heat of the African plains, the courage of these men and the greed that drew them.

"Of course there were other people seeking mineral concessions as well," Matthew went on. "We very nearly lost them."

"We?" Pitt interrupted.

Matthew grimaced. "As far as one can call Cecil Rhodes 'we.' He was—is—acting with the blessing of Her Majesty's government. We had a standing agreement, the Moffatt Treaty, made with Lobengula in February of the same year, that he would not give away any of his territories, I quote, 'without the previous knowledge and sanction' of the British government."

"You say we nearly lost them," Pitt brought the conversation back to the point. "Because of information going to the Germans?"

Matthew's eyes widened very slightly. "That's curious. The German Embassy certainly, but it began to look as if the Belgians might have known about it too. All of Central and East Africa is swarming with adventurers, hunters, mining prospectors and people hoping to be middlemen in all sorts of ventures." He leaned a little further forward across the desk. "Rudd was successful because of the advent of Sir Sidney Shippard, deputy commissioner for Bechuanaland. He is a great supporter of Cecil Rhodes, and believes in what he is trying to do. So does Sir Hercules Robinson at the Cape."

"What do you know that without question has passed from the Colonial Office to the German Embassy?" Pitt pressed. "For the time being, exclude suspicions. Tell me the information, and I'll find out how it came in, by word of mouth, letter, telegram, who received it and where it went after that."

Matthew reached out his hand and touched a pile of papers beside him.

"I have several things here for you. But there are other things also, which have very little to do with the Foreign Office, matters of money. A great deal of this rests on money." He looked at Pitt to see if he understood.

"Money?" Pitt did not know what he meant. "Surely money would be useless in buying land from native kings? And the government would equip explorers and scouts going to claim land for Britain?"

"No! That's the point," Matthew said urgently. "Cecil Rhodes is equipping his own force. They are well on their way even now. He put up the finance himself."

"One man?" Pitt was incredulous. He could not conceive of such wealth.

Matthew smiled. "You don't understand Africa, Thomas. No, actually he's not putting up all of it, but a great deal. There are banks involved, some in Scotland, and particularly Francis Standish. Now perhaps you begin to see the sort of treasures we are speaking of: more diamonds than anywhere else in the world, more gold, and a continent of land owned by people who live in the dark ages as far as weapons are concerned."

Pitt stared at him, ideas uncertain in his mind, cloudy images, remembered words of Sir Arthur's about exploitation, and the Inner Circle.

"When men like Livingstone went in, it was completely different," Matthew continued, his face bleak. "They wanted to take medicine and Christianity, get rid of ignorance, disease and slavery. They may have gained a certain immortality out of it, but they didn't look for anything for themselves. Even Stanley wanted glory more than any kind of material reward.

"But Cecil Rhodes wants land, money, power, and more power. We need men like him for this stage in the development of Africa."

His face shadowed over even more. "At least I think we do. Father and I argued about it. He thought the government should have taken a larger part in it and sent over our own men, openly, and to the devil with what the Kaiser or King Leopold thought. But of course Lord Salisbury never really wanted anything to do with it right from the beginning. He would have left Africa alone, if he could, but circumstances and history would not allow."

"You mean Britain is doing it through Cecil Rhodes?" Pitt still could not believe what Matthew seemed to be saying.

"More or less," Matthew agreed. "Of course there is quite a lot of other money as well, from London and Edinburgh. It is that information which has reached the German Embassy, at least some of it."

They heard footsteps in the corridor outside, but whoever it was did not stop.

"I see."

"Only part of it, Thomas. There are a lot of other factors as well: alliances, quarrels, old wars and new ones. There are the

Boers to consider. Paul Kruger is not a man ever to overlook with impunity. There is all the heritage of the Zulu Wars. There is Emin Pasha in Equatoria, and the Belgians in the Congo, the Sultan of Zanzibar in the east, and most of all there is Carl Peters and the German East Africa Company." He touched the pile of papers at his elbow again. "Read these, Thomas. I cannot allow you to take them with you, but it will show you what you are looking for."

"Thank you." Pitt reached his hand for them, but Matthew did not pass them across.

"Thomas . . ."

"Yes."

"What about Father? You said you would look into the accident." He was embarrassed, as if he were criticizing, and hated it, but was compelled by conviction to do it. "The longer you leave it, the harder it will be. People forget, they become afraid when they have time to realize that there are those who . . ." He took a deep breath and his eyes met Pitt's. They were bright hazel, full of pain and confusion.

"I have already started," Pitt said quietly. "I spoke to Sturges when I was in Brackley. He is convinced the business with the pups was Danforth's mistake. Danforth sent a letter saying he didn't want them, he'd changed his mind. At least it purported to come from Danforth, whether it did or not, but Sturges saw it, it was addressed to him. It had nothing to do with Sir Arthur."

"That's something." Matthew grasped onto it, but the anxiety did not leave his face. "But the accident? Was it deliberate? It was a warning, wasn't it?"

"I don't know. No one else saw it, as far as Sturges knows, though both the smith and the wheelwright saw the horseman careering up the street at a breakneck gallop, apparently completely out of control. But even a bolting horse won't usually charge into another it can clearly see, or go close enough for the rider to catch someone else with his whip. I think it was deliberate, but I don't know any way of proving it. The man was a stranger. No one knows who he was."

Matthew's face tightened. "And I suppose the same will be true of the underground railway. We'll never prove that either. From everything we can learn, no one he knew was with him." He looked down. "Clever. They know how to do it so if you say anything, tell anyone, it sounds absurd, like the ramblings of someone who has been eating opium, or lives permanently in his cups." He looked up suddenly, panic in his eyes. "It begins to make me feel helpless. I'm not consumed with hatred anymore. It has turned into something a lot more like fear, and a terrible weariness, as if it is all pointless. If it was anyone but Father, I might not even try."

Pitt understood the fear. He had felt it himself in the past, and now its cause was real. He also understood the enveloping exhaustion, now that the first shock of grief was over. Anger is a very depleting emotion; it burns up all the strength of the mind and the body. Matthew was tired, but in a while he would be renewed, and the anger would return, the sense of outrage, the passionate desire to protect, to prove the lie and restore some semblance of justice. He hoped profoundly that Harriet Soames was wise enough and generous enough to be gentle with him, to wait with patience for him to work his way through the tiredness and the confusion of feelings, that she would not just at that moment seek anything from him for herself beyond trust and the knowledge that he was willing to share all he was able to.

"Don't do anything alone," Pitt said very seriously.

Matthew's eyes widened a fraction, surprise and question in them, then after a moment, even a shadow of humor.

"Do you think I'm incompetent, Thomas? I've been fifteen years in the Foreign Office since we knew each other. I do know how to be diplomatic."

It had been a clumsiness of words rather than thought, and a desire to protect him which still lingered from youth.

"I'm sorry," Pitt apologized. "I meant that we could duplicate our efforts, and not only waste time but cause suspicion by it."

Matthew's face relaxed into a smile. "Sorry, Thomas. I am oversensitive. This has hit me harder than I could have foreseen." He gave Pitt the papers at last. "Look at these in the room next door, then give them back to me when you have finished."

Pitt rose and took them. "Thank you."

The room provided him was high ceilinged and full of sun from the long window, also facing the park. He sat in one of the three chairs and began. He made no notes but committed to memory the essence of what he needed. It took him to the middle of the day to be certain he knew precisely where to look to trace the information he could be quite certain had reached the German Embassy. Then he rose and returned the papers to Matthew.

"Is that all you require?" Matthew asked, looking up from his desk.

"For the moment."

Matthew smiled. "How about luncheon? There is an excellent public house just 'round the corner, and an even better one a couple of hundred yards along the street."

"Let's go to the even better one," Pitt agreed with an attempt at enthusiasm.

Matthew followed him to the door and along the corridor to the wide stairs down and into the bright busy street.

They walked side by side, occasionally jostled by passersby, men in frock coats with top hats, now and then a woman, highly fashionable, carrying a parasol and smiling and nodding to acquaintances. The street itself was teeming with traffic. Coaches, carriages, hansoms, broughams and open landaus passed by every few minutes, moving at a brisk trot, horses' hooves rapping smartly, harnesses jingling.

"I love the city on a fine day," Matthew said almost apologetically. "There is such life here, such a sense of purpose and excitement." He glanced sideways at Pitt. "I need Brackley for its peace, and the feel of permanence it has. I find I always remember it so clearly, as if I had only just closed my eyes from seeing it, smelling the sharp coldness of winter air, the snow on the fields, or the crackle of frost under my feet. I can breathe in and re-create the perfume of the summer wind from the hay, the dazzle of sunlight and the sting of heat on my skin, the taste of apple cider."

A handsome woman in pink and gray passed by and smiled at him, not as an acquaintance, but out of interest, but he barely noticed her.

"And the glancing light and sudden rain of spring," he went on. "In the city it's just wet or dry. There's no bursting of growth to see, no green haze over the fields, no strong, dark furrows of earth, no awareness at once of the turning seasons, and the timelessness of it all because it has happened since the creation, and presumably always will."

A coach rumbled by, close to the curb, and Matthew on the outside stepped in hastily to avoid being hit by the jutting lamps.

"Fool!" he muttered under his breath.

They were a dozen yards from the crossing.

"My favorite time was always autumn," Pitt said, smiling with recollection. "The shortening days, golden at the end where the long light falls across the stubble fields, the piled stooks against the sky, clear evenings where the clouds fall away towards the west, scarlet berries in the hedgerows, wild rose hips, the smell of wood smoke and leaf mold, the blazing colors of the trees." They came to the curb and stopped. "I loved the bursting life of spring, the flowers, but there was always something about autumn when everything is touched with gold, there is a fullness, a completion. . . ."

Matthew looked at him with a sudden, intense affection. They could have been twenty years younger, standing together at Brackley, gazing across the fields or the woods, instead of at Parliament Street, waiting for the traffic to allow them to cross.

A hansom went by at a brisk clip and there was a space. They set out smartly, side by side. Then out of nowhere, swinging around the corner, a coach and four came careering over the curb edge, horses wild-eyed, frightened and squealing. Pitt leaped aside, pushing Matthew as hard as he could. Even so Matthew was caught by the near side front wheel and sent sprawling across the road to fetch up with his head barely a foot from the gutter and the curb edge.

Pitt scrambled to his feet, whirling around to catch sight of the coach, but all that was visible was the back of it as it disappeared around the corner of St. Margaret Street heading towards the Old Palace Yard.

Matthew lay motionless.

Pitt went over to him. His own leg hurt and he was going to be bruised all down his left side, but he was hardly aware of it.

"Matthew!" He could hear the panic rising in his voice and there was a sick terror in his stomach. "Matthew!" There was no blood. Matthew's neck was straight, no twisting, no awkward angle, but his eyes were closed and his face white.

A woman was standing on the pavement sobbing, her hands up to her mouth as if to stifle the sound.

Another woman, elderly, came forward and knelt down beside Matthew.

"May I help?" she said calmly. "My husband is a doctor, and I have assisted him many times." She did not look at Pitt, but at Matthew. She ignored the permission she had not yet received, and touched Matthew's cheek lightly, taking her gloves off, then put her finger to his neck.

Pitt waited in an agony of suspense.

She looked up at him after a moment, her face quite calm.

"His pulse is very strong," she said with a smile. "I expect he will have a most unpleasant headache, and I daresay several bruises which will no doubt be painful, but he is very much alive, I assure you."

Pitt was overwhelmed with relief. It was almost as if he could feel the blood surge back into his own body and life into his mind and his heart.

"You should have a stiff brandy yourself," the woman said gently. "And I would recommend a hot bath, and rub your bruises with ointment of arnica. It will help, I promise you."

"Thank you. Thank you very much." He felt momentarily as if she had saved their lives.

"I suppose you have no idea who the driver was?" she went on, still kneeling at the roadside by Matthew. "He should be prosecuted. That sort of thing is criminal. It was only by the grace of God your friend avoided the curb stone, or he would have cracked his head open and might very well have been killed."

"I know." Pitt swallowed hard, realizing with force how true that was. Now that he knew Matthew was alive, he could see it more sharply, and begin to understand all that it meant.

She looked at him curiously, her brow puckered, sensing there was much more to it than the accident she had seen.

Other people were beginning to gather around. A stout man with splendid side-whiskers came forward, elbowing his way.

"Now then, what's happened here?" he demanded. "Need a doctor? Should we call the police? Has anyone called the police?"

"I am the police." Pitt looked up at him. "And yes, we need a doctor. I'd be obliged if anybody would send for one."

The man looked doubtful. "Are you indeed?"

Pitt went to fish in his pocket and produce his card, and to his disgust found that his hands were shaking. He pulled out the card with difficulty and passed it to the man without bothering to see his reaction.

Matthew stirred, made a little choking sound which turned into a groan, then opened his eyes.

"Matthew!" Pitt said stiffly, leaning forward, peering at him.

"Bloody fool!" Matthew said furiously. He shut his eyes in pain.

"You should lie still, young man," the elderly lady advised him firmly. "We are sending for a doctor, and you should receive his counsel before you make any attempt to rise."

"Thomas?"

"Yes ... I'm here."

Matthew opened his eyes again and focused them on Pitt's face. He made as if to speak, then changed his mind.

"Yes, exactly what you are thinking," Pitt said quietly.

Matthew took a very deep breath and let it out in a shudder. "I shouldn't have taken offense when you told me to be careful. I was childish, and as it turns out, quite mistaken."

Pitt did not reply.

The elderly lady looked around at the man with the whiskers. "May we take it that someone has been dispatched for a doctor, sir?" she enquired in much the manner a good governess might have used towards an indifferent butler.

"You may, madam," he replied stiffly, and moved away, Pitt was certain, in order to perform that task.

"I am sure that with a little help I could stand up," Matthew said. "I am causing something of an obstruction here, and making a spectacle of myself." He began to struggle to climb to his feet and Pitt was not able to prevent him, only to give him his arm and then catch him as he swayed and lost his balance. He clung on for several seconds before his head cleared and he was able, with concentration, to regain himself and stand, not unaided, but at least upright.

"I think we had better call you a hansom to take you home, and then send for our own physician as soon as possible," Pitt said decisively.

"Oh, I don't think that is necessary," Matthew argued, but was still swaying a trifle.

"You would be exceedingly unwise to ignore that advice," the elderly lady said severely. Now that Pitt and Matthew were both standing, she was considerably beneath their height, and obliged to look up at them, but her assurance was such that it made not the slightest difference. Pitt at least still felt as if he were in the schoolroom.

Matthew must have felt similarly, because he offered no argument, and when Pitt hailed a cab and it drew in, he thanked the lady profusely. They both took their leave and climbed in.

Pitt accompanied Matthew to his rooms and saw that the doctor was sent for, then went into the small sitting room to consider what he had read from the papers in the Foreign Office until the doctor should have been and delivered his opinion. Matthew was happy to relax and lie on his bed.

"A very ugly accident," the doctor said, some fifty minutes later. "But fortunately I think you have suffered no more than a slight concussion and some unpleasant bruising. Did you report the matter to the police?"

He was standing in Matthew's bedroom. Matthew was lying on the bed looking pale and still very shocked and Pitt was standing beside the door.

"Mr. Pitt is a policeman," Matthew explained. "He was beside me when it happened. He was knocked over as well."

"Were you? You said nothing." The doctor looked at him with raised eyebrows. "Do you need any attention, sir?"

"No thank you, just a few bruises," Pitt dismissed it. "But I'm obliged for your concern."

"Then I presume you will be reporting the matter to your superiors. To drive like that, to injure two men and simply keep on going, is a criminal offense," the doctor said sternly.

"Since neither of us knows who it was, nor do any of the other people in the street, there is very little that can be done," Pitt pointed out.

Matthew smiled wanly. "And Superintendent Pitt has no superiors, except the assistant commissioner. Do you, Thomas?"

The doctor looked surprised, and shook his head.

"Pity. People like that should be prosecuted. Like to see the man made to walk everywhere from now on. Still, there are a lot of things I'd like to see, and won't." He turned to Matthew. "Take a day or two's rest, and call on me again if the headache gets any worse, if your vision is affected, or if you are sick."

"Thank you."

"Good day, Sir Matthew."

Pitt conducted him out and returned to Matthew's room.

"Thank you, Thomas," Matthew said grimly. "If you hadn't pushed me I'd have been mangled to bits under those hooves. Do I presume it was the Inner Circle, warning me?"

"Or both of us," Pitt replied. "Or someone with a great deal of money at stake in Africa. Although I think that's less likely. Or it may have been simply an accident, and quite impersonal."

"Do you believe that?"

"No."

"Neither do I." Matthew made an attempt to smile. His long face with its hazel eyes was very pale indeed, and he made no effort to hide the fact that he was frightened.

"Leave it for a day or two," Pitt said quietly. "We can't accomplish anything by getting hurt or killed ourselves. Stay here. We'll think what our next move should be. We must make it count. This is not a battle where we can afford blows that do no damage."

"Not a lot I can do ... just yet." Matthew winced. "But I'm damned well going to think of nothing else."

Pitt smiled and took his leave. He could do no more now, and Matthew needed to sleep. He left with his mind still whirling and full of dark thoughts and fears.

It was nearly four o'clock when he walked across Downing Street and up the steps of the Colonial Office. He asked to see Linus Chancellor, and was told that if he was prepared to wait, that would be possible.

As it turned out, he waited only half an hour, and then was

shown into Chancellor's office. He was sitting at his desk, his broad brow puckered with interest and anxiety, his eyes keen.

"Afternoon, Pitt," he said without standing. He waved to the chair near the desk and Pitt took it. "I presume you have come to report your findings so far? Is it too soon to look for a suspect? Yes, I can see by your face that it is. What have you?" His eyes narrowed. "You look awkward, man. Very stiff. Are you hurt?"

Pitt smiled ruefully. In truth he was beginning to hurt very much. He had almost ignored his own injuries in his fear for Matthew. Now they were too sharp to be forgotten.

"I was hit by a coach a few hours ago, but I very much doubt it had anything to do with this."

Chancellor's face reflected real concern and a degree of shock. "Good God! You don't mean there is a possibility that someone deliberately tried to kill you?" Then his face tightened and a bleak, almost venomous look came into his eyes. "Although I don't know why I should be surprised. If a man will sell out his country, why should he balk at killing someone who looked like exposing him at it? I think my scale of values needs a little adjusting."

He leaned back in his chair, his face taut with emotion. "Perhaps violence offends our sensibility so profoundly we tend to think of it as worse than the unseen corruption of betrayal, which in some very essence is immeasurably worse. It is murder behind the smiling face, the thrust in the back"—his fist clenched as if he were dealing the blow himself—"when you are turned elsewhere, and then the sudden realization that all trust may be misplaced.

"It is robbery of everything that makes life worthwhile, the belief in good, the love of friends, honor itself. Why would I think he would not indulge in a simple push in a crowd? A man falls off the curb under the wheels of a carriage?" He looked at Pitt with concern on the surface over a passionate anger beneath. "Have you seen a physician? Should you be up and walking around? Are you sure there is no serious injury?"

Pitt smiled in spite of himself. "Yes, I have seen a doctor, thank you." He was stretching the truth. "I was with a friend who was considerably more hurt than I, and we shall both be well enough in a few days. But I appreciate your concern. I saw Sir Matthew Desmond this morning and he gave me details of the information which reached the Germans. I read it in the Foreign Office and left it there, but I can recall the essence of it, and I would be obliged if you could tell me if there is any common source or link, or at least anyone who would be excluded from possibility because they could not have known."

"Of course. Relate it to me." Chancellor leaned back in his seat and folded his hands, waiting.

With concentration Pitt recalled all the information he had gleaned from Matthew's papers, set it in an orderly fashion, progressing from one category to the next.

When he had finished Chancellor looked at him with puzzlement and renewed anxiety.

"What is it?" Pitt asked.

"Some of that is information I did not know myself," Chancellor replied slowly. "It doesn't pass through the Colonial Office." He let the words fall on silence, and stared at Pitt to see if he grasped the full implication of what he had said.

"Then our traitor has help, witting or unwitting," Pitt concluded reluctantly. Then a new thought came to him. "Of course that may be his weakness. . . ."

Chancellor saw what he meant instantly. The spark of hope leaped in his eyes and his body tensed. "Indeed it may! It gives you somewhere to start, to search for proofs, communications, perhaps even payments, or blackmail. The possibilities are considerable."

"Where do I begin?"

"What?" Chancellor was startled.

"Where else may the other information have come from?" Pitt elaborated. "What precisely is it that does not pass through this office?"

"Oh. Yes, I see. Financial matters. You have included details here of the various loans and guarantees given MacKinnon and Rhodes, among others. And backing from the City of London and from bankers in Edinburgh. The generalities any diligent person with a knowledge of finance might learn for himself, but the times, conditions, precise amounts could only have come from the Treasury."

His lips tightened. "This is very ugly indeed, Pitt. It seems there is a traitor in the Treasury as well. We shall owe you a great deal if you uncover this for us, and manage to do it discreetly." He searched Pitt's eyes. "Do I need to warn you how damaging this could be to the entire government, not only to British interests in Africa, if it becomes public that we are riddled with treason?"

"No," Pitt said simply, rising to his feet. "I shall do everything in my power to deal with it discreetly, even secretly if possible."

"Good. Good." Chancellor sat back and looked up at Pitt, his handsome, volatile face released of some of its tension at last. "Keep me aware of your progress. I can always make a few minutes in the day to see you, or in the evening if necessary. I don't imagine you keep exact hours any more than I do?"

"No, sir. I shall see you are acquainted with my progress. Good day, Mr. Chancellor."

Pitt went immediately to the Treasury, but it was nearly five o'clock, and Mr. Ransley Soames, the man he needed to see, had already left for the day. Pitt was tired and aching profoundly. He was not sorry to be thwarted in his diligence, and able to stop a hansom in Whitehall and return home.

He had debated whether or not to tell Charlotte the full extent of the incident with the coach. It would be useless trying not to mention it at all. She would be aware that he was hurt the instant she saw him, but it would not be necessary to mention the gravity of it, or that Matthew had been injured even more. He decided it would only worry her to no purpose.

"What happened?" she pressed him the moment he had finished telling her the barest outline. They were sitting in the parlor with a hot cup of tea. Both children were upstairs, having had their meal. Jemima was doing homework. There were only four more years to go before the examinations which would decide her educational future. Daniel, two years younger, was still excused such rigorous study. At five and a half he could read quite tolerably, and was learning multiplication tables by heart, and a great deal more spelling than he desired. But at this time in the early evening he was permitted simply to play. Jemima was endeavoring to master a list of all the Kings of England from Edward the Confessor in 1066 to the present Queen in 1890, which was a formidable task. But when it was time for her examinations she would be required to know not only their names and order of succession, but their dates and the outstanding events of their reigns as well.

"What happened?" Charlotte repeated, watching him closely.

"A coach had apparently run out of control, and brushed me when it came 'round the corner at close to a gallop. I was knocked over, but not hurt more than a few bruises." He smiled. "It is really nothing serious. I wouldn't have told you at all, except I don't want you to fear I am crippled with old age just yet!"

There was no answering smile in her face.

"Thomas, you look dreadful. You should see a doctor, just to make sure ..."

"It is not necessary."

She made as if to stand up. "I think it is!"

"No, it isn't!" He heard the edge to his voice, and was unable to curb it. He sounded sharp, frightened.

She stopped, looking at him with a pucker between her brows.

"I'm sorry," he apologized. "I have already seen a doctor." He told her the same stretching of the truth he had told Chancellor. "There is nothing at all except a few bruises, and a sense of shock and anger."

"It is not all. Why did you go to a doctor?" she asked, looking at him narrowly.

It was too complicated to lie, and he was too tired. It was only to protect her that he had evaded it. He wanted to tell her.

"Matthew was with me," he replied. "He was more seriously hurt. The doctor came for him. But he will be all right," he added quickly. "It was simply that he was insensible for a few moments."

She looked at him closely, her eyes clouded with worry.

"Was it an accident, Thomas? You don't think the Inner Circle came after Matthew as well, do you?"

"I don't know. I doubt it, because dearly as I would like to think he is a danger to them, I don't."

She looked at him doubtfully, but said no more on the matter. Instead she went to run him a hot bath and find some ointment of arnica.

"Good morning, Superintendent." Ransley Soames made it a question, although the wording was not such. He was a good-looking man with regular features and thick, wavy, fair hair brushed back off his brow. His nose was rather high at the bridge and his mouth had a hint of softness in it. Without self-discipline he might have been indulgent. As it was he had a considerable presence and he looked at Pitt steadily and with gracious interest. "What may I do for you?"

"Good morning, Mr. Soames," Pitt answered, closing the office door behind him and accepting the seat offered. Soames was sitting behind a high and very finely carved desk, a red box to one side, closed and with its ribbons tied. "I apologize for troubling you, sir, but I am enquiring, at the request of the Foreign Office, into certain information which has been very seriously misdirected. It is necessary that we know the source of the information, and all who may have been privy to it, in order to rectify the error."

Soames frowned at him. "Your language is very diplomatic, Superintendent, one might even say obscure. What sort of information are you referring to, and where has it gone that it should not?"

"Financial information regarding Africa, and I should prefer at this point not to say where it has gone. Mr. Linus Chancellor has asked that I be as discreet as possible. I expect you understand the necessity for that."

"Of course." But Soames did not look as if he thought well of being included in the proscription. "You will also understand, Superintendent, if I require some confirmation of what you say . . . simply as a formality?"

Pitt smiled. "Naturally." He produced a letter of authority Matthew had given him, with the Foreign Secretary's countersignature.

Soames glanced at it, recognized Lord Salisbury's hand, and sat up a little straighter. Pitt noticed a certain tension in him. Perhaps he was becoming aware of the gravity of the matter.

"Yes, Superintendent. Precisely what is it you wish to learn from me? An enormous amount of financial information passes across my desk, as you may appreciate. More than a little of it is to do with African matters."

"That which concerns me is to do with the funding of Mr. Cecil Rhodes's expedition into Matabeleland, which is presently taking place, among other things."

"Indeed? Are you not aware, Superintendent, that the greatest part of that has been funded by Mr. Rhodes himself, and his South Africa Company?"

"Yes sir, I am. But it was not always so. It would help me greatly if you could give me something of the history of the finances of the expedition."

Soames's eyes widened.

"Good gracious! Going back how far?"

The window was open, and amidst the faint rumble of traffic came the sound of a hurdy-gurdy, then it was gone again.

"Let us say, the last ten years," Pitt replied.

"What do you wish to know? I cannot possibly recount to you

the entire matter. I shall be here all day." Soames looked both surprised and irritated, as if he found the request unreasonable.

"I only need to know who dealt with the information."

Soames sighed. "You are still asking the impossible. Mr. Rhodes first tried to secure Bechuanaland from the Cape. Back in August of 'eighty-three he addressed the Cape Parliament on that issue." He sat back farther in his chair, folding his hands across his waistcoat. "It was the gateway to the enormous fertile northern plains of Matabeleland and Mashonaland. But he found Scanlen, the prime minister, to be quite uninterested. The Cape Parliament was in debt to an immense degree with a railway obligation of some fourteen million pounds, and having just suffered a war with Basutoland which had been a crippling additional expense. It was at that time that Rhodes first turned to London for finances ... unwillingly, I may say. Of course that was during Mr. Gladstone's Liberal government. Lord Derby was Foreign Secretary then. But he was no more interested than had been Scanlen of the Cape." Soames regarded Pitt narrowly. "Are you familiar with all this, Superintendent?"

"No sir. Is it necessary that I should be?"

"If you are to understand the history of the financing of this expedition." Soames smiled belatedly, and continued. "After our fearful losses at Majuba, Lord Derby wanted nothing to do with it. However, the following year there was a complete turn in events, largely brought about by fear of the Transvaal pushing northwards and eclipsing our efforts, our very necessary efforts for the safety of the Empire, the sea lanes 'round the Cape, and so on. We could not afford to allow the Cape ports to fall solely into the hands of the Afrikaners. Are you following me?"

"Yes."

"Kruger and the other Transvaal delegates sailed to London the following year, 'eighty-four, to renegotiate the Pretoria Convention. Part of this agreement—I won't bore you with the details—included Kruger letting go of Bechuanaland. Boer freebooters were moving northward." He was watching Pitt closely to see if he understood. "Kruger double-crossed Rhodes and annexed Goshen to the Transvaal, and Germany entered the scene. It became increasingly complicated. Do you begin to see how much information there is, and how difficult to ascertain who knew what?"

"I do," Pitt conceded. "But surely there are usual channels through which information passes which concerns Zambezia and Equatoria?"

"Certainly. What about the Cape, Bechuanaland, the Congo and Zanzibar?"

The sounds from the open window seemed far away, like another world.

"Exclude them for the time being," Pitt directed.

"Very well. That makes it easier." Soames did not look any less concerned or irritated. His brow was furrowed and there was a tension in his body. "There are only myself, Thompson, Chetwynd, MacGregor, Cranbourne and Alderley who are aware of all of the areas you mention. I find it hard to think that any of them have been careless, or allowed information to pass to anyone unauthorized, but I suppose it is possible."

"Thank you."

Soames frowned. "What do you intend to do?"

"Pursue the matter," Pitt replied with a noncommittal smile. He would have Tellman deal with it, see if there were any connections between one of these men and Miss Amanda Pennecuick, among other things.

Soames was regarding Pitt steadily. "Superintendent, I presume the information has been used inappropriately, for personal gain, speculation of some sort? I trust it in no way jeopardizes our position in Africa? I am aware of how serious it is." He leaned forward. "Indeed it is imperative that we obtain Zambezia and the entire Cape-to-Cairo route. If it falls to the wrong powers, God alone knows what harm may be done. All the work, the profound influence of men like Livingstone and Moffatt, will be overtaken by a tide of violence and religious barbarism. Africa may be bathed in blood. Christianity could be lost in the continent." His face looked bleak and sad. It was obviously something he believed in profoundly and without question.

Pitt felt a sudden wave of sympathy for the man. It was so far from the opportunism and the exploitation Sir Arthur had feared. Ransley Soames at least had no part in the Inner Circle and its manipulation. Pitt could like him for that alone. It was an overwhelming relief. After all, he was to be Matthew's father-in-law.

"I'm sorry. I wish I could say that it were," he answered gravely. "But it has been passed to the German Embassy."

The color drained from Soames's face and he stared at Pitt in horror. "Information ... accurate information? Are you sure?"

"It may not yet have done any irreparable harm," Pitt strove to reassure him.

"But ... who would do such a ... a thing?" Soames looked almost desperate. "Will the Germans press in from Zanzibar with armies? They do have men, weapons, even gunboats there, you know? There has already been rebellion, suppression and bloodshed!"

"That may be enough to prevent them pressing inland just yet," Pitt said hopefully. "In the meantime, Mr. Soames, thank you for this information. I shall take this with me." He rose to his feet and was at the door before he took a sudden chance. After all, Harriet Soames was a young woman of fashion and society. "Sir, are you by any chance familiar with the name of Miss Amanda Pennecuick?"

"Yes." Soames looked startled. "Whatever makes you ask such a question? She can have nothing to do with this. She is a friend of my daughter's. Why do you ask, Superintendent?"

"Is she acquainted with any of the gentlemen on this list?"

"Yes, yes I believe so. Alderley has met her in social circumstances in my house, that I am aware of. He seems very taken with her. Not unnaturally. She is an unusually charming young woman.

What has that to do with the financial information on Africa, Superintendent?"

"Possibly nothing." Pitt smiled quickly and opened the door. "Thank you very much, sir. Good morning."

The following day was Sunday, and for Nobby Gunne it was the happiest day she could remember. Peter Kreisler had invited her to go down the river with him, and had hired a small pleasure boat for the afternoon. They were to return by carriage through the long, late spring evening after supper.

Now she sat in the small craft on the bright water, the sun in her face, the breeze just cool enough to be pleasant, and the sounds of laughter and excited voices drifted across the river as women in pale muslin dresses, men in shirtsleeves, and excited children leaned over the rails of excursion boats, or looked down from bridges or across from either bank.

"All London seems to be out today," she said happily as their boatman steered dexterously between a moored barge and a fishing trawler. They had boarded at Westminster Bridge under the shadow of the Houses of Parliament, and were now well down the outgoing tide beyond Blackfriars, almost to the Southwark Bridge, with London Bridge ahead of them.

Kreisler smiled. "A perfect May day, why not? I suppose the virtuous are still in church?" They had earlier heard the sound of bells drifting across the water, and he had already pointed out one or two elegant Wren spires in the distance.

"I can be just as virtuous here," she replied with questionable truth. "And certainly a great deal better tempered."

This time he made no effort to hide his amusement. "If you are going to try to convince me you are a conventional woman, you are far too late. Conventional women do not paddle up the Congo in canoes."

"Of course not!" she answered happily. "They sit in pleasure boats on the Thames, and allow gentlemen of their acquaintance to take them up to Richmond or Kew, or down to Greenwich for the afternoon. . . ."

"Would you rather have gone up to Kew? I hear the botanical gardens are among the wonders of the world."

"Not in the least. I am perfectly happy going to Greenwich. Besides, on a day like this, I fear all the world and his aunt will be at Kew."

He settled a little more comfortably in his seat, relaxing back in the sun and watching the myriad other craft maneuvering the busy waterway, and the carriages and omnibuses on the banks, the stalls selling peppermint drinks, pies, sandwiches and cockles, or balloons, hoops, penny flutes and whistles, and other toys. A girl in a frilly dress was chasing a little boy in a striped suit. A black-and-white dog barked and jumped up and down in excitement. A hurdy-gurdy played a familiar tune. A pleasure boat passed by, its decks lined with people, all waving towards the shore. One man had a red bandanna tied around his head, a bright splash of color in a sea of faces.

Nobby and Kreisler glanced at each other. Speech was not necessary; the same amusement was in both their faces, the same wry enjoyment of humanity.

They had passed under the Southward Bridge. The old Swan Pier was to the left, London Bridge ahead, and then Custom House Quay.

"Do you suppose the Congo will ever become one of the great waterways of the world?" she said thoughtfully. "In my mind's eye I can only see it as a vast brown sliding stream hemmed in by a jungle so immense it covers nations, and just isolated canoes paddling a few miles from village to village." She trailed her hand gently in the water. The breeze was warm on her face. "Man seems so small, so ineffectual against the primeval strength of Africa. Here we seem to have conquered everything and bent it to our will."

"We won't ever conquer the Congo," he said without hesitation. "The climate won't let us. That is one of the few things we cannot tame or subdue. But no doubt we will build cities, take steamboats there and export the timber, copper and everything else we think we can sell. There is already a railway. In time I expect they will build another from Zambezia to the Cape, to take out gold, ivory and whatever else, more efficiently."

"And you hate the idea," she said with gravity, all the laughter vanished.

He looked at her steadily. "I hate the greed and the exploitation. I hate the duplicity with which we cheat the Africans. They've cheated and duped Lobengula, the king of the Ndebele in Mashonaland. He's illiterate, of course, but a wily old devil, I think perhaps even intelligent enough to understand some of his own tragedy."

The ebbing tide had them well in its grip and they passed under London Bridge. A girl in a large hat was staring down at them, smiling. Nobby waved to her and she waved back.

Custom House Quay was to their left, and beyond it Tower Hill and the Great Tower of London with its crested battlements and flags flying. Down at the water's edge was the slipway of Traitors Gate, where the condemned had been delivered by boat to their execution in days past.

"I wonder what he was like," Kreisler said quietly, almost as if to himself.

"Who?" Nobby asked, for once not following his thoughts.

"William of Normandy," he answered. "The last conqueror to subdue these lands and subjugate its people, set up his fortresses across the hills, and with armed soldiers to keep order and take profit from the land. The Tower was his." They were sliding past it as he spoke, on the swift ebbing water; the boatman had little to do to keep their speed.

She knew what Kreisler was thinking. It had nothing to do with William of Normandy or an invasion over eight centuries ago.

It was Africa again, and European rifles and cannons against the assegais of the Zulu impis, or the Ndebele, British formations across the African plains, black men ruled by white as the Saxons had been by the Normans. Only the Normans were blood cousins, allied by race and faith, different only in tongue.

She looked at him and held his gaze steadily. They were passing St. Catherine's Dock and heading towards the Pool of London. On either side of the river there were docks, wharves, and stairs going to the water's edge. Barges were moored, others moved out slowly into the stream and went up towards further docks, or down towards the estuary and the sea. Pleasure boats were fewer now; this was the commercial shore. Here was trade with all the world.

As if having taken her thoughts, he smiled. "Cargoes of silk from China, spices from Burma and India, teak and ivory and jade," he said, lying back a little farther. The sun on his brown face caught the pale color of his hair where it was already bleached by a far fiercer light than that of this gentle English afternoon with its dappled water. "I suppose it should be cedars of Lebanon and gold from Ophir! It won't be long before it's gold from Zimbabwe and mahogany and skins from Equatoria, ivory from Zanzibar and minerals from the Congo. And they will be traded for cotton from Manchester, and guns and men from half Europe. Some will come home again, many won't."

"Have you ever met Lobengula?" she asked curiously.

He laughed, looking up quickly. "Yes . . . I have. He's an enormous man, nearly twenty-two stones in weight, and over six feet tall. He wears nothing except a Zulu ring 'round his head and a small loincloth."

"Good heavens! Really? So big?" She regarded him closely to see if he was joking, although she knew almost certainly he was not.

His smile was steady, but his eyes were full of laughter. "The Ndebele are not a building people like the Shona, who created the city of Zimbabwe. They live by cattle raising and raiding, and making only villages of grass huts covered with dung. . . ."

"I know the sort," she said quickly, and memory returned so she could almost smell the dry heat in spite of the rushing and slapping of water all around her and the bright reflections dancing in her eyes.

"Of course you do," he apologized. "Forgive me. It is so rare a treat for me to be able to speak with someone who needs no explanation or word pictures to imagine what I'm describing. Lobengula holds a very formal court. Anyone seeking audience with him has to approach him crawling on hands and knees—and remain so throughout." He pulled a face. "It can be a very hot and exhausting experience, and not necessarily with any pleasure or profit at the end. He can neither read nor write, but he has a prodigious memory . . . for all the good that will do him dealing with Europe, poor devil."

She waited in silence. Kreisler was lost in thoughts of his own and she was content to allow it. She had no sense of being excluded; it was perfectly companionable. The light, the sound of the water, the wharves and warehouses of the Pool of London slipped by, and the shared dreams of the past in another land, the shared fears for its future as a different kind of darkness loomed over it.

"They duped him, of course," he said after a while. "They promised they would bring no more than ten white men to work in his country."

She sat upright suddenly, her eyes wide with disbelief.

"Yes." He looked at her through his lashes. "Unbelievable to you or me, but he accepted it. They also said they would dig nowhere near towns, and that they and their people would abide by the laws of the Ndebele, and behave generally as Lobengula's subjects." The bitterness crept in only at the end.

"And the price?" she asked quietly.

"A hundred pounds a month, a thousand Martini-Henry breach-locking rifles and a hundred thousand rounds of ammunition, and a gunboat on the Zambezi."

She said nothing. They were passing Wapping Old Stairs on their left as they sped downriver. The Pool of London was teeming with boats, barges, steamers, tugs, trawlers and here and there the odd pleasure boat. Would the brown, jungle-crusted Congo ever be like this, teeming with civilization and the goods of the world to be bought and sold, and consumed by men and women who had never left their own counties or shires?

"Rudd set off at a gallop to take the news to Rhodes in Kimberley," Kreisler went on, "before the king realized he had been cheated. The fool almost died of thirst in his eagerness to carry the news." There was disgust in his voice, but the only emotion registered in his face was a deep and acutely personal pain. His lips were stiff with the intensity of it as if it resided with him all the time, and yet for all his leanness of body and the strength she knew was there, he looked vulnerable.

But it was a private pain. She was perhaps the only person with whom he had or could share the full nature of it and expect any degree of understanding, yet she knew not to intrude into intimacy. Part of the sharing was the delicacy of the silence between them.

They were past the Pool and the London Docks and leaving Limehouse. Still the wharves and stairs lined either side, massive warehouses with painted names above them. The West India Docks were ahead, and then Limehouse Reach and the Isle of Dogs. They had already passed the old pier stakes sticking above the receding water, where in the past pirates had been lashed till the incoming tide drowned them. They had both seen them, glanced at each other, and said nothing.

It was very comfortable not to have to search for speech. It was a luxury she was not used to. Almost everyone else she knew would have found the silence a lack. They would have been impelled to say something to break it. Kreisler was perfectly happy just to catch her eye now and then, and know that she too was busy with the wind, the smell of salt, the noise and bustle around them, and yet the feeling of being detached from it by the small space of water that separated them from everyone else. They passed through it with impunity, seeing and yet uninvolved.

Greenwich was beautiful, the long green swell of ground rising from the river, the full leaf of the trees and the park beyond, the classical elegance of Vanburgh's architecture in the hospital and the Royal Naval Schools behind.

They went ashore, rode in an open trap up to the park and then walked slowly side by side through the lawns and flowers and stood under the great trees listening to the wind moving gently in the branches. A huge magnolia was in full bloom, its tulip flowers a foam of white against the blue sky. Children chased each other and played with hoops and spinning tops and kites. Nursemaids in crisp uniforms walked, heads high, perambulators in front of them. Soldiers in scarlet tunics lounged around, watching the nursemaids. Lovers, young and less young, walked arm in arm. Girls flirted, swinging parasols and laughing. A dog capered around with a stick in its mouth. Somewhere a barrel organ was playing a musical tune.

They had afternoon tea, and talked of frivolous things, knowing that darker matters were always there, but understood; nothing needed explaining. The sadness and the fear had all been shared and for this warm, familiar afternoon it could be left beneath the surface of the mind.

In the sunset, with the moth-filled air cooling and the smell of earth and leaves rising from the pathway, they found the carriage which was to take them on the long ride back westwards. He handed her in, and they drove home with only an occasional word as the dusk deepened. The light flared in apricot and amber and turquoise over the river, making it look for a brief moment as if it could have been as magical as the lagoons of Venice, or the seaway of the Bosphorus, the meeting of Europe and Asia, instead of London, and the heart of the greatest empire since Caesar's Rome.

Then the color faded to silver, the stars appeared to the south, away from the stir and lamps of the city, and they moved a little closer together as the chill of darkness set in. She could not remember a sweeter day.

CHAPTER
SIX

The Monday afterwards Nobby spent largely in her own garden. Of all the things she liked about England—and when she thought about it, there were really quite a few—its gardens gave her the greatest pleasure. There were frequent occasions when she loathed the climate, when the long, gray days of January and February depressed her and she ached for the African sun. The sleet seemed to creep between the folds of every conceivable garment designed against it. Icy water trickled down one's neck, onto one's wrists between glove and sleeve, no boots kept it all off the feet, skirt hems became sodden and filthy. Did the designers of gowns have the faintest idea what it was like to walk around carrying a dozen yards of wet fabric wrapped around one's torso?

And there were days, sometimes even weeks, when fog obliterated the world, clinging, blinding fog which caught in the throat, muffled and distorted sounds, held the smoke and fumes of a hundred thousand chimneys in a shroud like a cold, wet cloth across the face.

There were disappointing days in the summer when one longed for warmth and brilliance, and yet it persistently rained, and the chill east wind came in off the sea, raising goose pimples on the flesh.

But there were also the days of glory when the sun shone in a perfect sky, great trees a hundred, two hundred feet high soared into the air in a million rustling leaves, elms, whispering poplars, silver-stemmed birches, and the great beeches she loved most of all.

The land was always green; the depth of summer or the bleakest winter did not parch or freeze it. And the abundance of flowers must surely be unique. She could have named a hundred varieties without having to resort to a book. Now as she stood in the afternoon sunlight looking down her long, shaven velvet lawn to the cedar, and the elms beyond, an Albertine rose in a wild profusion of sprays was spilling over the old stone wall, uncountable buds ready to open into a foam of coral and pink blossom. The spires of delphiniums rose in front of it, ready to bloom in royal and indigo, and bloodred peonies were fattening to flower. The may blossom perfumed the air, as did pink and purple lilac.

On a day like this the empire builders were welcome to Africa, India, the Pacific, or the Spice Islands, or even the Indies.

"Excuse me, ma'am?"

She turned, startled out of her reverie. Her maid was standing looking at her with a surprised expression.

"Yes, Martha?"

"Please ma'am, there's a Mrs. Chancellor 'as called to see you. A Mrs. Linus Chancellor. She's very ..."

"Yes?"

"Oh, I think you'd better come, ma'am. Shall I say as you'll receive her?"

Nobby contained her amusement, and not inconsiderable surprise. What on earth was Susannah Chancellor doing paying an afternoon call here? Nobby was hardly in her social or her political sphere.

"Certainly tell her so," she replied. "And show her out onto the terrace."

Martha bobbed something like half a curtsy and hurried with

insufficient dignity back across the grass and up the steps to discharge her errand.

A moment later Susannah emerged from the French doors, by which time Nobby was coming up the shallow stone steps from the lawn, her skirt brushing against the urns with scarlet and vermilion nasturtiums spilling out of them, almost luminous in their brilliance.

Susannah was dressed very formally in white, trimmed with pale pink and a thread of carmine-shaded ribbon. White lace foamed at her throat and wrists and her parasol was trimmed with ribbon and a blush pink rose. She looked exquisite, and unhappy.

"Good afternoon, Mrs. Chancellor," Nobby said formally. This was an extremely formal time of the afternoon to call. "How very pleasant of you to come."

"Good afternoon, Miss Gunne," Susannah replied with less than her usual assurance. She looked beyond Nobby to the garden as if seeking someone else. "Have I interrupted you with . . . with other visitors?" She forced a smile.

"No, I am quite alone," Nobby replied, wondering what so troubled the younger woman. "I was simply enjoying the perfect weather and thinking what a delight it is to have a garden."

"Yes, isn't it," Susannah agreed, stepping farther across the terrace and starting down the steps to the lawn. "Yours is particularly beautiful. Would you think me discourteous to ask if you would show me 'round it? It is too much to take in at a glance. And it looks as if there is more of it yet, beyond that stone wall and the archway. Is that so?"

"Yes, I am very fortunate in its size," Nobby agreed. "Of course I should be delighted to show you." It was far too early to offer refreshment, and anyway that was not customary during the first hour of time appropriate for receiving. Although, of course, some fifteen minutes was all one stayed; it was also not done to walk around the garden, which would take half an hour at the very least.

Nobby was now quite concerned as to why Susannah had

come. It was impossible to imagine it was a simple call for the usual social purposes. Leaving her card would have been quite adequate, in fact the proper thing, since they were not in any real sense acquainted.

They walked very gently, Susannah stopping every few yards to admire something or other. Often she appeared not to know its name, simply to like its color, form, or its position complementing something else. They passed the gardener weeding around the antirrhinums and pulling a few long spears of grass from the mass of the blue salvia.

"Of course, as close to Westminster as we live," Susannah went on, "we do not have room for a garden such as this. It is one of the things I most miss. We do go down to the country when my husband can arrange it, but that is not so very often. His position is most demanding."

"I can imagine that it would be," Nobby murmured.

A brief smile touched Susannah's face and immediately vanished again. A curious expression followed, a softness in her eyes, at once pleasure and pain, yet her lips were pulled tight with some underlying anxiety which would not let her relax. She said the words "my husband" with the pride of a woman in love. Yet her hands fiddled incessantly with the ribbons on her parasol, her fingers stiff, as if she did not care if she broke the threads.

There was nothing Nobby could do but wait.

Susannah turned and began walking towards the great cedar and the white garden seat under its shade. The grass was thin where the needles had shed on it until the ground became bare altogether near the trunk, the roots having taken all the nourishment from the earth.

"You must have seen a great many wonderful things, Miss Gunne." Susannah did not look at her but through the stone archway beneath the roses. "Sometimes I envy you your travels. Then of course there are other times—most of them, I admit— when I am too fond of the comforts of England." She looked at

Nobby beside her. "Would it bore you to tell me something of your adventures?"

"Not at all, if that is really what you wish? But I assure you, you have no need of it in order to be polite."

"Polite?" Susannah was surprised, this time stopping to face Nobby. "Is that what you think?"

"A great many have thought it was the proper thing to do," Nobby replied with amusement and a flood of memory, much of it painful at the time, but merely absurd now.

"Oh, not at all," Susannah assured her. They were still in the shade of the cedar, and considerably cooler. "I find Africa fascinating. My husband has a great deal to do with it, you know?"

"Yes, yes I know who he is." Nobby was not sure what else to say. The more she knew of Linus Chancellor's backing of Cecil Rhodes, the less happy she was about it. The whole question of the settlement of Zambezia had troubled her ever since she had met Peter Kreisler. The thought of him brought a smile to her lips, in spite of the questions and the anxiety.

Susannah caught the intonation; at least it seemed as if she did. She looked around quickly, and was about to say something, then changed her mind and turned back to the garden again. She had been there ten minutes already. For a strictly formal call, she should now be taking her leave.

"I suppose you know Africa quite well—the people, I mean?" she said thoughtfully.

"I am familiar with them in certain areas," Nobby replied honestly. "But it is an inconceivably enormous country, in fact an entire continent of distances we Europeans can scarcely imagine. It would be ridiculous to say I know more than a fraction. Of course, if you are interested, there are people in London who know far more than I do and who have been there more recently. I believe you have already met Mr. Kreisler, for example?" She found herself oddly self-conscious as she spoke his name. That was foolish. She was not forcing him into the conversation, as a young woman does when in love, introducing a man's name into every possible subject. This was most natural; in fact it would have been unnatural not to have spoken of him.

"Yes." Susannah looked away from the arch and the roses and back down the lawn towards the house. "Yes, I have met him. A most interesting man, with vigorous views. What is your opinion of him, Miss Gunne?" She swiveled back again, her face earnest. "Do you mind my asking you? I don't know who else's opinion would be of the least worth, compared with yours."

"I think perhaps you overrate me." Nobby felt herself blushing, which made it even worse. "But of course what little I know you are most welcome to hear."

Susannah seemed to be most relieved, as if this were the real purpose of her visit.

"Thank you. I feared for a moment you were going to decline."

"What is it you are concerned about?" The conversation was becoming very stilted. Susannah was still highly nervous, and Nobby felt more and more self-conscious as time passed. The garden was so quiet behind the walls she could hear the wind in the tops of the trees like water breaking on a shore, gently as a tide on shingle. A bee drifted lazily from one open flower to another. The warmth of the afternoon was considerable, even under the shade of the cedar, and the air was heavy with the odor of crushed grass, damp leaves under the weight of foliage by the hedges, and the sweet pervasive blossom of lilacs and the may.

"His opinion of Mr. Rhodes is very poor," Susannah said at last. "I am not entirely sure why. Do you think it may be personal?"

Nobby thought she heard a lift of hope in her voice. Since Linus Chancellor had vested so much confidence in him, that would not be surprising. But what had Kreisler said to her which had caused her to doubt, and come seeking Nobby's opinion, and not her husband's? That in itself was extraordinary. A woman automatically shared her husband's status in life, his religious views, and if she had political opinions at all, they were also his.

"I am not sure whether he has even met Mr. Rhodes," Nobby replied slowly, hiding her surprise and feeling for words to convey the facts she knew, without the coloring of her own mistrust of the motives for African settlement and the fears she had of the exploitation of its people. "Of course he, like me, is a little in love with the mystery of Africa as it is," she went on with an apologetic smile. "We are apprehensive of change, in case something of that is lost. When you feel you were the first to see something, and you are excited and overwhelmed and deeply moved by it, you do feel as if no one else will treat it with the same reverence you do. And it causes one to fear, perhaps unjustly. Certainly Mr. Kreisler does not share Mr. Rhodes's dreams of colonization and settlement."

A smile flashed across Susannah's face and vanished.

"That is something of an understatement, Miss Gunne. If what he says is true, he fears it will be the ruination of Zambezia. I have heard some of his arguments, and I wondered if you would share with me your view of them."

"Oh . . ." Nobby was taken aback. It was too frank a question for her to answer without considerable thought, and a censorship of the emotions that came to her mind before she permitted them to anybody else, particularly Susannah Chancellor. There were many aspects to weigh. She must not, even accidently, betray a confidence Kreisler might have placed in her by allowing her to share emotions and fears which he might not have been willing to show others. The boat trip down the Thames had been an unguarded afternoon, not intended to be repeated to anyone else. She certainly would have felt deeply let down had he spoken of it freely, describing her words or experiences to friends, whatever the cause.

It was not that she thought for a moment that he was ashamed of any of his views. On the contrary. But one does not repeat what a friend says in a moment of candor, or on an occasion which is held in trust.

And yet she was painfully aware of a vulnerability in the woman who stood beside her gazing at the massed bloom of the lupines in colors of pinks and apricots, purples, blues and creams. Their perfume was almost overwhelming. Susannah was full of doubts so deep she had been unable to endure them in silence. Were they born of fear for the husband she loved, for the money invested by her mother-in-law, or by something in her own conscience?

And for Nobby, above even those considerations, was honesty, being true to her own vision of Africa and what she knew of it so deeply it had been part of her fiber, interwoven with her understanding of all things. To betray that, even for the sake of pity, would be the ultimate destruction.

Susannah was waiting, watching her face.

"You are unwilling to answer?" she said slowly. "Does that mean you believe he is right, and my husband is wrong in backing Cecil Rhodes as he does? Or is it that you know something to Mr. Kreisler's discredit, but you are unwilling to say it to another?"

"No," Nobby said firmly. "Nothing at all. It simply means that the question is too serious to be answered without thought. It is not something I should say lightly. I believe Mr. Kreisler holds his opinions with great depth, and that he is well acquainted with the subject. He is afraid that the native kings have been duped—"

"I know they have," Susannah interrupted. "Even Linus would not argue that. He says it is for a far greater good in the future, a decade from now. Africa will be settled, you know? It is impossible to turn back time and pretend that it has not been discovered. Europe knows there is gold there, and diamonds, and ivory. The question is simply who will do it. Will it be Britain, Belgium or Germany? Or far worse than that, possibly one of the Arab countries, who still practice slavery?"

"Then what is it in Mr. Kreisler's view that disturbs you?" Nobby asked with cutting frankness. "Naturally we would wish it to be Britain, not only for our benefit, quite selfishly, but more altruistically, because we believe we will do it better, instill better values, more honorable forms of government in place of what is there now, and certainly better than the slavery you mentioned."

Susannah stared at her, her eyes troubled.

"Mr. Kreisler says that we will make the Africans subject peoples in their own land. We have backed Mr. Rhodes and let him put in most of the money, and all of the effort and risk. If he succeeds, and he probably will, we shall have no control over him. We will have made him into an emperor in the middle of Africa, with our blessing. Can he be right? Does he really know so much and see so clearly?"

"I think so," Nobby said with a sad smile. "I think you have put it rather well."

"And perhaps those thoughts should frighten anyone."

Susannah twisted the handle of her parasol around and around between her fingers.

"Actually it was Sir Arthur Desmond who put it like that. Did you know him? He died about two weeks ago. He was one of the nicest men I ever knew. He used to work in the Foreign Office."

"No, I didn't know him. I'm very sorry."

Susannah stared at the lupines. A bumblebee drifted from one colored spire to another. The gardener passed across the far end of the lawn with a barrow full of weeds and disappeared towards the kitchen garden.

"It is absurd to mourn someone I only saw half a dozen times a year," Susannah went on with a sigh. "But I'm afraid that I do. I have an awful sadness come over me when I think that I shall not see him again. He was one of those people who always left one feeling better." She looked at Nobby to see if she understood. "It was not exactly a cheerfulness, more a sense that he was ultimately sane, in a world which is so often cheap in its values, shallow in its judgment, too quick to be crushed, laughs at all the wrong things, and is never quite optimistic enough."

"He was obviously a most remarkable man," Nobby said gently. "I am not surprised you grieve for him, even if you saw him seldom.

It is not the time you spend with someone, it is what happens in that time. I have known people for years, and yet never met the real person inside, if there is one. Others I have spoken with for only an hour or two, and yet what was said had meaning and honesty that will last forever." She had not consciously thought of anyone in particular when she began to speak, and yet it was Kreisler's face in the sunlight on the river that filled her mind.

"It was . . . very sudden." Susannah touched one of the early roses with her fingertips. "Things can change so quickly, can't they. . . ."

"Indeed." The same thought was filling Nobby's mind; not only circumstances but also emotions. Yesterday had been cloudless; now she was unable to prevent the flickers of doubt that entered her mind. Susannah was obviously deeply troubled, torn in her loyalties between her husband's plans and the questions that Kreisler had raised in her. She did not want to think he was right, and yet the fear was in her face, the angle of her body, the hand tight on the parasol, holding it as if it were a weapon, not an ornament.

Exactly what had he said to her, and perhaps more urgently than that, why? He was not naive, to have spoken carelessly. He knew who she was, and he knew Linus Chancellor's part in raising the additional financing and the government backing for Cecil Rhodes. He knew Susannah's relationship to Francis Standish and her own inheritance in the banking business. She had to have been familiar with at least some of the details. Was he seeking information from her? Or was he planting in her mind the seeds of disinformation, lies and half truths for her to take back to Linus Chancellor and the Colonial Office, ultimately the Prime Minister himself? Kreisler was a German name. Perhaps for all his outward Englishness, it was not Britain's interests in Africa he had at heart, but Germany's?

Maybe he was using them both, Susannah and Nobby?

She was surprised how profoundly that thought hurt, like a gouging wound inside.

Susannah was watching her, her wide eyes full of uncertainty, and the beginnings of just as deep a pain. There was a spirit between them of perfect understanding. For an instant Nobby knew that Susannah also was facing a disillusion so bitter the fear of it filled her mind with darkness. Then as quickly it was gone again, and a new thought took its place. Surely Susannah could not also be in love with Peter Kreisler? Could she?

Also? What on earth was she saying to herself? She was attracted ... that was all. She barely knew the man ... memories in common, a dream that had found them both in youth, enough to take them separately upon the same great adventure into a dark continent in which they had found a light and a brilliance, a land to love, and had come home with its fever and magic forever within them. And now they both feared for it.

One afternoon on the river when understanding had been too complete to need words, only a few hours out of a lifetime—enough to call enchantment, not love. Love was less ephemeral, less full of magic.

"Miss Gunne?"

She jerked herself back to the garden and Susannah.

"Yes?"

"Do you think Mr. Rhodes is just using us? That he will build his own empire in Central Africa, turn Zambezia into Cecil Rhodes land, and then cock a snook at us all? He would have the wealth to do it. No one can imagine the gold and the diamonds there, quite apart from the land, the ivory, timber and whatever else there is. It is teeming with beasts, so they say, creatures of every kind imaginable."

"I don't know." Nobby shivered involuntarily, as if the garden had suddenly become cold. "But it is certainly not impossible." There was no other answer she could give. Susannah did not deserve a lie, nor would she be likely to believe one.

"You say that very carefully." The ghost of a smile crossed Susannah's face.

"It is a very large thought, and one too dangerous to treat with less than care. But if you look back even a little way through history, many of our greatest conquests, and most successful, have been largely at the hands of one man," Nobby answered. "Clive in India is perhaps the best example."

"Yes, of course you are right." Susannah turned and looked up the long lawn towards the house. "And I have been here the better part of an hour. Thank you for being so . . . generous." But she did not say that she felt better or clearer in her mind, and Nobby was sure that it was not so.

She walked back towards the French doors to the house with her, not because she was expecting further callers, thank goodness——she was in no mood for them—but out of a sense of friendship, even a futile desire to protect someone she believed desperately vulnerable.

To those making the very most of the London Season, a night at the theater or the opera was positively a rest after the hectic round of riding in the park before breakfast, shopping, writing letters, seeing one's dressmaker or milliner in the morning, luncheon parties, making and receiving calls in the afternoon, or visiting dog shows, exhibitions, or galleries, garden parties, afternoon teas, dinners, *conversaziones*, soirees or balls. To be able to sit in one place without having to make conversation, even to drift off into a gentle doze if so inclined, while at the same time be seen to be present, was a luxury not to be overlooked. Without it one might have collapsed from the sheer strain of it all.

However, since Vespasia had long since given up such a frantic pattern of behavior, she visited the theater purely for the pleasure of seeing whatever drama was presented. This particular May the offerings included Lillie Langtry in a new play titled *Esther Sandraz*. She had no desire to see Mrs. Langtry in anything. Gilbert and Sullivan's *The Gondoliers* was naturally at the Savoy. She was not in the mood for it. She would have seen Henry Irving in a work called *The Bells*, or Pinero's farce *The Cabinet Minister*. Her opinion of cabinet ministers inclined her towards that. It looked more promising than the season of French plays, in French, currently at Her Majesty's, except that Sarah Bernhardt was doing *Joan of Arc*. That was tempting.

The operas were *Carmen*, *Lohengrin* or *Faust*. She had a love for Italian opera and was not fond of Wagner's, for all its current and surprising popularity. No one had expected it to be so. Had Simon Boccanegra been playing, or Nabucco, she would have gone even if she had to stand.

As it was she settled for *She Stoops to Conquer*, and found a remarkable number of her acquaintances had made the same decision. Although it was in many ways restful, the theater was still a place for which one dressed formally, at least for the three months of the Season, from May to July. At other times it was permissible to be rather more casual.

Theater outings were frequently organized in groups. Society seldom cared to do things in ones or twos. Dozens, or even scores, suited them better.

On this occasion Vespasia had invited Charlotte for pleasure, and Eustace as a matter of duty. He had been present when she made the decision to attend, and had shown so obvious an interest it would have been pointed not to include him, and for all the intense irritation he awoke in her from time to time, he was still part of her family.

She had invited Thomas also, of course, but he had been unable to come because of the pressure of work. He would not be able to leave Bow Street sufficiently early, and to enter one's box when the play was in progress was not acceptable.

Thus it was that, long before the curtain went up, she, Charlotte and Eustace were seated in her box indulging in the highly entertaining pastime of watching the other members of the audience arrive.

"Ah!" Eustace leaned forward slightly, indicating a gray-haired man of distinguished appearance entering a box to their left. "Sir Henry Rattray. A quite excellent man. A paragon of courtesy and honor."

"A paragon?" Vespasia said with slight surprise.

"Indeed." Eustace settled back and turned towards her, smiling with intense satisfaction. In fact he looked so well pleased with himself his chest had expanded and his face seemed to glow. "He embodies those knightly virtues of courage before the foe, clemency in victory, honesty, chastity, gentleness with the fair sex, protection of the weak, which are at the foundation of all we hold dear. That is what a knight was in times past, and an English gentleman is now—the best of them, of course!" There was absolute certainty in his voice. He was making a statement.

"You must know him very well to be so adamant," Charlotte said with wonder.

"Well you certainly know much of him that I do not," Vespasia said ambiguously.

Eustace held up one finger. "Ah, my dear Mama-in-law, that is precisely the point. I do indeed know much of him that is not known to the public. He does his greatest good by stealth, as a true Christian gentleman should."

Charlotte opened her mouth to make some remark about stealing, and bit it off just in time. She looked at Eustace's serene face and felt a chill of fear. He was so supremely confident, so certain he understood exactly what he was dealing with, who they were and that they believed the same misty, idealistic picture he did. He even thought in Arthurian language. Perhaps they held their meetings at round tables—with an empty seat for the "siege perilous" in case some wandering Galahad should arrive for the ultimate quest. The cleverness of it was frightening.

"A very perfect knight," Charlotte said aloud.

"Indeed!" Eustace agreed with enthusiasm. "My dear lady, you have it exactly!"

"That was said of Lancelot," Charlotte pointed out.

"Of course." Eustace nodded, smiling. "Arthur's closest friend, his right hand and ally."

"And the man who betrayed him," Charlotte added.

"What?" Eustace swung to face her, dismay in every feature.

"With Guinevere," Charlotte explained. "Had you forgotten that? In every way it was the beginning of the end."

Eustace obviously had forgotten it. The color spread up his cheeks, both with embarrassment at the indelicacy of the subject and confusion at having been caught in such an inappropriate analogy.

To her surprise Charlotte felt sorry for him, but she could not say anything which would be interpreted as praise for the Inner Circle, which was what the whole conversation was about. Eustace was so naive, sometimes she felt as if he were a child, an innocent.

"But the ideals of the Round Table were still the finest," she said gently. "And Galahad was without sin, or he would never have seen the Holy Grail. The thing is, one may find the good and the bad together, professing the same beliefs; all of us have weaknesses, vulnerabilities, and most of us have a tendency to see what we want to in others, most especially others we admire."

Eustace hesitated.

She looked at his face, his eyes, and saw for a moment his struggle to understand what she really meant, then he abandoned it and settled for the simple answer.

"Of course, dear lady, that is undoubtedly true." He turned to Vespasia, who had been listening without comment. "Who is that remarkable woman in the box next to Lord Riverdale? I have never seen such unusual eyes. They should be handsome, they are so large, and yet they are not, I declare."

Vespasia followed his gaze, and saw Christabel Thorne, sitting beside Jeremiah and talking to him with animation. He was listening with his gaze never wavering from her face, and with not only affection but very apparent interest.

Vespasia told Eustace who they were. Then she pointed out Harriet Soames in company with her father, and also displaying a most open affection and pride.

It was only a few moments after that when there was something of a stir in the audience. Several heads turned and there was a cessation of general whispering, but also a sudden swift commenting one to another.

"The Prince of Wales?" Eustace wondered with a touch of excitement in his voice. As a strict moralist he would have disapproved unequivocally of the Prince of Wales's behavior in anyone else. But princes were different. One did not judge them by the standards of ordinary men. At least Eustace did not.

"No," Vespasia said rather tartly. She applied the same standards to all; princes were not exempt, and she was also fond of the Princess. "The Secretary of State of Colonial Affairs, Mr. Linus Chancellor, and his wife, and I believe her brother-in-law, Mr. Francis Standish."

"Oh." Eustace was not sure whether he was interested or not.

Charlotte had no such doubts. Ever since she and Pitt had seen Susannah Chancellor at the Duchess of Marlborough's reception, she had found her of great interest, and overhearing her discussion with Kreisler at the Shakespearean bazaar had naturally added to it. She watched them take their seats, Chancellor attentive, courteous, but with the ease of one who is utterly comfortable in a marriage while still finding it of intense pleasure. Charlotte found herself smiling as she watched, and knowing precisely what Susannah felt with her turning of the head to accept his rearranging of the shawl across her chair, the smile on his lips, the momentary meeting of the eyes.

The lights dimmed and the music of the national anthem began. There was no more time for wandering attention.

When the applause died down and the first interval commenced it was a different matter.

Eustace turned to Charlotte. "And how is your family?" he enquired, but out of politeness, and to preempt any return to the subject of King Arthur, or any other society, past or present.

"They are all well, thank you," she replied.

"Emily?" he pressed.

"Abroad. Parliament is in recess."

"Indeed. And your mama?"

"Traveling also." She did not add that it was on honeymoon. That would be altogether too much for Eustace to cope with. She saw a twitch of laughter in Vespasia's mouth, and looked away. "Grandmama has moved into Ashworth House with Emily," she continued hastily. "Although of course she has no one there but the servants at present. She does not care for it at all."

"Quite." Eustace had the feeling that something had passed him by, but he preferred not to investigate it. "Would you care for some refreshment?" he offered gallantly.

Vespasia accepted, then Charlotte felt free to do so too. Obediently Eustace rose and took his leave to obtain it for them.

Charlotte and Vespasia glanced at each other, then both turned and looked, as discreetly as possible, at Linus and Susannah Chancellor. Francis Standish had gone, but there was nevertheless a third person in the box, and from the outline, quite obviously a man, tall, slender, of a very upright and military bearing.

"Kreisler," Charlotte whispered.

"I think so," Vespasia agreed.

A moment later as he half turned to speak to Susannah, they were proved right.

They could not possibly overhear the conversation, yet watching the expressions in their faces it was possible to draw very many conclusions.

Kreisler was naturally civil to Chancellor, but there was a pronounced coolness in both men, presumably due to their acknowledged political differences. Chancellor stood close to his wife, as though automatically including her in the opinions or arguments he expressed. Kreisler was not quite opposite them, a little to one side, so his face was invisible to Charlotte and Vespasia. He addressed Susannah with a sharpness of attention far more than mere good manners required, and seemed to direct his reasoning towards her rather than Chancellor, even though it was almost always Chancellor who answered.

Once or twice Charlotte noticed Susannah begin to speak, and Chancellor cut in with a reply, including her with a quick look or a gesture of the hand.

Again Kreisler would retort, always as much to her as to him.

Neither Charlotte nor Vespasia said anything, but Charlotte's mind was full of conjecture when Eustace returned. She thanked him almost absently, and sat with her drink, deep in thought, until the lights dimmed and the drama onstage recommenced.

During the second interval they left the box and went out into the foyer, where Vespasia was instantly greeted by several acquaintances, one in particular, an elderly marchioness in vivid green, with whom she spoke for some time.

Charlotte was very happy to spend her time merely watching, again finding a most absorbing subject in Linus and Susannah Chancellor and Mr. Francis Standish. She was most interested when she observed Chancellor's attention distracted for several minutes, and Standish alone with Susannah seeming to be arguing with her. From the expression on her face, she stood her ground, and he glanced angrily more than once in the direction of the far side of the foyer where Peter Kreisler was standing.

Once he took Susannah by the arm, and she shook him off impatiently. However when Chancellor returned Standish seemed to be quite satisfied that he had won, and led the way back towards their box. Chancellor smiled at Susannah with amusement and affection, and offered her his arm. She took it, moving closer to him, but there seemed to be a distress in her, some shadow across her face which haunted Charlotte so deeply she was unable to rid herself of it and enter into the rest of the play.

———

The next day was gusty but fine, and a little after midmorning Vespasia ordered her carriage to take her to Hyde Park. It was not necessary to stipulate that it must be near the corner by the Albert Memorial. There was only the choice between that and Marble Arch if one were to meet the members of Society who customarily took their morning rides or walks in the park. In the walk between the Albert and Grosvenor Gate one could meet everyone in Society who had elected to take the air.

Vespasia would have been perfectly happy anywhere, but she had come specifically to find Bertie Canning, an admirer. At the theater last evening her friend the marchioness had mentioned that he had a vast knowledge of people, especially those whose fame or notoriety rested on exploits in the greater part of the Empire, rather than in the confines of England. If anyone could tell her what she now quite urgently desired to know about Peter Kreisler, it was he.

She did not wish to ride: she could too easily miss Canning, and it offered no opportunity for conversation. She alighted and walked slowly and with the utmost elegance towards one of the many seats along the north side of the Row. Naturally, it was the fashionable side, where she would be able to watch in reasonable comfort as the world passed by. It was an entertainment she would enjoy at any time, even were there no purpose to it, but her observations last night, coupled with what she had overheard at the bazaar, had woken in her an anxiety she wished to satisfy as soon as possible.

She was dressed in her favorite silver-gray with touches of slate blue, and a hat of the very latest fashion. It was not unlike a riding hat, with a high crown and very slightly curled brim, and it was swathed with silk. It was extraordinarily becoming. She noticed with satisfaction that she drew the interest of several of those passing by in the lighter carriages customary at this hour, uncertain who she was, or if they should bow to her.

The Spanish ambassador and his wife were walking in the opposite direction. He touched his hat and smiled, sure he must know her, or if he did not, then he ought to.

She smiled back, amused.

Other vehicles passed by, tilburies, pony chaises, four-in-hands; small, light and elegant. Every one was exquisitely turned out, leather cleaned and polished, brasses gleaming, horses groomed to perfection. And of course the passengers and drivers were immaculate, servants in full livery, if indeed there were servants present. Many gentlemen cared to drive themselves, taking great pride in their handling of the "ribbons." Several she knew, in one way or another. But then Society was so small almost everyone had some degree of acquaintance.

She saw a European prince she had known rather better some thirty years ago, and as he strolled past they exchanged glances. He hesitated, a flash of memory in his eyes, a momentary laughter and warmth. But he was with the princess, and her peremptory hand on his arm prevailed. And perhaps the past was better left in its own cocoon of happiness, undisturbed by present realities. He passed on his way, leaving Vespasia smiling to herself, the sunlight gentle on her face.

It was nearly three quarters of an hour, spent agreeably enough, but not usefully, before she at last saw Bertie Canning. He was strolling alone, not unusually, since his wife did not care to leave the house except by carriage and he still preferred to walk. Or at least that was what he claimed. He said it was necessary for his health. Vespasia knew perfectly well he treasured the freedom it gave him, and he would still have done so had he needed two sticks to prop himself up.

She thought she might be obliged to approach him, and if so she would have done it with grace, but fortunately it was not necessary. When he saw her she smiled with more than the civility good manners required, and he seized the opportunity and came over to where she was sitting. He was a handsome man in a smooth, hearty way, and she had been fond of him in the past. It was no difficulty to appear pleased to see him.

"Good morning, Bertie. You look very well."

He was in fact nearly ten years younger than she, but time had been less generous to him. He was undeniably growing portly, and his face was ruddier than it had been in his prime.

"My dear Vespasia. How delightful to see you! You haven't changed in the least. How your contemporaries must loathe you! If there is anything a beautiful woman cannot abide, it is another beautiful woman who bears her years far better."

"As always, you know how to wrap a compliment a little differently," she said with a smile, at the same time moving a trifle to one side in the smallest of invitations for him to join her.

He accepted it instantly, not only for her company, but very possibly also to rest his feet. They spoke of trivia and mutual acquaintances for a few moments. She enjoyed it quite genuinely. For that little time the passage of years had no meaning. It could have been thirty years ago. The dresses were wrong—the skirts too narrow, no crinolines, no hoops; there were far too many fashionable demimondaines about, too many women altogether—but the mood was the same, the bustle, the beauty of the horses, the excitement, the May sunshine, the scent of the earth and the great trees overhead. London Society was parading and admiring itself with self-absorbed delight.

But Nobby Gunne was not twenty-five and paddling up the Congo River in a canoe; she was fifty-five, and here in London, far too vulnerable, and falling in love with a man about whom Vespasia knew very little, and feared too much.

"Bertie . . ."

"Yes, my dear?"

"You know everyone who has anything to do with Africa. . . ."

"I used to. But there are so remarkably many people now." He shrugged. "They appear out of nowhere, all kinds of people, a great many of them I would rather not know. Adventurers of the least attractive kind. Why? Have you someone in mind?"

She did not prevaricate. There was no time, and he would not expect it.

"Peter Kreisler."

A middle-aged financial magnate drove past in a four-in-hand, his wife and daughters beside him. Neither Vespasia nor Bertie Canning took any notice. An ambitious young man on a bay horse doffed his hat and received a smile of encouragement.

A young man and woman rode by together.

"Engaged at last," Bertie muttered.

Vespasia knew what he meant. The girl would not have ridden out with him were they not.

"Peter Kreisler?" she jogged his memory.

"Ah, yes. His mother was one of the Aberdeenshire Calders, I believe. Odd girl, very odd. Married a German, as I recall, and went to live there for a while. Came back eventually, I think. Then died, poor soul."

Vespasia felt a jar of sudden coldness. In other circumstances to be half German would be irrelevant. The royal family was more than half German. But with the present concern over East Africa high on her mind, and acutely relevant to the issue, it was a different matter.

"I see. What did his father do?"

A popular actor rode by, handsome profile lifted high. Vespasia thought very briefly of Charlotte's mother, Caroline, and her recent marriage to an actor seventeen years her junior. He was less handsome than this man, and a great deal more attractive. It was a scandalous thing to have done, and Vespasia heartily wished her happiness.

"No idea," Bertie confessed. "But he was a personal friend of the old chancellor, I know that."

"Bismarck?" Vespasia said with surprise and increasing unhappiness.

Bertie looked at her sideways. "Of course, Bismarck! Why are you concerned, Vespasia? You cannot know the fellow. He spends all his time in Africa. Although I suppose he could have come home. He's quarreled with Cecil Rhodes—not hard to do—and with the missionaries, who tried to put trousers on everybody and make Christians out of them . . . much more difficult."

"The trousers or the Christianity?"

"The quarrel."

"I should find it very easy to quarrel with someone who wants to put trousers on people," Vespasia replied. "Or make Christians out of them if they don't want it."

"Then you will undoubtedly like Kreisler." Bertie pulled a face.

A radical member of Parliament passed them, in deep conversation with a successful author.

"Ass," Bertie said contemptuously. "Fellow should stick to his last."

"I beg your pardon?"

"Politician who wants to write a book and a writer who wants to sit in Parliament," Bertie replied.

"Have you read his book?" Vespasia asked.

Bertie's eyebrows rose. "No. Why?"

"Terrible. And John Dacre would do less harm if he gave up his seat and wrote novels. Altogether I think it would be an excellent idea. Don't discourage them."

He stared at her with concern for a moment, then started to laugh.

"He quarreled with MacKinnon as well," he said after a moment or two.

"Dacre?" she asked.

"No, no, your fellow Kreisler. MacKinnon the money fellow. Quarreled over East Africa, of course, and what should be done there. Hasn't quarreled with Standish yet, but that's probably due to his relationship with Chancellor." Bertie frowned thoughtfully. "Not that there isn't something in what he says, dammit! Bit questionable, this chap Rhodes. Smooth tongue, but a shifty eye. Too much appetite for power, for my taste. All done in a hurry. Too fast. Too fast, altogether. Did you know Arthur Desmond, poor devil? Sound fellow. Decent. Sorry he's gone."

"And Kreisler?" She rose to her feet as she said it. It was growing a little chilly and she preferred to walk a space.

He stood and offered her his arm.

"Not sure, I'm afraid. Bit of a question mark in my mind. Not certain of his motives, if you understand?"

Vespasia understood very well.

A famous portrait artist passed by and tipped his hat to her. She smiled in acknowledgment. Someone muttered that the Prince of Wales and the Duke of Clarence were coming and there was a rustle of interest, but since they rode here fairly often, it was no more than a ripple.

An elderly man with a sallow face approached and spoke to Bertie. He was introduced, and since he obviously intended staying, Vespasia thanked Bertie Canning and excused herself. She wished to be alone with her thoughts. The little she had learned of Peter Kreisler was no comfort at all.

What were his motives in pursuing Susannah Chancellor? Why did he argue his point so persistently? He could not be so naive as to think he could influence Chancellor. He was already publicly committed to Cecil Rhodes.

Where were Kreisler's own commitments? To Africa and the self-determination he spoke of, or to German interests? Was he trying to provoke an indiscretion from which he could learn something, or to let slip his own version of facts, and mislead?

And why did he court Nobby Gunne?

———

Vespasia would have been a great deal unhappier had she been in the Lyric music hall and seen Nobby and Kreisler together in the stalls laughing at the comedian, watching the juggler with bated breath as he tossed plate after plate into the air, groaning at the extraordinary feats of the yellow-clad contortionist, tapping their feet with the dancing girls.

It was definitely slumming, and they were enjoying it enormously. Every few moments they exchanged glances as some joke delighted or appalled them. The political jokes were both vicious and ribald.

The last act, top of the bill, was an Irish soprano with a full, rich voice who held the audience in her hands, singing "Silver Threads Among the Gold," "Bedouin Love Song," Sullivan's "The Lost Chord," and then, to both smiles and tears, Tosti's "Good-bye."

The audience cheered her to the echo, and then when at last the curtain came down, rose from their seats and made their way outside into the warm, busy street where gas lamps flared, hooves clattered on the cobbles, people called out to passing cabs and the night air was balmy on the face and damp with the promise of rain.

Neither Nobby nor Kreisler spoke. Everything was already understood.

CHAPTER
SEVEN

"Nothing," Tellman said, pushing out his lip. "At least nothing that helps." He was talking about his investigation into Ian Hathaway of the Colonial Office. "Just a quiet, sober, rather bookish sort of man of middle years. Doesn't do anything much out of the ordinary." He sat down in the chair opposite Pitt without being asked. "Not so ordinary as to be without character," he went on. "He has his oddities, his tastes. He has a fancy for expensive cheeses, for example. Spends as much on a cheese as I would on a joint of beef. He hates fish. Won't eat it at any price."

Pitt frowned, sitting at his desk with the sun on his back.

"Buys plain shirts," Tellman went on. "Won't spend a farthing extra on them. Argues the toss with his shirtmaker, always very politely. But he can insist!" Tellman's face showed some surprise. "At first I thought he was a bit of a mouse, one of the quiet little men with nothing to say for themselves." His eyes widened. "But I discovered that Mr. Hathaway is a person of enough resolve when he wants to be. Always very quiet, very polite, never raises his voice to anyone. But there must be something inside him, something in his look, because the tailor didn't argue with him above a minute or two, then took a good stare at him, and all of a sudden backed down sharply, and it was all 'yes sir, Mr. Hathaway; no sir, of course not; whatever you wish, sir.' "

"He does hold a fairly senior position in the Colonial Office," Pitt pointed out.

Tellman gave a little snort, fully expressive of his derision. "I've seen more important men than him pushed around by their tailors! No sir, there's a bit more steel to our Mr. Hathaway than first looks show."

Pitt did not reply. It was more Tellman's impression than any evidence. It depended how ineffectual Tellman had originally thought him.

"Buys very nice socks and nightshirts," Tellman went on. "Very nice indeed. And more than one silk cravat."

"Extravagant?" Pitt asked.

Tellman shook his head regretfully. "Not the way you mean. Certainly doesn't live beyond his income; beneath it if anything. Takes his pleasures quietly, just the occasional dinner at his club or with friends. A stroll on the green of an evening."

"Any lady friends?"

Tellman's expression conveyed the answer without the need for words.

"What about his sons? Has he any other family, brothers or sisters?"

"Sons are just as respectable as he is, from all I can tell. Anyway, they both live abroad, but nobody says a word against them. No other family as far as I know. Certainly he doesn't call on them or write."

Pitt leaned backwards farther into the sun. "These friends with whom he dines once a week or so, who are they? Have they any connection with Africa or Germany? Or with finance?"

"Not that I can find." Tellman looked both triumphant and disgusted. It gave him some satisfaction to present Pitt with a further problem, and yet he resented his own failure. His dilemma amused Pitt.

"And your own opinion of him?" Pitt asked with the shadow of a smile.

Tellman looked surprised. It was a question he apparently had not foreseen. He was obliged to think hastily.

"I'd like to say he's a deep one with a lot hidden under the surface." His face was sour. "But I think he's just a very ordinary, bald little man with an ordinary, open and very tedious life; just like ten thousand others in London. I couldn't find any reason to think he's a spy, or anything else but what he looks."

Pitt respected Tellman's opinion. He was bigoted, full of resentments both personal and rooted in his general social status, but his judgment of crime, and a man's potential for it, was acute, and seldom mistaken.

"Thank you," he said with a sincerity that caught Tellman off guard. "I expect you are right."

Nevertheless he contrived an occasion to go to the Colonial Office and meet Hathaway for himself, simply to form an impression because he did not have one. Not to have spoken with him again would have been an omission, and with as little certainty in the case as he had, he could not afford omissions, however slight.

Hathaway's office was smaller than Chancellor's or Jeremiah Thorne's, but nevertheless it had dignity and considerable comfort. At a glance it looked as if nothing in it were new; everything had a gentle patina of age and quality. The wood shone from generations of polishing, the leather gleamed, the carpet was gently worn in a track from door to desk. The books on the single shelf were morocco bound and gold lettered.

Hathaway sat behind the desk looking benign and courteous. He was almost completely bald, with merely a fringe of short, white hair above his ears, and he was clean-shaven. His nose was pronounced and his eyes a clear, round blue. Only when one had looked at him more closely did their clarity and intelligence become apparent.

"Good morning, Superintendent," he said quietly. His voice was excellent and his diction perfect. "How may I be of assistance to you? Please, do sit down."

"Good morning, Mr. Hathaway." Pitt accepted the offer and sat in the chair opposite the desk. It was remarkably comfortable; it seemed to envelop him as soon as he relaxed into it, and yet it was firm in all the right places. But for all the apparent ease, Hathaway was a government servant of considerable seniority. He would have no time to waste. "It is regarding this miserable business of information going astray," Pitt continued. There was no point in being evasive. Hathaway was far too clever not to have understood the import of the investigations.

There was no change whatever in Hathaway's face.

"I have given it some thought, Superintendent, but unfortunately to no avail." The shadow of a smile touched his mouth. "It is not the sort of news one can ever forget. You made fairly light of it when you spoke to me before, but I am aware that it is anything but a light matter. I do not know precisely what the material is, nor to whom it has been passed, but the principle is the same. Next time it could be something vital to British interests or well-being. And of course we do not always know who our enemies are. We may believe them friends today . . . and yet tomorrow . . ."

It was a chilling thought. The bright, comfortable room only seemed to add to the reality of it. Pitt did not know whether Hathaway was speaking in the narrow sense of Britain's enemies, or in the more general breadth of enemies in general. Arthur Desmond's face came sharply to his mind. How many of his enemies had he guessed at? How surprised would he have been had he heard the evidence at his own inquest? What faces there would have startled him, what testimony?

It was the worst of a secret society, the everyday masks behind which were hidden such different faces. There were executioners in the Inner Circle, although *murderers* would be a more honest word. They were men set apart to exact the punishment the society had deemed in its best interests. Sometimes it was merely personal or financial ruin, but on rare occasions, like that of Arthur Desmond, it was death.

But who were the executioners? Even the members of his own ring almost certainly did not know. That would be necessary, both for the executioner's protection and for the efficiency of his work. He could face the victim with a smile and a handshake, and at the same time deal him a death blow. And the rest of the Inner Circle would be sworn on covenant of blood to assist him, protect him, keep silence as commanded.

Hathaway was staring at him, waiting patiently. Pitt forced his mind back to the African information.

"Of course, you are quite right," he said hastily. "It is one of the bitterest of realities. We have traced a great deal from its arrival in the Colonial Office until it is stored permanently. I believe I know everyone who has access to it. . . ."

Hathaway smiled sourly. "But of course it is more than one person. I presume I am suspect?"

"You are one of those who is privy to the information," Pitt conceded guardedly. "I have no more cause to consider you than that. I believe you have a son in Central Africa?"

"Yes, my son Robert is in the mission field." There was very little expression in Hathaway's face. It was impossible to tell if he were proud of his son's vocation or not. The light in his eyes might have been pleasure, or love, or indulgence, or merely a reflection of the sunlight streaming through the window to his left. There was nothing in his gentle voice but good manners, and the slight anxiety the subject of Pitt's call required.

"Where?" Pitt asked.

This time a flicker crossed Hathaway's face. "The shores of Lake Nyasa."

Pitt had been studying the atlas. The coast of Africa was fairly well charted, with some few exceptions, but there were vast areas inland which were crossed by only a few tracks. Features were put in tentatively: tracks from east to west, the trails of the great explorers, a lake here, a range of mountains there. But most of it was borderless, regions no cartographer had seen or measured, perhaps no white man had trodden. He knew Lake Nyasa was close to the area which Cecil Rhodes would claim, and where Zimbabwe, the city of black gold, was fabled to be.

Hathaway was watching him closely, his round, pale eyes seeing everything.

"That is the area with which you are concerned." He made it a statement rather than a question. He did not move, nor did his face change appreciably, but there was a sudden deepening of his concentration. "Superintendent, let us stop playing games of words with each other. Unless you correct me, I shall assume that it is the German interest in Mashonaland and Matabeleland which concerns you. I am aware we are negotiating a new treaty on the zones of influence, that Heligoland is involved, that the fall of Chancellor Bismarck has affected matters substantially, and that Carl Peterson and the German presence in Zanzibar, the rebellion there and its swift and bloody repression, are features of great importance. So also must be Mr. Rhodes's expedition from the Cape, and his negotiations with Mr. Kruger and the Boers. We should be considerably disadvantaged in our position if all we know were also to be known to the Kaiser."

Pitt said nothing. There was no sound from beyond the windows, which overlooked not the street or the park but a more enclosed courtyard.

Hathaway smiled a little and settled farther back in his seat. "This is not merely a matter of someone seeking a dishonest personal advantage in gold or diamond investments," he said gravely. "This is treason. All private considerations must be forgotten in an effort to find the man who would do this." His voice was no louder, no higher, yet there was a subtle change in its timbre, a passionate sincerity. He had not moved, but his physical presence was charged with energy.

It would have been pointless to deny the truth. Pitt would not have been believed; he would simply have insulted the man opposite him and driven a wedge of evasion between them.

"One of the problems with treason," Pitt replied slowly, choosing his words with care, "is that once we know it is there, it makes us distrust everyone. Sometimes the suspicion will do almost as much damage as the act itself. Our fears may cripple us as effectively as the truth."

Hathaway's eyes widened. "How perceptive of you, Superintendent. Indeed, that is so. But are you saying that you consider it possible there is no treason, simply a clever semblance of it, in order that we should so maim ourselves?" There was surprise in his voice, but also a slow realization that it could be the truth. "Then who has planted it?"

Footsteps passed by in the corridor, hesitated, then continued.

Pitt shook his head fractionally. "I meant only that we must not make it worse than it is, not do his work for him by causing suspicion where there are no grounds. Those with access to the information are few."

"But they are highly placed," Hathaway deduced immediately. "Thorne, myself, or Chancellor! Dear heaven, if it is Chancellor, we are in a desperate pass." There was humor in his face. "And I know it was not I."

"There are other possibilities," Pitt said quickly. "But few. Aylmer, for example. Or Arundell. Or Leicester."

"Aylmer. Ah yes, I had forgotten him. A young man, relatively speaking, and ambitious. He has not yet fulfilled all his family expects of him. That can be a powerful spur to a man." His eyes did not move from Pitt's face. "I am increasingly grateful as I grow older that my mother was a mild creature whose only dream for her sons was that they marry agreeable women, and I was fortunate to oblige her in that while still in my twenties." He smiled for a moment with recollection, but his unusual eyes met Pitt's again with total directness. "I don't doubt that you are here to speak to me in an effort to make some assessment of my character, but beyond that elementary exercise, is there some practical way in which I can assist you?"

Pitt had already made up his mind.

"Yes, Mr. Hathaway, if you would. I have ascertained that much of this information comes first to you, even before it reaches Mr. Chancellor."

"It does. I think I perceive what you have in mind: to change it in some way that will not cause great damage, and disseminate different versions of it to Chancellor, Aylmer, Thorne, Arundell and Leicester, and yet keep the original for Lord Salisbury, to prevent the possibility of a serious error." He pushed out his lip. "It will need some thought, I shall have to find just the right piece of information, but I can see it has to be done." He looked eager as he said it, almost relieved to have some part to play.

Pitt could not help smiling. "If it would be possible? And the sooner it is done, the sooner we may achieve a result."

"Indeed! Yes, it must be done with care, or it will be obvious." He sat forward in his chair again. "It must tally with all the information we already possess, or at least it must not contradict it. I shall keep you informed, Superintendent." He smiled with frankness and a kind of intense, energetic happiness brimming inside him.

Pitt thanked him again and rose to take his leave, still uncertain if he had been wise, but knowing of nothing better to precipitate matters. He had not yet told Matthew or Assistant Commissioner Farnsworth of his intention.

"You did what?" Farnsworth said, his face aghast. "Good God, man, do you realize what could happen as a result of this ... this ..."

"No," Pitt said brazenly. "What could happen?"

Farnsworth stared at him. "Well the very least of it is that misinformation could be passed to ministers of Her Majesty's government! In fact it most certainly will be!"

"Only to Chancellor . . ."

"Only? Only Chancellor!" Farnworth's face was deep pink. "Do you realize he is the senior minister responsible for colonial affairs? The British Empire covers a quarter of the face of the earth! Have you no sense of what that means? If Chancellor is misinformed, heaven knows what damage could follow."

"None at all," Pitt replied. "The information being changed is trivial. Hathaway knows the truth, and so will the Foreign Secretary. No decisions will be implemented without reference to one or the other of them, probably to both."

"Possibly," Farnsworth said reluctantly. "All the same, it was damned high-handed of you, Pitt. You should have consulted me before you did this. I doubt the Prime Minister will approve of it at all."

"If we don't provoke something of the sort," Pitt replied, "we are unlikely to find out who is passing information before the treaty has to be concluded."

"Not very satisfactory." Farnsworth bit his lip. "I had hoped you would have learned something definite by ordinary investigation." They were in Farnsworth's office. He had sent for Pitt to report on his progress so far. The weather had changed and sharp spring rain was beating against the windows. Pitt's trouser bottoms were damp from the splashing of passing carriages and cabs. He sat with his legs crossed, deliberately relaxed.

Farnsworth leaned over his desk, his brows drawn down. "You know, Pitt, you've made one or two foolish mistakes, but it is not too late to amend them."

"Too late?" For a moment Pitt did not understand him.

"You have had to do this alone, against a largely hostile and suspicious background," Farnsworth went on, watching Pitt's face earnestly. "You have gone in as an intruder, a policeman among diplomats and politicians, civil servants."

Pitt stared at him, not sure if he were leaping to absurd conclusions, a familiar darkness now at the edge of his mind.

"There are those who would have helped you!" Farnsworth's voice dropped, a more urgent note in it, deeper, wavering between harshness and hope. "Men who know more than you or I could expect to learn in a year of investigation with questions and deductions. I offered it to you before, Pitt. I'm offering it again."

The Inner Circle. Farnsworth was pressing him to join the Inner Circle, as he had almost as soon as Pitt had succeeded Micah Drummond. Pitt had refused then, and hoped the offer would not be repeated or referred to. Perhaps he should have known that was a willful blindness, a foolishness in which he should not have indulged. It was always there to be faced now or later.

"No," Pitt said quietly. "My reasons are still the same. The help would be at too high a price."

Farnsworth's face hardened. "You are very unwise, Pitt. Nothing would be asked of you that a decent, patriotic man would not willingly give. You are denying yourself success, and promotion when the time comes." He leaned forward a fraction farther. "With the right help, you know, there is no limit to where you could go. All manner of doors would eventually be opened to you! You would be able to succeed on merit. And you have merit! Otherwise the rules of Society will make it impossible for you. You must be aware of that! How can you not see the good in such a thing?" It was a demand for an answer, and his blue-gray eyes met Pitt's unflinchingly.

Pitt was aware not only of the strength of will behind the calm, almost bland countenance, but suddenly of an intelligence he had not previously suspected. He realized that until that moment he had had a certain contempt for Farnsworth, an unconscious assumption that he held office because of birth, not ability. Farnsworth's lack of understanding of certain issues, certain characteristics or terms of phrase, he had taken for slowness of mind. It came to him with a jolt that it was far more probably a narrowness of experience.

He was one of the vast numbers of people who cannot imagine themselves into the class or gender, least of all the emotions, of a different person. That is lack of vision or sensitivity, even compassion, but it is not stupidity.

"You are favoring one closed group which favors its own, over another doing just the same," he replied with a candor he had not shown Farnsworth before, and even as he said it he was aware he was treading on the edge of danger.

Farnsworth's impatience was weary and only peripherally annoyed. Perhaps he had expected little more. "I'm all for idealism, Pitt, but only to a point. When it becomes divorced from reality it ceases to be any use and becomes an encumbrance." He shook his head. "This is how the world works. If you don't know that, I confess I don't understand how you have succeeded as far as you have. You deal with crime every day of your life. You see the worst in humanity, the weakest and the ugliest. How is it you are so blind to higher motives, men who cooperate together to bring about a greater good, from which in the end we shall all benefit?"

Pitt would like to have said that he did not believe the motives of the leaders of the Inner Circle were anything of the sort. Originally, perhaps, they had had a vision of good, but it was now so interwoven with their own power to bring it about, and their own glory in its achievement, that too much of it was lost on the way. But he knew that saying as much would not sway Farnsworth, who had too much invested in believing as he did. It would only produce denial and conflict.

And yet for an instant there was understanding on the edge of his mind, a moment when some sympathy between them was possible. He should grasp it. There was a moral and a human imperative to try.

"It is not a question of the justice or honor of those goals," he replied slowly. "Either for themselves or for others. And I don't doubt that many people would benefit from much of what they bring about. . . ."

Farnsworth's face lit with eagerness. He almost interrupted, then disciplined himself to wait for Pitt to finish.

"It is that they decide what is good, without telling the rest of us," Pitt continued, choosing his words with great care. "And they bring it about by secret means. If it is good, we benefit, but if it is not, if it is not what we wanted, by the time we know, it is too late." He leaned forward unconsciously. "There is no stopping it, no redress, because we don't know who to blame or to whom we can appeal. It denies the majority of us, all of us outside the Circle, the right or the chance to choose for ourselves."

Farnsworth looked puzzled, a crease between his brows.

"But you can be in the Circle, man. That is what I'm offering you."

"And everyone else?" Pitt said. "What about their choices?"

Farnsworth's eyes widened. "Are you really suggesting that everyone else, the majority"—he raised his hand to indicate the mass of population beyond the office walls—"are able to understand the issues, let alone make a decision as to what is right, wise, profitable . . . or even possible?" He saw Pitt's face. "No, of course you aren't. What you're suggesting is anarchy. Every man for himself. And God knows, perhaps every woman and every child too?"

Until now Pitt had acted on a passionate instinct, not needing to rationalize what he thought; no one had required it of him.

"There is a difference between the open power of government and the secret power of a society whose members no one knows," he said with commitment. He saw the derision in Farnsworth's face. "Of course there can be oppression, corruption, incompetence, but if we know who holds the power, then they are to some degree accountable. We can at least fight against what we can see."

"Rebellion," Farnsworth said succinctly. "Or if we fight against it secretly, then treason! Is that really what you prefer?"

"I don't want the overthrow of a government." Pitt would not be goaded into taking a more extreme position than he meant. "But I have no objection to its downfall, if that is what it merits."

Farnsworth's eyebrows rose.

"In whose judgment? Yours?"

"The majority of the people who are governed."

"And you think the majority is right?" Farnsworth's eyes were wide. "That it is informed, wise, benevolent and self-disciplined or, God damn it, even literate—"

"No, I don't," Pitt interrupted. "But it can't ever be if it is governed in secret by those who never ask and never explain. I think the majority have always been decent people, and have the right, as much right as you or anyone else, to know their own destiny and have as much control over it as is possible."

"Consistent with order"—Farnsworth sat back, his smile sardonic—"and the rights and privileges of others. Quite. We have no difference in aim, Pitt, only in how to achieve it. And you are hopelessly naive. You are an idealist, quite out of touch with the reality both of human nature and of economics and business. You would make a good politician on the hustings, telling the people all the things they want to hear, but you'd be hopeless in office." He crossed his hands, interlacing his fingers, and gazing at Pitt with something close to resignation. "Perhaps you are right not to accept the offer of membership in the Inner Circle. You haven't the stomach for it, or the vision. You'll always be a gamekeeper's son at heart."

Pitt was not certain whether that was intended as an insult or not; the words were, judging from Farnsworth's voice, and yet the tone was disappointed rather than deliberately offensive.

He stood up. "I expect you're right," he conceded, surprised that he minded so little. "But gamekeepers protect and preserve what is good." He smiled. "Is that not what you have been talking about?"

Farnsworth looked startled. He opened his mouth to dismiss the idea, then realized its truth and changed his mind.

"Good day, sir," Pitt said from the doorway.

There was only one thing Pitt could profitably do regarding the Colonial Office. The routine investigation of associates, personal habits, the search for weakness, could be accomplished as well by Tellman and his men as by Pitt himself. Not that he expected any of it to yield much of value. But quite apart from that, Arthur Desmond's death still filled his thoughts in every quiet moment and the underlying sadness was with him all the time. It grew gradually more compelling that he should resolve what he could, for Matthew's sake and for his own.

Charlotte had said little to him on the subject, but her unusual silence was more eloquent than speech. She had been gentle with him, more patient than was characteristic, as if she were sensitive not only to his loss but to his awareness of guilt. He was grateful for it. He would have found her criticism painful, because it would have been fair, and when one is most vulnerable, one is also the least able to bear the wound.

But he also longed to return to the frankness that was more natural to both of them.

He began with General Anstruther, and was obliged to pursue him from one of his clubs to a second, and ultimately find him in a quiet reading room of a third. Or it would be more accurate to say he was informed by the steward that General Anstruther was there. Pitt, not being a member, was not permitted into that very private and privileged sanctuary.

"Would you please ask General Anstruther if he can spare me a few moments of his time?" Pitt said politely, hating having to beg. He had no authority in this case, and could not use his office to insist. It galled him far more than he should have allowed it to.

"I will ask him, sir," the steward replied expressionlessly. "Who may I say is asking?"

"Superintendent Pitt, of Bow Street." Pitt handed him his card.

"Very well, sir. I shall enquire." And leaving Pitt standing in the large and extremely opulent hall, he retreated upstairs, carrying the card on a silver tray.

Pitt gazed around the walls at the marble busts of long dead soldiers and saw Marlborough, Wellington, Moore, Wolfe, Hastings, Clive, Gordon, and two he did not recognize. It crossed his mind with amusement, but no surprise, that Cromwell was not there. Above the doors were the arms of Richard Coeur de Lion, and Henry V. On the farther wall was a somber and very fine painting of the burial of Moore after Corunna, and opposite, another of the charge of the Scots Greys at Waterloo. More recent battle honors hung from the high ceiling, from Inkermann, the Alma and Balaclava.

General Anstruther came down the stairs, white whiskers bristling, his face pink, his back stiff as a ramrod.

"Good day to you, sir. What can I do for you?" He made it almost a demand. "Must be damned urgent to seek a fellow out at his club, what?"

"It is not urgent, General Anstruther, but I think it is important," Pitt replied respectfully. "And I can get the information accurately from no one else, or I should not have troubled you."

"Indeed! Indeed. And what is it, Mr. . . . Superintendent? Unless it is very brief, we can hardly stand around here like a couple of butlers, what. Come into the guests' room." He waved a heavy, florid hand towards one of the many oak doors off the hallway, and Pitt followed him obediently.

The room was filled with extremely comfortable armchairs, but the pictures and general decor were forbidding, perhaps to remind visitors of the military grandeur of the club's members and the utter inferiority of civilians permitted in on sufferance.

General Anstruther indicated one of the chairs, and as Pitt sat down, took the one opposite him and leaned back, crossing his legs.

"Well then, Superintendent, what is it that troubles you?"

Pitt had thought carefully what he should say.

"The matter of the death of the late Sir Arthur Desmond," he replied candidly. He saw Anstruther's face tighten, but continued speaking. "There have been certain questions asked, and I wish to be in possession of all the facts so that I can refute any unpleasant or unwarranted suggestions that may be made."

"By whom, sir? Suggestions of what?" Anstruther demanded. "Explain yourself, sir. This is most unfortunate."

"Indeed it is," Pitt agreed. "The suggestions are concerning his sanity, and the possibility of either suicide or—just as bad—murder."

"Good God!" Anstruther was genuinely shocked; there was nothing assumed in the horror in his face, the slackness of initial disbelief, and then the growing darkness in his eyes as all the implications came to him. "That's scandalous! Who has dared to say such a thing? I demand to know, sir!"

"At the moment it is no more than suggestion, General Anstruther," Pitt replied, somewhat mendaciously. "I wish to be in a position to refute it decisively if it should ever become more."

"That's preposterous! Why should anyone murder Desmond? Never knew a more decent chap in my life."

"I don't doubt that is true, until the last few months," Pitt said with more confidence than he felt. He had a growing fear in his mind that Anstruther's outrage might be so deep as to prompt him to complain in a manner which would reach Farnsworth's ears, and then Pitt would be in serious trouble. Perhaps he had overstated his case and brought about more harm than good?

It was too late to go back.

"Well . . ." Anstruther said guardedly. "Ah—yes." He was obviously remembering what he had said at the inquest. "That is true—up to a point."

"That is what I am worried about." Pitt felt he had regained a little ground. "Just how erratic was his behavior, sir? You were naturally very discreet at the inquest, as becomes a friend speaking in a public place. But this is private, and for quite a different purpose."

"Well ... I hardly know what to say, sir." Anstruther looked confounded.

"You said earlier that Sir Arthur was forgetful and confused," Pitt prompted him. "Can you give me instances?"

"I ... er. One doesn't choose to remember such things, man! For heaven's sake, one overlooks the failings of one's friends. One does not commit them to memory!"

"You don't remember any instance?" Pitt felt a stirring of hope, too thin to rely on, too bright to ignore.

"Well ... er ... it is more of an impression than a catalog of events, don't you know, what?" Anstruther was now thoroughly unhappy.

Pitt had the sudden sharp impression that he was lying. He did not actually know anything at all. He had been repeating what he had been told by fellow members of the Inner Circle.

"When did you last see Sir Arthur?" he asked quite gently. Anstruther was embarrassed. There was no point in making an enemy of him; then he would learn nothing.

"Ah ..." Anstruther was pink-faced now. "Not certain. Events put it rather out of my mind. I do recall quite plainly dining with him about three weeks before he died, poor fellow." His voice gained in confidence. He was on firm ground now. "Seemed to me to have changed a lot. Rambling on about Africa."

"Rambling?" Pitt interrupted. "You mean he was incoherent, disconnected in his ideas?"

"Ah—that's a little steep, sir. Not at all. I mean simply that he kept returning to the subject, even when the rest of us had clearly passed on to something else."

"He was a bore?"

Anstruther's eyes widened. "If you like, sir, yes. He didn't know when to leave the matter alone. Made a lot of accusations that were most unfortunate. Quite unfounded, of course."

"Were they?"

"Good heavens, of course they were." Anstruther was appalled. "Talked about secret plots to conquer Africa, and God knows what else. Quite mad—delusory."

"You are profoundly familiar with Africa, sir?" Pitt did his best to keep every shred of sarcasm out of his voice and thought he succeeded.

"What?" Anstruther was startled. "Africa? What makes you say that, Superintendent?"

"That you know that there are no conspiracies regarding the financial backing of settlement there. There is a great deal of money involved, and presumably fortunes to be made by those who obtain mineral rights."

"Ah ... well ..." Anstruther had been about to dismiss the idea in anger, then just in time realized that he had no grounds for it at all, however repugnant the idea was to him. Pitt watched the changing emotions in his face, and knew that his reactions to Sir Arthur's charges were from the heart rather than the head, a plain man's disbelief and horror of intrigue, complexities he did not understand and corruption he despised.

"I hope it is not true," Pitt said gently. "But the belief in it does not seem so farfetched to me that one might consider it madness. Boundless wealth usually draws adventurers and thieves as well as honest men. And the prospect of such power has corrupted people before. Sir Arthur, as a politician, would be familiar with some of the scandals of the past, and not unnaturally fear for the future."

Anstruther drew in his breath. His face was even pinker and he was obviously struggling between loyalties. Pitt did not know whether one of them was to the Inner Circle, but he believed it was. In all probability he saw it as Farnsworth had described it to Pitt: an organization of intelligent, enlightened men banded together to bring about the best good of the country, including the majority of blind and foolish men and women who could not decide for themselves, having neither the knowledge nor the wisdom.

Honor and duty required that those who had these qualities should protect them for their own good. Anstruther would have given oaths of loyalty, and he was a man born and bred to unquestioning loyalties. A lifetime in the army had ingrained in his being obedience without question. Desertion was a capital offense, the last and most terrible sin of which a man was capable.

And yet now he was faced with truth he could not deny, and both his innate sense of honor and his general decency were at war with his sworn allegiances and his lifetime habit.

Pitt waited for him to find his resolution.

Outside in the street a hansom drew up and a short man in military uniform stepped out, paid the driver, and came up the stairs to the club. A four-in-hand drove by at a brisk trot.

"What you say, sir, is probably true," Anstruther conceded with great difficulty, the words forced out of him. "Perhaps it was not so much that poor Desmond was convinced of conspiracy that was ridiculous, as it was the men whom he charged. That, sir, was undoubtedly beyond the bounds of reason. Decent men, fine and honorable men I have known all my life." His face was suffused with color, and his voice rang with the absolute conviction that he was right. "Men who have served their fellows, their country, their queen, without recognition or gain, sir."

Only secret and unquestioned power, Pitt thought to himself, perhaps the headiest reward of all. But he did not say so.

"I can imagine that that was extremely offensive to you, General," he said instead.

"Extremely, sir," Anstruther agreed vehemently. "Most distressing. Liked Desmond for years. Most agreeable chap. Decent, what. Tragedy he should come to such an end. Damned tragedy." He was at last satisfied with his own resolution to the dilemma, and he faced Pitt squarely, allowing his emotion to fire his words. That at least was unquestioned and presented no problems at all. "Very sorry," he went on. "Sorry for the family, dammit. I hope you manage to keep this thing quiet, sir. Use your discretion. Nobody needs to know. Let it be buried. Best thing. Best thing altogether, for everyone. Nobody believed the nonsense he spoke in the end. No harm done, what!"

Pitt rose. "Thank you for your time, General Anstruther. You have been most frank, and I appreciate it, sir."

"Least I can do. Painful matter." Anstruther rose also and accompanied Pitt to the door and into the hallway. "Best set to rest. Good day to you, Superintendent."

"Good day, General Anstruther."

Outside in the street in the broad May sunshine Pitt had a strange feeling of light-headedness. He barely noticed the carriages and horses passing by, or the fashionable woman who brushed his elbow as he strode along the footpath. He was just off Piccadilly, and there was a faint sound of music coming from Green Park.

He walked rapidly without realizing it, a spring in his step. Anstruther had said what he had most hoped. Sir Arthur was not irrational; simply startling, disturbing and profoundly unwelcome. Anstruther was a decent man caught in a situation he could not handle. He was not used to complex loyalties which vied with each other. He was incapable of rethinking his values, his friendships and his trust without a wrench to his mind he would do everything in his power to avoid.

There was no proof in what he had learned, except in his own mind, and perhaps his emotions would be more at rest. Sir Arthur was vindicated . . . at least so far.

Next he found the Honorable William Osborne. He was an entirely different manner of man. It was late afternoon before he would receive Pitt, and then it was at his own house in Chelsea. It was opulent, close to the banks of the Thames and in a lushly shaded garden along a quiet tree-lined street. He greeted Pitt with impatience. Obviously he had an engagement for the evening and resented the interruption.

"I have no idea what I can do for you, Mr. Pitt." He was standing in his oak-paneled library, into which Pitt had been shown, and he did not sit down himself nor offer a seat. There was no mistaking that he did not intend the interview to be long enough to require one. "I said all I know about this unfortunate affair at the inquest, which is a matter of public record. I know nothing else, nor would I be inclined to discuss it if I did."

"You testified that Sir Arthur had recently expressed some irrational opinions," Pitt said with an effort to keep his temper.

"As I have just said, Mr. Pitt, that is a matter of public record." He was standing in the middle of the blue Turkish carpet, rocking very slightly on the balls of his feet. He reminded Pitt vaguely of a more ill-tempered Eustace March.

"Can you tell me what these opinions were, sir?" Pitt asked, looking directly at him but keeping his voice light and his tone courteous.

"I don't wish to repeat them," Osborne replied. "They were ludicrous, and to no one's credit."

"It is important that I know," Pitt insisted.

"Why?" Osborne's rather thin eyebrows rose. "The man is dead. How could it matter now what nonsense he said in his last few months?"

"Since he is dead," Pitt said quietly and very firmly, "he cannot now withdraw them." He made a rash decision. He smiled very slightly. "There are men of goodwill, honorable men who prefer to remain anonymous, whose names he has slandered, by implication if not directly. I know that you understand what I am saying, sir. Mr. Farnsworth . . ."—he pronounced the name carefully—"is concerned that no taint should linger. . . ." He let the suggestion speak for itself.

Osborne stared at him, his dark gray eyes hard and level.

"Then why the devil didn't you say so, sir? There's no need to be so coy."

Pitt felt his stomach lurch. Osborne had understood him and

believed the lie. He thought he was speaking to a fellow member of the Inner Circle.

"I am used to being careful," Pitt replied with a modicum of truth. "It is a habit hard to forget."

"Has its uses," Osborne conceded. "Very bad business. Of course the wretched fellow was making all sorts of rash accusations. Had hold of the wrong end of the stick altogether." His face was tight, his lips a thin line. "No vision. No vision at all. Decent enough chap, but bourgeois at heart. Totally impractical. A well-intentioned fool can do more real harm than a wagonload of villains who know what they are about!" He looked at Pitt dourly. There was still a suspicion in him. In his judgment Pitt was not Inner Circle material. He was neither a gentleman nor a loyal servant.

On both points he had made, he was correct. Pitt had no desire to argue the first. The second was another matter.

"I agree with you, sir," he said honestly. "A well-intentioned fool can be extremely dangerous, if given power, and frequently brings about the downfall of many others, although it may be the last of his intentions."

Osborne looked surprised. Apparently he had not expected Pitt to agree with him. He grunted. "Then you will take my point, sir." He stopped abruptly. "Precisely what is it you wish to know, and who is in danger of being slandered by all this wretched nonsense?"

"I should prefer not to give names," Pitt answered. "And in truth, I do not know them all. In the interest of discretion, much of it was kept from me."

"Rightly so." Osborne nodded. After all, Pitt might be a member, but he was merely a person of use. "The charges Sir Arthur made were that certain gentlemen, our friends, were secretly organized together to fund a settlement expedition in Central Africa," he explained, "which would at once exploit both the native African tribal leaders and the British government's financial and moral backing in the venture. The suggestion was that when the settlement proved successful, and vast wealth was found, both real and potential, then they would profit unfairly, in terms of money and of political power in the new country to be established, nominally under British suzerainty, but in fact a law unto itself. And then they would prevent others from sharing in this fortune by excluding them, by means of these secret dealings and agreements." Osborne's face was bleak and angry, and he stared at Pitt, waiting for his response.

"That was a very foolish thing to have said," Pitt replied with honesty, even though he believed it was almost certainly true. "He had undoubtedly lost a grip upon reality."

"Absolutely," Osborne agreed fervently. "Totally absurd! And irresponsible, dammit. He might have been believed."

"I doubt it," Pitt said with a sudden rush of bitterness. "It is a truly appalling thought, and very few people believe what they do not wish to, particularly if it is nothing they have feared before, even in nightmare, and there is no evidence of it to prove it true."

Osborne looked at him narrowly, as if he suspected sarcasm, but Pitt's eyes were guileless. He felt no compunction at all in being as devious as he could, or in quite plainly lying.

Osborne cleared his throat.

"That is all I have to tell you, Pitt. I know of nothing else. Africa is not my field of expertise."

"That has been most helpful, thank you, sir," Pitt conceded. "I think it possible I may be able to establish the truth with a little more assistance from others. Thank you for your time, sir. Good day."

"Good day to you." Osborne drew breath as if to add something further, then changed his mind.

By the time Pitt had found Calvert, the third man who had given evidence at the inquest, it was late, and in spite of being mid-May, nearly dark. He heard a similar story from him, full of hearsay, confusion, accusations repeated with outrage, ignorance of Africa except that somehow it should be British by right, moral if not political.

Pitt was so weary his feet were sore and he found he had unconsciously clenched his shoulders and his jaw till his throat ached. It was all nebulous, a matter of impressions, assumptions springing from anger, and a sense of having been betrayed by someone they should have been able to trust. For all the words of pity, the blame was there all the time. Arthur Desmond had made public suggestions, true or false, that they were corrupt. Men who should have given them respect would now not do so. People who should not even have guessed at the existence of the Inner Circle would wonder and speculate about it. That had been the greatest sin in the man's view, the spreading before the general gaze of that which should have been private. No matter what the sin or the crime, one did not wash one's linen in public. It was not the act of a gentleman. If you could not rely upon a gentleman to behave like one, what was there left of worth?

Pitt did not know if the man was a member of the Inner Circle or not. What he had said could simply have been a class loyalty. So could what Osborne had said, for that matter, but he was almost certain of Osborne.

Who else? Hathaway, Chancellor, Thorne, Aylmer? Of Farnsworth there was no doubt, and he loathed Farnsworth. But he had loved Arthur Desmond all his life, and he had been a member. So had Micah Drummond, whom he had grown to like immensely and to trust without question. He should talk to him. He was probably the only person who could help. Even as he lengthened his stride along the footpath, his decision was made. He would go now!

Membership had now been offered to Pitt. It was not exclusive to gentlemen. Anyone might be a member, might even be the executioner. It could have been the steward of the club, or the manager. Or the doctor who was called.

He was walking briskly and the night was balmy. He should have been warm, but he was not. He was chilled inside, and his legs were so tired every step required an effort of will, but he was determined to see Drummond, and the sense of purpose lent him strength.

A hansom came around the corner too quickly and he was obliged to move sharply out of its way, knocking into a stout man who had not been looking where he was going.

"Have a care, sir!" he said furiously, facing Pitt with bulging eyes. He held a heavy carved walking stick in one hand, and he gripped it tightly as if he would have raised it to defend himself if necessary.

"Look where you are going, and I won't need to!" Pitt said.

"Why you ruffian!" The man lifted the end of the stick a foot off the ground in a threatening gesture. "How dare you speak to me like that. I'll call the police, sir! And I'll warn you, I know how to use this, if you force me."

"I am the police! And if you touch me with that thing, I'll arrest you and charge you with assault. As it is, keep a civil tongue in your head or I'll charge you with being a public nuisance."

The man was too startled to retaliate, but he kept his hand hard on his stick.

Had Pitt gone too far with Osborne? Perhaps Osborne was high enough in the Inner Circle to know perfectly well who were members and who were not. Pitt had damaged the Inner Circle before. It was naive to imagine they would not know him. They had killed Arthur Desmond—why not Pitt? An attack in the street, a quick push under the wheels of a vehicle. A most regrettable street accident. It had already happened once, with Matthew—hadn't it?

He turned on his heel and strode away, leaving the man gibbering with outrage.

This was absurd. He must control his imagination. He was seeing enemies everywhere, and there were above three million people in London. There were probably no more than three thousand of them members of the Inner Circle. But he could never know which three thousand.

Around the corner he took a cab, giving Micah Drummond's address, and sat back, trying to compose himself and master his flying thoughts. He would ask him if he had any idea how large the Circle was. He was frightened of the answer, yet it could be helpful to know. On thinking of it now, he was foolish not to have gone to him for help as soon as he knew of Sir Arthur's death. Drummond had been naive to begin with, and perhaps he still only half understood the evil even now, but he had been a member for many years. He might recall incidents, rituals, and see them in a different light with the wisdom of hindsight.

Even if he had no new insights, no concrete suggestions, Pitt would feel less alone simply to talk to him.

The cab pulled up and he alighted and paid the driver with something close to a sense of elation.

Then he saw that there were no lights in the house, at least not at the front. Drummond and Eleanor might be out for the evening, but the servants would have left on the outside lamps if that were so. They could not have retired this early. The only answer was that they must be away. Disappointment overwhelmed him, engulfing him like a cold tide.

"Was they expectin' you, sir?" the cabby said from behind him. He must have seen the darkness and reached his own conclusion. Possibly it was compassion which kept him, equally possibly the hope of another immediate fare. "Shall I take you somewhere else, then?"

Pitt gave him his home address, then climbed in and shut the door.

"Thomas, you look terrible," Charlotte said as soon as she saw him. She had heard his key in the lock and came into the hall to meet him. She was dressed in deep pink, and looked warm, almost glowing, and when he took her in his arms there was an air of may blossom about her. He could hear one of the children upstairs calling out to Gracie, and a moment later Jemima appeared on the landing in her nightgown.

"Papa!"

"What are you doing out of bed?" he called up.

"I want a drink of water," she answered with assurance.

"No you don't." Charlotte disengaged herself and turned around. "You had a drink before you went to bed. Go back to sleep."

Jemima tried another avenue. "My bed's all untidy. Will you come and make it straight for me, please, Mama?"

"You're big enough to make it straight for yourself," Charlotte said firmly. "I'm going to get some supper for Papa. Good night."

"But Mama . . ."

"Good night, Jemima!"

"Can I say good night to Papa?"

Pitt did not wait for Charlotte's answer to this, but strode up the stairs two at a time and picked up his daughter in his arms. She was so slight, so delicately boned she felt fragile as he held her, even though she clung to him with surprising strength. She smelled of clean cotton and soap, and the hair around her brow was still damp. Why on earth did he challenge the Inner Circle? Life was too precious, too sweet to endanger anything. He could not destroy them, only bruise himself trying. Africa was half the earth away.

"Good night, Papa." Jemima made no move to be put down.

"Good night, sweetheart." He let her go gently, turned her around, and gave her a little push on her way.

This time she knew she was beaten, and disappeared without further argument.

Pitt came downstairs too full of emotion to speak. Charlotte looked at his face, and was content to bide her time.

———

In the morning he slept in, then ignored Bow Street entirely and went directly to the Morton Club to look for Horace Guyler, the steward who had given evidence at the inquest. He was too early. The club was not yet open. Presumably there were maids and footmen cleaning the carpets, dusting and polishing. He should have thought of that. He was obliged to kick his heels for an hour, and then he was allowed in, and had to wait a further thirty minutes before Guyler was given the freedom to see him.

"Yes sir?" Guyler said with some apprehension. They were standing in the small steward's room, at present empty but for the two of them.

"Good morning, Mr. Guyler," Pitt replied casually. "I wonder if you would tell me a little more about the day Sir Arthur Desmond died here."

Guyler looked uncomfortable, but Pitt had a strong feeling it was not guilt so much as a deep-seated fear of death and everything to do with it.

"I don't know what else I can say, sir." He shifted from one foot to the other. "I already said all I know at the inquest."

If he were an Inner Circle member, he was a consummate actor. Or perhaps he was a cat's paw? Perhaps the executioner simply used him?

"You answered all you were asked." Pitt smiled, although no smile was going to put him at his ease. "I have a few questions the coroner did not think to ask you."

"Why, sir? Is something wrong?"

"I want to make sure that nothing becomes wrong," Pitt said ambiguously. "You were serving gentlemen in the drawing room that day?"

"Yes, sir."

"Alone?"

"Beg pardon, sir?"

"Were you the only steward on duty?"

"Oh no, sir. There's always two or three of us at least."

"Always? What if someone is ill?"

"Then we hire in extra staff, sir. Happens quite often. Fact, I saw one that day."

"I see."

"But I was looking after that part o' the room, sir. I was the one what served Sir Arthur, at least most o' the time."

"But someone else did for part of it?" Pitt kept the rising urgency out of his voice as much as possible, but he still heard it there, as Guyler did. "One of these extra staff, perhaps?"

"I don't know for sure, sir."

"What do you mean?"

"Well . . . I can't really see what other stewards are doing if I'm pouring drinks for someone, taking an order or an instruction, sir. People is every so often coming and going. Gentlemen go to the cloakroom, or to the billiard room, or to the library, or the writing room or the like."

"Did Sir Arthur move around?"

"Not as I recall, sir. But I don't rightly know. I wouldn't swear to nothing."

"I certainly wouldn't press you," Pitt tried to reassure him.

Guyler's anxious expression did not change in the slightest.

"You said that Sir Arthur drank a great deal of brandy that day," Pitt pursued.

"Yes, sir. At my judgment, I would say five or six glasses at any rate," Guyler replied with conviction.

"How many of those did you serve him?"

"About four, sir, clear as I can remember."

"So someone else served him one, perhaps two?"

Guyler heard the lift of hope, even excitement in Pitt's voice.

"I don't know that, sir. I'm just supposing," he said quickly, biting his lip, his hands clenched.

"I don't understand. . . ." Pitt was genuinely confused; he had no need to pretend.

"Well, sir, you see . . . I'm saying Sir Arthur had about five or six glasses o' brandy because that's what I counted from what people said—"

"From what people said?" Pitt broke in sharply. "What people? How many glasses did you serve him yourself, Guyler?"

"One, sir. One glass o' brandy a little before dinner. The last one . . ." He gulped. "I suppose. But I swear before God, sir, that I never put nothing in it but brandy out o' the best decanter, exactly as I'm supposed to!"

"I don't doubt that," Pitt said steadily, looking at Guyler's frightened face. "Now explain to me these other four or five brandies you say Sir Arthur had. If you did not serve them, and you don't know whether any of the other stewards did, what makes you assume they existed at all?"

"Well, sir . . ." Guyler's eyes met Pitt's with fear, but no evasion. "I remember Sir James Duncansby saying as Sir Arthur wanted another drink, and I poured one and gave it to him to take to Sir Arthur. Seeing as Sir James had one at the same time, and said as he'd take it back to Sir Arthur. It isn't done to argue with gentlemen, sir."

"No, of course it isn't. That accounts for one. What about the others?"

"Well, er . . . Mr. William Rodway came and ordered a second one from me, saying as the first, which he'd had from one of the other stewards, he'd given to Sir Arthur."

"That's two. Go on."

"Mr. Jenkinson said as he'd treat Sir Arthur, and 'e took two, one for himself like."

"Three. You want one or two more."

"I'm not really sure, sir." Guyler looked unhappy. "I just overheard Brigadier Allsop saying as he'd seen Sir Arthur ordering one from one of the other stewards. At least I think it was one, I'm not sure. It could have been two."

Pitt felt a curious sense of lightness. The steward had served Sir Arthur only one drink! All the rest were hearsay. They might never have reached him at all. Suddenly the confusion and nightmare were sorting into some kind of sense. Sanity was returning.

And with sanity were the darker, uglier, but so much less painful conclusions that if this were not the truth but a conspiracy, then Sir Arthur had been murdered, just as Matthew believed.

And perhaps if Pitt had been there, if he had been home to Brackley and Sir Arthur had been able to turn to him in the first place with his terrible suspicion of the Inner Circle, then maybe Pitt could have warned him, have advised him, and he would not now be dead.

He thanked Guyler and left him, anxious and more puzzled than when he had come in.

Dr. Murray was not a man to be so easily led or persuaded. Pitt had been obliged to make an appointment to see him in Wimpole Street and to pay for the privilege, and Murray was not amused when he discovered that the purpose for Pitt's presence in his surgery was to ask questions, rather than to seek aid for some complaint. The rooms were imposing, soberly furnished, exuding an air of well-being and confidence. It crossed Pitt's mind to wonder what had drawn Arthur Desmond to such a man, and how long he had consulted him.

"Your request was somewhat misleading, Mr. Pitt, at the outset, and that is the kindest I can say for it." Murray leaned back from his huge walnut desk and looked at Pitt with disfavor. "What authority have you for enquiring into the unfortunate death of Sir Arthur Desmond? The coroner has already given his judgment on the causes and closed the case. I fail to see what good can be done by further discussion of the matter."

Pitt had expected some difficulty, and even if Murray were a member of the Circle, as he suspected, he knew his trick with Osborne would not work a second time. Murray was far too confident to be duped. And he thought it likely he was also much more senior in the hierarchy which governed it, and might well know who Pitt was, his past enmity to the Circle and his very recent refusal to join. He forced from his mind the further possibilities that Murray himself was the executioner, though as he sat in the consulting room with the door closed behind him, and the windows with their thick, velvet curtains, he could see the bright street beyond and carriages passing to and fro in the sunlight. But the glass was so thick and so well fitted he could hear nothing of the rattle and bustle of life. He felt suddenly claustrophobic, almost imprisoned.

He thought of lying about the coroner's being dissatisfied, but then he dared not. The coroner might be an Inner Circle member as well. In fact almost anyone might be, even among his own men. He had always felt Tellman was too angry, too full of resentment to lend himself to anything so dedicated to the power of governing. But perhaps that was blind of him.

"I am a personal friend of Sir Matthew's," he said aloud. That at least was perfectly true. "He asked me to make a few further enquiries on his behalf. He is not well at the moment. He met with an accident in the street a few days ago, and was injured." He watched Murray's face intently, but saw not even a flicker in his eyes.

"I am so sorry," Murray sympathized. "How very unfortunate. I hope it was not serious?"

"It seems not, but it was very unpleasant. He could have been killed."

"I am afraid it happens all too often."

Was that a veiled threat? Or only an innocent and truthful observation?

"What is it you wish to know, Mr. Pitt?" Murray continued, folding his hands across his stomach and looking at Pitt gravely. "If you are indeed a friend of Sir Matthew's, you would do him the greatest service by persuading him that his father's death was in many ways a mercy, before he became sufficiently ill to damage his reputation beyond recall, and possibly to have suffered greatly in his more lucid moments. It is most unpleasant to face, but less damaging in time than to go on fighting against the truth, and possibly causing a great deal of unpleasantness along the way." A smile flickered across his face and disappeared. "Men of goodwill, of whom there are many, wish to remember Arthur as he was, but to rake the matter up over and over will not allow that to happen." His eyes did not waver from Pitt's.

One moment Pitt was sure it was a warning; the men of goodwill he referred to were members of the Circle, large in number, but immeasurably more powerful than number alone would suggest. They would retaliate if Matthew pressed them.

Then the next moment he knew there was no proof of that. Murray was simply a doctor stating the obvious. Pitt was developing a delusion about being persecuted himself, seeing plots everywhere, accusing innocent people.

"I shall be better able to convince him if I have some facts and details to tell him," he replied, not moving his gaze either. "For example, had you ever prescribed laudanum for Sir Arthur before? Or was this his first experience with it, as far as you were aware?"

"It was his first experience," Murray replied. "He told me that himself. But I did explain to him most carefully both its properties and its dangers, Mr. Pitt. I showed him precisely how and when to take it, and how much would produce a sleep of reasonably natural depth and duration."

"Of course," Pitt agreed. "But in his confused state . . . he was confused, was he not? Irrational and contradictory at times?"

"Not with me." Murray said what he had to, to protect himself, as Pitt had expected. "But I have subsequently learned from others that he had some strange obsessions, not altogether rational. I take your point, Mr. Pitt. He may have forgotten what I told him and taken a lethal dose, thinking it would merely give him an afternoon nap. We can't know what was in his mind at the time, poor man."

"How was the laudanum made up?"

"In powders, which is the usual way." He smiled very slightly. "Each dose separated and in a folded paper. It would be difficult to take more than one dose, Mr. Pitt, unless one had forgotten and taken a second in absentmindedness. I regret it could not more satisfactorily fill your theory. It is a precaution I usually take."

"I see." It did not affect Pitt's real belief. It would still have been perfectly possible for Murray to make up a dose that was lethal and put it in with the others. He kept the look of agreeable enquiry on his face. "When did Sir Arthur come to you, Dr. Murray?"

"He first consulted me in the autumn of 1887, over a congestion of the lungs. I was able to help him and he effected a complete cure. If you are referring to this last visit, that was ... let me see." He looked through a calendar of appointments on his desk. "April twenty-seventh." He smiled. "At four-forty in the afternoon, to be precise. He was here some half hour or more. He was very troubled indeed, I regret to say. I did all I could to reassure him, but I am afraid he was beyond my ability to help this time. I don't think I flatter myself if I say he was past the help of any man of medicine."

"Did you make up the laudanum yourself, Dr. Murray?"

"No, no. I don't keep supplies of all the drugs I prescribe for my patients, Mr. Pitt. I gave him a prescription which I presume he took to an apothecary. I recommended Mr. Porteous of Jermyn Street. He is an excellent man, both knowledgeable and extremely careful. I am most particular, for the very cause you mention, that the laudanum should be precisely measured and each dose separately wrapped. Sir Arthur had been to him on several previous occasions, and said that he would indeed use him."

"I see. Thank you very much, Dr. Murray. You have been most patient." Pitt rose to his feet. He had learned only little that was of use, but he could think of no more to ask without raising suspicion, if not actual certainty, that he was pursuing the Inner Circle again, and that he was convinced of murder. That would achieve nothing, and he was acutely aware of his own danger.

As it was, he was absurdly relieved to be outside in the bright air amid the rattle of hooves and hiss of carriage wheels and the vitality and movement of the street.

He went straight to Jermyn Street and found the apothecary's shop.

"Sir Arthur Desmond?" The old man behind the counter nodded benignly. "Such a nice gentleman. Sorry to hear about his death. Very sad. So unfortunate. What may I do for you, sir? I have just about everything a body can need to repair or ease whatever troubles you. Have you seen a physician, or may I advise you?"

"I don't need to purchase anything. I'm sorry for misleading you. It is your memory I need to consult." Pitt did feel guilty for offering no business, but there was nothing he needed. "When was Sir Arthur last in here?"

"Sir Arthur? Why do you wish to know that, young man?" He squinted at Pitt curiously but not unkindly.

"I—I am concerned about his death . . . the manner of it," Pitt answered a little awkwardly. The old man looked not unlike Sir Arthur, and it brought an odd twist of memory back, seeing him behind the counter of the dark shop.

"Oh. Well, so am I, and that's the pity of it. If he'd come here with his writ from the doctor, as he usually did, I'd have given him the laudanum all wrapped separately, as I always do for all my customers, and then this dreadful accident would never have happened." The old man shook his head sorrowfully.

"He didn't come here?" Pitt said sharply. "You are sure?"

The old gentleman's eyebrows rose. "Of course I am sure, young man. Nobody serves behind this counter but myself, and I did not serve him. I haven't seen Sir Arthur since last winter. About January, it would be. He had a cold. I gave him some infusion of herbs to put in hot water, to clear his head. We talked about dogs. I recall it very well."

"Thank you. Thank you, Mr. Porteous. I am greatly obliged to you, sir. Good day."

"Good day, young man. I shouldn't run like that, sir, if I were you. No good for the digestion. You'll get overexcited. . . ."

But Pitt was out of the door and off down Jermyn Street at a flying pace.

He was halfway along Regent Street before he realized he did not know where he was going. Where had Sir Arthur obtained the laudanum? If not in Jermyn Street, then from some other apothecary. Or had Murray given it to him after all? Was there any way whatever of proving it?

Perhaps Matthew would know? Apothecary's papers frequently had their names on them. It was both a safeguard and a means of advertising. He retraced his steps and called a cab to take him to Matthew's apartments.

"What is it?" Matthew asked quickly. He was sitting up at his desk in the small room which served him as dining room and study. He was wearing a dressing robe, and still looked very pale. There were shadows around his eyes as if latent bruises were at last beginning to show.

"You look ill," Pitt said anxiously. "Should you be up?"

"I have nothing worse than a headache," Matthew dismissed it quickly. "What is it? What have you found?"

Pitt sat on one of the other chairs. "I've been to see several people. It seems all of Sir Arthur's irrational behavior is either hearsay or based on the fact he upset people's prejudices and desires. . . ."

"I told you!" Matthew said triumphantly, light and eagerness in his face for the first time since he had come to Pitt's house with the news of Sir Arthur's death. "He wasn't the least confused or senile. He knew only too well what he was saying. What else? What about the brandy, and the laudanum? Have you proved that wrong yet?" He smiled apologetically. "I'm sorry, I'm expecting miracles. You've done brilliantly, Thomas. I am grateful."

"The brandy is hearsay too. The steward only served him one glass; the rest were ordered by other people on his behalf . . . perhaps."

Matthew frowned. "Perhaps? What do you mean?"

Pitt recited what Guyler had told him.

"I see," Matthew said quietly, leaning back. "God, isn't it frightening. The Inner Circle is all over the place. But surely not everyone you've spoken to can be members, can they? Or can they?" His face looked pale again at the thought.

"I don't know," Pitt confessed. "I presume members can be summoned if they are needed. And this was something of an emergency for them. After all, Sir Arthur was breaking the covenant of secrecy and accusing them of conspiracy to commit fraud, and in some senses even treason."

Matthew sat silent, deep in thought.

"Matthew . . ."

He looked up.

"I went to see Dr. Murray as well. He says he recommended Sir Arthur to get the laudanum he prescribed at the usual apothecary in Jermyn Street, but Porteous is quite certain that Sir Arthur did not go to him. Have you any idea where else he might have got it?"

"Does it matter? Do you think it was wrong dosages or something? An apothecary who was the executioner of the Circle?" His face was pinched with revulsion. "What an appalling thought . . . but it makes excellent sense."

"Or the doctor himself," Pitt added. "Do you know?"

"No. But if we could find one of the papers it would probably tell us." He stood up. "There may be some left among his effects. I'll look. Come, we'll both go."

Pitt rose. "He only had them two or three days. It was April twenty-seventh he went to see Murray for the consultation."

Matthew stood and turned to face Pitt.

"The twenty-seventh. Are you sure?"

"Yes. Why?"

"He said nothing about it to me. He can't have got them that day, because we went to Brighton in the afternoon."

"What time?"

"To Brighton? About half past two. Why?"

"And what time did you get back?"

"We didn't. We dined with friends and came back the following morning."

"Murray said that was the day he saw Sir Arthur—at four-forty in the afternoon. Are you sure it was the twenty-seventh you went to Brighton, not the day before, or after?"

"Absolutely certain. It was Aunt Mary's birthday and we had a party. We always do on the twenty-seventh of April, every year."

"Then Murray lied. He never saw Sir Arthur!"

Matthew frowned. "Could he have misunderstood the date?"

"No. He looked it up in his book. I saw him."

"Then the whole consultation was a lie," Matthew said, curiously melancholy. "And if that is so, then where did the laudanum come from?"

"God knows!" Pitt whispered huskily. "Someone in that club room . . . someone who took him a brandy he didn't order."

Matthew swallowed hard and said nothing.

Pitt sat down again, feeling curiously weak and frightened, and looking across at Matthew's white face, he knew he felt just the same.

CHAPTER
EIGHT

Pitt woke up slowly, the thumping in his head becoming more persistent till it dragged him to the surface of consciousness and forced him awake. He opened his eyes. The bedroom was barred with sunlight where the curtains did not quite meet. Charlotte was still asleep beside him, warm and hunched up, her hair in loose braids beginning to come undone.

The banging was still going on. There was no sound in the street outside, no carriages, no drays, no noise of footsteps or voices.

He turned over and looked at the clock beside the bed. It was ten minutes before five.

The banging was getting worse. It was downstairs at the front door.

He sat up reluctantly and pushed his fingers through his hair, then put his jacket on over his nightshirt and walked barefoot across the floor to open the window. Charlotte stirred but did not fully waken. He pushed up the sash and looked out.

The banging stopped and a foreshortened figure stepped back from the door and looked up. It was Tellman. His face was very white in the early morning light and he had come without his usual bowler hat. He looked disheveled and upset.

Pitt indicated that he would come down, and after closing the window again, he walked as quietly as he could back to the door to the landing and went down the stairs into the hall. He undid the lock and pulled the door open.

Tellman looked even worse closer to. His face was ashen and what little flesh there was seemed to be sunken away. He did not wait to be asked.

"Something terrible has happened," he said as soon as he saw Pitt. "You'd better come and deal with it yourself. I haven't told anybody yet, but Mr. Farnsworth's going to be in a right state when he hears."

"Come in," Pitt ordered, standing back. "What is it?" All sorts of fears whirled around in his head; presumably some terrible news had come from the German Embassy. Although how would Tellman know that? Had someone absconded, taking papers with them? "What is it?" he demanded more urgently.

Tellman remained on the step. He was so pale he looked as if he might collapse. That in itself alarmed Pitt. He would have thought Tellman inured to anything.

"Mrs. Chancellor," Tellman said, and coughed painfully, then gulped. "We've just found her body, sir."

Pitt was stunned. His breath caught in his throat and the words came out in a whisper. "Her body?"

"Yes sir. Washed up in the river at the Tower." He watched Pitt with hollow eyes.

"Suicide?" Pitt said slowly, unable to believe it.

"No." Tellman stood motionless except that he shivered very slightly although the morning was mild. "Murder. She'd been strangled, and then put in the water. Sometime last night by the looks of it. But you'll need the medical examiner to tell you for sure."

Pitt felt a sorrow so sharp it exploded in him in a kind of wild anger. She had been such a beautiful, vulnerable woman, so full of life, so highly individual. He remembered her vividly at the Duchess of Marlborough's reception. He could picture her face in his mind as Tellman was talking. It was so seldom he had known a victim in life, the sense of loss was personal, different from the pity that he usually felt.

"Why?" he said violently. "Why would anyone want to destroy a woman like that? It doesn't make any kind of sense." Without realizing it he had clenched his fists and his body was tight with rage under his jacket. He was not even aware of his bare feet on the step or the fact he had no trousers on.

"The treason at the Colonial Office . . ." Tellman said unhappily. "Maybe she knew something?"

Pitt thumped the door lintel with the heel of his clenched fist, and swore.

"You'd better get dressed, sir, and come," Tellman said quietly. "There's no one knows about it yet, except the boatman as found her and the constable who reported it to me, but we can't keep it that way for long. Don't matter what you say to 'em, discretion and all that, somebody'll talk to someone."

"They know who she is?" Pitt was startled.

"Yes sir. That's why I was called."

Pitt was irritated with himself; he should have thought of that before.

"How?" he demanded. "How could riverboat men know her?"

"The constables," Tellman explained patiently. "They were the ones who knew who she was. She was obviously someone of quality, any fool could see that, but she had a locket 'round her neck, little gold thing that opened up, with a picture in it." He sighed and there was a sadness for a moment in his eyes. "Linus Chancellor, it was, clear as you like. That's why they called us. Whoever she was, they knew that picture meant something that could only mean trouble."

"I see. Where is she now?" Pitt looked back at him.

"Still at the Tower, sir. I had 'em cover her up, and left her where she was, more or less, so as you could see."

"I'll be down," Pitt said, and left Tellman on the step. He went back upstairs, taking off his jacket as he reached the landing and pulling off his nightshirt as soon as he was through the bedroom door.

Charlotte had drifted back to sleep and it seemed cruel to waken her, but he had to give her some account of where he had gone. He finished dressing first. There was no time to shave. A brisk splash of cold water in the basin and a rubdown with the towel would have to do.

He reached over and touched her gently.

There must have been some rigidity in him, or perhaps the coldness of his hands after the water, but she woke immediately.

"What is it? What's wrong?" She opened her eyes and saw him dressed. She struggled to sit up. "What's happened?"

He had no time to tell her gently. "Tellman's come to say they have found Susannah Chancellor's body washed up from the river."

She stared at him, unable for a moment to comprehend what he had said.

"I have to go." He bent to kiss her.

"She committed suicide?" she said, her eyes still fixed on his. "The poor creature . . . I . . ." Her face was wrenched with pity.

"No . . . no. She was murdered."

There was both shock and a kind of relief in her face.

"Why did you think she committed suicide?" he asked.

"I . . . I don't know. She seemed so troubled."

"Well there was no doubt about it, from what Tellman says."

"How was she killed?"

"I haven't been there yet," he answered, not wanting to tell her. He kissed her quickly on the cheek and stepped back.

"Thomas!"

He waited.

"You said 'from what Tellman said.' What did he say?"

He let out his breath slowly. "She was strangled. I'm sorry. He's waiting for me."

She sat still, her face full of grief. There was nothing he could do. He went out feeling sad and helpless.

Tellman was waiting in the hall and he turned and led the way out into the street as soon as Pitt appeared. Pitt closed the door and hastened to catch him up. At the corner they crossed into the main thoroughfare, and it was only a matter of minutes before they hailed a hansom and Tellman directed it to the Tower of London.

It was a long journey from Bloomsbury. They went south first to Oxford Street, and then east until it turned into High Holborn and then for nearly a mile before turning right farther towards the river down St. Andrews Street, Shoe Lane and St. Bride's to Ludgate Circus.

Tellman sat in silence. He was not a companionable man. Whatever his thoughts were he was disinclined to share them and he sat uncomfortably, staring straight ahead.

Several times it was on the edge of Pitt's tongue to ask him something, but he could think of nothing that would be useful. Tellman had already said all he knew for certain. The rest would be only speculation. Anyway, Pitt was not sure he wanted to hear Tellman's ideas on Susannah Chancellor. Her lovely, intelligent face with its capacity for pain was too sharp in his mind, and he knew what he was going to see when they got to the Tower.

They turned along Ludgate Hill and swung around St. Paul's churchyard with the giant mass of the cathedral above them. Its dome was dark against the pale, early sky, which was marked only by a few shreds of cloud like banners across its limpid blue. There were very few people about. Down the whole length of Canon Street they passed only half a dozen cabs, two drays and a dung cart. Canon Street turned into East Cheap and then into Great Tower Street.

Tellman leaned forward and suddenly banged sharply against the roof for the cabby's attention.

"Turn right!" he ordered. "Turn down Water Street to Lower Thames Street."

"Ain't nothing down there but Queen's Stairs and Traitors Bridge," the cabby replied. "If you want the Tower, like you said, you'd be better off in Trinity Square, which is up to the left."

"Just take us to Queen's Stairs and then go about your business," Tellman said curtly.

The cabby muttered something inaudible, but obeyed.

They glimpsed the Custom House to the west, already busy with men coming and going. Then they turned right facing the great medieval bastion of the Tower of London, a stone memory of a conquest that spanned back to the Dark Ages and a history recorded only in brief bursts by illuminated writing and quaint works of art and tales of bloody battles and exquisite, passionate islands of Christianity.

The hansom stopped at Queen's Stairs. Pitt paid the cabby and he turned and left, his horses moving into a brisk trot.

It was two minutes before six. The great silver sheet of the river was utterly calm. Even the cargo barges, dark against the bright surface, barely made a ripple. The air was fresh and slightly damp and smelled of salt from the tide.

Tellman led the way along the water's edge to the stairs, where a boatman was waiting for them. He looked up without a change of expression and deftly maneuvered the small craft around so they could get in.

Pitt looked questioningly at Tellman.

"Traitors Gate," he said succinctly, climbing in ahead of Pitt and sitting down. He disliked boats, and it showed in his face.

Pitt followed him easily and thanked the boatman as he pulled away.

"She was washed up at Traitors Gate?" he asked with a catch in his voice.

"Tide left her there," Tellman replied. It was only a few yards down the river to the gate itself, the entrance to the Tower by which condemned people had been brought to their execution, and which opened directly onto the water.

Pitt could see the little knot of people already gathered around: a constable in uniform looking cold in spite of the mildness of the morning, a scarlet tunic of a Yeoman of the Guard, the traditional Beefeaters who man the Tower, and the other of the two boatmen who had first found her.

Pitt climbed ashore, only just avoiding getting his feet wet on the slipway. Susannah was lying on the waterline where the high tide had left her, only her feet below the surface, a long, slender form barely crumpled, turned over half onto her face. One white hand was visible protruding from the wet, dripping cloth of her gown. Her hair had come unraveled from its pins and lay like seaweed around her neck, spilling onto the stone.

The constable turned as Pitt came ashore, recognized him and stepped back from the body.

"Morning, sir." He looked very pale.

"Good morning, Constable," Pitt replied. He did not remember the man's name, if indeed he knew it. He looked down at Susannah. "When was she found?"

" 'Bout 'alf past three, sir. High tide 'd be just before three, 'cording to the boatman 'ere. Reckon as they were the first past 'ere on this side o' the river after she were washed up, poor creature. Weren't no suicide, sir. Poor soul was strangled, no two ways about that." He looked sad and very solemn for his twenty-odd years. His beat was on the river's edge, and this was not the first body he had seen, nor the first woman, but she was perhaps the first he had seen with beautiful clothes and—when the hair was pulled back, as it was now—such a passionate, vulnerable face. Pitt knelt down to look at her more closely. He saw the unmistakable finger marks purple on her throat, but from the lack of swelling or bloating on her face, he thought perhaps she had actually died of a broken neck rather than suffocation. It was a tiny thing, very tiny, but the fact that she was not disfigured eased the hurt. Possibly she had suffered only very briefly. He would think that as long as he could.

"We didn't touch her, sir," one of the boatmen said nervously.

" 'Cept to make sure as she was dead, and we couldn't 'elp 'er, poor creature." He knew enough of the circumstances which drive people to suicide to have no judgment over it. He would have put them all in consecrated ground and left the decision to God. But he was not a churchgoing man by choice. He went only to please his wife.

"Thank you," Pitt said absently, still looking at Susannah. "Where would she have been put in the water to be washed up here?"

"That depends, sir. Currents is funny. 'Specially in a river like this where it twists and turns, like. Most often bodies sink at first, then come up again right about where they went in. But if she was put in on the turn o' the tide, into the water, like, if she moved at all it could a' bin upriver from 'ere. That's if she were put in off a boat. But if she were put in off the shore, more like it were on the incoming tide, and she came upriver from below. And that would depend on when she were put in, as to where, if you follow me, guv?"

"So all we know for sure is that she was here when the tide turned?"

"Yer got it right," the boatman agreed. "Bodies stay in the water different sorts of times. Depends on what passes making a wake, or if they bump summink. Things get caught and pulled sometimes. There's eddies and currents you can't always account for. Maybe the doc can tell yer 'ow long she's been gone, poor thing. Then we can tell yer if she were put in then, like, just about where it would be."

"Thank you." Pitt looked up at Tellman. "Have you sent for the mortuary wagon?"

"Yes sir. It will be waiting up in Trinity Square. Didn't want a whole lot of talk going on," Tellman answered without glancing at the boatmen. If they didn't know who she was, so much the better. The news would spread fast enough. It would be an appalling way for Chancellor to learn, or anyone else who had cared for her.

Pitt straightened up with a sigh. He should tell Chancellor

himself. He knew the man, and Tellman did not. Apart from that it was not a duty to delegate.

"Get them down here to take her to the medical examiner. I must report it as soon as possible."

"Yes sir, of course." Tellman glanced once more at Susannah, then turned on his heel and went back to the boat, his face twisted with distaste.

A few moments later Pitt left also, climbing up the Queen's Stairs and walking slowly around to Great Tower Hill. He was obliged to walk as far as East Cheap before he found another cab. The morning was beginning to cloud over from the north and now there were more people about. A newsboy shouted some government difficulty. A running patterer had an early breakfast at a pie stall while he studied the day's events, getting ready to compose his rhymes. Two men came out of a coffee shop, arguing animatedly with each other. They were looking for a cab, but Pitt reached it just before them, to their considerable annoyance.

"Berkeley Square, please," he directed the driver, and climbed in. The driver acknowledged him and set off. Pitt sat back and tried to compose in his mind what he would say. It was useless, as he had known it would be. There was no kind or reasonable way in which to break such news, no way to take the pain out of it, no way even to lessen it. It was always absolutely and unequivocally terrible.

He tried to think at least what questions to ask Chancellor, but it was of little use. Whatever he decided now, he would still have to think again when he saw Chancellor's state of mind, whether he was able to retain sufficient composure to answer anything at all. People were affected differently by grief. With some the shock was so deep it did not manifest itself to begin with. They might be calm for days before their grief overcame them. Others were hysterical, torn with helpless anger, or too racked with weeping to be coherent, or think of anything but their loss.

"What number, sir?" the cabby interrupted his thoughts.

"Seventeen," he replied. "I think."

"That'll be Mr. Chancellor, sir?"

"That's right."

The cabby seemed about to add something more, but changed his mind and closed the trapdoor.

A moment later Pitt alighted, paid him and stood on the doorstep, shivering in spite of the early morning sun. It was now after seven. All around the square maids were busy bringing out carpets to the areaways to be beaten and swept, and bootboys and footmen went in and out on errands. Even a few early delivery boys pushed carts, and news vendors handed over their papers for the maids to iron so they could be presented at breakfast before the masters of the houses left for the day's business in the city.

Pitt rang the doorbell.

It was answered almost immediately by a footman who looked surprised to see someone at the front door so very early.

"Yes sir?" he said politely.

"Good morning. My name is Pitt." He produced his card. "It is imperative I see Mr. Chancellor immediately. It is on a matter that cannot wait. Will you tell him so, please."

The footman had worked for a cabinet minister for some time and he was not unused to matters of dire emergency.

"Yes sir. If you will wait in the morning room, I will inform Mr. Chancellor that you are here."

Pitt hesitated.

"Yes sir?" the footman said politely.

"I am afraid I have some extremely unpleasant news. Perhaps you would send the butler to me first."

The footman paled.

"Yes sir, if you think that's necessary?"

"Has he been with Mr. Chancellor long?"

"Yes sir, some fifteen years."

"Then please send him."

"Yes sir."

The butler came within moments, looking anxious. He

closed the morning room door behind him and faced Pitt with a frown.

"I'm Richards, sir, Mr. Chancellor's butler. I gather from Albert that something distressing has happened. Is it one of the gentlemen in the Colonial Office? Has there been a . . . an accident?"

"No, Richards, I am afraid it is far worse than that," Pitt said quietly, his voice rough at the edges. "I am afraid Mrs. Chancellor has met with . . . has met with a violent death." He got no further. The butler swayed on his feet as if he were about to faint. Every vestige of color fled from his skin.

Pitt lunged forward and grasped him, guiding him backwards towards one of the chairs.

"I'm . . . I'm sorry, sir," Richards gasped. "I don't know what came over me. I . . ." He looked up at Pitt beseechingly. "You are sure, sir? There could not be some error . . . some mistake as to identity?" Even as he said it his face reflected his knowledge that it could not be so. How many women were there in London who looked like Susannah Chancellor?

Pitt gave no answer. None was necessary.

"I think it would be wise if you were to make yourself available close at hand when I have to break the news to Mr. Chancellor," Pitt said gently. "Perhaps a decanter of brandy. And you might make sure that there are no callers and no messages until he feels able to deal with them."

"Yes. Yes, of course. Thank you, sir." And still looking very shaken and uncertain in his step, Richards rose and left the room.

Linus Chancellor came in a moment or two later, an eagerness in his step and a directness in his eyes that gave Pitt a bitter jolt. He realized Chancellor was expecting news about the African information that was being passed. And with that keenness in his eyes, he also realized, if he had ever doubted it, that Chancellor was innocent of any involvement.

"I'm sorry, sir. I have very grave news," he said almost before

Chancellor had closed the door. He could not bear the misapprehension.

"Is it one of my senior colleagues?" Chancellor asked. "It is good of you to come here to tell me in person. Who is it? Aylmer?"

Pitt felt cold in spite of the warmth of the room and the sun now bright outside.

"No, sir. I am afraid it is about Mrs. Chancellor I have come." He saw the surprise in Chancellor's face and did not wait. "I am profoundly sorry, sir, but I have to tell you that she is dead."

"Dead?" Chancellor repeated the word as though he did not know its meaning. "She was perfectly well last evening. She went out to . . ." He turned and went to the door. "Richards?"

The butler appeared immediately, the salver with brandy decanter and glass in his hands, his face ashen white.

Chancellor looked back at Pitt, then at the butler again.

"Have you seen Mrs. Chancellor this morning, Richards?"

Richards looked enquiringly at Pitt.

"Mr. Chancellor, there is no doubt," Pitt said gently. "She was found at the Tower of London."

"The Tower of London?" Chancellor said incredulously. His eyes were wide with disbelief, and there was a look on his face that seemed close to laughter, as if the sheer idea of it were too absurd to be true.

Pitt had seen hysteria before; it was not altogether unexpected.

"Please sit down, sir," he asked. "You are bound to feel unwell."

Richards set the tray down and offered a glass of brandy.

Chancellor took it and drank it all, then coughed severely for several seconds until he managed to regain control of himself.

"What happened?" he asked slowly, fumbling to get his tongue around the words. "What could she possibly have been doing at the Tower of London? She went out to visit Christabel Thorne. I know Christabel is eccentric . . . but the Tower of London? Where, for heaven's sake? She can surely not have been inside it at that time of night?"

"Could she and Mrs. Thorne have taken a trip on the river?" Pitt asked, although it seemed a strange thing for two ladies to do alone. Would they find Christabel's body also, on some further stretch of the riverbank?

"And what . . . a boating accident?" Chancellor said doubtfully. "Did Mrs. Thorne suggest such a thing?"

"We have not yet enquired of Mrs. Thorne. We did not know Mrs. Chancellor had been with her. But it was not an accident, sir. I am deeply sorry, but I am afraid it was murder. The only comfort I can offer is that it would have been very quick. It is unlikely she suffered."

Chancellor stared at him, his face white, then red. He seemed about to choke on his own breath.

Richards offered him another glass of brandy and he drank it. The blood left his face and he looked ill.

"And Christabel?" he whispered, staring at Pitt.

"So far we know nothing about her, but we will naturally make enquiries."

"Where . . . where was she found . . . my . . . wife?" Chancellor seemed to have difficulty saying the words.

"At Traitors Gate. It has a slipway down—"

"I know! I know, Superintendent. I have seen it many times. I know what it is." He swallowed again, gulping in air. "Thank you for coming to tell me yourself. It must be one of your most unpleasant tasks. I appreciate that you came in person. I imagine you will be in charge of the case? Now if you don't mind, I would prefer to be alone. Richards, please inform the Colonial Office that I shall not be in this morning."

Pitt walked from Linus Chancellor's to the home of Jeremiah Thorne, across the square and along to the far end of Mount Street, and north to Upper Brook Street. It took him less than twenty minutes to reach the front door and ring the bell. His heart was pounding as if he had run twice the distance, his tongue dry in his mouth.

The bell was answered by a footman who enquired as to his business, and when presented with his card, showed him into the library and asked him to wait. He would enquire whether Mrs. Thorne was at home. At this time in the morning it was a ridiculous pretense. He could hardly fail to know if she were at home, but he had been trained to use the polite fiction before allowing any visitor in. If it were inconvenient, or his employer did not wish to see someone, he could hardly return and say so as bluntly.

Pitt waited with a tension so severe he was unable to sit down or even to stand in one spot. He paced back and forth, once catching his knuckles on the edge of a carved table as he turned, oblivious of his surroundings. He was aware of the pain, but only dimly. His ears strained to hear the sound of footsteps. Once when a maid passed he went to the door and was on the point of flinging it open, when he realized he was being absurd. Then he heard giggling and a male voice answering back. It was a simple piece of domestic flirtation.

He was still close to the door when Christabel came in. She was wearing a pale gray morning dress and looked in excellent health, but very questionable temper. Although curiosity was holding it in check, at least until she had ascertained the cause of his call at such a time.

"Good morning, Superintendent," she said coolly. "You alarmed my footman by your rather vehement insistence upon speaking to me. I hope your reason is adequate to justify it. This is a very uncivil time to call."

He was too shaken to respond sharply; the tragedy was real. His mind's eye was still filled with Susannah's face as she lay in the silence of Traitors Gate, the water of the river lapping over her feet.

"I am extremely relieved to see you well, Mrs. Thorne."

Something in the gravity of his face frightened her. Quite suddenly her manner altered entirely, the anger evaporated.

"What is it, Mr. Pitt? Has something happened?"

"Yes, ma'am. I am very sorry indeed to have to tell you that

Mrs. Chancellor met her death last night. Mr. Chancellor had believed she was with you, so I naturally came immediately to make sure you were not ..."

"Susannah?" She looked stricken, staring at him with her enormous eyes, the arrogance fled out of her. "Susannah is dead?" She took a step backwards, then another until she found the chair behind her and sank into it. "How? If ... if you feared for me also, then it was ... violent?"

"Yes, Mrs. Thorne. I am afraid she was murdered."

"Oh, dear God!" She put her hands up to her face and sat quite motionless for several moments.

"May I call someone for you?" he offered.

She looked up. "What? Uh—no, no thank you. My poor Susannah. How did it happen? Where was she, for heaven's sake, that she could be ... was she attacked? Robbed?"

"We don't yet know. She was found in the river, washed up on the shore."

"Drowned?"

"No, she was strangled, so violently that her neck may well be broken. It was probably very quick. I'm sorry, Mrs. Thorne, but since Mr. Chancellor had believed she was coming to visit you, I have to ask you if you saw her last evening."

"No. I dined at home, but Susannah did not come here. She must have been attacked before she ..." She sighed and a shadow of a smile, small and very sad, touched her lips. "That is, if, of course, she intended to come here. Perhaps she went somewhere else. It would be unwise to suppose it had to be here she had in mind. Although I do not believe it would be an assignation. She was too much in love with Linus for that to be ... likely."

"You don't say 'possible,' Mrs. Thorne?" he said instantly.

She rose to her feet and turned to look out of the window, her back to him. "No. There is not much that is impossible, Superintendent. That is something you learn as you get older. Associations are not always what you suppose, and even when you love one person, you may not necessarily behave in a manner other people would understand."

"Are you speaking in generalities, or do you have Mrs. Chancellor in mind?" Pitt asked quietly.

"I don't really know. But Linus is not an easy man. He is witty, charming, handsome, ambitious, and certainly extremely talented. But I have always wondered if he was capable of loving her as much as she loved him. Not that many marriages are composed of two people who love each other equally, except in fairy stories." She kept her back to him and her voice suggested she was indifferent whether he understood her or not. "Not everyone is able to give so much. There is usually one party who has to compromise, to accept what is given and not be bitter or lonely for the rest. That is especially true for women who are married to powerful and ambitious men. Susannah was clever enough to know that, and I think wise enough not to fight against it and lose what there was for her . . . which I believe was much."

"But you do not think it impossible she may have found some friendship or admiration elsewhere?"

"Not impossible, Superintendent, but unlikely." She turned back to face him. "I liked Susannah very much, Mr. Pitt. She was a woman of intelligence, courage, and great integrity. She loved her husband, but she was well able to speak and act for herself. She was not . . . dominated. She had spirit, passion and laughter. . . ." Suddenly her eyes filled with tears and they spilled down her cheeks. She stood quite still and wept without screwing up her face, simply lost in a deep and consuming grief.

"I am so sorry," Pitt said quietly, and went to the door. He found Jeremiah Thorne in the hall outside, looking surprised and a little anxious.

"What the devil are you doing here?" he demanded.

"Mrs. Chancellor has been murdered," Pitt replied without preamble. "I had reason to believe your wife might also have been harmed. I am delighted that she is not, but she is distressed and in need of comfort. Mr. Chancellor will not be in to the Colonial Office today."

Thorne stared at him for a moment, barely comprehending what he had heard.

"I'm sorry," Pitt said again.

"Susannah?" Thorne looked stricken; there was no mistaking the reality of his emotion. "Are you sure? I'm sorry, that's an absurd question. Of course you are, or you would hardly have come here. But how? Why? What happened? Why in God's name did you think Christabel was involved?" He searched Pitt's face as if he might have seen some answer in it more immediate than words.

"Mr. Chancellor had been under the impression that his wife was intending to visit Mrs. Thorne yesterday evening," Pitt replied. "But apparently she did not reach here."

"No! No . . . she was not expected."

"So Mrs. Thorne told me."

"Dear God, this is dreadful! Poor Susannah. She was one of the loveliest women I ever knew—lovely in the truest sense, Pitt. I am not thinking of her face, but of the spirit that lit her inside, the passion and the courage . . . the heart. Forgive me. Come back and ask anything you like later on, but now I must go to my wife. She was deeply fond of Susannah. . . ." And without adding anything further he turned and went towards the library, leaving Pitt to find his own way out.

It was far too soon to expect any information from the medical examiner. The body would barely have reached him. The physical evidence was slight. As the boatman had said, she could have been put into the water upstream after the tide had turned at about two-thirty and drifted down, or downstream on the flood tide, and have been carried up, and thus left when the ebb began. Or as likely as either of those, she could have gone in roughly where she was found. Below the Tower were only Wapping, Rotherhithe, Limehouse, the Surrey Docks, and the Isle of Dogs. Deptford and Greenwich were too far for the brief time before the change from flow to ebb. What on earth would Susannah Chancellor have been doing in any of those places?

Above were much more likely sites: London Bridge, Blackfriars, Waterloo; even Westminster was not so far. He was talking about miles. Although she was probably put in either from a bridge or from the north bank to have washed up on the north side as she was.

To have gone in where she was found, at the Tower of London, seemed impossible. What could she have been doing there? Nor could she have been in the immediate area. There was only Customs House Quay on one side and St. Catherine's Docks on the other.

The best thing would be to find out what time she left her home in Berkeley Square, and how. No one had mentioned if she took one of her own carriages; presumably they had at least one. Where had the coachman left her? Was it conceivable she had been killed by one of her own servants? He could not imagine it, but it had better be eliminated all the same.

He was already retracing his steps to Berkeley Square and it took him only another few minutes to reach number seventeen again. This time he went down to the areaway steps rather than disturb them at the front door.

It was opened by the bootboy looking white-faced and frightened.

"We ain't buyin' nuffink today," he said flatly. "Come back another time." He made as if to close the door.

"I am the police," Pitt told him quietly. "I need to come in. You know what has happened. I have to find out who did it, so I must discover all you know."

"I don't know nuffink!"

"Don't you know what time Mrs. Chancellor went out?"

"Who is it, Tommy?" a man's voice called from somewhere behind him.

"It's the rozzers, George."

The door opened wider and a servant with his right arm in a sling faced Pitt suspiciously.

Pitt handed him his card.

"You'd better come in," the man said reluctantly. "I don't know what we can tell you."

The bootboy stood aside to allow Pitt in. The scullery was full of vegetables, pots and pans, and a small maid with red eyes and her apron bunched up in one hand.

"Mr. Richards is busy," the man went on, leading Pitt through the kitchen and into the butler's pantry. "And the footmen are in the hall. The maids are all too upset to answer the door."

Pitt had assumed he was a footman, but apparently he was mistaken.

"Who are you?" he asked.

"Coachman, George Bragg."

Pitt looked at the arm. "When did you do that?"

"Last night." He smiled bitterly. "It's only a scald. It'll mend."

"Then you did not drive Mrs. Chancellor when she went out?"

"No sir. She took a hansom. Mr. Chancellor went with her to get one. She was going to be some time, and Mr. Chancellor himself was planning to go out later, in the carriage."

"They keep only one carriage?" Pitt was surprised. Carriages, horses and general harness and livery were marks of social standing. Most people kept as many and of as high a quality as they could, often running into debt to maintain them.

"Oh no sir," Bragg said hastily. "But Mrs. Chancellor hadn't been planning to go out, and so we hadn't got the big carriage harnessed up, and Mr. Chancellor was going to use the brougham himself, later. She was going only less than a mile away. I daresay she'd have walked it in daylight."

"So it was after dark when she left?"

"Oh yes sir. About half past nine, I would say. And looked like it could come on to rain. But Lily saw her go. She would tell you more exact. That is if she can pull herself together long enough. She was very fond of Mrs. Chancellor, and she's in a terrible state."

"If you can find her, please," Pitt requested.

George left Pitt alone to do as he asked, and was gone nearly a quarter of an hour before he returned with a red-faced, puffy-eyed girl of about eighteen, who was obviously extremely distressed.

"Good morning, Lily," Pitt said quietly. "Please sit down."

Lily was so unused to being asked to sit in the presence of superiors, she did not comprehend the order.

"Sit down, Lily." George pushed her with a gentle hand into the chair.

"George says you saw Mrs. Chancellor leave the house last night, Lily," Pitt began. "Is that so?"

"Yes sir." She sniffed.

"Do you know what time that was?"

"About half past nine, sir. I'm not sure exact."

"Tell me what happened."

"I were up on the landing, from turning down the beds, an' I saw the mistress going across the 'all to the front door." She gulped. "She were wearin' her blue cloak which she's so fond of. I saw her go out the front door. That's the truth. I swear it is." She started to cry again, quietly and with surprising dignity.

"And you usually turn the beds down at half past nine?"

"Yes, yes ... sir ..."

"Thank you. That's all I need to trouble you for. Oh—except, you saw Mrs. Chancellor. Did you see Mr. Chancellor as well?"

"No, sir. 'E must a' gone out already."

"I see. Thank you."

She stood up with a little assistance from George, and left the room, closing the door behind her.

"Is there anyone else you need to see, sir?" the coachman asked.

"You said Mr. Chancellor went out later?"

"Yes sir."

"But you didn't drive him?" Pitt looked at the arm in the sling.

"No, sir. I hurt my arm before he went out, in fact just before. Mr. Chancellor drove himself. He's quite good with a light vehicle. He could manage the brougham easily, and of course he'd called down before, so it was already harnessed."

"I see. Thank you. Do you know what time he came back?"

"No sir. But he's often late. Cabinet meetings and the like can go on half the night, if the government's got troubles . . . and when hasn't it?"

"Indeed. Thank you, I don't think there is anything else I need to ask here, at least for the moment. Unless you can tell me anything you think may be of use?"

"No sir. It's the most terrible thing I ever heard. I don't know what can have happened." He looked grieved and confused.

Pitt left, his mind full of doubts and ugly speculation. He walked back along Bruton Street deep in thought. Susannah had told her husband that she was going to see Christabel Thorne, but apparently that was untrue; unless she had been waylaid somewhere along Mount Street, within ten minutes of leaving home?

But why lie, unless it was something she did not wish him to know? Where could she be going, and with whom, that she felt compelled to keep it from him? Was it possible she knew who the traitor was in the Colonial Office? Or at least that she suspected? Was it even conceivable that it was she herself, stealing information from Chancellor without his knowledge? Did he take papers home with him, and she had somehow seen them? Or did he discuss such matters with her, since her family was so prominent in banking? Could she have been on the way, even then, to the German Embassy? Then who had stopped her? Who had found her between Berkeley Square and Upper Brook Street, and taken her to the riverbank and killed her? He must have been waiting for her, if that were true.

Or was it a far simpler, more ordinary explanation, one of an assignation with a lover? Christabel Thorne had doubted it, but she had not thought it impossible. Was that what lay between Susannah and Kreisler, and all the arguments about Africa were of only secondary importance, or even none at all? Was the emotion that racked her guilt?

And why had the hansom driver not come to the police? Surely he would do once the discovery of the body was broadcast throughout London when the newspapers reached the streets. That could only be a matter of hours. The early editions would have it now, and by lunchtime newsboys would be shouting it.

It was a bright day, people were smiling in the sun, women in frocks of muslin and lace, parasols spread, carriage harnesses shining, and yet he felt none of it as he walked, head down, towards Oxford Street.

Was it even imaginable that it was anything to do with the Inner Circle? She had known Sir Arthur, and apparently liked him profoundly. Could she possibly have known anything about his death? Was that the secret that troubled her, some dreadful suspicion which she had at last realized?

If so, who was it? Not Chancellor. Pitt would be prepared to swear Chancellor was not a member. What about Thorne? Susannah was a close friend of Christabel. She would feel she was betraying a relationship that was dear to her, and yet she would feel equally unable to keep her silence in the face of murder. No wonder Charlotte had said she looked tormented.

Two young women passed him, laughing, their skirts brushing his feet. They seemed a world away.

Did Christabel know anything about it? Or was she speaking the truth when she said Susannah had not been there? Perhaps she had no idea that the husband she seemed so close to was capable of murdering her friend to prevent her from exposing the Circle. How would she bear it when she was forced to know?

Was Jeremiah Thorne, in his own way, another victim of the Inner Circle, destroyed by a covenant made in ignorance, if not innocence, a man who dared not be true to himself, for fear of losing ... what? His position, his social standing, his financial credit, his life?

In Oxford Street he hailed a cab and gave the driver the address of the Bow Street station. The medical examiner might have made a preliminary report, at least, a guess as to the time of death, and apart from that, he should see Farnsworth.

He spent the journey considering what steps to take next. It would be difficult. One did not lightly investigate the wife of a cabinet minister, and one of the most popular at that. People would have their own ideas as to what had happened to her, fundamental beliefs they would not wish challenged. Emotions would be raw. He would present an easy target, someone to blame for the grief and the anger, and for the fear which would follow. If a cabinet minister's wife, in a hansom in Mayfair, could be murdered, who is safe?

By the time he alighted in Bow Street the late editions of the newspapers were on sale, and a boy was shouting in a clear, penetrating voice.

"Extra! Terrible murder! Minister's wife! Linus Chancellor's wife found dead at Tower o' London! Extra! Extra!" His voice dropped. " 'Ere, Mr. Pitt. You wanna copy? It's all 'ere!"

"No thank you," Pitt refused. "If I don't know it already, then it is a lie." And leaving the boy giggling, he walked up the steps and into the police station.

Farnsworth was already there, tight faced and less immaculate than usual. He was coming down the stairs as Pitt reached the bottom to go up.

"Ah, good," Farnsworth said immediately. "I've been waiting for you. Good God, this is awful!" He bit his lip. "Poor Chancellor. The most brilliant colonial secretary we've had in years, possibly even a future prime minister, and this had to happen to him. What have you learned?" He turned on the steps and started back up again towards Pitt's office.

Pitt followed him up, closing the door before replying.

"She left the house at half past nine yesterday evening, Chancellor with her, but he only went so far as to call her a hansom and put her in it. She said she was going to visit Christabel Thorne, in

Upper Brook Street, about fifteen minutes away at the most. But Mrs. Thorne says she never reached there, nor was she expecting her."

"Is that all?" Farnsworth said grimly. He was standing with his back to the window, but even so his expression was unmistakable, a mixture of shock and despairing anxiety.

"So far," Pitt replied. "Oh, she was wearing a blue cloak when she left home, according to the maid who saw her go, but it wasn't on her when we found her. Possibly it's still in the river. If it is washed up somewhere else, it might provide an indication as to where she went in."

Farnsworth thought for a moment. He opened his mouth to say something, then possibly realized the answer, and merely grunted. "Suppose it could have been anywhere, depending on the tide?"

"Yes, although according to the river boatmen, more often than not they surface again more or less where they went in."

Farnsworth pulled a face of distaste.

"The time of death may help with that," Pitt went on. "If it is early enough it had to be well before the tide turned."

"When did it turn?"

"About half past two."

"What a damnable thing! I suppose you have no idea as to motive? Was she robbed . . . or . . ." His face crumpled and he refused to put words to the second thought.

Pitt had not even entertained that idea. His mind had been too full of treason, and knowledge of the murder of Arthur Desmond.

"I don't know, sir," he confessed. "The medical examiner will tell us that. I haven't a report from him yet. It is a little early."

"Robbery?" Farnsworth looked hopeful.

"I don't know that either. There was a locket 'round her neck when she was found. That was how they knew who she was. I didn't ask Chancellor if she were wearing anything else of value."

Farnsworth frowned. "No, perhaps not. Poor man. He must be devastated. This is terrible, Pitt! For every reason, we must clear this up as soon as possible." He came forward from the window. "You'd better leave the Colonial Office business to Tellman. You concentrate on this. It's dreadful . . . quite dreadful. I can't remember a case so . . . so shocking since . . ." He stopped.

Pitt would have said, The autumn of 'eighty-eight, and the Whitechapel murders, but there was no point. One did not compare horrors one with another.

"Unless they are connected," he said instead.

Farnsworth's head jerked up. "What?"

"Unless Mrs. Chancellor's death and the Colonial Office treason are connected," he elaborated.

Farnsworth looked at him as if he had spoken blasphemy.

"It is not impossible," Pitt said quietly, meeting his eyes. "She may quite accidentally have discovered something, without any guilt on her part."

Farnsworth relaxed.

"Or she may very possibly be involved," Pitt added.

"I hope you have sufficient intelligence not to say that anywhere but here?" Farnsworth said slowly. "Not even hint that you have thought it?"

"Of course I have."

"I trust you to deal with this, Pitt." It was something of a question, and Farnsworth stared at him with entreaty in his face. "I don't always approve of your methods, or your judgments, but you've solved some of the worst cases in London, at one time or another. Do everything you can with this. Think of nothing else until it is finished . . . do you understand?"

"Yes, of course." He would not have done anything else regardless of what Farnsworth had said, and perhaps Farnsworth knew that.

Further discussion was preempted by a sharp knock on the door, and a constable poked his head around the moment Farnsworth answered.

"Yes?" Farnsworth said abruptly.

The constable looked embarrassed. "There's a lady to see Mr. Pitt, sir."

"Well tell her to wait!" Farnsworth snapped. "Pitt is busy."

"No, sir. I—I mean a real lady." The constable did not move. "I daren't tell 'er that, sir. You haven't seen 'er."

"For heaven's sake, man! Are you scared of a woman just because she thinks she's important?" Farnsworth barked. "Go and do as you're told!"

"But, sir, I . . ." He got no further. An imperious voice behind him interrupted his embarrassment.

"Thank you, Constable. If this is Mr. Pitt's office, I shall tell him myself that I am here." And the moment after the door swung wide and Vespasia fixed Farnsworth with a glittering eye. She looked magnificent in ecru lace and silk, and pearls worth a fortune across her bosom. "I don't believe I have your acquaintance, sir," she said coolly. "I am Lady Vespasia Cumming-Gould."

Farnsworth took a deep breath and gulped, swallowed the wrong way and relapsed into a fit of coughing.

Vespasia waited.

"Assistant Commissioner Farnsworth," Pitt said for him, hiding both his astonishment and his amusement with some difficulty.

"How do you do, Mr. Farnsworth." Vespasia swept past him into the office and sat down on the chair in front of Pitt's desk, resting her parasol, point down, on the carpet and waiting until Farnsworth should have recovered himself, or taken his leave, or preferably both.

"Have you come to see me, Aunt Vespasia?" Pitt asked her.

She looked at him coldly. "Of course I have. Why on earth else should I come to this unfortunate place? I do not frequent police stations for my amusement, Thomas."

Farnsworth was still in considerable difficulty, gasping for breath, tears running down his cheeks.

"How may I be of service?" Pitt asked Vespasia as he took his place behind his desk, Micah Drummond's very beautiful oak desk with the green leather inlay. Pitt was very proud to have inherited it.

"You may not," she replied, a slight melting in her silver eyes. "I have come in order to help you, or at least to give you further information, whether it helps or not."

Farnsworth was still unable to stop coughing. He stood with his handkerchief to his scarlet face.

"In relation to what?" Pitt enquired.

"For heaven's sake, assist that man before he chokes himself!" she ordered. "Haven't you brandy, or at least water to offer him?"

"There's a bottle of cider in the corner cupboard," Pitt suggested.

Farnsworth grimaced. Micah Drummond would have kept brandy. Pitt could not afford it, and had no taste for it anyway.

"If . . . you will . . . excuse me . . ." Farnsworth managed to get out between gasps.

"I will." Vespasia inclined her head sympathetically, and as soon as Farnsworth was gone, she looked back at Pitt. "Regarding the murder of Susannah Chancellor. Can anything else be on your mind this morning?"

"No. I had not realized you would have heard of it already."

She did not bother to reply to that. "I saw her the evening before last," she said gravely. "I did not overhear her conversation, but I observed it, and I could not help but see that it aroused the profoundest emotions."

"With whom?"

She looked at him as if she knew exactly what he feared. There was profound sorrow in her face.

"Peter Kreisler," she replied.

"Where was this?"

"At Lady Rattray's house in Eaton Square. She was holding a musical evening. There were fifty or sixty people there, no more."

"And you saw Kreisler and Mrs. Chancellor?" he prompted, a

sinking feeling of disappointment inside him. "Can you describe the encounter for me, as precisely as possible?"

A flicker of disapproval crossed her face and disappeared. "I do understand the importance of the issue, Thomas. I am not inclined to embroider it. I was some ten or twelve feet away, half listening to an extremely tedious acquaintance talking about her health. Such a tasteless thing to do. No one wishes to know the details of somebody else's ailments. I observed Mrs. Chancellor first. She was talking very earnestly to someone whose face was mostly hidden behind a very luxuriant potted palm. The wretched place was like a jungle. I was forever expecting insects to drop out of the trees down my neck. I did not envy the young women with deep décolletages!" She shrugged very slightly.

Pitt could picture it, but it was not the time to comment.

"Her face wore an expression of deep concern, almost anguish," Vespasia continued. "I could see that she was on the verge of a quarrel. I moved so as to learn who her companion was. He seemed to be pleading with her, but at the same time adamant that he would not change his own mind. The course of the argument altered, and it seemed she was the one entreating. There was an appearance of something close to desperation in her. But judging from her face, he could not be moved. After the course of some fifteen minutes or so, they parted. He looked well pleased with himself, as if he found the outcome quite acceptable. She was distraught."

"But you have no idea of the subject of this conversation?" he asked, though he already knew the answer.

"None at all, and I refuse to speculate."

"Was that the last time you saw Mrs. Chancellor?"

"Yes. And also the last time I saw Mr. Kreisler." She looked profoundly unhappy, and the depth of her sadness troubled him.

"What is it you fear?" he asked frankly. She was not someone with whom subtlety or evasion would be successful. She could read him far too well.

"I am afraid Mr. Kreisler's love for Africa, and what he sees as its good, far outweigh any other consideration with him, or any other loyalty," she replied. "It is not a quality which will leave Nobby Gunne unhurt. I have known several men during my life whose devotion to a cause would excuse in their minds any behavior towards a mere individual, in the firm belief that it is a nobler and greater ideal." She sighed and allowed her parasol to fall sideways against her skirt.

"They all had an intense vitality about them, a charm based upon the fire and bravado of their nature, and an ability to treat one, for a short time, as if all the ardor of their spirit were somehow reachable to others, to love, if you like. Invariably I found there was a coldness at the core of them, an obsession which fed upon itself and which consumed sacrifices without return. That is what I am afraid of, Thomas—not for myself, but for Nobby. She is a fine person, and I am extremely fond of her."

There was nothing to say, no argument to make that was honest.

"I hope you are mistaken." He smiled at her gently. "But thank you very much for coming to tell me." He offered his hand, but she rose, disregarding it. She walked, stiff backed, head erect, to the door, which he opened for her, and then he conducted her downstairs and out into the street, where he handed her up into her waiting carriage.

"Before she went into the water, without doubt," the medical examiner said, pushing his lower lip out and taking a deep breath. He looked up at Pitt, waiting for criticism. He was a long-faced, dour man who took the tragedies of his calling seriously. "One thing to be said for the swine that did this, though, he was quick. Hit her a couple of times, very hard."

"I don't see it!" Pitt interrupted.

"You wouldn't. Side of the head, mostly hidden by her hair. Then he throttled her so violently he broke the bone"—he touched his own neck—"and killed her almost immediately. Doubt she felt more than the first blow, and then a moment's choking before it was all over. Wasn't strangled to death."

Pitt looked at him with a sense of chill. "Very violently?"

"Very. Either he meant to kill her, or he was in such a monumental fury he didn't realize his own strength. You're looking for a very dangerous man, Pitt. Either he's completely merciless and he kills to rob, even when there's no need—he could have silenced her perfectly well without doing this to her—or else he's someone with such a hatred in him it erupts in something close to madness, if not actually into it."

"Was she . . . molested?"

"Good God, of course she was molested! What do you call that?" He jerked his head towards the body on the table, now covered with a sheet. "If you mean was she raped, don't be so damned lily-livered about it. God, I hate euphemisms! Call a crime by its ugly name, and be honest with the victim. No she wasn't."

Pitt let out a sigh of relief. He had cared about that more than he realized. He felt the knots in his shoulders easing a little and something of the pain inside him dulled.

"When did she die? Can you judge a time?" he asked.

"Not close enough to be of much use to you," the medical examiner replied with a snort. "Anything between eight and midnight, I should think. Being put into the river doesn't help. Cold, even at this time of the year. Makes a mess of rigor mortis. Makes a damned mess of everything! Actually, talking about a mess . . ." He frowned, looking across at Pitt with a puzzled expression. "Found some odd marks on her body, very slight, 'round her shoulders. Or to be more accurate, under her arms and across the back of her neck. She'd been dragged around in the water a lot. Could have been her clothes got caught up in something, pulled tight and caused it. When was she found?"

"About half past three."

"And when was the last time she was seen alive?"

"Half past nine."

"There you are then. You can work out for yourself almost as much as I can tell you. You've got a very dangerous man to look for, and good luck to you. You'll need it. Lovely woman. It's too bad." And without waiting for anything further he turned back to the body he was presently examining.

"Can you tell how long she was in the water?" Pitt asked.

"Not any closer than you can work out for yourself. I should say more than thirty minutes, less than three hours. Sorry."

"Was she killed manually?"

"What? Oh yes. He killed her with his bare hands, no ligature, just fingers around the throat. As I already said, a very powerful man, or one driven by a passion the like of which I hope never to see. I don't envy you your job, Pitt."

"Nor I yours," Pitt said sincerely.

The medical examiner laughed with a short barklike sound. "It's all over when I get them, no more pain, no more violence or hatred left, just peace and a long silence. The rest is up to God . . . if He cares."

"I care," Pitt said between his teeth. "And God has got to be better than I am."

The medical examiner laughed again, and this time there was a softer tone to it. But he said nothing.

It was a surprisingly long time from half past nine in the evening until about midnight. Not many people could account for their whereabouts for those two and a half hours, beyond possible dispute. Pitt took two men from other cases, leaving Tellman on the matter of the Colonial Office, and also diverted his own time to questioning and checking, but he found no evidence that was conclusive of anything.

Linus Chancellor said that he had gone out, driving his own carriage owing to the accident to his coachman. He had gone to deliver a package of crucial importance to Garston Aylmer, who had apparently been out when he got there. He was most annoyed about it, but had left it with Aylmer's footman, who upon being asked, confirmed that Chancellor had indeed called at a little before eleven o'clock.

Chancellor's own servants had not heard him come in, but they had been instructed not to wait up for him.

Susannah's maid had sat up for her mistress, naturally, as was her duty, so that she might assist her to undress when she returned, and hang up her clothes. She had fallen asleep in her chair about half past three, and only realized Susannah's failure to return in the morning. She refused to say anything about it, or to explain why she had not raised any alarm earlier.

It was apparent to Pitt that she had assumed her mistress had kept an assignation, and while she desperately disapproved of it, she was too loyal to betray it either. No pressure from Pitt, or the butler, would make her alter her account.

Pitt went to find Peter Kreisler and require him to account for his movements, but when he presented himself at Kreisler's rooms he was informed that Kreisler was out, and not expected home for several hours. He was obliged to wait for that answer.

Aylmer said he had been out looking at the stars. He was an enthusiastic astronomer. No one could confirm it. It was not an avocation shared by many, and could be conducted excellently alone. He had taken a small telescope on a tripod to Herne Hill, away from the city lights. He had driven himself in a gig which he kept for such purposes, and saw no one he knew. If his story were true, one would not have expected him to. There would not be many gentlemen from the Colonial or Foreign Offices wandering around Herne Hill in the small hours of the morning.

Jeremiah and Christabel Thorne had spent the evening at home. She had retired early. He had stayed up till past midnight reading official papers. The servants agreed that this was true. They also agreed that had either Mr. or Mrs. Thorne left the house by the garden door to the dining room, none of them would have been aware of it, having all retired beyond the baize door to their own quarters after dinner was cleared away. There were no fires to stoke, no visitors to show in or out, and Mr. Thorne had said he would draw the curtains himself and make sure the doors were fast.

Ian Hathaway had dined at his club and left at half past eleven. He said he had gone straight home, but since he lived alone, and he had not required his servants to wait up for him, there was no one to corroborate his word. He might as easily have left again, had he chosen to.

As a matter of course Francis Standish, Susannah's brother-in-law, was also informed of her death, and probably asked if he would tell them where he had spent the evening. He replied that he had come home early, changed his clothes, and gone out to the theater alone. No, there was no one who could corroborate that.

What had he seen?

Esther Sandraz. He could describe the play in very general terms, but that meant nothing. A newspaper review would give him that.

Naturally every effort was made to find the driver of the hansom who had picked up Susannah Chancellor in Berkeley Square. He was the only one who knew what had happened to her after that, until she had met her murderer.

The constable deputed by Pitt spent all afternoon and all evening searching for him, and failed completely. The following day Pitt withdrew Tellman from the Colonial Office matter and put him to the task. He was equally unsuccessful.

"Perhaps it wasn't a real hansom?" Tellman said sourly. "Perhaps it was our murderer, dressed up to look like a cabby?"

It was a thought which had already occurred to Pitt. "Then find out where he got the hansom from," he instructed. "If that is the case, then it cuts down the possibilities for time. We know that most of the people we have suspected so far in the Colonial Office matter can account for themselves at half past nine."

Tellman snorted. "Did you really think it was one of them?" he said with contempt. "Why? Why would any of them kill Mrs. Chancellor?"

"Why would anybody at all kill her?" Pitt countered.

"Robbery. There are two rings missing, Bailey said. He checked with her maid."

"What about the locket? Why didn't they take that?" Pitt pursued it. "And did the maid say she was wearing her rings that night?"

"What?"

"Did the maid say she was wearing her rings that evening?" Pitt repeated patiently. "Ladies have been known to lose jewelry, even valuable pieces, or to pawn them, or sell them, or give them away."

"I don't think he asked." Tellman was annoyed because he had not thought of that. "I'll send him back."

"You'd better. But keep looking for that cabdriver all the same."

The last person Pitt found was Peter Kreisler. Three times the previous day Pitt had called upon him, and on each occasion he had still been absent, and his manservant had had no idea if he would be back at all that day. On the second occasion of Pitt's calling the footman informed him that Mr. Kreisler had been deeply upset by the news of Mrs. Chancellor's death, and had left the building almost immediately, without giving any indication as to where he was bound and when he intended to return.

When Pitt went again on the afternoon after Tellman's unsuccessful search for the cabdriver, Kreisler was at home, and received Pitt immediately and with some eagerness. His face was tired, as if he had slept little, and there was an intense nervous energy about him, but his grief, whatever its depth or extent, was well in control. But then Pitt imagined Kreisler was a man who masked his emotions at any time, and was used to both triumph and tragedy.

"Come in, Superintendent," he said quickly, showing him into a surprisingly charming room with a polished wooden floor and delicate African carvings on the mantel. There were no animal skins or horns, but one very fine painting of a cheetah. He waved to one of the chairs. "Dobson, bring the Superintendent a drink. What would you like, ale, tea, something stronger?"

"Have you cider?"

"Certainly. Dobson, cider for Superintendent Pitt. I'll have some too." He waved at the chair again, and himself sat opposite, leaning forward towards Pitt, his face earnest. "Have you found anything of importance yet? I have been studying the tides of the river to see where she could have been put in. That may help to discover where she was killed, and thus of course where she went from Berkeley Square, which I believe she left in the mid-evening, alone." His hands were clenched in front of him. "At least, alone as soon as Chancellor had called a cab for her and seen her into it. If she was bound for Upper Brook Street, she must have been waylaid almost immediately. Do you think it was meant to be an abduction, and somehow it went wrong?"

It was actually a thought which had not occurred to Pitt, and there was a glimmer of sense in it.

"For ransom?" he asked, aware that the surprise was in his voice.

"Why not?" Kreisler pointed out. "It seems to me to make more sense than to murder her, poor woman. Chancellor has both wealth and a great deal of power. So has her brother-in-law, Standish. Possibly it was intended to try to coerce him in some way. Which is an extremely ugly thought, but not an impossible one."

"No ... indeed," Pitt agreed reluctantly. "Although it must have gone very badly wrong to end like this. She was certainly not killed by accident."

"Why?" Kreisler looked at him intently, his face tight with emotion. "Why do you say that, Superintendent?"

"The manner of her death made that apparent," Pitt replied. He did not intend to discuss it further with Kreisler, who was in many ways a principal suspect.

"Are you sure?" Kreisler pressed. "Whose good could her death serve? Surely it would . . ." His voice trailed off.

"If I knew whose good it served, Mr. Kreisler, I should be a great deal further towards finding her murderer," Pitt answered. "You seem very profoundly concerned in the matter. Did you know her better than I had supposed?" He watched Kreisler closely, the pallor of his skin, the brilliance of his eyes, the tiny muscles flickering in his jaw.

"I have met her several times, and found her charming and intelligent, and a woman of great sensitivity and honor," he replied with a tensely loud voice. "Is that not more than enough reason to be horrified at her death and to wish passionately that her murderer should be found?"

"Of course it is," Pitt said very quietly. "But most people, however profound their feelings, are content to leave it to the police to bring that about."

"Well I am not," Kreisler stated fiercely. "I will do everything in my power to learn who it is, and make damned sure the world knows it too. And frankly, Superintendent, I don't care whether that pleases you or not."

CHAPTER
NINE

Pitt arrived home late after a day which was exhausting both physically and emotionally. He was looking forward to putting the whole matter out of his mind for a space, and sitting in the parlor with his feet up and the doors to the garden open to let in the late spring evening air. It was fine and balmy, the sort of day when the smells of the earth linger heavily and overtake the awareness of a mighty city beyond the garden walls. One could think only of flowers, cut lawns, shady trees and moths drifting lazily in the stillness.

However as soon as he entered the hallway he knew that was not to be. Charlotte came out of the parlor, her face grave, a warning in her eyes.

"What is it?" he said with apprehension.

"Matthew is here to see you," she replied softly, aware of the open door behind her. "He looks very worried, but he wouldn't tell me anything about it."

"You asked him?"

"No, of course I didn't. But I made . . . listening noises."

He smiled in spite of himself, touched her gently as he passed, and went into the parlor.

Matthew was sitting in Pitt's favorite chair, staring out of the open French windows across the lawn towards the apple tree. As soon as he felt Pitt's presence in the room, even though there had been no sound, he turned around and stood up. His face was pale and there were still shadows around his eyes. He looked as if he had suffered a long illness and was only barely well enough to be out of his bed.

"What's happened?" Pitt demanded, closing the door behind him.

Matthew seemed startled, as though the directness of the question had been unexpected.

"Nothing, at least nothing new. I . . . I wondered if you had been able to learn anything more about Father's death." He opened his eyes wide and stared at Pitt questioningly.

Pitt felt guilty, even though he had every reason for having been unable to even think of the matter.

"No, I . . . I am afraid not. The assistant commissioner has given me the murder of Susannah Chancellor, and it has driven—"

"I understand. Of course I do," Matthew interrupted. "You don't need to explain it to me, Thomas. I am not a child." He walked towards the French doors as if he meant to go outside into the evening air. "I just . . . wondered."

"Is that what you came for?" Pitt asked doubtfully. He joined Matthew in the doorway.

"Of course." Matthew stepped across the threshold and out onto the paved terrace.

Pitt followed, and together they walked very slowly over the grass towards the apple tree and the shaded section of the wall. There was deep green moss on the stones, rich as velvet, and low down near the ground a creeping plant with yellow starlike flowers.

"What else has happened?" Pitt repeated. "You look dreadful."

"I had a crack on the head." Matthew pulled a face and winced. "You were there."

"Is it worse? Have you had the doctor back?"

"No, no it's getting better. It's just slow. This is a fearful business about Chancellor's wife." He frowned and took another step across the soft grass. It was thick within the shade of the tree and spongy under the feet. The white drift of the apple blossom was faintly sweet in the air, a clean, uncloying smell. "Have you any idea what happened?"

"Not yet. Why? Do you know anything?"

"Me?" This time Matthew looked genuinely surprised. "Nothing at all. I just think it's a dreadful stroke of fate for a man so brilliant, and whose personal life was so unusually happy. There are many politicians who could have lost their wives and been little the worse for it at heart, but not Chancellor."

Pitt stared at him. The remark was curiously uncharacteristic, as if only half his mind were on his words. Pitt was becoming more and more certain that there was in fact something troubling him.

"Did you know Chancellor well?" he asked aloud.

"Moderately," Matthew replied, continuing to walk, and not looking at Pitt. "He's one of the most accessible men of high rank. Agreeable to talk to. He comes from a fairly ordinary family. Welsh, I believe, at least originally. They may have been in the Home Counties a while now. It wasn't political, was it?" He turned to Pitt, curiosity and puzzlement in his face. "I mean, it couldn't be, surely?"

"I don't know," Pitt replied candidly. "At the moment I have no idea at all."

"None?"

"What did you have in mind when you asked?"

"Don't play games with me, Thomas," Matthew said irritably. "I'm not one of your damned suspects!" Then a moment later he was struck with contrition. "I'm sorry. I don't know what I meant. I'm still plagued by Father's death. Part of my mind is convinced he was murdered, and by the Inner Circle, both to keep him from saying anything more about them and as a warning to other would-be traitors to the oaths. Loyalty's a hell of a thing, Thomas. How much loyalty can you demand of anyone? I'm not even sure I know what loyalty is. If you had asked me a year ago, or six months ago,

I would have been quite convinced it was a stupid question, not even worth asking because the answer was so obvious. Now I can't answer it." He stood still on the grass, his face full of confusion, his eyes searching Pitt's. "Can you?"

Pitt thought for a long time before he replied, and even then it was tentative.

"I suppose it is honoring your promises," he said slowly. "But then it is also honoring your obligations, even if there have been no specific promises made."

"Exactly," Matthew agreed. "But who sets out what those obligations are, or to whom? Whose is the first claim? What when people assume you have some obligation to them, and you don't assume it? They can, you know."

"Sir Arthur and the Inner Circle?"

Matthew lifted his shoulders in a gesture of vague assent. "Anyone. Sometimes we take for granted things, and imagine that other people do too ... and perhaps they don't. I mean ... how well do we know each other, how well do we even know ourselves, until we are tested? You imagine you will behave in a certain way if you are faced with a choice, but when the time comes, you find you don't."

Pitt was even surer that Matthew had something specific in mind. There was too much passion in his voice for it to be mere philosophizing. But equally obviously, he was not yet ready to speak of it openly. Pitt did not even know if it was actually to do with Sir Arthur, or if he had merely mentioned that as something they had in common from which to begin.

"You mean a division of loyalties?"

Matthew moved a step away. Pitt knew he had touched a nerve, and it was too soon.

Matthew waited a moment before he replied. The garden was silent. Somewhere beyond the hedges a dog barked. A tortoiseshell cat walked along the wall and dropped soundlessly into the orchard.

"Some of those men at the inquest genuinely felt as if he had betrayed a trust," Matthew said at last. "A loyalty to their secret society, perhaps in a way to their class. Somebody in the Colonial Office is betraying their country, but perhaps they don't see it like that." He took a deep breath, his eyes on the wind in the apple leaves. "Father felt that to keep silent about the Inner Circle was to betray all that he felt most important in life, although he might never have thought to give it a name. I'm not sure I like giving things names. Does that sound like evasion? Once you give things a name and promise allegiance, you've given part of yourself away. I'm not prepared to do that." He looked at Pitt with a frown. "Can you understand that, Thomas?"

"Most things don't ask for an unlimited allegiance," Pitt pointed out. "That is what is wrong with the Inner Circle; it asks men to promise loyalty in advance of knowing what will be asked of them."

"A sacrifice of conscience, Father called it."

"Then you have answered your own question," Pitt pointed out. "You didn't need to ask me, and you shouldn't care what my answer would have been."

Matthew flashed him a sudden, brilliant smile. "I don't," he confessed, putting his hands into his pockets.

"Then what still troubles you?" Pitt asked, because the shadow and the tension were still in Matthew, and the smile faded as quickly as it had come.

Matthew sighed, turning away from the orchard wall and beginning to walk slowly along it. "Yes, you and I can say that comfortably because we have no issue between us that we see differently. But how would you feel if my course led me to do something which you felt betrayed you? Wouldn't you hate me for it?"

"Are you talking about all this in theory, Matthew, or is there something specific you are trying to find the courage to say?" Pitt fell in step beside him.

Matthew looked away, facing back towards the house. "I don't even know of anything about which I believe all that differently from you. I was thinking of Father, and his friends in the Inner Circle." He glanced sideways for a moment at Pitt. "Some of them were his friends, you know? That is what he found so terribly difficult."

Nothing that Matthew said was untrue, but Pitt still had the feeling that in some way Matthew was lying. They walked up the lawn towards the house together but they did not touch on the subject again. Charlotte invited Matthew to stay and dine with them, but he declined, and took his leave, his face still shadowed with anxiety, and Pitt watched him go with a sadness he could not rid himself of all evening.

Charlotte looked at Pitt enquiringly when they were done. "Is he all right? He looked ..." She searched for a word.

"Troubled," Pitt supplied it for her, sitting down in his chair and leaning back, stretching a little. "Yes, I am almost sure there is something else, but he cannot bring himself to say it."

"What sort of thing?" She looked at him anxiously. He was not sure whether she was concerned for Matthew or for both of them. He could see in her eyes the knowledge of his own regret mixed so heavily with his loss.

He turned his gaze away. "I don't know, something to do with loyalties. . . ."

She drew in her breath sharply, as if to speak, then changed her mind tactfully. He almost laughed, it was so unlike her, but it would too easily have broken into misery.

"I suppose it is to do with the Circle," he said, although he was not at all sure that was what had gnawed at Matthew so painfully. But either way, this evening he preferred not to think of it any further. "What is for dinner?"

"That's not much," Farnsworth said grimly when Pitt reported to him next. "The wretched man cannot have disappeared from the face of the earth." He was referring to the driver of the hansom cab which had picked up Susannah Chancellor in Berkeley Square. "Who did you say you had on it?"

They were in his own office rather than Pitt's room in Bow Street, and he stood by the window looking towards the Embankment of the river. Pitt sat in the chair opposite. Farnsworth had invited him to sit when he had first come in, and then a moment later had risen himself. It gave him a physical advantage he seemed to prefer.

"Tellman," Pitt replied, sitting back a little farther. He did not in the least mind looking up. "And I tried myself. I know the man may be crucial, but so far we have found no trace of him, which leads me to—"

"If you are going to say Chancellor was lying, then you are a fool," Farnsworth said irritably. "You surely cannot be so out of touch with reality as to imagine Chancellor would—"

"The whole question is irrelevant," Pitt interrupted in his turn. "Chancellor went straight back to his house and was seen within ten minutes of having put her in the hansom. I already know that from his own household staff. Not that I suspected him anyway. It is merely a matter of form to ascertain where everyone was at the relevant time."

Farnsworth did not reply to that.

"Which leads me to suppose," Pitt finished the sentence Farnsworth had broken into, "that the driver was in some way implicated. Possibly he was not a regular cabby at all, but someone dressed as one."

"Then where did he get the hansom from?" Farnsworth demanded. "Chancellor said it was a hansom. He would know the difference between a cab and a private carriage."

"I've got Tellman looking into that now. So far we don't know, but it must have come from somewhere, either hired or stolen. He's going around to all the companies."

"Good. Good. That could be the break we are needing."

"Kreisler thought it might have been an attempt at kidnapping that went wrong," Pitt suggested.

Farnsworth was startled and a flicker of irritation crossed his face.

"What? Who the devil is Kreisler?"

"Peter Kreisler. Something of an expert on African affairs." Pitt spoke thoughtfully. "He seems to be very concerned about the case. In fact he has spent a lot of time pursuing it himself."

"Why?" Farnsworth demanded, coming back to his desk and sitting opposite Pitt. "Did he know her?"

"Yes."

"Then he's a suspect, dammit!" His fist clenched. "I assume you are investigating him very thoroughly indeed?"

"Yes, of course I am." Pitt's voice rose in spite of his efforts to keep it level. "He says he was at home that evening, but he cannot prove it. His man had the evening off."

Farnsworth relaxed. "Well that may be all there is to it! It may be as simple as that, no abduction, nothing political, simply a jealous man, infatuated and rejected." There was considerable satisfaction in his voice. It would be an ideal solution.

"Possibly," Pitt agreed. "Lady Vespasia Cumming-Gould saw them in a heated discussion the previous night. But that is a long way from proving that Kreisler is violent and unstable enough to have murdered her simply because she refused him."

"Well find out, man!" Farnsworth said sharply. "Look into his past. Write to Africa, if you have to. He must have been attracted to other women at some time or another. See how he behaved then. Learn everything about him, his loves, hates, quarrels, debts, ambitions, everything there is to know about him! I am not going to allow the murder of a cabinet minister's wife to remain an unsolved case . . . and neither are you!"

It sounded like a dismissal. Pitt rose to his feet.

"And the Colonial Office," Farnsworth went on. "How are you progressing with that? Lord Salisbury asked me only yesterday if we had learned anything of use." His face tightened. "I did not inform him of your machinations to pass various different versions of false figures. God knows what he would have said if I had. I assume you have achieved nothing with that ploy or you would have told me?"

"It is too early yet," Pitt replied. "And the Colonial Office is in something of an upheaval with Chancellor himself not present."

"When do you expect that little piece of deception to bear fruit?" Farnsworth asked, not without sarcasm.

"In the next three or four days at the outside," Pitt replied.

Farnsworth frowned. "Well, I hope you are right. Personally I think you are a little too sanguine about it altogether. What do you propose to do next, if it fails?"

Pitt had not thought that far. His mind was taken up with Susannah Chancellor, and always at the back of his thoughts, intruding at every opportunity, was the death of Arthur Desmond—and, since he had seen Dr. Murray, the near certainty that he had been murdered by the Inner Circle. He still intended to prove that, as soon as the urgency of the Chancellor case allowed.

"I have no further ideas," he admitted. "Beyond continuing with usual police routine, to learn all I can of every possible suspect, in the hope that some fact, or lie, will prove who is guilty, both in the Colonial Office and in the Treasury. A connection that is not openly acknowledged would be indicative."

"Not very satisfactory, Pitt. What about this woman Pennecuick?" He stood up again and walked restlessly over towards the window. "It still looks to me as if Aylmer is your man."

"Possibly."

Farnsworth put his hands into his pockets and looked thoughtful. "You told me Aylmer could not account for his time that evening. Is it possible Mrs. Chancellor had in some fashion discovered his guilt, and that he was aware of this, and that he murdered her to protect himself? And had he, for example, any connection with Kreisler?"

"I don't know. . . ." Pitt began.

"Then find out, man! That shouldn't be beyond your wit to do." He looked at Pitt coldly, regret in his eyes.

Pitt was sure he was thinking of the Inner Circle, and how much easier such investigations might be with the help of a wide-spread, covert network to call on. But who would know, with all the interlocking covenants and obligations, the hierarchy of loyalties, who was bound to whom, what lies or silences were promised? Even which officers in the police might be involved, a thought which was peculiarly frightening. He met Farnsworth's stare with bland denial.

Farnsworth grunted and looked away.

"Then you had better be about it," he said, then turned to the river again, and the bright light on the water.

"There is another possibility," Pitt said quietly.

Farnsworth did not look around, but kept his back to the room and to Pitt.

"Yes?"

"That she did in fact visit the Thorne house," Pitt replied. "We are still looking for her cloak. She was wearing it when she left, but it was not with her body. If we find it, it may tell us something."

"Depending on where, I suppose," Farnsworth conceded. "Go on. What if she did visit the Thorne house?"

Farnsworth's shoulders tightened.

"Then either Thorne murdered her," Pitt answered, "or he and his wife did together, although I find that harder to believe. I think Mrs. Thorne was genuinely grieved and shocked when I told her."

"Why on earth would Thorne kill Mrs. Chancellor? You're not suggesting an affair, are you?" This time there was mockery in Farnsworth's voice.

"No." Pitt did not bother to add how unlikely he thought it.

Farnsworth turned to look at him. "Then what?" His eyes widened. "The Colonial Office treason? Thorne?"

"Possibly. But there is another solution, which may not be unconnected. . . ."

"What do you mean, not unconnected?" Farnsworth frowned. "Explain yourself, Pitt. You are talking in circles. Do you mean it is connected, or don't you?"

Pitt gritted his teeth. "I think the death of Arthur Desmond may have been connected with his beliefs—"

He got no further. Farnsworth's face darkened and his eyes narrowed. "I thought we had already dismissed that, and put it to rest. Arthur Desmond was a good man who unfortunately, tragically if you like, became senile towards the end of his life and suffered from serious delusions. The kindest thing one can assume is that he accidentally took an overdose of his sleeping draft."

His lips tightened. "Less kindly, one might conclude that he knew he was losing his mind and had already seriously compromised his reputation and slandered many of his erstwhile friends, and in a moment of lucid realization of just what was happening to him, took his own life."

He swallowed. "Perhaps I should not say that is an unkind solution. On second thoughts it was a highly honorable thing to do, and most like him." His eyes met Pitt's for a moment. "Yes, I'm sure that is the man you knew also. It required a considerable courage. If you have the regard for him that you profess, you will leave it at that and let him rest in peace. By keeping on raking up the matter you are prolonging the pain for his family and seriously misadvising them. I cannot warn you more gravely that you are making a profound mistake. Do I make myself clear?"

"Perfectly," Pitt agreed, staring back at him, sensing the power of his resolve, and driven to ignore it. "But none of that is relevant to what Mrs. Chancellor may have thought, which is what we are concerned with."

"You didn't discuss this farrago of nonsense with Mrs. Chancellor, for God's sake!" Farnsworth was aghast. He was still standing with his back to the window, his face in his own shadow from the sunlight, throwing its lines and planes into sharp relief.

"No I didn't," Pitt replied steadily. "But I am aware that Mrs.

Chancellor knew Sir Arthur and thought very highly of him, and that he discussed his beliefs about Africa with her. Lady Vespasia Cumming-Gould told me so."

Farnsworth pulled a face at the mention of Vespasia's name again. He was beginning to dislike her intensely.

"And how did she know that, pray? I suppose she is acquainted with Mrs. Chancellor? She is something of a busybody, and I think not to be taken seriously." The moment he had said that he regretted it. It was a mistake, and he not only saw it in Pitt's face, but his own social background was sufficient to have heard her name before, and to have recognized a true aristocrat when he met one. His temper had spoken before his intellect.

Pitt merely smiled, which was patronizing. Losing his own temper would have placed him in an equal position; this was superior.

"Well?" Farnsworth snapped. "Are you suggesting on the strength of that, that Mrs. Chancellor believed Mr. Thorne murdered Desmond, and that in fact he did, and felt compelled to murder her to keep her silent about it? Wouldn't simply denying it have been just as effective, and a great deal less trouble?" His voice was dripping sarcasm.

Put as baldly as that, it did sound absurd. Pitt felt the color rush up his face, and saw the satisfaction in Farnsworth's eyes. Farnsworth's shoulders relaxed and he turned back towards the window.

"You are losing your grip, Pitt. That was unworthy of you."

"That was your suggestion, not mine," Pitt denied it. "What I am suggesting is that possibly Sir Arthur knew something about the missing information from the Colonial Office. After all, he often went in to the Foreign Office, and still had close connections there at the time of his death. He may not have realized the full importance of what he knew, but if he mentioned it to Susannah Chancellor, and she did understand it, because of Standish, and her family background in African finance, and Chancellor's knowledge in the Colonial Office, and her friendship with Mrs. Thorne, then . . ."

"She put it all together and tackled Thorne with it?" Farnsworth was staring at him with growing interest. "And if Thorne is the traitor after all . . . yes, yes, you have a possibility!" His voice lifted a little. "Look into that, Pitt, but very carefully. For heaven's sake remain discreet, both not to offend Thorne if he is innocent, and possibly more important, not to warn him if he is guilty."

He made an effort of will. "I apologize to you, Pitt. I should not have leapt to such a hasty conclusion as to what you were saying. This does indeed make sense. You'd better get to it straightaway. Go and see the servants at the Thorne household. And keep on looking for that cabdriver. If he delivered her there, then he has nothing to fear, and will be a witness at Thorne's undoing."

"Yes, sir." And Pitt rose from the chair to obey. It was what he had been intending to do anyway.

But the servants in the Thorne household could tell him nothing of use. He questioned them each, but no one had seen or heard Susannah Chancellor on the evening of her death. He pressed them as to the possibility of her having called without their knowledge. But it required a stretch of the imagination beyond reason to suppose that she had, unless she had specifically been asked to alight short of the house and not to present herself at the front door; instead to walk around the side, through the garden to the doorway to the back, and then make her way across the lawn to the French doors of the study and let herself in that way. Or possibly someone had been waiting for her.

Of course that was perfectly possible, but why should she do such a thing? If anyone had asked her to come secretly, without any of the servants seeing her, what explanation could they give for such an extraordinary request? Had it been Thorne, or Christabel, or both?

If indeed they had anything to do with it, it seemed far more likely one of them had gone out and met her in the street and taken her to wherever she had been killed, then left and returned to the house through the side entrance.

But looking at Christabel Thorne's clear, wide eyes, full of intelligence, anger and grief, he could not imagine that she had taken part in anything so duplicitous.

But then again, if she loved her husband, perhaps he had persuaded her it was necessary, either for some higher good politically or morally, or simply to save him from discovery and disgrace.

"I really am sorry to be of so little assistance, Superintendent," she said earnestly. They were in the study, where the doors led into the garden and he could see the flowering shrubs beyond her from where he sat. "Believe me," she continued, "I have racked my brains to think of anything that could possibly be relevant. Mr. Kreisler was here, you know, and asked me all the same questions you are doing, and I could offer him nothing."

"Kreisler was here?" he said quickly.

Her eyes widened.

"You didn't know? He seems most concerned to learn the truth. I confess, I had not realized he cared so much for Susannah." Her expression was difficult to read; there was confusion, surprise, sadness, even a faint shred of wry, hurt amusement.

Pitt had other thoughts on the subject. He was beginning to wonder which motives lay behind Kreisler's enquiries. Was it a passion to avenge Susannah, either through assisting the police or privately? Or was it in order to learn how much they knew, so he might guard either himself or someone else? Or was it to lay false information, to mislead and even further confuse the search? The more he knew of Kreisler, the less certain he was about him.

"No," he said aloud. "I think there is a lot yet to be learned on that matter."

She looked at him with a sudden quickening of interest. "Do you suspect him, Superintendent?"

"Of course, Mrs. Thorne."

There was a flash of humor across her face, this time undisguised. "Oh no," she replied. "I am not going to give words to any speculation. You must imagine what you will. I enjoy trivial gossip, but I abhor it when it touches on things that matter."

"And Mr. Kreisler matters?"

Her high eyebrows arched. "Not in the slightest, Superintendent. But accusations of complicity in murder matter very much." Her face darkened. "And Susannah mattered, to me. I liked her profoundly. Friendship matters, almost as much as honor."

She had spoken with intense seriousness, and he answered her in equal vein.

"And when the two conflict, Mrs. Thorne?"

"Then you have one of life's tragedies," she replied without hesitation. "But fortunately I am not placed in that situation. I know nothing about Susannah to her dishonor. Or about Linus either, for that matter. He is a man of deep conviction, and he always openly and honestly proclaimed both his intent and the means by which he would bring it to pass.

"And believe me, Superintendent, he has never entertained the slightest improper intentions towards another woman." It was a simple and rather obvious statement, one any friend might make in the circumstances, and frequently did. Normally it sounded trite, it was merely an exercise in loyalty, but looking at Christabel's face with its fierce intelligence and almost disdainful pride, he was unable to dismiss it so lightly. There was no sentimentality in her; it was not an emotional response, but one born of observation and belief.

They were both oblivious of the quiet room or the sunlit garden beyond, even of the wind moving the leaves to cast the occasional shadows on the glass.

"And Mr. Kreisler?" he asked.

"I have no idea. A contentious man," she said after a moment's consideration. "I had thought him attracted to Miss Gunne, which would be most understandable. But certainly he pursued Susannah as well, and even with his undoubted arrogance, I doubt he can have deluded himself he could achieve anything of a romantic nature with her."

Pitt was less certain. No matter how much Susannah might still be in love with her husband, people were capable of all sorts of strange acts where passion, loneliness, and physical need were concerned. And Susannah had certainly gone somewhere she preferred not to tell anyone about.

"Then what?" he asked, watching her expression as she sought for an answer.

The veil came down over her thoughts again. Her eyes were bright and direct, but no longer revealing anything unguarded of herself.

"That is your profession to find out, Superintendent. I know nothing that would help you, or I should already have told it to you."

And Pitt learned nothing further from Thorne himself when he visited him at the Colonial Office. Garston Aylmer was more forthcoming.

"Absolutely frightful," he said with deep emotion when Pitt said that he was now here in connection with Susannah's murder. "Quite the most personally shocking thing I have ever heard." And indeed he looked very shaken. Seeing his pale face, slightly sunken eyes and yet the steadiness of his gaze when he met Pitt's, it would be difficult to imagine it was assumed, or indeed that it had anything to do with guilt.

"I knew her quite well, naturally," Aylmer went on, his short thick fingers playing absently with a pencil on the desk in front of him. "One of the most charming of women, and with an unusual integrity." He looked up gravely, the pencil frozen in mid-motion. "There was an inner honesty in her which was both very beautiful and at times quite disconcerting. I really am profoundly sorry she is gone, Superintendent."

Pitt believed him entirely, and felt naive even while he did so.

"What do you know of the relationship between her and Mrs. Thorne?" Pitt asked.

Aylmer smiled. "Ah—Christabel. A very rare type of lady ... thank goodness! A couple of dozen of her, and London would be revolutionized and reformed to within an inch of its life." He shrugged his heavy shoulders. "No, Superintendent, that is unfair. Christabel is charming at times, and always interesting. But women with quite such a driving force for good terrify me. It is a little like finding oneself accidentally in the path of a tornado."

"Tornados are destructive forces," Pitt pointed out, looking clearly at Aylmer to see if he intended the analogy.

"Only to one's peace of mind." Aylmer smiled ruefully. "At least as far as Christabel is concerned. She has a passion for educating women which is most disturbing. It genuinely frightens a great many people. And if you know her at all, you will know she does nothing in half measures."

"What is it she wishes to reform?"

Aylmer spread his hands in a gesture of abandonment. "Just about everything. Attitudes, beliefs, the entire role of women in the world, which of course means of men as well." He smiled. "Specifically? Improve radically the role of the odd women ..."

"The odd women?" Pitt was totally confused. "What odd women?"

Aylmer's smile grew broader. "All odd women. My dear fellow, odd women are all women who are not 'even,' that is to say, married. The women, of whom there are a large and ever-increasing number who have no man to provide for them financially, make them socially respectable and give them something to do, namely to care for him and whatever children there may be."

"What on earth does she propose to do about it?"

"Why, educate them! Have them join the professions, the arts, the sciences, anything they wish. The odd women, if that is where their abilities or their desires lead them. If Christabel succeeds, next time you call your dentist, your plumber, your banker or your architect, you may find it is a woman. Heaven help us when it is your doctor or your priest!"

Pitt was dumbfounded.

"Precisely," Aylmer agreed. "Apart from women's complete unsuitability both emotionally and intellectually—not to mention physically—for such tasks, that will throw thousands of men out of work. I told you, she is a revolutionary."

"And ... people allow it?" Pitt was amazed.

"No of course they don't. But have you ever tried to stop a truly determined woman? Any woman, never mind Christabel Thorne?"

Pitt thought of trying to stop Vespasia, and knew precisely what Aylmer meant.

"I see," he said aloud.

"I doubt it." Aylmer shook his head. "To see the full enormity of it, you would have to know Christabel. Incredible courage, you know. Doesn't give a damn about the scandal."

"Was Mrs. Chancellor also involved?" Pitt asked.

"Good gracious, what an appalling thought! I have no idea. I don't think so. No ... Susannah's interests were all to do with her family, banking, investment, finances and so on. If she had any radical ideas, it was about that sort of thing. But she was far more conventional, thank God." His brow darkened suddenly. "That is what she quarreled with Kreisler about, so far as I can recall. Curious man. He was here, you know, asking me questions about her. In fact, Superintendent, he was rather more pressing than you are!"

Pitt sat a little farther upright. "About Mrs. Chancellor's death?"

"Yes. Yes, he seemed most concerned. I couldn't tell him anything I haven't told you ... which is almost nothing at all. He also wanted to know about both Mr. and Mrs. Thorne." He laughed a little self-consciously. "And about me. I am not sure if he suspected

I might have some involvement, or if he was simply desperate enough to pursue anything at all."

Pitt was wondering the same thing, both about Aylmer and about Kreisler. This information that he had been to see Aylmer was most disquieting.

He was further disturbed when he saw Ian Hathaway, ostensibly to ask if there had been any progress with the falsified figures, but also to see if he could learn anything more about either Mr. or Mrs. Thorne and their possible connection with Susannah or with Arthur Desmond.

Hathaway looked puzzled. He sat in his quiet, discreet office with its slightly faded good taste and solidity.

"No, Superintendent. That is what is so very curious, and, I admit, beyond me to understand. I would have called you this afternoon had you not come here to see me. We do have information from the German Embassy. . . ."

Pitt drew in his breath involuntarily, his heart beating a little faster, in spite of his effort to remain perfectly composed.

Hathaway saw it and smiled, his small, clear blue eyes steady.

"The message includes figures quite specifically, and this is what is incomprehensible. They are not any of those which I distributed, nor are they the genuine figures which I retained and passed to Lord Salisbury."

"What?" Pitt could scarcely believe what he had heard. It made no sense whatever. "I beg your pardon?"

"Precisely," Hathaway agreed. "I can see no sense in it at all. That is why I delayed contacting you." He sat motionless. Even his hands on the desk were quite still. "I made doubly sure that I had received the message correctly. It was my first thought that somehow figures had been transposed or misunderstood; but it was not so. The message was clear and correct, the figures are quite different, and indeed if acted upon, seriously misleading. I have no desire whatever to disabuse the German Embassy of its error. I am also, at this stage, at a loss to understand what has happened. I did take the liberty of informing Lord Salisbury of the matter, to be sure he had the correct figures himself. I need hardly say that he has."

Pitt sat in silence, digesting what Hathaway had told him and trying to think of some explanation. None came to his mind.

"We have failed, Superintendent, and I confess to total confusion," Hathaway said ruefully, leaning back in his chair again and regarding Pitt steadily. "I am perfectly prepared to try again, if you think there is any purpose to it?"

Pitt was more disappointed than he cared to admit. He had been counting on this producing some result, however small or difficult to follow. He had no idea where to turn next, and he dreaded confessing to Farnsworth that what had seemed such an excellent plan had failed so completely. He could already imagine his response, and the contempt with which it would be delivered.

"About the death of Mrs. Chancellor," Hathaway said quietly. "I fear I can be of little help there either. I wish I knew something of service to you. It seems such a pointless tragedy." He looked totally sincere, a decent man expressing a profoundly felt regret for grief, and yet Pitt also sensed in him a reasoning in his brain that superseded emotion. Was he distinguishing between pointless tragedies and those which were necessary, and had meaning?

"Did she ever mention Sir Arthur Desmond to you, Mr. Hathaway?" Pitt asked.

Not a flicker crossed Hathaway's face.

"Sir Arthur Desmond?" he repeated.

"Yes. He used to be at the Foreign Office. He died recently at his club."

"Yes, yes I know who you mean." He relaxed so slightly it was barely noticeable, a mere shift of the muscles in his shoulders. "Most unfortunate. I suppose such things tend to happen from time to time, when a club's membership is on the elderly side. No, I cannot recall her having mentioned him. Why? Surely he can have nothing whatever to do with this latest business? His death was a very ordinary sort of misfortune. I was at the club that afternoon myself, in the writing room with a business colleague."

He let out his breath in a very gentle sigh. "As I understood it from the newspapers, Mrs. Chancellor was attacked very violently, presumably while in her hansom cab, and then put in the river afterwards. Is that so?"

"Yes, that is correct," Pitt conceded. "It is simply that Sir Arthur was vehemently against the development of Central Africa as planned by Mr. Rhodes, and so is Mr. Kreisler, who ..." He stopped. Hathaway's face had changed noticeably.

"Kreisler?" Hathaway said slowly, watching Pitt very closely. "He came to see me, you know? Also regarding Mrs. Chancellor's death, although that was not the reason he gave. He concocted some story about mineral rights and leases and so on, but it was Mrs. Chancellor and her opinions which seemed to concern him. A most unusual man. A man of powerful passions and convictions."

He had a curious habit of stillness which conveyed an intense concentration. "I assume you have naturally considered him as a possible suspect, Superintendent? I don't mean to tell you your business, but anyone who asks as many questions as to detail as does Mr. Kreisler has a far more than passing interest in the outcome."

"Yes, Mr. Hathaway, I have considered him," Pitt replied with feeling. "And by no means discounted the possibility that they quarreled, either about Africa and Mr. Chancellor's backing of Mr. Rhodes, or about something else, possibly more personal, and that that quarrel became a great deal more savage than either of them intended. I imagine Mr. Kreisler is well able both to attack and to defend himself as the situation may require. It is possible he may do either instinctively when aroused to uncontrolled rage, and far too late to realize he has committed murder."

Hathaway's face pinched with distress and distaste.

"What a very grave and uncivilized way to behave. Temper of

such violence and complete lack of control is scarcely a characteristic of a human being, let alone a man of honor or intellect. What a dismal waste. I hope that you are not correct in your assumption, Superintendent. Kreisler has real possibilities for better ends than that."

They spoke a little further, but ten minutes later Pitt rose to leave, having learned nothing about Susannah Chancellor, and in a state of confusion about the information from the German Embassy.

"And what has that to do with anything at all?"

Charlotte was paying a duty call upon her grandmother, who, now that Charlotte's mother was recently remarried (a fact which Grandmama disapproved of with almost apoplectic fury), was obliged to live with Charlotte's sister and her husband. Emily and Jack found this arrangement displeasing; the old lady was of an exceedingly difficult temperament. But she could no longer remain at Cater Street with Caroline and Joshua—in fact she had refused point-blank to do so, not that the opportunity had been offered. And there was certainly no room in Charlotte's house, although in fact she had refused to consider that either. She would not dream of living in the house of a person of the police, even if he was recently promoted and now on the verge of respectability. That, when all was said and done, was only marginally better than being on the stage! Never in all the history of the Ellison family had anyone married an actor until Caroline had lost her wits and done so. But then of course she was an Ellison only by marriage. What poor Edward, Charlotte's father, would have said could only be guessed at. It was a mercy he was in his grave.

Charlotte had pointed out that were he not, the question of Caroline's remarrying anyone would not have arisen. She was told curtly not to be impertinent.

Now since Emily and Jack were on holiday in Italy, and Grandmama was thus alone, apart from the servants, Charlotte felt duty-bound to call upon her at least once a fortnight. She had kept a treat for herself after honor was satisfied. She was going out with Harriet Soames to visit the flower show.

Grandmama was keen to hear all the gossip Charlotte could think of. In fact, with Caroline living in Cater Street and seldom calling (being newly married and much occupied with her husband), and Emily and Jack abroad, she was starved for something to talk about.

Charlotte had idly mentioned Amanda Pennicuick and Garston Aylmer's pursuit of her, and that Mr. Aylmer was unusually homely.

"It has quite a lot to do with many things, if one is to consider marrying him," Charlotte replied candidly. They were sitting in Emily's large, airy, rather ornate withdrawing room. There were portraits of past Ashworths on all the walls and an Aubusson carpet specially woven for the room.

"Stuff and nonsense!" the old lady snapped. "That just goes to show how light-minded you are! A man's looks do not matter in the slightest." She glared at Charlotte. "Anyway, if they did, why on earth did you marry Thomas? He is hardly handsome, or even graceful. Never seen a man so badly dressed in my life! He could make the best Saville Row suit look like a rag bag, once he had it on his back. His hair is too long, he keeps enough to stock a curiosity shop in his pockets, and I've never seen him with his tie on straight since the day he arrived."

"That is not the same thing as being homely!" Charlotte argued.

"Then I should like to know what the difference is," Grandmama retorted. "Except, of course, that a man cannot help his features, whereas he can most certainly help his dress. Untidy clothes are the sign of a slovenly mind, I always say."

"You don't always say it. In fact you've never said it before."

"Only to save your feelings, but since you raised the matter, you have brought it upon yourself. Who is this Amanda Shilling, or Sixpence, or whatever her name is?"

"Pennecuick."

"Don't quibble. That is not an answer. Who is she?" the old lady demanded.

"I don't know, but she's extremely pretty."

"That also is totally immaterial. Who are her family? Has she any breeding, any manners, any money? Does she know how to behave? Has she any relations worth mentioning?"

"I don't know, and I don't suppose Mr. Aylmer cares. He is in love with her, not her relatives," Charlotte pointed out. "He will make quite sufficient money of his own. He is a senior official in the Colonial Office, and much is expected of him."

"Then you have answered your own question, you stupid girl. What on earth does it matter what he looks like? He has good breeding and excellent prospects. He is a very good catch for the Penny-whatever girl, and she has enough sense to see it. Is he of agreeable temperament?" Her small, black eyes were bright with interrogation. "Does he drink to excess? Does he keep bad company?"

"He seems very agreeable, and I have no idea whether he drinks or not."

"Then as long as he is satisfactory in those areas, he is not to be dismissed." She spoke as if that were an end to the matter. "I don't know why you mentioned it. It is not remarkable in any way."

Charlotte tried again. "She is interested in astronomy."

"In what? Why can you not speak plainly? You are mumbling badly these days. You have become slipshod in your speech since you married and left home. It must be associating with poor types. You can always tell a person's breeding by their speech."

"You have just contradicted yourself," Charlotte pointed out, referring to the fact that the old lady was her direct ancestor.

"Don't be impudent!" the old lady said tartly, but from the flush of annoyance in her face, Charlotte knew that she had perceived the flaw in her argument. "Every family has its occasional black sheep," she added with a vicious glare. "Even our poor dear Queen has her problems. Look at the Duke of Clarence. I ask you. He doesn't even choose well-bred women to keep as his mistresses, or so I've heard. And you come here wittering on about some wretched girl, who is nobody at all, marrying a man who is well-bred, has an excellent position, and even better prospects. Just because he is unfortunate enough to be a little plain. What of it?"

"She is not marrying him."

The old lady snorted fiercely. "Then she is a fool, that is all I can say! Now why don't you talk about something sensible? You have barely asked me how I am. Do you know that that wretched cook of Emily's sent me boiled fowl for my dinner last night. And baked mackerel the night before. And there was no forcemeat stuffing, and very little wine. It tasted of fish, and precious little else. I should have liked baked lobster. We have that when Emily is at home."

"Perhaps there were no good lobsters at the fishmongers'," Charlotte suggested.

"Don't tell me she tried, because I shan't believe you. I should have liked a little jugged hare. I am very partial to a well-jugged hare."

"It is out of season," Charlotte pointed out. "Jugged hare doesn't begin until September."

The old lady looked at her with acute disfavor and dropped the subject. She returned instead to Amanda Pennecuick. "What makes you suppose she is a fool, this Moneyfast girl?"

"You said she was a fool, not I."

"You said she was not marrying the man because he was homely, in spite of being in every way that matters an excellent catch. That makes her a fool, on your description. How do you know she is not marrying him? That she may have said so is neither here nor there. What else would she say, I ask you! She can hardly say that she is. That would be premature, and vulgar. And vulgarity, above all things, is unforgivable. And extremely unwise."

"Unwise?" Charlotte questioned.

The old lady looked at her with open disgust. "Of course it would be unwise, you stupid girl. She does not wish him to take her lightly." She sighed noisily with impatience. "If she allows him to undervalue her now, it will set the pattern for the rest of their lives. Let him think her reluctant. Let him woo her so diligently that when he finally wins her he feels he has achieved a great victory, not merely picked up something no one else wished for anyway.

"Really, there are times when I despair of you, Charlotte. You are clever enough at book learning, but what use is that to a woman? Your career is in your home, married to the best man you can find who will have you. You should make him happy, and see that he rises as high in his chosen profession as his abilities, and yours, will allow him. Or if you are clever enough to marry a gentleman, then see that he rises in Society and does not run into debt."

She grunted, and shifted her position with a rustle of skirts and creak of stays. "No wonder you had to settle for a policeman. A girl as naturally unintelligent as you are was fortunate to find anyone at all. Your sister Emily, on the other hand, has all the brains for both of you. She takes after her father, poor man. You take after your fool of a mother."

"Since you are so clever, Grandmama, it is really a great misfortune we don't have a title, an estate in the country and a fortune to match," Charlotte said waspishly.

The old lady looked at her with malicious delight. "I had not the advantages of your good looks."

It was the first compliment Charlotte could ever recall the old lady paying her, especially on such a subject. It quite robbed her of a reply, which—she realized a moment later—had been the intention.

Nevertheless in leaving her and riding in a hansom to Harriet Soames's house, in order to go together to the flower show, she did wonder if Amanda Pennecuick was doing what the old lady had suggested, and actually intended in due course to accept Mr. Aylmer's attentions.

She mentioned it to Harriet as they admired some magnificent early blooms arranged in a crystal bowl.

At first Harriet looked amazed, then as the thought took firmer hold in her mind, her attitude changed.

"You know . . ." she said very slowly. "You know that is not as absurd as it sounds. I have noticed in Amanda a certain inconsistency in disclaimers about Mr. Aylmer's attentions. She says she has nothing in common with him but an interest in the stars. But I never before suspected it was powerful enough to induce her to accept the company of anyone she genuinely disliked." She giggled. "What a delicious thought. Beauty and the Beast. Yes, I do think you might be right. In fact I hope so." She was beaming with pleasure as they walked in to admire a bowl of gaudy tulips whose petals opened like lilies in brilliant scarlets, oranges and flames.

Pitt arrived home late and tired to find Matthew Desmond there waiting for him, pale faced, his fair streaked hair flopping forward as if he had been running his fingers through it in nervous distraction. He had declined to sit in the parlor with Charlotte but had begged to be allowed to walk alone in the garden, and seeing his distress so plainly in his face, she had not tried to dissuade him. This was obviously not a time for the usual rigors of courtesy.

"He has been here nearly an hour," she said quietly when Pitt stood in the parlor looking out of the French doors at Matthew's lean figure pacing back and forth under the apple tree. Obviously he had not yet realized Pitt was there.

"Did he say what has happened?" Pitt asked. He could see that it was something that caused Matthew keen torment of mind. Had it been merely grief he would have sat still in the parlor; probably he would have shared it with Charlotte, knowing Pitt would certainly tell her afterwards anyway. He knew Matthew well enough to be certain that this was no longer the indecision which he felt had touched him last time he had been there, but something far stronger, and as yet unresolved.

"No," Charlotte replied, her face puckered with concern, probably for Matthew, but also for Pitt. Her eyes were tender and she seemed on the verge of saying something else, and then realized it would not help. Whatever the matter was, it could not be avoided, and to make suggestions that it could or should would make it harder, not easier.

He touched her gently in a silent acknowledgment, then went out through the door and over the lawn. The soft grass masked his footsteps so that Matthew did not know he was there until he was only three yards away.

Matthew turned suddenly. His face for an instant registered something close to horror, then he masked his feelings and tried to compose himself to his more usual courtesy.

"Don't," Pitt said quietly.

"What?"

"Don't pretend. Something is very seriously wrong. Tell me what it is."

"Oh. I . . ." Matthew made an attempt to smile, then closed his eyes. His face flooded with pain.

Pitt stood by helplessly, filled with apprehension and the sort of fierce protectiveness one feels only towards a younger child whom you have watched and known through all the vulnerable years. Standing together under the apple tree it was as if all the intervening time had fled away and left them as they were a quarter of a century ago, when his single year's advantage had meant so much. He ached to do something, even as elemental as reaching out his arms to hold him, as if they were still children. But there were too many years between them, and he knew it would be unacceptable. He could only wait.

"The Colonial Office . . ." Matthew said at last. "You don't know who it is yet, do you?"

"No."

"But some of the information comes . . ." He stopped as if even now he hesitated on the verge of whatever it was he was compelled to say, and could not bear to.

Pitt waited. A bird was chirping in the apple tree. Somewhere beyond the wall a horse whinnied.

"From the Treasury," Matthew finished.

"Yes," Pitt agreed. He was about to add the names of the men to whom Ransley Soames had narrowed it down, then he realized that would be an intrusion, and not helpful. Better to allow Matthew to say uninterrupted whatever it was.

Matthew stared at a twig of apple blossom which had fallen on the grass, his back half turned towards Pitt.

"Two days ago Harriet told me that she had overheard her father, Ransley Soames, in a conversation. She went to speak to him in his study, not aware that he was using the telephone." Again Matthew stopped.

Pitt did not speak.

Matthew took a deep breath and continued in a quiet, husky voice, as if his throat were so tight he could barely get the words through it.

"He was speaking to someone about government finances for the exploration and settlement of Zambezia, and as Harriet recounted it, it concerned several aspects, from Cecil Rhodes to MacKinnon, Emin Pasha and the Cape-to-Cairo possibilities, and the importance of a naval base at Simonstown. What it might cost Britain if we were to lose it."

So far what Matthew was saying was what Soames might have been expected to say to a colleague, and not of itself remarkable.

Matthew was still staring at the apple twig on the grass.

"Then he went on to say, 'This is the last time I can tell you anything. That man Pitt from the police has been here, and I dare not continue. You will have to do all you can with what you already have. I'm sorry.' And then apparently he replaced the re-

ceiver. She did not realize what she was telling me—but I knew."
At last Matthew turned and faced Pitt, his eyes agonized, as if waiting for a blow to be struck at him.

Now it was only too obvious why. Ransley Soames was the traitor in the Treasury. Unwittingly his daughter had betrayed him to Matthew, and after torment of indecision, Matthew had come to Pitt. Only he had not come in ignorance; he knew all that it meant, and could foresee the consequences of his act, and yet he felt unable to do otherwise.

Pitt did not speak. It was not necessary to say that he must use the knowledge he had. Matthew had known that when he came. It was also pointless to say that he would keep Matthew's name, or Harriet's, out of the issue, because Matthew knew that was impossible also. Nor did he need to make any sympathetic sounds of understanding. He knew what it meant. What Matthew was feeling, or what it would cost him, no one would know, or ever do more than guess.

He simply held out his hand in companionship for a brother, and in admiration for a man whose integrity was brighter than any comfort of his heart.

CHAPTER
TEN

Pitt could not sleep. At first he lay silently in bed, uncertain whether Charlotte was also awake and loath to disturb her, but eventually he decided she was asleep and would not be aware if he got up and left the room.

He crept downstairs and stood in the parlor looking at the soft light of the quarter moon over the garden. He could dimly see the pale drift of the apple blossom and the dark shadow of the tree on the grass. There were shreds of cloud in the sky, masking some of the stars. Others he could see in tiny pinpoints of light. The night air was warm. In a few weeks it would be midsummer and there were hardly any fires lit in all the million houses, only the cooking ranges, the .gasworks and factory chimneys. Even the slight wind smelled clean.

Of course it was nothing like Brackley, where you could breathe in the scent of hay and leaves and damp woods and turned earth all in one great gasp. But it was better than usual, and there was a stillness that should have brought a sense of calm. In other circumstances it would have.

But tomorrow he would have to go and confront Ransley Soames. There really was no alternative. He knew all the information which had been passed from the Treasury. Matthew himself had given him that. Soames had been privy to all of it. So had several others, but he could recount precisely what he had overheard him say, and the specific reference to Simonstown and the Boers, even the exact words he had used regarding Pitt himself.

It would be an ugly scene; it was bound to be. Tomorrow was Saturday. Pitt would find him at his home, which was about the only good thing in the whole matter. He could be arrested and charged discreetly, not in front of his colleagues.

Of course for Harriet it would be close to unbearable. But then, anyone's fall hurt others. There was always a wife, a child or a parent, someone to be horrified, disillusioned, torn with amazement and grief and shame. One could not allow it to impinge too far, or one would be so racked with pity it would be impossible to function.

It was after nine o'clock when Pitt stood in Ransley Soames's hallway. The butler looked at him with curiosity.

"I am afraid it is a matter which cannot wait," Pitt said gravely. He had brought Tellman with him, in case the scene became uglier than he could handle alone, but he had left him outside, reluctant to call him unless it became unavoidable.

"I will see if Mr. Soames is able to receive you," the butler replied. It was not the customary euphemism, but it served the same purpose.

He was gone only a few moments and returned with an expressionless face.

"If you care to come this way, sir, Mr. Soames will see you in the study."

But actually it was a further ten minutes before Soames appeared. Pitt waited in the quiet, pale green room set with ornate furniture, too many pictures and photographs, and a potted plant which had been overwatered. Normally he might have looked at the bookcases. They were usually indicative of a man's character and interests. But today he could not concentrate his mind on more than the immediate future. He saw two rather idealistic books concerning Africa. One was a novel by H. Rider Haggard, the other a collection of letters from a missionary.

The door opened and Soames came in, closing it behind him. He looked mildly irritated, but not concerned.

"How may I help you, Mr. Pitt?" he said tersely. "I imagine it is urgent, or you would not have come to my home on a Saturday morning."

"Yes, Mr. Soames, it is," Pitt acknowledged. "There is no pleasant way of dealing with this, so I shall be direct. I have cause, sir, to know that it is you who has been passing financial information from the Treasury to someone in the Colonial Office, for them to pass on to the German Embassy."

The blood rushed scarlet to Soames's face, and then after a moment of terrible silence, fled, leaving him pasty white. He opened his mouth to say something, perhaps a denial, but the words died on his tongue. He might have had some conception of the guilt in his face, and how futile, even ridiculous, such a denial would be.

"It—it's not . . ." he began, and then faltered to a stop. "You don't understand," he said wretchedly. "It's not . . ."

"No," Pitt agreed. "I don't."

"It is not accurate information!" Soames looked as if he were in danger of fainting, his skin was so white, and there was a chill sweat standing out on his lip and brow. "It was to mislead Germany!"

Pitt hovered for a moment on the edge of believing him, then realized how easy that was to say, and how unlikely.

"Indeed," he said coldly. "Perhaps you will give me the names of the government ministers who are aware of this. Regrettably they do not include the Foreign Secretary, the Colonial Secretary, or the Prime Minister."

"It was not done . . . like . . . like that." Soames looked agonized and his eyes were desperate, and yet there was somewhere a shred of honesty in them. Was it a terrified last attempt to convince himself?

"Then you had better explain precisely how it was done, and who else is involved," Pitt suggested.

"But you know . . ." Soames stared at him, for the first time realizing that he did not know just how much Pitt was aware of, nor had he so far explained how he had learned it.

"If it is not what I think, Mr. Soames, then you will have to tell me precisely what it is," Pitt said, retrenching his position quickly. "It looks to me like simple treason, the handing over of privileged government information to someone you knew would pass it to Britain's enemies, or at best rivals. What consideration you received in return is a matter yet to be discovered."

"None!" Soames was indignant. "Good God, there is . . . that is a heinous suggestion! I passed on information to a man of subtlety and brilliance who distorted it just sufficiently to be misleading, but not so much as to be unbelievable. Not against Britain's interests, but very much to preserve them, in both East and Central Africa, but also in the North Sea. I would not expect you to understand. . . ."

"Heligoland," Pitt said succinctly.

Soames was transparently surprised. "Yes. Yes, that is right."

"You gave this man correct information for him to distort it?"

"Precisely."

Pitt sighed. "And how do you know he did that?"

"What?"

"How do you know that he distorted it before he passed it on?"

"I have his word. . . ." He stopped, his eyes sick with sudden comprehension. "You don't believe me. . . ."

"I think the kindest thing I can say for you, Mr. Soames," Pitt said wearily, "is that you are naive." Soames pushed backwards into the chair behind him.

"Who is it?" Pitt asked.

"I . . . I can't believe it." Soames made one last effort to cling to his innocence. "He . . . was . . ."

"Plausible," Pitt finished for him. "I find it hard to credit that you were so easily duped." Although even as he said it, it became a lie. Looking at Soames's face, ashen and wretched, he thought he was indeed naive.

"His reasons were . . ." Soames began again, still struggling. "His reasoning was so logical. They are not fools, the Germans." He brushed his hand across his sweating lip. "The information had to be very close to accurate. Inventions would not do."

"That I can easily accept," Pitt agreed. "Even the need to give misinformation is understandable. They are acutely involved with East Africa, Zambezia, Zanzibar especially, and I know we are in negotiations with them over a major treaty."

Soames's face brightened a little.

"But we have a secret service for that kind of thing," Pitt went on.

"Which works through the Foreign and Colonial offices!" Soames sat forward, his eyes brighter. "Really, Superintendent, I think you have misjudged the affair."

"No I have not, Mr. Soames," Pitt replied sharply. "If that kind of information were required of you, for that purpose, then you would have been asked for it by either Mr. Chancellor or Lord Salisbury. You would not have been required to do it covertly, and to be afraid of my enquiries. In fact I would have had no enquiries, because they were instigated by the Foreign Office, as you must recall, and assisted by the Colonial Office, who were most worried by the information passing to the Germans, and quite unaware that it is not correct."

Soames sat on the edge of the chair, his body slack in a moment's despair. Then he straightened up and shot to his feet, lunging at the telephone, and picked it out of its cradle, staring at Pitt defiantly. "I can explain!" He spoke to the operator and asked to be connected with Lord Salisbury's home, giving the number. All the time his eyes were on Pitt.

A part of Pitt felt pity for him. He was arrogant and gullible, but he was not an intentional traitor.

There was a crackle at the other end of the line.

Soames drew in his breath to speak, then realized the futility of it. Slowly he replaced the receiver.

There was no need for Pitt to make a comment. Soames looked as if his knees would buckle under him.

"Who did you give the information to?" Pitt asked again.

"Jeremiah Thorne," Soames replied with stiff lips. "I gave it to Jeremiah Thorne."

Before Pitt had time to respond, even to wonder if it were the truth, the door opened and Harriet Soames stood in the entrance, her face pale, her eyes wide and ready to accuse. She looked first at her father and saw his extreme distress, bordering on the edge of collapse, and then she glared at Pitt.

"Papa, you look ill. What has happened? Mr. Pitt, why have you come here, and at this hour of the day? Is it to do with Mrs. Chancellor's death?" She came in and closed the door.

"No, Miss Soames," Pitt answered her. "It is a matter, so far as I know, quite unconnected. I think it would be better if you were to permit us to conclude it privately, and then Mr. Soames can tell you afterwards, as seems good to him."

She moved closer to her father, her eyes blazing, in spite of the alarm in her which was rapidly turning to fear.

"No. I will not leave until I know what has happened. Papa, what is wrong?" Her voice was rising with fear. He looked so desperate, so drained of all the buoyancy and confidence he had had only an hour ago. It was as if the vitality had bled out of him.

"My dear ... I ...." He attempted some explanation, but the test was too great for him. The truth weighed on him till it drove out everything else. "I have made a terrible mistake," he tried again. "I have been very ... naive.... I have allowed someone to use me, and to deceive me with a very plausible lie, a man whose honor I never questioned."

"Who?" Her voice rose close to panic. "Who has used you? I don't understand what you mean. Why is Mr. Pitt here? Why did you call in the police? If someone has defrauded you, can he help? Would it not be better to . . . I don't know . . . to deal with it privately?" She looked from her father to Pitt, and back again. "Was it much money?"

Soames seemed incapable of a coherent explanation. Pitt could not bear the agony any longer. To see him at once struggling and despairing was an intrusion into the man's shame which was unnecessary. A clean blow would be more merciful.

"Mr. Soames has been passing secret information to a spy," he said to Harriet, "in his belief that the man was using it to help Britain's interests in Africa by falsifying it before relaying it to the Germans. However the plan was not approved by either the Colonial Office or the Foreign Office. On the contrary, they had called me and empowered me to investigate where the information was coming from."

She looked at him with disbelief.

"You are wrong! You must be wrong." She swung around to her father, her mouth open, to ask him to explain; then she saw the full depth of his distress. Suddenly she knew that in some terrible way there was truth in it. She turned back to Pitt. "Well whatever happened," she said furiously, "if my father has been deceived by someone, it was not a dishonorable act, and you should be very careful what you say to him." Her voice shook and she stepped closer to Soames, as if he needed some physical protection and she would give it.

"I have not made an accusation of dishonor, Miss Soames," Pitt said gently. "At least not on your father's part."

"Then why are you here? You should be looking for whoever it is that lied to him and passed on the information."

"I did not know who, until your father told me."

Her chin came up. "If you didn't know who it was, then how

could you know it had anything to do with my father? Perhaps it hasn't. Have you thought of that, Superintendent?"

"I had thought of it, Miss Soames, and it is not so."

"Prove it," she challenged, staring at Pitt with brilliant eyes, her face set, jaw tight, her remarkable profile as stiff as if carved in almond-tinted stone.

"It's no use, Harriet," Soames interrupted at last. "The Superintendent overheard my conversation when I was passing the information. I don't know how, but he was able to recite it back to me."

She stood as if frozen. "What conversation? With whom?"

Soames glanced at Pitt, a question in his eyes.

Pitt shook his head.

"With the man at the Colonial Office," Soames replied, avoiding using his name.

"What conversation?" Her voice was strangled in her throat. "When?"

"On Wednesday, late afternoon. Why? What difference can it make now?"

She turned very slowly to look at Pitt, horror in her eyes and disgust so absolute and so terrible her face was made ugly with it.

"Matthew," she whispered. "Matthew told you, didn't he?"

Pitt did not know what to say. He could not deny it, and yet neither could he bear to confirm that her charge was true. It would be fatuous and unbelievable to suggest that Matthew might not have understood the meaning of what he said, or what the result would be.

"You can't deny it, can you!" she accused him.

"Harriet . . ." Soames began.

She swung around to him. "Matthew betrayed you, Papa . . . and me. He betrayed both of us for his precious Colonial Office. They'll promote him, and you'll be ruined." There was a sob in her voice and she was so close to tears she barely had control.

Pitt wanted to defend Matthew, even to plead his cause, but he knew from her face that it would be useless, and anyway, Matthew had the right to say what he could to explain himself. Pitt should not preempt that, no matter how intensely he felt. He met Harriet's eyes, full of overwhelming hurt, anger, confusion and the passion to protect. He understood it far more deeply than reason or words could have conveyed. He wanted to protect Matthew from the hurt he knew was inevitable, and with the same fierce instinct to save the weaker, the more vulnerable, that burned in her.

And both of them were powerless.

"It is despicable," she said, catching her breath and almost choking. "How could anyone be so . . . so beneath contempt?"

"To give away their country's secrets, with which they had been entrusted, or to report that treason to the authorities, Miss Soames?" Pitt said quietly.

She was white to the lips. "It . . . it is not . . . treason." She found it difficult to say the word. "He . . . he . . . was deceived. . . . That is not treason . . . and . . . and you will not excuse Matthew to me—not ever!"

Soames climbed to his feet with difficulty. "I shall resign, of course."

Pitt did not demur, nor point out that he would be extremely unlikely to have any option.

"Yes sir," he agreed. "In the meantime, I think it would be advisable if you were to come to the Bow Street station and make a statement in respect of what you have just told me."

"I suppose that is inevitable," Soames agreed reluctantly. "I'll . . . I'll come on Monday."

"No, Mr. Soames, you will come now," Pitt said firmly.

Soames looked startled.

Harriet moved closer to her father, putting her arm through his. "He has already told you, Superintendent, he will go on Monday! You have had your victory. What else do you need? He is ruined! Isn't that enough for you?"

"It is not I who has to be satisfied, Miss Soames," Pitt replied with as much patience as he could muster. He was not sure whether she was so naive. "Your father is not alone in this tragedy. There are other people to arrest. . . ."

"Then go and arrest them! Do your duty! There's nothing more to keep you here!"

"The telephone." Pitt looked at the instrument where it sat on its cradle.

"What about it?" She regarded it with loathing. "If you want to use it, you may!"

"So may you," he pointed out. "To warn others, and when I arrive there, they will be gone. Surely you can see the necessity for action now, and not Monday morning?"

"Oh . . ."

"Mr. Soames?" He waited with growing impatience.

"Yes . . . I er . . ." He looked confused, broken, and for that moment at least, Pitt was almost as sorry for him as Harriet, even though he also felt a contempt for his foolishness. He had been arrogant enough to think he knew better than his colleagues, and no doubt a little self-importance had played its part, the knowledge that he knew secrets others did not. But he was going to pay an uncommon price for a very common sin.

Pitt opened the door for him.

"I'm coming with him!" Harriet declared defiantly.

"No, you are not," Pitt said.

"I . . ."

"Please!" Soames turned to look at her. "Please . . . leave me a little dignity, my dear. I should rather face this alone."

She fell back, the tears spilling over her cheeks, and Pitt escorted Soames out, leaving her standing in the doorway, her face filled with anger and overwhelming grief.

Pitt took Soames to Bow Street and left him there with Tellman, to take all the details of precisely what information he had passed to Thorne and when. He had hesitated to take him directly to the police station; it was a sensitive matter and he had been directly commissioned from higher up. But he could not take him to Matthew, the person who had originally instigated the investigation, because of the relationship between them. Nor could he take him to Linus Chancellor, who would be at home at this hour on a Saturday, and in no frame of mind to deal with such a matter. And he did not entirely trust any of the other people concerned, nor was he certain to find them in the Colonial Office, even if he had.

He had not the power to go directly to Lord Salisbury, and certainly not to the Prime Minister. He would arrest Thorne, and then make a complete report of the matter for Farnsworth.

He took two constables with him, just in case Thorne should prove violent. It was not beyond possibility. Secondly they would be necessary to conduct a search of the premises and prevent any destruction of further evidence which would no doubt be required if the matter came to trial. It was always possible the government might prefer to deal with it all discreetly, rather than expose its error and vulnerabilities to public awareness.

He arrived by hansom with the constables, and posted one at the back door, just in case of attempted flight. That would be undignified and absurd, but not beyond possibility. All kinds of people can panic, sometimes those one least expects.

A footman opened the front door, looking extremely sober—in fact the pallor of his face suggested he had already received some kind of shock and was still reeling from its effects.

"Yes sir?" he enquired without expression.

"I require to see Mr. Thorne." Pitt made it a statement, not a request.

"I'm sorry sir, he is not at home," the footman replied, still no emotion whatever in his face.

"When are you expecting his return?" Pitt felt a surprising frustration, probably because he had liked both Thorne himself and

Christabel, and he loathed having to come on this errand. Being faced with postponing it made it even worse because it prolonged it.

"I am not, sir." The footman looked confused and distressed, his eyes meeting Pitt's directly for the first time.

"What do you mean, you are not?" Pitt snapped. "You mean you don't know at what hour he will return? What about Mrs. Thorne? Is she at home?"

"No, sir, both Mr. and Mrs. Thorne left for Portugal yesterday evening, and my information is that they are not returning to England."

"Not . . . at all?" Pitt was incredulous.

"No, sir, not at all. The household staff have been dismissed, except myself and the butler, and we are here only to take care of things until Mr. Thorne's man of affairs can dispose of the house and its effects."

Pitt was stunned. Thorne had fled. And if Thorne had gone last night, then it was not Soames's doing. In fact Thorne had left without warning Soames, and he could have.

"Who was here yesterday?" he said sharply. "Exactly who called at this house yesterday?"

"Mr. Aylmer, sir. He came in the afternoon shortly after Mr. Thorne returned from the Colonial Office, about four o'clock, and half an hour after that, a Mr. Kreisler—"

"Kreisler?" Pitt interrupted immediately.

"Yes sir. He was here for about half an hour, sir."

Pitt swore under his breath. "And when did Mr. Thorne inform you he was leaving for Portugal? When were those arrangements made?"

A delivery cart rumbled along the street behind them and fifty yards away a maid came up the area steps with a mat and began to beat it.

"I don't know when he made the arrangements, sir," the footman answered. "But he left about an hour after that, maybe a little less."

"Well, when did he pack? When did he give the servants notice?"

"They only took two large cases with them, sir, and so far as I know, they were packed just after Mr. Kreisler arrived. Mr. Thorne gave us notice at the same time, sir. It was all very sudden—"

"Last night?" Pitt interrupted. "They gave you all notice last night? But the other staff cannot all have gone last night. Where would they go to?"

"Oh no sir." He shook his head. "One of the upstairs maids was at her sister's anyway, there being a death in the family, like. So the other one went this morning. They were sisters. Mrs. Thorne's ladies' maid had been sent on holiday. . . ." He sounded surprised as he said it. It was an extraordinary thing to do. Servants did not have holidays. "And the cook is going this afternoon. She is a very good cook indeed, and much sought after." He said that with some satisfaction. "Lady Brompton'll be only too glad to have her. She's been angling after her for years. They need a new boot boy next door, and Mrs. Thorne said as she'd called someone for the scullery maid and found her a place."

So it was not completely sudden! They had been prepared for the eventuality. Kreisler had merely told him the time was come. But why? Why did Kreisler warn him instead of allowing him to be caught? His part in it, and in Susannah Chancellor's death, was becoming less clear all the time.

The footman was staring at him.

"Excuse me, sir, but you are Superintendent Pitt, aren't you?"

"Yes."

"Then, sir, Mr. Thorne left a letter for you. It is on the mantelpiece in the withdrawing room. If you'll wait a moment, sir, I'll fetch it."

"There's no need," Pitt said quickly. "I am afraid I am obliged to search the house anyway."

"Search the house?" He was startled. "What for? I don't know that I can allow that . . . except . . ." He stopped, uncertain what he meant. Now that his master was gone, apparently never to return, he was about to be without a position, although he had been given handsome notice and an excellent reference. And Pitt was the police.

"A wise decision," Pitt said, reading his face. He called the constable standing just beyond the step. "Fetch Hammond from the back, and then begin to look through the house. I shall be in the withdrawing room."

"What about Mr. Thorne, sir?"

Pitt smiled ruefully. "I am afraid that Mr. and Mrs. Thorne left London bound for Portugal last night. And they are not expected to return."

The constable's face fell; he made as if to say something, then changed his mind. "Yes, sir. I'll fetch Hammond, sir."

"Thank you." Pitt came into the hall and then followed the footman to the withdrawing room.

It was a comfortable room, unostentatious, with dark green curtains and pale, damasked walls. The pictures were arranged oddly, and it was only after a moment or two he realized that it was because three or four had been removed. Presumably they were either the most valuable or those of greatest sentimental worth. The furniture was old; the mahogany bookcase shone with generations of polishing, and one of its glass panes was cracked. The chairs were a trifle scuffed, as if sat in for long evenings beside the fire; the fender around the hearth had a dent in it and there was a tiny brown mark on the carpet where a spark had caught it. A vase of late tulips, gaudy and wide open like lilies, gave a heart and a perfume to the room.

A very small marmalade-and-white kitten lay curled into a ball on one of the cushions, apparently sound asleep. Another kitten, equally small, perhaps only nine or ten weeks old, lay in the seat of the chair, but he was smoky black, his shadowy, baby stripes still visible. He lay not curled up but stretched out his full length, and he was equally fast asleep.

The letter caught Pitt's eye straightaway. It was propped up on the mantelpiece, and his name was written on the front.

He picked it up, tore it open, and read.

My dear Pitt,

By the time you read this, Christabel and I shall be on the boat across the Channel on our way to Portugal. Which will, of course, mean that you are aware that it is I who have been passing information from the Colonial Office and the Treasury to the German Embassy.

What you do not know is my reason for doing so. Nor, I think, do you know that it was almost all false. Naturally to begin with, it had to be genuine, and then later, when I had earned their trust, it was false only to a very minor degree, but sufficient to do them a considerable disservice.

I have never been to Africa myself, but I know a great deal about it from my years in the Colonial Office. I know from letters and dispatches more assuredly than you can appreciate, just what atrocities have been committed by white men in the name of civilization. I am not speaking of the occasional murder, or even massacre. That has occurred throughout history, and possibly always will. Certainly the black man is quite as capable of atrocities of that order as anyone else. I am speaking of the greed and the stupidity, the rape of the land and the subjugation, even the destruction of a nation of people, the loss of their culture and their beliefs, the degrading of a race.

I do not hold out great hope that Britain will settle either wisely or fairly. I am certain we shall do neither. But there will be those among us who will make the attempt, and we have a certain humanity, standards of conduct and honor which will mitigate the worst of it.

If, on the other hand, Germany takes East Africa, Zanzibar and the whole of that coast—which they are quite capable of doing, especially in our undecided state—then there will certainly be war between Britain in Central Africa and Germany in the east. Belgium in the west will be drawn in, and no doubt what is left of the old Arab Sultanates as well. What was once only tribal skirmishes with spears and assegais will become a full-scale war of machine guns and cannons as Europe turns Africa into a bloodbath to settle its own old rivalries and new greeds.

One European power dominant enough to prevent that is a better alternative, and quite naturally, I wish it to be Britain, for both moral and political reasons. To that end I have sent to the German Embassy misinformation regarding mineral deposits, endemic disease and its spread, the areas affected, the cost of various expeditions, their losses, the enthusiasm or disillusion of financial backers. I think you now see my purpose?

Is it necessary to explain to you why I did not do this through the Colonial Office's official channels? Surely not! Apart from the obvious danger that the more people who knew of it, the less likely it was to remain undetected and have any chance of success, I am quite sure Linus Chancellor would have had no part in such a scheme. I did sound him out, very tentatively.

Also Lord Salisbury is, as you well know, very ambivalent in his attitude towards Africa, and not to be trusted to remain in his present ebullient mood.

Poor Ransley Soames is very gullible, as easily duped as any man I know. But he has no worse sin than an overbearing vanity. Do not be too hard upon him. The fact that he is a fool will be punishment enough for him. He will not recover from that.

I have no knowledge as to who murdered poor Susannah, or why. Had I, I should most certainly have told you.

Be careful of the Inner Circle. Their power is wider

than you know, and their hunger is insatiable. Above all they never forgive. Poor Arthur Desmond is witness to that, and one you will not forget. He betrayed their secrets and paid with his life. But again, I know that only because he spoke to me of his convictions, and I know enough of the Circle to be convinced his death was not accidental. He knew he was in danger. He had been threatened before, but he considered the game worth the stake. He was one of the best of men, and I miss him sorely. I do not know who contrived his death, nor how ... only why.

I have given all my servants notice, a month's pay and good references. My man of affairs will dispose of the house and its contents, and the proceeds are to be given to Christabel's charity. It will do much good. Since you cannot prove treason against her, I think you will not interfere with that bequest?

My household staff are good, but they will be confused and alarmed. Therefore I have a personal favor to ask of you. Christabel's two kittens, Angus and Archie, have perforce been left behind. I do not feel at ease that they will be taken with any of my staff, who have no facilities to care for them. Will you please take them with you and see that they are found a good home ... together, if you don't mind. They are devoted to each other. Archie is the marmalade one, Angus the black. I am greatly obliged to you. To say 'yours' seems absurd, when I am most patently not! But I write candidly, as one man of conviction to, I believe, another.

Jeremiah Thorne

Pitt stood with the paper in his hands as if he could scarcely comprehend what was written. And yet now that he saw it, it all made excellent sense. He could not condone what Thorne had done, nor could he entirely condone the means he had employed.

His battle was as much against the Inner Circle as against Germany, yet there he was helpless. All he could do was warn as explicitly as possible.

He had known Sir Arthur. If there had been even a vestige of doubt lingering, that would have swept it away.

Yet he still believed British dominion of Africa was better than German, or a divided nation. What he said about war was almost surely true, and that would be a disaster of immeasurable proportions.

Why had Kreisler warned him? Their beliefs were not the same. Or was it not deliberate? Had Kreisler asked his questions and Thorne understood the meaning behind them?

It was all academic now. It explained why none of Hathaway's figures had reached the German Embassy. Thorne had altered them all anyway.

He looked around him at the gracious, comfortable room: the ormolu clock ticking on the mantelshelf from which he had taken the letter, the pictures on the walls, mostly dark Dutch scenes of landscapes with animals and water. He had never before appreciated how beautiful cows were, how a body with so many protruding bones could still have about it such an air of peace.

On the chair beside his elbow, Archie, the orange kitten, uncurled himself, stretched out a silken paw with claws spread, gave a little squeak of satisfaction, and began to purr.

"What on earth am I going to do with you?" Pitt asked, unconsciously admiring the perfection of the creature. It had a star-shaped face with bright, sea-blue–green eyes and enormous ears. It was watching him with curiosity, and no fear whatever.

He put out his hand and rang the bell. The footman appeared immediately. He had obviously been waiting in the hall.

"Mr. Thorne has requested that I take these two cats," Pitt said with a frown.

"Oh, I am glad," the footman responded with relief. "I was afraid we were going to have them disposed of. That would be a terrible shame. Nice little things, they are. I'll get a basket for you, sir. I'm sure there'll be one suitable."

"Thank you."

"Not at all, sir. I'll do it right away."

Pitt took them home because he had very little alternative. Also he wanted to tell Charlotte about Soames, and knew it would devastate Matthew. Last night he had not told her of it, hoping in some way it would prove mistaken, although she knew there was something deeply wrong. Matthew had left without waiting to eat, or to speak with both of them, and she had watched him leave with anxious face and troubled eyes.

First he presented her with the cats. They were angry in the basket and in a considerable temper to be out, which took precedence over news of any other thought.

"They're beautiful," she exclaimed with delight, putting the basket on the kitchen floor. "Oh, Thomas, they're exquisite! Where on earth did you get them? I wanted a cat as soon as we moved, but no one has had any." She looked up at him with delight filling her face, then immediately turned back to the basket. Archie was playing with her finger, and Angus was staring at her with round, golden eyes. "I shall think of names for them."

"They are already named," he said quickly. "They belonged to Christabel Thorne."

"Belonged?" She jerked her head up. "Why do you say that? What has happened to her? You said she is all right!"

"I expect she is. Jeremiah Thorne is the traitor at the Colonial Office, if *traitor* is the right word. I'm not sure that it is."

"Jeremiah Thorne?" She looked crushed, her face filled with sudden sadness. The kittens were temporarily forgotten, in spite of the fact that Archie was quietly biting her finger, and then licking it, holding it between his paws. "I suppose you are sure? Have you arrested him?"

He sat down on one of the wooden chairs beside the kitchen table.

"No. They have both gone to Portugal. They left last night. I think Kreisler's constant questions warned them."

"They've got away?" Then her expression sobered. "Oh. I'm sorry. I . . ."

He smiled. "There's no need to apologize for feeling relieved. I am myself, for a lot of reasons, not least because I liked them."

Her face was filled with a mixture of curiosity, guilt and confusion. "What other news? Is it not bad for you, for England, that they escaped?"

"For me, possibly. Farnsworth may be angry, but he may also come to realize that if we had caught them there would have been a considerable conflict as to what to do with them."

"Try them," she said instantly. "For treason!"

"And expose our own weakness?"

"Oh. Yes, I see. Not very good, when we are busy negotiating treaties. It makes us look incompetent, doesn't it?"

"Very. And actually all the information he gave was inaccurate anyway."

"On purpose? Or was he incompetent too?" She sat down opposite him, temporarily leaving the kittens to explore, which they did with enthusiasm.

"Oh, no, definitely on purpose," he replied. "So if he defended himself by saying that, then we ruin the good he has done, as well as making ourselves look stupid. No, on the whole, I think it is best he goes to Portugal. Only he left his cats behind, and asked me if I would look after them so their servants don't dispose of them. Their names are Archie and Angus. That is Archie, presently trying to get into the flour bin."

Her face softened into pure pleasure again as she looked down at the little animal, then at the other one, whose soft, black face was wide-eyed and filled with interest. He moved a step closer, then jumped back, then took another step forward, tail high.

It was hard to spoil the moment.

"I shall probably go and see Matthew this evening. . . ." he began.

She froze, her fingers motionless above the kitten, then she looked up at him, waiting for him to tell her.

"Soames was the traitor in the Treasury," he said. "Matthew knew it."

Her face filled with pain. "Oh, Thomas! That's dreadful! Poor Harriet. How is she taking it? Did you have to arrest him? Can Matthew be with her? Wouldn't it be better if . . . if you didn't go?" She leaned across the table, putting her hand over his. "I'm sorry, my dear, but he is not going to find it easy to understand that you had to arrest Soames. In time, I expect he will realize . . ." She stopped, seeing from his face that there was something she had not understood. "What? What is it?"

"It was Matthew who told me," he said softly. "Harriet Soames confided to him, in ignorance, a telephone call she had overheard her father make, not understanding its meaning, and he felt honor-bound to repeat it to me. I am afraid she will not forgive him for it. In her eyes he has betrayed both herself and her father."

"That's not fair!" she said instantly, then closed her eyes and shook her head from side to side in a sharp little movement of denial. "I know it is natural to feel that way, but it is still not fair. What else could he do? She cannot expect him to deny his own life's work and belief and be party to Mr. Soames's treason! It's not Matthew!"

"I know that," he said softly. "And perhaps there is part of her which knows it too, but that doesn't help. Her father is disgraced, ruined. The Colonial Office won't prosecute, or the Treasury either, because of the scandal, but it will become known."

She looked up. "What will happen to him?" Her face filled with a cold, bleak sadness. "Suicide?" she whispered.

"It's not impossible, but I hope not."

"Poor Harriet! Yesterday she had everything and the future

looked endlessly bright. Today there is nothing at all, no marriage, no father, no money, no standing in Society, only the few friends who have the courage to remain by her, and no hope for anything to come. Thomas, it's sad, and very frightening. Yes, of course, she cannot forgive Matthew, and that will be a wound he will never be healed of either. What a terrible, terrible mess. Yes, go to Matthew; he will need you more than ever before."

Pitt had stopped by at Matthew's office and found him white to the lips, hollow-eyed and barely able to function in his duty. He had known the danger of such rejection when he had first gone to Pitt, but part of him had clung to the hope that it would not be so, that somehow Harriet would, in her despair and shame, turn to him, in spite of what he had done, what he had felt compelled to do. Given his own sense of honor he had had no choice.

He had begun to tell Pitt some of this, but Pitt had understood it without the necessity of words. After a few moments Matthew had ceased trying to explain, and simply let the subject fall. They sat together for some time, occasionally speaking of things of the past, happy, easy times remembered with pleasure. Then Pitt rose to leave, and Matthew returned to his papers, letters and calls. Pitt took a hansom to Farnsworth's office on the Embankment.

"Soames?" Farnsworth said with confusion, anger and distress conflicting in his face. "What a damn fool thing to have done. Really, the man is an ass. How could he credit anything so—so totally beyond belief? He is a cretin."

"The curious thing," Pitt said flatly, "is that it is largely true."

"What?" Farnsworth swung around from the bookshelf where he was standing, his eyes wide and angry. "What are you driveling on about, Pitt? It's an absurd story. A child wouldn't have accepted that explanation."

"Probably not, but then a child would not have the sophistication . . ."

"Sophistication!" Farnsworth grimaced with disgust. "Soames is about as sophisticated as my boot boy. Although even he wouldn't have swallowed that, and he's only fourteen."

". . . to be misled by an argument about the results of a clash of European powers in black Africa, and the need to prevent it in the interests of morality in general, and the future of all of us," Pitt finished as if he had not been interrupted.

"Are you making excuses for him?" Farnsworth's eyes widened. "Because if you are, you are wasting your time. What are you doing about it? Where is he?"

"At Bow Street," Pitt replied. "I imagine his own people will deal with him. It is not my domain."

"His own people? Who do you mean? The Treasury?"

"The government," Pitt answered. "It will no doubt be up to them to decide what to do about it."

Farnsworth sighed and bit his lip. "Nothing, I imagine," he said bitterly. "They will not wish to admit that they were incompetent enough to allow such a thing to happen. That is probably true of the whole issue. To whom did he give his information? You haven't told me that yet. Who is this altruistic traitor?"

"Thorne."

Farnsworth's eyes widened.

"Jeremiah Thorne? Good heavens. I had my money on Aylmer. I knew it wasn't Hathaway, in spite of that lunatic scheme to disseminate false information to all the suspects. Nothing ever came of that!"

"Yes it did, indirectly."

"What do you mean, indirectly? Did it, or didn't it?"

"Indirectly," Pitt repeated. "We got the information back from the German Embassy, and it was none of the figures Hathaway had given, which supports what Soames said of Thorne. He was giving misinformation all the time."

"Possibly, but I shall want proof of that before I believe it. Is he at Bow Street as well?"

"No, he's probably in Lisbon by now."

"Lisbon?" A range of emotions fought in Farnsworth's face. He was furious, contemptuous, and at the same time aware of the embarrassment saved by the fact that Thorne could not now be tried.

"He left last night," Pitt went on.

"Warned by Soames?"

"No. If anyone, Kreisler . . ."

Farnsworth swore.

". . . but I imagine unintentionally," Pitt went on. "I think Kreisler was more concerned with finding out who murdered Susannah Chancellor."

"Or finding out how much you knew about the fact that he killed her," Farnsworth snapped. "All right, well at least you have cleared up the treason affair—not very satisfactorily, I might add, but this is better than nothing. And I suppose it could have been very ugly if you had arrested Thorne. You are due some credit for it."

He sighed and walked over to his desk. "Now you had better return to the tragedy of Mrs. Chancellor. The government, not to mention the press, want to see a solution to that." He looked up. "Have you anything at all? What about the cabdriver? Do you have him yet? Do you know where she was put into the river? Have you found her cloak? Do you even know where she was killed? I suppose it would be by Thorne, because she discovered his secret?"

"He said he knew nothing about it."

"Said? You just told me he had left for Portugal last night, and you got there this morning!"

"He left me a letter."

"Where is it? Give it to me!" Farnsworth demanded.

Pitt passed it across and Farnsworth read it carefully.

"Cats!" he said at the end, putting it down on his desk. "I suppose you believe him about Mrs. Chancellor?"

"Yes, I do."

Farnsworth bit his lip. "Actually, I am inclined to myself. Pursue Kreisler, Pitt. There is a great deal that is not right about that man. He has made enemies. He has an unreliable temper and is acquainted with violence. Seek out his reputation in Africa; nobody knows what he stands for or where his loyalties are. That much I have learned for myself." He jerked his hand sharply. "Forget the connection with Arthur Desmond. That's nonsense, always was. I know it is painful for you to accept that he was senile, I can understand that, but it is incontrovertible. I'm sorry. The facts are plain enough. He cadged brandy from everyone he knew, and when he was too fuddled to have any clarity of thought at all, he took an overdose of laudanum, probably by accident, possibly intending to make an honorable end of it before he became even more uncontrolled and finally said something, made some accusation or slander he could not live down."

Pitt froze. Farnsworth had used the word *cadged*. How did he know Sir Arthur had not ordered every brandy himself in the usual way? There was one answer to that—because he knew what had happened that afternoon in the Morton Club. He had not been there. It had not come out in testimony at the inquest; in fact the opposite had been said, that Sir Arthur had ordered the drinks himself.

Pitt opened his mouth to ask Farnsworth if he had spoken to Guyler himself, then just in time, with the words on the edge of his tongue, he realized that if he had not, the only way he could have known would be if he were part of the same ring of the Inner Circle which had ordered Sir Arthur's death.

"Yes?" Farnsworth said impatiently, his blue-gray eyes staring at Pitt. It seemed at a glance as if he spoke in temper, but behind the surface emotion, the exterior that Pitt could see—and had seen so often before he could picture it with his eyes closed, so familiar was it—he saw for a moment that colder, cleverer mind, far more watchful, waiting for Pitt to betray himself.

If Pitt asked the question, Farnsworth would know exactly what he suspected, how far he had moved already. He would know Pitt was looking for the executioner and that he knew Farnsworth was part of that ring.

Pitt veiled his eyes and lied, the fear breaking out in a cold sweat on his skin. Someone could so easily brush against him and push him in front of the oncoming wheels of a carriage, or pass their hand over his mug of cider in a tavern, and he would drink a fatal dose.

"Well?" Farnsworth said with something close to a smile.

Pitt knew if he gave in too easily Farnsworth would see through it and know he had understood. Suddenly he was aware of the possibility that Farnsworth was far cleverer than he had thought. He had never excelled at police procedure; he was too arrogant to take the pains. But he knew how to use the men whose skill it was: Tellman, Pitt, even Micah Drummond in his time. And how many had he inducted into the Circle? Who were they? Probably Pitt would never know; even when it was too late, he might not know who had struck the blow.

He was waiting, the afternoon sunlight shining through the windows on his fair hair.

"Do you really think that it could have been suicide?" Pitt asked as if he were accepting the idea with deep reluctance. "A matter of death rather than dishonor . . . to himself, I mean?"

"Would you prefer that?" Farnsworth countered.

"Not prefer, I don't think." Pitt forced himself to say the words, to act the part, even to believe it himself while he spoke. He was cold inside. "But it is easier to fit into the facts we know."

"Facts?" Farnsworth was still staring at him.

"Yes . . ." Pitt swallowed. "Taking a dose of laudanum at all in the afternoon, in your club. One would have to be very fuddled indeed to do it by accident, it's . . . it's bad form. But a suicide would be more understandable. He wouldn't want to do it at home." He knew he was rambling, saying too much. He felt a little dizzy; the room seemed enormous. He must be careful. "Where his servants would find him," he went on. "And perhaps be distressed. A woman servant—maybe that was when the realization came to him of just how ruinous his behavior had been?"

"I should think that it was like that," Farnsworth agreed. His body relaxed indefinably. Once again he looked irritable and impatient. "Yes, I daresay you have it, Pitt. Well, let go of it, man. Get back to work on the Chancellor case. That is your absolute priority. Do you understand me?"

"Yes sir. Of course I do." Pitt rose to his feet and found his knees unaccountably weak. He was forced to stand still for several seconds before he could master himself and take his leave, closing the door behind him and starting down the stairs holding on to the banister.

CHAPTER
ELEVEN

Nobby Gunne was deeply distressed by the death of Susannah Chancellor, not only because she had found her a charming and unique person, but also, with an intense sense of guilt, because she was terrified that Peter Kreisler had some involvement in it. In her worst moments she even feared he might have been directly responsible.

She did not see him for at least three days, and that only added to her anxiety and the hideous ideas that danced in her head. His presence might have been reassuring. She might have looked at his face and seen the ultimate sanity in it, and known her fears were ugly and unjust. She would have been able to speak with him and hear his sorrow for Susannah. Perhaps he might even say where he had been that night and prove his innocence.

But all she received from him was a short note saying how grieved he was, and that business to do with it kept him occupied to the exclusion of all else, at least for the present. She could not imagine what business he could have as a result of Susannah's death, but possibly it concerned African finance and the banking which so involved her family.

When she did see him it was because he had called upon her in the afternoon. It was a most unconventional thing to do, but then convention had never bothered either of them. He found her in the garden picking early roses. Most of them were still in bud, but there were one or two open. She had already chosen some leaves from a copper beech tree which were a deep purpley red and set off the pink petals in a way no ordinary green leaf could.

He was walking across the lawn, unannounced, a fact over which she would have words with her maid later on. Now all she could think of was her pleasure in seeing him and the brooding anxiety which made her heart beat faster and tightened her throat.

He did not bother with formal greetings, enquiries for health, or remarks about delightful weather. He stopped in front of her, his eyes direct and troubled, but his delight in her company undisguised.

For a moment her fears were swallowed up in the inner surge of happiness at the sight of his face and the confidence in him which she had in part forgotten.

"I'm sorry to intrude on you uninvited," he said, holding out his hands, palms upwards.

She placed her own in his and felt the warmth of his fingers close over hers. For an instant she forgot her fears. They were absurd. He would never have done anything so appalling. If he had been involved at all, then there would be some innocent explanation of it, whether she ever heard it or not.

She did not reply with the cliché she might have said to anyone else.

"How are you?" She searched his face. "You look very tired."

He let go of her hands and fell into step beside her, walking very slowly along the herbaceous border. "I suppose I am," he admitted. "I seem to have slept very little in the last few days, since the death of Mrs. Chancellor."

Although the subject was at the forefront of her thoughts, yet still she was startled to hear him raise it so soon, too soon for her to have prepared what she meant to say, in spite of having turned it over in her mind through every wakeful hour since it had happened.

She looked away from him, as if to some point on the far side of the garden, although nothing was happening more important than a small bird hopping from one twig to another.

"I had not realized you were so fond of her." She stopped, afraid that she sounded petulant and he would misunderstand. Or was it misunderstanding? Was she not jealous? How absurd, and worse that that, how ugly. "She was indeed extremely charming." That sounded trite and flat. "And so very alive. I find it painful to acknowledge that she is gone. I should very much have liked to know her better."

"I liked her," he replied, staring at the spires of the delphiniums. They were already in bud heavily enough to tell which were the dark blue, which sky blue, and which either white or pink. "There was an honesty in her which is all too rare. But that is not why I lie awake over her death." He frowned, turning to face her. "Which I thought you knew. You are less direct than goes with your intelligence. I shall have to remember that. It is most feminine. I think I like it."

Now she was thoroughly confused, and felt the color burning up her cheeks. She avoided his eyes. "I am not at all sure I know what you mean. Why are you so distressed by her death, if it is not offensive to ask? I cannot believe it is pain for Linus Chancellor. I formed the distinct impression you did not care for him at all."

"I don't," he agreed. "At least, I have no objection to the man himself. In fact I admire him intensely. He has energy, intelligence, talent, and the will to harness them to a purpose, which is the key to it all. Many men have all the attributes for success except that. Will and discipline can make a man." He walked another few steps before continuing, his hands thrust into his pockets. "But I disagree passionately with his beliefs and plans for Africa. But you already know that."

"So why are you so distraught?" she asked.

"Because I quarreled with her the evening before the night she died."

Nobby was startled. She had not believed him a man to have such a tender, even superstitious conscience. It sat ill with everything else she knew of him. Of course there were incongruities in people's characters, sudden traits that seemed quite contradictory, but this caught her completely by surprise.

"That's foolish," she said with a smile. "I doubt you were so unpleasant as to give you cause to feel guilty, just because it was not resolved. You differed in view about settlement in Zambezia. It was an honest difference. I am sure she would not—"

"For heaven's sake!" he interrupted with a laugh of derision. "I will stand by what I said to God himself! Certainly to Susannah Chancellor, dead or alive! No—it was a public place, and I am quite certain I was thoroughly observed, and the matter will have been reported to the police. Your diligent friend Pitt will be very aware of it. He has already been to see me. He was polite, of course, but also, underneath the good manners, very suspicious. It would suit a good many people if I were charged with murdering her. It would . . ." He stopped, seeing the alarm in her face.

He smiled self-mockingly. "Oh come, Nobby. Don't pretend you don't know that. The sooner the matter is settled, the greater honor there will be for the police, the press will leave them alone, and no one will need to look too exhaustively into poor Susannah's life. Although I am sure it was as pure as most people's; still it is an unpleasant exercise, and bound to offend a few whose lives touched hers, perhaps less than honorably."

" 'Less than honorably'?" She was surprised, and not sure what he meant.

He smiled ruefully. "Mine to begin with," he confessed. "The quarrel was innocent enough, not personal, a matter of conviction; but viewed by others who did not know what was said, it might look otherwise. I have no doubt there will be other people who would not care to have every word or gesture examined by the prurient and unkind." He looked at her with a gentleness touched with humor which set her pulses racing. "Have you not been guilty of foolishness now and then which you would rather remained private? Or a word or an act that was hasty, shabbier than you wished?"

"Yes of course I have." She did not need to add more; the understanding was complete, without the necessity of words.

They walked a few paces farther and then turned along the path towards the stone wall and the early roses spilling over it. The archway was in dappled sunlight, picking out the flat surfaces of the individual stones, and the tiny plants in the crevices low down where it was moist, ferns and mosses with flowers like pinprick stars. Above them there was a faint rustle in the leaves of the elm trees as a breeze moved, laden with the smell of grass and leaf mold.

She looked at his face and knew he was thinking of the pleasures of being home in England, the timeless grace of old gardens. Africa with its savagery, its gaudy vegetation, so often seared and withered by relentless sun, its teeming wildlife, all seemed unreal in this ancient certainty where the seasons had come and gone with the same nurturing pattern for a hundred generations.

But Susannah's death would not go away. Law was also a thing more certain here, and Nobby knew Pitt well enough to have no doubt that he would pursue it to the end, no matter what that end might be. He did not bow to coercion, expediency, or even emotional pain.

If the truth were unbearably ugly, she did not know if he would make public all the evidence. If the answer proved to be too desperately tragic, if it would ruin others for no good cause, if the motive caught his pity hard enough, he might relent. Although she could not imagine a reason that could ever mitigate the murder of someone like Susannah.

But that argument was pointless. It was not Pitt she was afraid of, or prosecution or justice, it was truth. It would be equally terrible to her if Kreisler were guilty, whether he were charged or not.

But why did she even entertain the thought? It was hideous, terrible! She felt guilty that it even entered her mind, let alone that she let it remain there.

As if reading her thoughts, or seeing the confusion in her face, he stopped just beyond the arch in the small shade garden with its primroses and honesty and arching Solomon's seal.

"What is it, Nobby?"

She was abashed to find an answer that was neither a lie nor too hurtful to both of them.

"Did you learn anything?" She seized upon something useful to ask.

"About Susannah's death? Not much. It seems to have happened late in the evening and when she was alone in a hansom cab, no one knows where. She had said she was going to visit the Thornes, but never arrived, as far as we know. Unless, of course, the Thornes are lying."

"Why should the Thornes wish her harm?"

"It probably goes back to the death of Sir Arthur Desmond—at least that is what Pitt has apparently suggested. It makes little sense to me."

They were standing so still a small, brown bird flew out of one of the trees and stood on the path barely a yard from them, its bright eyes watching curiously.

"Then why?" she said quietly, the fear still large within her. She knew enough of men who traveled the wild places of the earth to understand that they have to have an inner strength in order to survive, a willingness to attack in the need to defend themselves, the resolve to take life if it threatened their own, a single-mindedness that brooked nothing in its way. Gentler people, more circumspect, more civilized at heart, all too often were crushed by the ferocity of an unforgiving land.

He was watching her closely, almost searchingly. Slowly the happiness and the sense of comfort drained out of him, replaced by pain.

"You are not convinced that I did not do it, are you, Nobby?"

he said with a catch in his voice. "You think I could have murdered that lovely woman? Just because . . ." He stopped, the color washing up his face in guilt.

"No," she said levelly, the words difficult to speak. "Not just because she differed with you over settlement in Africa, of course not. But then we both know that would be absurd. If you had, it would be because of the shares she has in one of the great banking houses and the influence she might have over Francis Standish, and of course because of her husband's position. She supported him fully, which meant she was against you."

He was very pale, his features twisted with hurt.

"For God's sake, Nobby! How would my murdering her help?"

"It is one supporter less. . . ." She trailed off, looking away from him. "I am not supposing you killed her, only that the police might think so. I am afraid for you." That was the truth, but not the whole truth. "And you were angry with her."

"If I killed everyone I was angry with, at one time or another, my whole career would be littered with corpses," he said quietly, and she knew from the tone in his voice that he had believed only the truth she had spoken; the lies and the omissions he understood for what they were.

The bird was still on the path close to them, its head cocked to one side.

He put his hands on her arms and she felt the warmth of him through the thin sleeves of her dress.

"Nobby, I know that you understand Africa as I do, and that at times men are violent in order to survive in a violent and sudden land, where the dangers are largely unknown and there is no law but that of staying alive, but I have not lost my knowledge of the difference between Africa and England. And morality, the underlying knowledge of good and evil, is the same everywhere. You do not kill people simply because they stand in your way, or believe differently over an issue, no matter how big. I argued with Susannah, but I did not hurt her, or cause her to be hurt. You do me an injustice if you do not believe that ... and you cause me deep pain. Surely I do not need to explain that to you? Do we not understand each other without the need for speeches and declarations?"

"Yes." She answered from the heart, her head ignored, silenced in a deeper, more insistent certainty. "Yes of course we do." Should she apologize for even having entertained the thought? Did he need her to?

As if he had read it in her eyes, he spoke, smiling a little.

"Good. Now let us leave it. Don't go back over it. You had to acknowledge what passed through your mind. Don't let there be dishonesty between us, the need to hide behind deceit and politeness for fear of the truth."

"No," she agreed quickly, a ridiculous smile on her face in spite of all that common sense could tell her. "Of course I won't."

He leaned forward and kissed her with a gentleness that took her by blissful surprise.

Pitt was sitting at the breakfast table slowly eating toast and marmalade. The toast was crisp and the butter very mildly salted. Altogether it was something to be savored to the last crumb.

And he had been out until nearly midnight the previous evening, so if he were late at Bow Street this morning, it was justifiable. The children had left for school and Gracie was busy upstairs. The daily woman was scrubbing the back steps, and would presently put black lead on the range, after cleaning it out, a job which Gracie was delighted to have got rid of.

Charlotte was making a shopping list.

"Are you going to be late again this evening?" she asked, looking up at him.

"I doubt it," he replied with his mouth full. "Although we still haven't found the hansom driver yet. . . ."

"Then he's involved," she said with certainty. "If he were innocent he would have come forward by now. If he doesn't want to be found, how will you get him?"

He finished the rest of his tea. "By the long, slow process of questioning every driver in London," he assured her. "And proving whether they were where they say. And if we are lucky, by someone informing. But we don't know where she went into the water. It could have been upriver or down. All we do know is that she seems to have been dragged some distance by her clothes being caught in something." Charlotte winced. "I'm sorry," he apologized.

"Have you found her cloak?" she asked.

"No, not yet."

He ate the last of his toast with satisfaction.

"Thomas . . ."

He pushed out his chair and stood up. "Yes?"

"Do bodies often wash up at Traitors Gate?"

"No—why?"

She took a deep breath and let it out.

"Do you think it is possible that whoever it was intended her to end up there?"

The idea was puzzling, and one which had not occurred to him before.

"Traitors Gate? I should doubt it. Why? It's more likely that he cared where he put her in, close to where he killed her, and unobserved. It would be chance, tide and the currents which took her to the slipway at the Tower. And, of course, whatever dragged her."

"But what if it wasn't?" she insisted. "What if it was intended?"

"It doesn't honestly make a lot of difference, except that he would have had to find the right place to put her in, which might have meant moving her. But why would anyone care enough to take the risk?"

"I don't know," she confessed. "Only because she betrayed someone."

"Who? Not her husband. She was always loyal to him, not as

a matter of course, but because she truly loved him. You told me that yourself."

"Oh, yes," she agreed. "I didn't mean that kind of betrayal. I thought perhaps it might be back to the Inner Circle again."

"There are no women members anyway, and I'm convinced Chancellor is not a member either."

"But what about her brother-in-law, Francis Standish?" she pressed. "Could he not be involved in Sir Arthur's death, and somehow she found out? Susannah was very fond of Sir Arthur. She wouldn't keep silent, even to protect her own. Perhaps that was what troubled her so much."

"Family loyalty . . . and betrayal," Pitt said slowly, turning the idea over in his mind. Harriet Soames's face was sharp in his inner eye, in passionate defense of her father, even knowing his guilt. "Possibly . . ."

"Does it help?"

He looked at her. "Not a lot. Intentional or not, she will have been put in at the same place." He pushed his chair back in, kissed her cheek before going to the door. His hat was on the rack in the hall. "It's something I shall search for with more diligence today. I think it is time I forgot the hansom driver and concentrated on finding a witness to her body being put into the water."

"Nothing except what didn't happen," Tellman said with disgust when Pitt asked him to report his progress so far. They were standing in Pitt's office in the early light, the noise from the street drifting up through the half-open window.

Tellman was tired and frustrated. "No one has seen the damned hansom, either in Berkeley Square or Mount Street, or anywhere else," he went on. "At least, no one who has it in mind to tell us. Of course all London is crawling with cabs, any one of which could have had Mrs. Chancellor in it!" He leaned against the bookcase behind him. "Two were seen in Mount Street about the right time, but both of them have been accounted for. One was a Mr. Garney going out to dine with his mother. His story is well vouched for by his servants and hers. The other was a Lieutenant Salsby and a Mrs. Latten, going to the West End to dine. At least that is what they said."

"You disbelieve them?" Pitt sat down behind his desk.

" 'Course I disbelieve them!" Tallman smiled. "Seen his face, and you would have too. Seen hers, and you'd know what they were going to do! She's no better than she should be, but not party to abducting a cabinet minister's wife. That's not how she makes her living!"

"You know her?"

Tellman's face registered the answer.

"Anything else?" Pitt asked.

"Don't know what else to look for." Tellman shrugged. "We've spent days trying to find the place she went in. Most likely Lime-house. More discreet than upriver. It'd be eleven or so before he put her into the water, maybe. That'd be four hours before she was found. Don't really matter whether she hit the slipway on the in-coming tide or went past farther into the current and was washed up on the outgoing. Still means she put in somewhere south." He breathed out slowly and pulled a face. "And that's a long stretch of river with a dozen wharves and steps, and as many streets that lead to them. And you'll get no help from the locals. The people that spend their time waiting around there aren't likely to speak to us if they can help it. Slit your throat for the practice."

"I know that, Tellman. Have you a better idea?"

"No. I tried them all and they don't work, but I'm known 'round there. Used to be at that station. You might do better." His expression and his voice both denied it.

But Pitt was not satisfied. According to the river police, if she had been put into the water within an hour or so of having been killed, which the medical examiner had said could be no later than eleven, or at a stretch half past, then the incoming tide could only have carried her from the Limehouse area, at the farthest. It was more likely to have been closer, except that that made it Wapping, right on the Pool of London.

Tellman had already tried the Thames police, whose station was on the river's edge. They were extremely helpful, in an utterly negative way. Their patrols were excellent. They knew every yard of the waterfront, and they were sure no woman of Susannah Chancellor's description and status had been put into the river there that night. It was an extravagant claim, but Pitt was inclined to believe them. The Port of London was always busy, even as late as midnight. Why should anyone take such a risk?

Which always brought him back to the question as to why anyone should murder Susannah Chancellor anyway. Was it an abduction that had gone tragically wrong?

Then was it simply greed, imagining Chancellor would pay a fine ransom? Or was the motive political . . . . which brought him back to Peter Kreisler again.

Tellman had already spent fruitless days in Limehouse and learned nothing of use. If anyone had seen a body put into the water, they were not saying so. If they had seen a hansom, and a man carrying a woman, they were not saying that either. He had even been south of the river to Rotherhithe, but that yielded no conclusion, except that it was not impossible that someone could have taken a small boat from one of the hundred wharves or stairs and carried a body in it. He had even considered if Tellman could be part of the conspiracy, a subtle and brilliant Inner Circle member. But looking at the anger in his face, hearing the brittle edge in his voice, he could not believe his own judgment to be so wrong.

"What now?" Tellman said cynically, interrupting Pitt's thoughts. "You want me to try the Surrey Docks?"

"No, there's no point." An idea was forming in Pitt's mind from what Charlotte had said about betrayals and Traitors Gate. "Go and see what you can find out about her brother-in-law."

Tellman's eyebrows rose. "Mrs. Chancellor's brother-in-law—

Francis Standish? Why? Why in the name of Hell would he want to murder her? I still think it was Kreisler."

"Possibly. But look at Standish anyway."

"Yes sir. And what will you be doing?"

"I shall try upriver, somewhere like the stretch between Westminster and Southwark."

"But that would mean someone'd waited with her after she was dead and before they put her into the water," Tellman pointed out incredulously. "Why would anyone do that? Why take that risk?"

"Less chance of being seen, closer to midnight," Pitt suggested.

Tellman gave him a look of total scorn. "There's people up and down the river all the time. Anything after that'd be as good. Better get rid of it as soon as possible. Easier to travel about in a hansom when they're all over the streets," he said reasonably. "Who'd notice one in the many? Notice one at one o'clock in the morning. Too late for theaters. People who go to late parties and balls have their own carriages."

Pitt was uncertain whether to share Charlotte's idea with Tellman or not. On the face of it, it sounded absurd, and yet the more he thought of it, the more it seemed possible.

"What if he intended her to be washed ashore at Traitors Gate?"

Tellman stared at him. "Another warning to anyone minded to betray the Circle?" he said with a spark of fire in his eyes. "Maybe. But that'd take some doing! No reason why she should come ashore at all. Often they don't. And even if he knew the tides, she could have been dragged; as it happens, she was! He'd have to wait for the ebb, in case she washed off again." His voice was gathering enthusiasm. "So he waits somewhere, and puts her in at high water, then he'd be certain positive she'd not go off again."

Then his face darkened. "But there's no way, even if he put her in above the Tower, that she'd be sure to go ashore there. She could have gone all the way down to the next big curve, around Wapping, or further, to the Surrey Docks." He shook his head. "He'd have to put her there himself, by boat, most likely. Only a madman would risk carrying her there down at Queen's Steps, the way we went to find her."

"Well he wouldn't come from the north bank upriver," Pitt thought aloud. "That's Custom House Quay, and then the Billingsgate Fish Market. He'd have been seen for sure."

"Other side of the river," Tellman said instantly, standing upright, his thin body tense. "Horseley Down. Nobody 'round there! He could have put her in a small boat and ferried her across. Just left her more or less where we found her. Outgoing tide wouldn't touch her."

"Then I'm going to the south bank," Pitt said decisively, standing up and moving away from the desk.

Tellman looked doubtful. "Sounds like a lot of trouble, not to say danger, just to make sure she fetched up at the Tower. Can't see it, myself."

"It's worth trying," Pitt answered, undeterred.

"The medical examiner said she was dragged," Tellman pointed out, the last shreds of reluctance still clinging. "Clothes caught on something! He couldn't have just put her there!"

"If he brought her from the other side, perhaps he dragged her?" Pitt replied. "Behind his boat, to make it look as if she'd been in the water some time."

"Geez!" Tellman sucked his breath in between his teeth. "Then we're dealing with a madman!" He caught sight of Pitt's face. "All right—even madder than we thought."

Pitt took a hansom. It was a long ride. He went south and east along the river, crossed at London Bridge and then turned east again immediately into Tooley Street.

"What ezac'ly are yer lookin' fer?" the cabby asked dubiously. It was not that he objected to a fare that lasted several hours, and was willing to pay him to stand around, but he liked to know what was wanted of him, and this was a most peculiar request.

"I'm looking for a place where someone could have waited in a carriage until a quiet time just after the tide had turned, and then rowed a body across the river and left it on the slipway at Traitors Gate," Pitt replied.

The cabby let out an incredulous blasphemy under his breath. "Sorry, guv," he apologized the moment after. "But you ain't 'alf got a nasty turn o' mind." He looked nervously around at the quiet bank and the empty stretch of river in the sun.

Pitt smiled sadly. "The murder of Mr. Chancellor's wife," he explained, showing the man his card.

"Oh! Oh, yeah! That was terrible, poor lady." The man's eyes widened. "Yer reckon as she was killed over 'ere, and taken across after, like?"

"No, I think she was brought over here in a carriage, someone waited until the tide turned, and then rowed across and left her on the slipway at the Tower."

"Why? That don't make no sense! Why not just stick 'er in the water and scarper! Daft ter be seen. 'Oo cares where she fetches up?"

"I think he may have cared."

"Why wait for the tide to turn? I'd just a' put 'er in there as quick as possible and got goin' afore anyone saw me." He shivered. "You looking for a madman?"

"A man with an insane hatred, perhaps, but not mad in any general sense."

"Then he'd a' gone ter 'Orsley Steps and rowed up a fraction on the incoming tide and left 'er there," the cabby said with decision. "An' rowed back ter Little Bridge, further up, ter keep goin' with the tide, like, instead o' rowin' agin it." He looked satisfied with his answer.

"If he'd left her on the incoming tide," Pitt reasoned, "she might have been floated off again, and finished up somewhere else."

"True," the cabby agreed. "Still an' all, I'd a' taken the chance."

"Perhaps. But I'll see if anyone saw a carriage standing waiting that night. Horsley Down Steps and Little Bridge Stairs, you said?"

"Yes, guv. Yer want ter go there ter them places?"

"I do."

"It would take an awful long time!"

"It probably will," Pitt agreed with a tight smile. "Don't worry, I'll take you to lunch. Do you know a good pub close by?"

The cabby's face brightened. " 'Course I do! Bin 'ere before, or 'ereabouts. There's the Black Bull up over London Bridge, bit over the other side. Or the Triple Plea down Queen Elizabeth Street, just over there." He pointed with a gnarled hand. "Or over the railway line"—he swiveled farther around—"yer could go into Bermondsey and find anything yer like."

"We'll try the Triple Plea," Pitt promised. "First we'll go to the Horsley Down Steps."

"Right, guv. Right y'are." And he urged his horse forward with something almost close to anticipation.

They went down Tooley Street at a brisk trot until it became Queen Elizabeth Street, then the cab turned sharply left towards the river. There was a large building on the right side of the road which looked like a school. The street bore the dismal name of Potters' Fields. Pitt wondered if it struck the cabby's macabre sense of humor. They followed it a hundred yards or so until it ended at the road, little more than a path, which ran along the riverbank. There was only a sloping margin between them and the water, and it was deserted, even at this time of day. They passed two more roads leading up towards Queen Elizabeth Street before they came to the Horsley Down Steps, from where it would have been easy enough to get into a boat.

There was a small open area, less than a square, at the end of Freeman's Lane. A couple of men stood around idly, watching whoever might pass, mainly the traffic along the water.

Pitt got out of the hansom and approached them. Several possible opening gambits occurred to him; the one he least favored was admitting who he was. It was one of those occasions when his sartorial inelegance was an advantage.

"Where would I get a boat around here?" he asked bluntly.

"What kind of a boat?" one of them asked, removing the clay pipe from between his teeth.

"Small one, only to cross the river," Pitt replied.

"London Bridge, jus' up there." The man gestured with his pipe. "Why don't yer walk?"

The other one laughed.

"Because I might meet someone I don't wish to," Pitt replied without a flicker of humor. "I might be taking something private with me," he added for good measure.

"Might yer, then?" The first man was interested. "Well I daresay as I could rent yer a boat."

"Done it before, have you?" Pitt asked casually.

"Wot's it ter you?"

"Nothing." Pitt affected indifference and turned as if to leave.

"Yer want a boat, I'll get yer one!" the man called after him.

Pitt stopped. "Know the tides, do you?" he enquired.

" 'Course I know the tides! I live 'ere!"

"What tide's best for going across to the Tower?"

"Geez! Yer planning to rob the Tower? After the crown jools, are yer?"

Again the second man laughed uproariously.

"I want to take something, not fetch it back," Pitt answered, hoping he had not gone too far.

"Slack water," the first man replied, watching him closely. "Stands ter reason. No current pullin' yer."

"Is the current strong?"

" 'Course it's strong! It's a tidal river, ain't it! Geez, w'ere you bin? Yer stupid or summink?"

"If I got here early, where could I wait?" Pitt ignored the insult.

"Well not 'ere, if yer don't want to be seen, that's fer sure," the man said dryly, and clasped his pipe between his teeth again.

"Why? Who'd see me?"

"Well I would, fer a start!"

"Slack water's in the middle of the night," Pitt argued.

"I know when slack water is! I come down 'ere middle o' the night often enough."

"Why?"

" 'Cause there ain't much right 'ere, but a hundred yards or so"—he pointed along the bank—"there's dozens o' wharfs. There's Baker's Wharf, Sufferance, Bovel and Sons, Landells, West Wharf, the Coal Wharf and a lot o' steps. And that's before yer gets to Saint Saviour's Dock. There's always summink ter be 'ad down there."

"In the middle of the night?"

" 'Course in the middle o' the night. Look, guv, if yer wants to take summink across the river as yer shouldn't, this in't the right place for yer. If yer got to get to the Tower, then go upstream, the Little Bridge Stairs. That's quieter, and there's often the odd boat moored up there as yer could take fer nuffink, if yer brought it back again. No trouble. I'm surprised yer didn't see it from London Bridge if yer came over that way. Only a quarter of a mile or so. Yer can see if there's a boat."

"Thank you," Pitt said with a lift in his voice he could barely control. "That's excellent advice." He fished in his pocket and found a shilling. "Have a pint each. I'm obliged to you."

"Thanks, guv." The man took the shilling and it disappeared into his pocket. He shook his head as Pitt turned away. "Nutter," he said to himself. "Right nutter."

"Back to Little Bridge Stairs," Pitt told the cabby.

"Right y'are."

They went back up to Tooley Street and then down Mill Lane towards the river. This time there was no road beside the water. Mill Lane ended abruptly at the bank and Little Bridge Stairs. There was a narrow dock a few yards upriver, and nothing else but the water and the bank. Pitt alighted.

The cabby wiped the side of his nose and looked expectantly at him.

Pitt looked around him, then down at the ground. Nothing would pass that way, except to go to the steps and the water. A carriage could wait here for hours without necessarily being remarked.

"Who uses these stairs?" Pitt asked.

The cabby looked affronted.

"Y'askin' me? 'Ow the 'ell would I know? Be fair, guv, this ain't my patch."

"I'm sorry," Pitt apologized. "Let's have luncheon at the nearest public house, and they may be able to tell us."

"Now that sounds like a very sensible idea," the cabby agreed with alacrity. "I saw one jus' 'round the corner. Called the Three Ferrets, it were, and looked quite well used, like."

It proved to be more than adequate, and after a meal of tripe and onions, followed by steamed spotted dick pudding and a glass of cider, they returned to the stairs armed with even more information than Pitt had dared hoped for. It seemed very few people used the stairs, but one Frederick Lee had passed by that way on the night in question and had seen a carriage waiting sometime before midnight, the coachman sitting on his box, smoking a cigar, the carriage doors closed. On his way home, more than an hour later, the man had seen it again. He had thought it odd, but none of his business, and the coachman had been a big fellow, and Lee was not inclined to make trouble for no good reason. He believed in minding his own business. He despised nosiness; it was uncivil and unhealthy.

Pitt had thanked him heartily, treated him to a glass of cider, then taken his leave.

But at the narrow, riverside end of Mill Lane, overlooking the water and the stairs down, Pitt walked back and forth slowly, eyes downcast, searching the ground just in case there were any signs of the carriage that had waited there so long, while the tide reached its height, hung slack, and then began the ebb. The surface of the road bore no trace; it was rutted stone sloping away to gutters at the side.

But it was summer. There had been only a brief shower or two of rain in the last week, nothing to wash away debris. He walked slowly up one side, and was partway down the other, about twenty yards from the water, when he saw a cigar butt, and then another. He bent down and picked them up, holding them in the palm of his hand. They were both coming unraveled from the leaf at the charred end, the tobacco loose and thready. He pulled it gently. It was distinctive, aromatic, certainly costly, not the sort of a cigar a cabdriver or waterside laborer would smoke. He turned it over carefully, examining the other end. It was curiously cut, not by a knife but by a specifically designed cigar clipper, the blades meeting equidistantly from either side. There was a very slight twist to it, and the mark of an uneven front tooth where someone had clenched a jaw on it in a moment of emotional tension.

He took out his handkerchief and wrapped them both carefully and placed them in his pocket, then continued on his way.

But he found nothing else of interest, and returned to the hansom, where the cabby was sitting on the box, watching every move he made.

"Got summink?" he asked with excitement, waiting to be told what it was and what it meant.

"I think so," Pitt replied.

"Well?" The man was not going to be shut out of the explanation.

"A cigar butt," Pitt said with a smile. "An expensive one."

"Gawd . . ." The cabby let out his breath in a sigh. " 'Er murderer sat an' smoked, with 'er corpse in his carriage, awaiting to take 'er across the river. 'E's a cool bastard, in't 'e?"

"I doubt it." Pitt climbed into the cab. "I rather think he was in the grip of a passion possibly greater than ever before in his life. Take me to Belgravia please, Ebury Street."

"Belgravia! Yer never thinking 'im what done it lives in Belgravia, are yer?"

"Yes I am. Now get started will you!"

It was a long ride back across the river and westwards, and in places the traffic was heavy. Pitt had plenty of time to think. If

Susannah's murderer had thought of her as a traitor, and felt it so passionately he had killed her for it, then it could only be someone to whom she could be considered to owe an intense loyalty. That must be either her family, represented by Francis Standish, or her husband.

What betrayal could that be? Had she believed Arthur Desmond and Peter Kreisler, after all? Had she questioned Standish's investment with Cecil Rhodes, the whole manner in which the Inner Circle was involved? If Standish were a member, possibly a prominent one, could he even be the executioner? And had Susannah known, or guessed that? Was that why she had to be killed, for her knowledge, and because she was bent on sharing it rather than remaining loyal to her family, her class, and its interests?

That made a hideous sense. Standish could have met her in Mount Street. She would have expected a quarrel, a plea, but not violence. She would have been quite unafraid of anything but unpleasantness, and climbed into his carriage without more than a little coercion on his part. It satisfied all the facts he knew.

Except for what had happened to her cloak. Now that he was sure she had not been put in the river at all, simply made to look as if the receding tide had left her there by chance, it was no longer a reasonable explanation that her cloak had become lost as the current took her one way and then another.

Had he dropped it in the river for that purpose? Why? It proved nothing. And if he had, why had it not been washed up somewhere, or tangled in some rudder or oar? It would not have sunk with no body in it to carry it down. Anyway, it was a stupid thing to do; simply one more article for the police to search for, and meaning nothing one way or the other.

Unless, of course, the cloak did mean something! Could it be in some way marked, which would incriminate Standish?

Pitt could think of nothing. No one was pretending it was suicide or accident. The method and means were plain enough, even the motive was plain. He had defiantly and unnecessarily drawn attention to it!

The more he thought about it, the more sense it made. Sitting in the hansom, in spite of the mildness of the day, he shivered as he felt the power of the Inner Circle everywhere around him, not only making threats of financial and political ruin, but when betrayed, ruthlessly murdering its own, even a woman.

"Ebury Street, guv!" the cabby called out. "What number do you want?"

"Twelve," Pitt replied with a start.

" 'Ere y'are then, twelve it is. D'yer want me to wait for yer?"

"No thank you," Pitt replied, climbing out and closing the door. "I could be some time." He looked in his pocket for the very large sum he now owed for having had the cab out most of the day.

The cabby took it and counted it. "No offense," he apologized before putting it into his pocket. "That don't matter," he said referring back to the time. "I'd kinda like to see this to the end, if yer don't mind, like?"

"As you please." Pitt gave a slight smile, then turned and went up the steps.

The door was opened by a tall footman in livery. "Yes sir?"

"Superintendent Pitt, from Bow Street. Is Mr. Standish at home?"

"Yes sir, but he has a gentleman with him. If you care to wait, I will ask if he is able to see you." He stood aside to allow Pitt in, and then showed him to the study. Apparently Standish and his visitor were in the withdrawing room.

The study was a small room by the standards of houses in Belgravia, but graciously proportioned and furnished in walnut wood with a red Turkey carpet and red curtains, giving it an air of warmth. It was obviously a room in which work was carried out. The desk was functional as well as handsome; and there were inkwells, pens, knives, blotting powder and seals neatly placed ready for use. And there was paper splayed out, as if only recently left. Perhaps Standish had been interrupted by the arrival of his present visitor. A large red jasper ashtray sat on one corner of the desk, a heavy coil of ash lying in the center, and one cigar stub, burned right down to within half an inch of the end.

Gingerly Pitt picked it up and put it to his nose. It was quite unlike the one from Little Bridge Stairs, both in aroma and texture of tobacco. Even the end was different—cut with a knife—and the faint teeth marks were very even.

He reached for the bell rope and pulled it.

The footman came, looking a little startled at being summoned by a guest whom he knew to be a mere policeman. "Yes sir?"

"Does Mr. Standish have any cigars other than these?" Pitt asked, holding up the butt for the man to see.

The footman hid his distaste for such a display of peculiar manners as well as he was able, but some shadow of it was visible in his eyes.

"Yes sir, I believe he does keep some others for guests. If you care to have one, sir, I shall see if I can find them."

"Yes please."

With raised eyebrows the footman went to a drawer in the desk, opened it, and produced a box of cigars which he offered to Pitt.

Pitt took one, although he knew before smelling it that it was not like the butt in his pocket. It was narrower, darker in color and of a bland, unremarkable odor.

"Thank you." He replaced it in its box. "Does Mr. Standish ever drive his own carriage, say a four-in-hand?"

The footman's eyebrows were so high they furrowed his brow. "No sir. He has a touch of rheumatism in his hands, which makes it most uncomfortable, indeed extremely dangerous, when trying to control horses."

"I see. What are the symptoms of the rheumatism?"

"I think he is better placed to tell you such things, sir, than I. And I am sure that he will not be above an hour or so with his present business."

"What are the symptoms?" Pitt persisted, and with such urgency in his voice that the footman looked taken aback. "If you can tell me, I may not need to bother Mr. Standish."

"I'm sure, sir, it would be much better if you were to consult a physician. . . ."

"I don't want a general answer," Pitt snapped. "I want to know precisely how it affects Mr. Standish. Can you tell me or not?"

"Yes sir." The footman backed away a step. He regarded Pitt with considerable apprehension. "It shows itself with a sudden, sharp pain in the thumbs, and loss of strength."

"Enough to lose grip upon whatever he is holding, for example, the reins of the carriage?"

"Precisely. That is why Mr. Standish does not drive. I thought I had explained that, sir."

"You have, indeed you have." Pitt looked towards the door. "I shall not now have to bother Mr. Standish. If you feel it necessary to say I called, tell him you were able to answer my questions. There is no cause for alarm."

"Alarm?"

"That's right. None at all," Pitt replied, and walked past him to the hallway and the front door.

It was not Standish. He did not believe it was Kreisler—he had no cause for the passion in it—but he had to make certain. He found the cabdriver waiting for him, surprised to see him back so soon. He offered no explanation, but gave him Kreisler's address and asked him to hurry.

"Mr. Kreisler is out," the manservant informed him.

"Does he have any cigars?" Pitt asked.

"I beg your pardon, sir?"

"Does he have any cigars?" Pitt repeated tartly. "Surely the question is plain enough?"

The man's face stiffened. "No he does not. He does not smoke, sir. He finds the smell of tobacco offensive."

"You are quite sure?"

"Of course I am sure. I have worked for Mr. Kreisler for several years, both here and in Africa."

"Thank you, that is all I needed to know. Good day."

The manservant muttered something under his breath along the general lines of a parting, but less polite than he would have wished to be heard.

It was now early evening. Pitt got back into the hansom. "Berkeley Square," he ordered.

"Right y'are, guv."

It was not far, and Pitt rode deep in thought. There was one more thing he wanted to find, and if it was as he now expected, then there was only one conclusion that fitted all he knew, all the material evidence. And yet emotionally it was a tragedy out of proportion to anything he had foreseen or imagined. The thought of it saddened him, even touched him with a dark fear of the mind, a confusion of ideas and beliefs, as well as a very immediate apprehension about his own actions and the course that lay before him now.

The cabby peered in. "What number, guv?"

"No number. Just stop by the nearest manhole down into the sewers."

"What did yer say? I didn't 'ear yer right. Sounds like yer said the sewers!"

"I did. Find me a manhole," Pitt agreed.

The cab moved forward thirty or forty yards and stopped again.

"Thank you." Pitt climbed out and looked back at the hansom. "This time I definitely want you to wait. I may be a little while."

"I wouldn't leave yer now if yer paid me to go," the cabby said vehemently. "I never 'ad a day like this in me life before! I can get free dinners on this fer a year or more. Yer'll want a light, guv?" He scrambled down and detached one of his carriage lamps, lit it and gave it to Pitt.

Pitt took it and thanked him, then pulled up the manhole lid and very carefully climbed into the hole down the rungs into the bowels of the sewer system. The daylight decreased to a small round hole above him, and he was glad of the lamp and its pool of light. He turned to make his way along through the round brick-lined tunnel, moisture dripping onto the path and echoing eerily as it struck the rancid waterway between. Tunnel led off tunnel, down steps and over sluices and falls. Everywhere was a sound of water and the sour smell of waste.

"Tosher!" he called out, and his voice echoed in all directions. Finally he fell silent and there was no more sound than the incessant dripping, broken by the squeak of rats, and then nothing again.

He walked a dozen more yards, and then shouted again. "Tosher" was the general cant term for the men who made their living scavenging the sewers. He was close to a great sluice that must have spilled water over a drop of a dozen feet onto a lower level. He moved on, and called a third time.

"Yeh?"

The voice was so close and so harsh it startled him and he stopped and nearly fell into the channel. Almost at his elbow a man in thigh-high rubber boots came out of a side tunnel, his face grimy, his hair smeared across his forehead.

"Is this your stretch?" Pitt jerked his arm backwards towards the way he had come.

" 'Course it is. What d'yer think I'm doin' 'ere, lookin' for the source o' the Nile?" the man said with contempt. "If yer lookin' fer a stretch o' yer own, this ain't it. It's not fer sale."

"Police," Pitt said succinctly. "Bow Street."

"Well, yer off yer beat," the man said dryly. "Watcher want 'ere?"

"A woman's blue cloak, maybe put down a manhole almost a week ago."

In the dim light the man's face had a guarded look, devoid of surprise. Pitt knew he had found it, and felt a sudden breathlessness as the reality of his belief swept over him.

"Maybe," the man said cautiously. "Why? What's it werf?"

"Accessory after the fact of murder, if you lie about it," Pitt replied. "Where is it?"

The man drew in his breath, whistling a little between his teeth, looked at Pitt's face for several seconds, then changed his mind about prevaricating.

"There weren't nothing wrong with it at all, not even wet," he said with regret. "I gave it to me woman."

"Take it to Bow Street. Maybe if you're lucky you'll get it back after the trial. The most important thing is your evidence. Where did you find it, and when?"

"Tuesd'y. Early mornin'. It were 'ung up on the stairs up inter Berkeley Square. Someone must a' dropped it in and not even waited to see if it fell all the way down. Though why the devil anyone'd want ter do that I dunno."

"Bow Street," Pitt repeated, and turned to find his way back. A rat scuttered past him and plopped into the channel. "Don't forget," he added. "Accessory to murder will get you a long stretch in the Coldbath. Helpfulness will get you an equally long stretch of undisturbed prosperity."

The man sighed and spat, muttering something under his breath.

Pitt retraced his steps back to the ladder and daylight. The cabby was waiting for him with burning curiosity in his eyes.

"Well?" he demanded.

Pitt replaced the light in its bracket.

"Wait for me outside number fourteen," he replied, breathing in deeply and looking for his handkerchief to blow his nose. He set out at a brisk walk across the square to Chancellor's house, mounted the steps and knocked at the door. The lamplighter was busy at the far side and a carriage swept past, harness jingling.

The footman let him in with a look of surprise and distaste, not only at his appearance but also at the distinctive and highly unpleasant odor surrounding him.

"Good evening, Superintendent." He opened the door wide and Pitt stepped inside. "Mr. Chancellor has just returned from the

Colonial Office. I shall tell him you are here. May I say, sir, that I hope you have some good news?" It seemed he had not read the shadows in Pitt's face.

"I have much further information," Pitt replied. "It is necessary that I speak with Mr. Chancellor. But perhaps before you bother him, I might have another word with the maid—Lily, I think her name is—who saw Mrs. Chancellor leave."

"Yes sir, of course." He hesitated. "Superintendent, should I know . . . er . . . should I have Mr. Richards present this time?" Perhaps after all he had seen something of the emotions Pitt felt with such intensity, the sadness, the knowledge that he was in the presence of overwhelming passions of violence and tragedy.

"I think not," Pitt replied. "But thank you for the thought." The man had served Chancellor for fifteen years. He would be confused, torn with horror and conflicting loyalties. There was no need to subject him to what was bound to ensue. He would be little likely to be of any use.

"Right sir. I'll get Lily for you. Would you like to see her in the housekeeper's sitting room?"

"No thank you, the hall would be better."

The footman turned to leave, hesitated for a moment, perhaps wondering if he should offer Pitt some opportunity to wash, or even clean clothes. Then he must have considered the situation too grave for such small amenities.

"Oh—" Pitt said hastily.

"Yes sir?"

"Can you tell me what happened to Bragg's arm?"

"Our coachman, sir?"

"Yes."

"He scalded it, sir. Accident, of course."

"How did it happen, exactly? Were you there?"

"No sir, but I got there just after. In fact we were all there then, trying to clean up, and to help him. It was a pretty right mess."

"A mess? Did he drop something hot?"

"Not exactly. It was Mr. Chancellor himself who dropped it. It just sort of slipped out of his hands, so Cook said."

"What did?"

"A mug o' hot cocoa. Boiling milk is awful hot, makes a terrible scald, it does. Poor George was in a right state."

"Where did it happen?"

"Withdrawing room. Mr. Chancellor had sent for George to harness up the brougham and come and tell him when it was done. He wanted to know something about one o' the horses, so he wanted George hisself, like, not just the message. He was having a mug o' cocoa—"

"Warm weather for cocoa, isn't it?"

"Yes, it is. I would sooner have had a lemonade, myself," the footman agreed. His face was puzzled, but he still obediently answered every question.

"Is Mr. Chancellor fond of cocoa?"

"Never 'eard that he was. But he certainly had cocoa that evening. I'd swear to that. I've seen poor George. Anyway, seems Mr. Chancellor's foot slipped, or summink, and George moved rather sudden like, and got himself scalded. Mr. Chancellor rang the bell immediately, and Mr. Richards came and saw what had happened. Then before you know what's what, we're all in the kitchen trying to help poor George, getting his coat off, ripping his shirtsleeves, putting this and that on his arm, Cook and the housekeeper arguing fit to bust whether butter's best, or flour, maids shrieking and Mr. Richards saying as we should get a doctor. Housemaids is upstairs in bed, in the attic, so they didn't know a thing, and nobody even thought of them to clean up. And with Mr. Chancellor needing to go out."

"So he drove himself?"

"That's right."

"What time did he get home?"

"Don't know, sir. Late, because we went to bed just before midnight, poor George being in state, and the mistress not home yet. . . ." His face fell as he remembered all that he had learned since the panic of that night.

"Where was Lily during this upheaval?"

"In the kitchen with the rest of us, till Mr. Chancellor sent her to the landing to tear up the old sheets to make bandages for George."

"I see. Thank you."

"Shall I get Lily, sir?"

"Yes please."

Pitt stood in the fine hallway, looking about him, not at the pictures and the sheen on the parquet flooring, but at the stairway and the landing across the top, and then at the chandelier hanging from the ceiling with its dozen or so lights.

Lily came through the green baize door looking anxious and still profoundly shaken.

"Y-you want to see me, sir? I didn't know anything, I swear, or I'd have told you then. I don't know where the mistress went. She never said a thing to me. I didn't even know she was going out!"

"No, I know that Lily," he said as gently as he could. "I want you to think back very carefully. Can you remember where you were when you saw her leave? Tell me exactly what you saw . . . absolutely exactly."

She stared at him. "I just came along the landing after turning down the beds an' looked down to the hallway. . . ."

"Why?"

"Beg pardon, sir?"

"Why did you look down?"

"Oh—I suppose 'cause I saw someone moving across towards the door. . . ."

"Exactly what did you see?"

"Mrs. Chancellor going to the front door, sir, like I said."

"Did she speak to you?"

"Oh no, she was on 'er way out."

"She didn't say good night, or tell you when she expected to come back? After all, you would have to wait up for her."

"No sir, she didn't see me 'cause she didn't turn 'round. I just saw her back as she went out."

"But you knew it was her?"

"O' course I knew it was her. She was wearin' her best cloak, dark blue velvet, it is, lined with white silk. It's the most beautiful cloak. . . ." She stopped, her eyes filling with tears. She sniffed hard. "Yer didn't ever find it, did you, sir?"

"Yes, we found it," Pitt said almost in a whisper. He had never before felt such a complex mixture of grief and anger about any case that he could recall.

She looked at him. "Where was it?"

"I don't think you need to know that, Lily." Why hurt her unnecessarily? She had loved her mistress, cared for her in her day-to-day life, been part of it in all its intimacies. Why tell her it had been pushed down into the sewers that wove and interwove under London?

She must have understood his reasons. She accepted the answer.

"You saw the back of Mrs. Chancellor's head, the cloak, as she went across the hall towards the front door. Did you see her dinner gown beneath it?"

"No sir, it comes to the floor."

"All you could see would be her face?"

"That's right."

"But she had her back to you?"

"If you're going to say it weren't her, sir, you're wrong. There weren't no other lady her height! Apart from that, there weren't no other lady here, sir, then nor ever. Mr. Chancellor isn't like that with other ladies. Devoted, he was, poor man."

"No, I wasn't thinking that, Lily."

"I'm glad. . . ." She looked uncomfortable. Presumably she was thinking of Peter Kreisler, and the ugly suspicions that had crossed their minds with regard to Susannah.

"Thank you, Lily, that's all."

"Yes sir."

As soon as Lily had gone the footman appeared from the recess beyond the stairs. No doubt he had been waiting there in order to conduct Pitt to his master.

"Mr. Chancellor asked me to take you to the study, Superintendent," he instructed Pitt, leading the way through a large oak door, along a passage into another wing of the house, and knocking on another door. As soon as it was answered, he opened it and stood back for Pitt to enter.

This was very different from the more formal reception rooms leading off the hall where Pitt had seen Chancellor before. The curtains were drawn closed over the deep windows. The room was decorated in yellows and creams, with touches of dark wood, and had an air of both graciousness and practicality. Three walls had bookcases against them, and there was a mahogany desk towards the center, with a large chair behind it. Pitt's eyes went straight to the humidor on top.

Chancellor looked strained and tired. There were shadows around his eyes, and his hair was not quite as immaculate as when Pitt had first known him, but he was perfectly composed.

"Further news, Mr. Pitt?" he said with a lift of his eyebrows. He only glanced at Pitt's grimy clothes and completely disregarded the odor. "Surely anything now is academic? Thorne has escaped, which may not be as bad as it first appears. It will save the government the difficulty of coming to a decision as to what to do about him." He smiled with a slight twist to his mouth. "I hope there is no one else implicated? Apart from Soames, that is."

"No, no one," Pitt replied. He hated doing this. It was a cat-and-mouse game, and yet there was no other way of conducting it. But he had no taste for it, no sense of achievement.

"Then what is it, man?" Chancellor frowned. "Quite frankly, I am not in a frame of mind to indulge in lengthy conversation. I commend you for your diligence. Is there anything else?"

"Yes, Mr. Chancellor, there is. I have learned a great deal more about the death of your wife. . . ."

Chancellor's eyes did not waver. They were bluer than Pitt had remembered them.

"Indeed?" There was a very slight lift in his voice, an unsteadiness, but that was only natural.

Pitt took a deep breath. His own voice sounded strange in his ears when he spoke, almost unreal. The clock on the Pembroke table by the wall ticked so loudly it seemed to echo in the room. The drawn curtains muffled every sound from the garden or the street beyond.

"She was not thrown into the river and washed up by chance of tide at Traitors Gate. . . ."

Chancellor said nothing, but his eyes did not leave Pitt's.

"She was killed before, early in the evening," Pitt went on, measuring what he was saying, choosing his words, the order in which he related the facts. "Then taken in a carriage across the river to a place just south of London Bridge, a place called Little Bridge Stairs."

Chancellor's hand closed tight above the desk where he was sitting. Pitt was still standing across from him.

"Her murderer kept her there," Pitt continued, "for a long time, in fact until half past two in the morning, when the tide turned. Then he placed her in the small boat which is often tied up at the steps, the boat he had seen when crossing London Bridge. It is a few hundred yards away."

Chancellor was staring at him, his face curiously devoid of expression, as if his mind were on the verge of something terrible, hovering on the brink.

"When he had rowed out a short way," Pitt went on, "he put her over the stern, tied across her back and under her arms with a rope, and rowed the rest of the way, dragging her behind, so her body would look as if it had been in the water a long time. When he got to the far side, he laid her on the slipway at Traitors Gate, because that was where he wished her to be found."

Chancellor's eyes widened so imperceptibly it could have been a trick of the light.

"How do you know this? Do you have him?"

"Yes, I have him," Pitt said softly. "But I know it because the carriage was seen."

Chancellor did not move.

"And during the long wait, he smoked at least two cigars," Pitt went on, his eyes going for a moment to the humidor a few inches from Chancellor's hand, "of a curiously aromatic, pungent brand."

Chancellor coughed and caught his breath. "And you ... worked all this out?"

"With difficulty."

"Was ..." Chancellor was watching Pitt very closely, measuring him. "Was she killed in the hansom cab? Was she ever really going to Christabel Thorne's?"

"No, she was never going to Christabel Thorne's," Pitt replied. "There was no hansom cab. She was murdered here in this house."

Chancellor's face tightened, but he did not move. His hand on the desk opened and closed, but he did not touch the cigar box.

"Her maid saw her leave," he said, swallowing with difficulty.

"No, Mr. Chancellor, she saw you leave, wearing Mrs. Chancellor's cloak," Pitt corrected him. "She was a very tall woman, as tall as you are. You walked along the street to the manhole at the corner of the square, then you opened it and pushed the cloak down. You returned here and went upstairs saying you had put her in the hansom. You rang the bell and ordered your own carriage. Shortly after that you contrived an accident in which you scalded your coachman's arm, and while everyone was attending to that, you carried Mrs. Chancellor's body downstairs and put it into your own carriage, which you drove east and south until you crossed the river, as I have already said, and waited until the tide turned, so you could leave her at Traitors Gate, when the water would not rise any further and take her away again."

Pitt reached forward and opened the cigar box, taking out one of the rich cigars. The aroma of it was sickeningly familiar. He held it to his nose, and looked over it at Chancellor.

Suddenly the pretense was gone. A passion flooded Chancellor's face that was so savage and so violent it altered him utterly. The assurance, the urbanity, were vanished, his lips drawn back revealing his teeth, his cheeks white; there was a burning outrage in his eyes.

"She betrayed me," he said harshly, his voice still high with the incredulity of it. "I loved her absolutely. We were everything to each other. She was more than just my wife, she was my companion, my partner in all my dreams. She was part of everything I did, everything I've admired. She always believed exactly as I did . . . she understood . . . and then she betrayed me! That's the worst sin of all, Pitt . . . to betray love, to betray trust! She fell away, she couldn't trust me to be right. A few rambling, ill-informed, hysterical conversations with Arthur Desmond, and she began to doubt! To doubt me! As if I didn't know more about Africa than he did, than all of them! Then Kreisler came along, and she listened to him!" His voice was rising with the fury which consumed him till it was close to a shriek.

Pitt moved a step forward but Chancellor ignored him. The wound he felt engrossed him so he was barely aware of Pitt as anything more than an audience.

"After all I had told her, all I had explained," he went on, risen to his feet now behind the desk, staring at Pitt, "she didn't trust me, she listened to Kreisler—Peter Kreisler! A mere adventurer! He sowed a few seeds of doubt in her, and she lost her faith! She told me she was going to have Standish remove his backing from Rhodes's venture. That in itself wouldn't have mattered. . . ."

He laughed savagely, a wild note of hysteria rising in it. "But when people knew about it . . . that my own wife no longer supported me! Dozens would have withdrawn—hundreds! Soon everyone would have doubted. Salisbury's only looking for an excuse. I would have looked a complete fool, betrayed by my own wife!"

He threw himself back into the chair and pulled the desk

drawer open, still staring at Pitt. "I never thought you'd work it out! You liked her ... you admired her! I didn't think you'd ever believe she was a traitor to her husband, to all we had both believed, even though I left her at Traitors Gate. It was the perfect place ... she deserved that."

Pitt wanted to say that if he had not, he might never have found the truth, but it was pointless now.

"Linus Chancellor—"

Chancellor pulled his hand out of the desk drawer. There was a small black pistol in it. He turned the barrel on himself and pulled the trigger. The shot was like a whip crack in the room and exploded in his head, splattering blood and bone everywhere.

Pitt was numb with horror. The room rocked like a ship at sea; the light from the chandelier seemed to splinter and break. There was a terrible smell in the air, and he felt sick.

He heard a running of feet outside. A servant threw open the door and someone screamed, but he did not know if it was a man or a woman. He stumbled over the other chair, bruising himself violently as he made his way out, and heard his own voice like a stranger's sending someone for help.

CHAPTER
TWELVE

"Why?" Nobby Gunne stood in Charlotte's front parlor, her face twisted with anxiety. Of course the newspapers had been full of the tragedy of Linus Chancellor's death. Whatever discretion or pity may have dictated, it was impossible to conceal the fact that he had taken his life suddenly and violently in the presence of a superintendent of the police. No euphemistic explanation would have satisfied even the most naive person. It had to be because the police had brought him some news which was not only unbearable, but so threatening that his response was immediate.

Were it a normal tragedy, some solution to his wife's death which destroyed the faith and trust he had had in her, or which implied some further disaster, he might well have felt there was no alternative but to take his own life; but he would have done it later, after contemplation, and in the privacy of his own company, perhaps late at night. He would not have done it in the police superintendent's presence unless he had not only brought shattering news but also a threat to arrest him and place him under such immediate restraint as to make instant action the only possible way of escape.

There might have been other answers, but no one thought further than the murder of Susannah and that Chancellor himself was guilty.

"Why?" Nobby repeated, staring at Charlotte with urgency and mounting distress. "What did she do that he could not possibly have forgiven her? He did love her, I would have sworn to that. Was it—"she swallowed with great difficulty, as though there were something blocking her throat"—another man?"

Charlotte knew what she feared, and wished intensely that she could have given an answer which would have been painless. But lies were no use.

"No," she said quickly. "No, it was not another man. You are quite right, I believe they did love each other, each in their own way. Please . . ." She indicated the closest chair. "It seems . . ."

"Yes?"

"I was only going to say that it seems so . . . formal, so cold, to stand here face-to-face across the carpet discussing something so terribly important."

"Is it . . . important?" Nobby asked.

"People's feelings are always important."

Reluctantly Nobby sat down, a matter of perching on the edge of one of the chairs. Charlotte sat in another opposite her, but farther back in it, less uncomfortably.

"You do know why, don't you?" Nobby pressed. "Superintendent Pitt will have told you. I remember you used to be most involved in his cases . . . at the time of . . ."

"Yes, he told me."

"Then please, it is of the utmost importance to me. Why did Mr. Chancellor kill Susannah?"

Looking at Nobby's earnest face, Charlotte was deeply afraid that the answer she had to give was not the one Nobby most feared, but one that would in a way be every bit as hard.

"Because he felt she betrayed him," she said gravely. "Not with another man! At least not in the way one would usually take that to mean: with another man's ideas. And he found that intolerable. It would have become public, because she was intending to withdraw her support, and that of the part of the family banking business which was still in her influence. That could not remain private." She looked at Nobby's pale face. "You see, she had been one of his most fervent supporters and admirers all the way along. Everyone would know, and would talk about it."

"But . . . if she felt . . . differently . . ." Nobby started a train of thought, but it died even as she tried to give it words. It was indefinable, something no one had even bothered to express because it was taken for granted. Women owed their husbands their loyalty, not only of supporting them in all they aspired to do, but more subtly than that, going far deeper into the assumptions of man and woman, of trusting their judgment in all matters that lay in the male domain, matters of thought, philosophy, politics and finance. It was taken for granted married women did not require a vote since they were naturally represented by their husbands. It was not open to question, even in the privacy of the home. To challenge publicly was a betrayal of all unspoken agreements everyone assumed, even in a marriage where there was no love, let alone in one where there was love both long-standing and still intense.

"It was a matter of conscience with her," Charlotte added. "She was not willingly disloyal. I even remember seeing her try to argue with him once. He simply did not hear her, because the idea that she thought differently was inconceivable to him. Heaven knows how many times she tried."

Nobby looked almost as if it had been she who was bereaved. She seemed stunned, her eyes focusing far away, her attention inward. She even swayed a little when she stood up.

"Yes . . . yes, of course. I know she did nothing out of malice, or lightly. Thank you. You have been most generous to me. Now, if you will excuse me . . . I think I have a further call to make. . . ."

Charlotte hesitated on the brink of asking her if she was all right, but she knew the wound was an emotional one and must be endured. No one else could help. She murmured some sort of farewell and watched Nobby go, very upright and fumbling a little, out of the parlor and to the front door.

Nobby rode home barely aware of where she was going. Half of her wanted to go now to see Kreisler, to speak to him in the shadow-thin hope there was some other answer. A far larger part knew it was not only pointless but also absurd. She would only embarrass them both. One did not call upon a man in his rooms to inform him that you were ... What? Disillusioned? Heartbroken? That you loved him, which subject had never been discussed between you, never given such words, but that you could not condone what he had done.

He had not asked her to.

She went home engulfed in misery, and it was late in the afternoon, after the time when social calls of a formal nature were paid, when the maid told her that Mr. Kreisler was there to see her.

She considered receiving him in the withdrawing room. The thought of the garden was too painful, too full of memories of a different mood, a closeness and an hour of intimacy and hope.

And yet the withdrawing room—any room in the house—was too small. They would have to stand too close to each other; turning away would be obvious.

"I shall be in the garden," she replied, and walked quickly out of the door as if, even before he entered, it could be some kind of escape.

She was standing by the border, the roses now in bloom, when he reached her. He did not bother with preamble. They had never spoken to each other in trivialities.

"I imagine you have heard about Linus Chancellor?" he said quietly. "All London has. I wish I could be sure it would mean some space, some interim of relief for Africa, but the treaty will go ahead, and by now I daresay Rhodes is already in Mashonaland."

She kept her back towards the lawn and did not turn sideways to face him.

"Is that why you did it?"

"Did what?" He sounded genuinely puzzled. There was no evasion in his voice, no pretense.

She had expected to sound querulous, even tearful, but her question, when it came, was level and surprisingly strong.

"Drove Susannah until she broke."

He was startled. There was a moment's silence. She was acutely aware of his physical presence beside her.

"I didn't!" he said with amazement. "I just ... just argued my case!"

"Yes, you did," she replied. "You pressed her relentlessly, tearing away Chancellor's reasoning, painting word pictures of greed and ruin in Africa, the ultimate immorality of the destruction of a whole race of people. . . ."

"You know that's true!" he challenged her. "That is what will happen. You, of all people, know as well as I do what will happen to the Mashona and the Matabele when Rhodes settles there. Nothing can make them obey Lobengula's laws! It's laughable ... at least it would be if it were not so bloody tragic."

"Yes I do know that, but that is not the point!"

"Isn't it? I think it's precisely the point!"

She turned to face him. "It is not your beliefs I challenged. I wouldn't even if I didn't share them. You are entitled to believe as you will. . . ."

His eyebrows rose and his eyes widened, but she ignored him. Sarcasm was beneath the passions and the seriousness of her argument.

"It is the methods you used. You attacked Chancellor where he was vulnerable."

"Of course," he retorted with surprise. "What would you have me do, attack him where he is best defended? Give him a sporting chance? This is not a game, with chips to be won or lost at the end. This is life, with misery and destruction the price of losing."

She was quite sure of what she meant. She faced him without a flicker.

"And the destruction of Susannah, pressing her heart and her loyalties until they broke, and broke her with them, was it a fair price?"

"For God's sake, Nobby! I didn't know he was going to kill her!" he protested, his face aghast. "You surely cannot imagine I did. You know me better than that!"

"I don't imagine you knew it," she continued, the ache of misery inside her temporarily subsiding under the force of her certainty. "I think you didn't particularly care."

"Of course I care!" His face was white to the lips. "I wouldn't have had it this way. I didn't have options."

"You did not have to press her till she had no way out but to choose between her loyalty to the husband she loved or to her own integrity."

"That's a luxury. The stakes are too high."

"Central Africa, against the turmoil and death of one woman?"

"Yes . . . if you like. Ten million people against one."

"I don't like. What about five million against twenty?"

"Yes . . . of course." There was no wavering in his eyes.

"One million against a hundred? Half a million against a thousand?"

"Don't be absurd!"

"When does it even out, Peter? When does it stop being worth it? When the numbers are the same? Who decides? Who counts?"

"Stop it, Nobby! You are being ridiculous!" He was angry now. There was no apology in him, no sense that he had to defend himself. "We are talking about one person and a whole race. There is no counting to be done. Look, you want the same things for Africa that I do. Why are we quarreling?" He put his hands up as if to touch her.

She stepped back.

"You don't know, do you?" she said with slow understanding, and a sadness that tore at her emotions and left her reason like a shining, solitary light. "It is not what you want I cannot tolerate, it is what you are prepared to do to attain it, and what that doing makes of you. You spoke of the end and the means as if they were separate. They are not."

"I love you, Nobby. . . ."

"I love you also, Peter. . . ."

Again he made a move towards her, and again she stepped back, only a few inches, but the gesture was unmistakable.

"But there is a gulf between what you believe is acceptable and what I believe, and it is one I cannot cross."

"But if we love each other," he argued, his face pinched with urgency and incomprehension, "that is enough."

"No it isn't." There was finality in her voice, even a bitter irony. "You counted on Susannah's love of honor, her integrity, to be greater than her love for Chancellor . . . and you were right. Why is it you do not expect mine to be also?"

"I do. It's just that . . ."

She laughed, a funny, jerky sound, harshly aware of the irony. "It's just that, like Linus Chancellor, you never thought I could disagree with you. Well I do. You may never know how much I wish I did not."

He drew in his breath to speak, to argue one more time, and then saw in her eyes the futility of it, and saved himself the indignity and her the additional pain of refusing him again.

He bit his lip. "This is a price I did not expect to have to pay. It hurts."

Suddenly she could not look at him. Humility was the last thing she had expected. She turned to the roses, and then right around towards the apple tree, so he would not see the tears on her face.

"Good-bye, Nobby," he said softly, his voice husky, as if he too were in the grasp of an emotion almost beyond his bearing, and she heard his footsteps as he walked away, no more than a faint whispering over the grass.

Charlotte's mind was preoccupied with Matthew Desmond and the terrible, consuming loneliness he felt because Harriet could not forgive him for having repeated the telephone conversation she had overheard. She would not even have him received in the house. There was no way he could plead his case or offer any comfort or explanation to her. She had shut herself away with her shame, her anger and her sense of being unforgivably betrayed.

Charlotte turned it over and over in her mind; never for a moment did she doubt that what Matthew had done was right. If he made that choice, he lost Harriet, but had he not done so, had he kept silent against his own conscience, to please her, he could not have kept faith with himself. He would have lost what was best in him, that core of truth which in the end is the key to all decisions, all values, the essence of identity. To deny the knowledge of right is something one does not forgive oneself. Ultimately that would have destroyed their love anyway.

But all the time she was about her own chores, simple or complicated, kneading bread or cutting pastry frills for a pie, watching Gracie peel the vegetables, sorting the linen and mending Pitt's frayed shirt cuffs, finding buttons to replace the lost ones, every time her mind could wander, she could think of nothing but Matthew's pain, his loneliness and the sense of utter bereavement he must be feeling. Even watching Archie and Angus careering around the kitchen floor after each other brought only a brief smile to her face.

In the few evenings they had together she watched Pitt's face in repose, and saw the tension which never left him lately, even after the solution to Susannah's death, and she knew the pity for that ached within him, and the remnants of guilt which still shadowed his thoughts of Arthur Desmond. She longed to be able to help, but putting her arms around him, telling him she loved him, were only palliative, on the surface, and she knew better than to pretend they reached the hurt.

It was the same day that Nobby had called, when she realized what had really hurt her, and what Charlotte was convinced she was going to do about it, that she determined to go and see Harriet herself. Whatever happened, she could hardly make matters any worse, and Harriet, just as much as Matthew, deserved to be told the truth. Her happiness, however much was possible—and that could be a great deal in time—depended on the decision she must make now. She could choose courage, understanding and forgiveness; or she could retreat behind blame, consume herself with anger and outrage, and become a bitter and lonely woman, unloving and unlovely.

But she had the right to know what her choice was in its reality, not the reassuring words of lying comfort.

Charlotte dressed accordingly in a modest but becoming gown of forest green muslin trimmed with blue. It was unusually dark for the summer, and therefore the more striking. She took a hansom to Matthew's rooms, whose address she had found in Pitt's desk, and asked the cabby to wait.

He was startled to see her, but made her welcome. He still looked ill and profoundly unhappy.

Briefly she told him her plan and asked him to accompany her, not into Harriet's home, but at least as far as the street outside.

"Oh no!" He rejected her plan immediately, pain and defeat filling his face.

"If I cannot persuade her, she will never know you were there," she pointed out.

"You won't succeed," he said flatly. "She'll never forgive me."

"Were you wrong?" Charlotte challenged.

"I don't know. . . ."

"Yes you do! You did the only possible thing that was honorable, and you should never doubt it. Think of the alternative. What would that be? To have lied by silence to cover Soames's treason, not because you believed it was right but because you were afraid Harriet would reject you. Could you live with that? Could you keep your love for Harriet if you had paid that price for it?

"No . . ."

"Then come with me and try. Or are you absolutely sure she is too shallow to understand?"

He smiled thinly and picked up his jacket. There was no need to say anything.

She led the way out and this time gave the cabby Harriet Soames's address. When they arrived she gave Matthew's hand a quick squeeze, then alighted, leaving him inside the cab, and climbed the steps. She did not intend to allow herself to be turned away if it was humanly possible, short of creating a scene. She knocked, and when the door was opened, looked the maid very directly in the eye and announced her name, adding that she had something of importance of which she wished to inform Miss Soames, and would be greatly obliged if Miss Soames would consent to receive her.

The maid was gone rather a long time, about five minutes, before returning and saying that she regretted that Miss Soames was unwell and would not be receiving today. If Mrs. Pitt cared to leave a note, she would take it to her mistress.

"No thank you," Charlotte said briskly, but forcing a rather desperate smile. "The matter is personal and very delicate. I shall call again, and again, until Miss Soames is well enough to receive me. I am not prepared to pass it through a third person, nor to commit it to paper. Would you please inform her of that? I am sure Miss Soames is a lady of courage. She could not have the countenance she does and wish to hide from the world forever. To the best of my knowledge, she has not yet anything whatsoever of which to be ashamed—only shame itself, and the desire to run away."

The maid blanched. "I—I can't tell her that, ma'am!"

"Of course you can't." Charlotte smiled even more encouragingly. "But you can tell her that I said so. And if you have any regard for her at all, which I am sure you have, then you will wish her to face the world and defy it. Everyone who is worth anything at all will admire her for it. People take you largely at your own estimation, you know. If you think yourself unworthy, they will assume that you know what you are about, that you are indeed unworthy. Carry your head high and look them in the eye, and unless the evidence is overwhelming, they will assume you are as innocent as you seem. Now please go and tell her what I have said."

"Yes ma'am. Yes, right away, ma'am." And she retreated hastily to do so, her heels clicking on the polished floor.

Charlotte let her breath out in a sigh of momentary relief. That had been a speech worthy of Great-Aunt Vespasia! What she said she believed to be true, but she had spoken with an incredible arrogance and a confidence in herself she was far from feeling.

She stood just inside the entrance in the sunlight, declining to take a seat in the handsome hall, although there were several provided. It seemed an age until the maid returned, although it was probably no more than ten minutes.

"Yes ma'am," the maid said, coming back almost at a trot, her face pink, her manner showing considerable respect. "Miss Soames said that she would make the effort to see you. If you will come this way, please."

Charlotte followed her to a small private sitting room at the back of the house where Harriet was lying on a gold-colored velvet chaise longue, looking dramatically wan, in an afternoon gown of white muslin, her dark hair around her shoulders in undress. It would have been more becoming had there been color in her skin, instead of the rather sallow look it had, indicating a real malady, even if one born of despair.

She looked up at Charlotte and invited her to be seated, dismissing the maid. She made no pretense of offering refreshment.

"Your message was candid to the point of offense, Mrs. Pitt. It is remarkable of you to have felt you had any right to insist upon seeing me. We had the slightest of acquaintance; a few pleasant occasions together do not give you the right to intrude on my grief with threats of harassing me, or calling me a coward. What is it you wish to say that you think warrants such behavior? I cannot imagine what it can be."

Charlotte had thought long and hard about what she would say, but now that the moment was come, it was far more difficult than her worst thoughts had foreseen.

"You have an extremely important choice to make," she began, her voice low and gentle. "One which will affect the rest of your life . . ."

"I have no choice whatsoever," Harriet said bluntly. "Matthew Desmond has removed them all from me. There is only one path open to me now. But that does not concern you, Mrs. Pitt. I suppose I cannot blame your husband for what has happened. After all, he is a policeman and bound to follow his duty. However, I cannot like him for it, nor you, because you are his wife. If we are to speak so plainly, which seems to be your wish, then I will be plain."

"The matter is far too important to be anything less than plain," Charlotte agreed, changing her mind suddenly as to how she would say what she had to. "But if you think I agree with my husband's actions out of loyalty to him, you are mistaken. There are certain things we must believe for ourselves, regardless of what any others may think, be they fathers, husbands, political leaders or men of the church. There is an inner self, a soul, if you like, which is answerable to God, or if you do not believe in Him, then to history, or to life, or merely to yourself, and loyalty to that must supersede all other loyalties. Whatever light of truth you have glimpsed, that must never be betrayed, whatever or whoever else must fall because of it."

"Really, Mrs. Pitt, you—"

"That sounds extreme?" Charlotte cut across her. "Of course there are ways of doing things. If you have to let someone down, deny their beliefs, you owe it to them to do it openly and honorably, to their faces and not their backs, but no one has the right to demand of you a loyalty to them above that to your own conscience. . . ."

"No, of course not, I mean . . . I . . ." Harriet stopped, unsure where her agreement was leading her.

"I used to know a poem at school, written during the Civil War," Charlotte went on. "By Richard Lovelace. It was called 'To Lucasta, Going to the Wars.' There was a line in it—'I could not love thee, dear, so much,/Loved I not honor more.' I laughed at it then. My sister and I would ask, 'Who is Honor Moore?' But I am beginning to understand what it means; at least in my better moments I have a glimpse of it."

Harriet frowned at her, but she was listening.

"The finer a person is," Charlotte continued, "then the more integrity, compassion, and courage they have, and the finer the love they can give you, and I honestly believe also the deeper the love. A shallow vessel holds less, has less from which to give, and you can reach the bottom a lot sooner than you expect or wish to."

Harriet's eyes had not moved from Charlotte's face.

"What are you trying to tell me, Mrs. Pitt?"

"Do you admire a man who does what he believes to be right, indeed knows to be, only when it does not cost him anything?"

"Of course not," Harriet replied quickly. "Anyone can do that. Most people do. Indeed it is in one's own interest to do so. It is only when there is cost involved that there is any nobility, any honor."

"Then your answer in words is quite different from the answer in your acts," Charlotte pointed out, but gently, and with a look of sadness that held no criticism.

"I don't understand you," Harriet said slowly, but her very hesitation showed that perhaps she was beginning to.

"Don't you? Would you have had Matthew do something he knew to be wrong in order to please you? Would you have admired that, loved him for it? If he could do something wrong, betray his country's trust and his colleagues' honor to please you, what else would he betray, to save himself pain or loneliness, if the occasion arose?"

Harriet's face pinched with distress and a terrible conflict of decision.

"Would he lie to you," Charlotte went on, "to save himself from your anger or rejection? Where does he make a stand? What truths or promises are sacred? Or can anything be broken if the pain of keeping it is sharp enough?"

"Stop it!" Harriet said. "You don't need to go on. I know what you mean." She drew in a long breath, twisting her fingers in her lap. "You are telling me I am wrong to blame Matthew for doing what he believed was right."

"Don't you believe it was right?" Charlotte pressed.

Harriet was silent for a long time.

Charlotte waited.

"Yes . . ." Harriet said at last, and Charlotte could guess how much it hurt her. She was in a sense turning her back on her father, admitting he was wrong. And yet it was also a kind of release from the effort of trying to maintain a fiction that tore her reason from her emotion in a conflict which would erode her as long as it lasted. "Yes, yes you are right." She looked at Charlotte through a frown of anxiety. "Do you think he will . . . forgive me for my hasty judgment . . . and anger?"

Charlotte smiled with absolute certainty.

"Ask him," she replied.

"I . . . I . . ." Harriet stammered.

"He is outside." Charlotte smiled in spite of herself. "Shall I ask him to come in?" Even as she said it she moved towards the door. She barely waited to hear Harriet's husky assent.

Matthew was sitting hunched up in the hansom, peering out, his face haggard. He saw Charlotte's expression and eagerness and hope fought with reason in his eyes.

Charlotte stopped beside him. "Harriet says will you please

come in," she said gently. "And Matthew . . . she . . . she has realized her mistake. I think the less that is said of it, the more easily will it have some chance to heal."

"Yes. Yes, of course. I . . ." He gulped. "Thank you!" And then he forgot Charlotte and strode to Harriet's front door and through it without bothering to knock or wait for any answer.

Charlotte walked back down the pavement and quite unashamedly stared in through the front window, where she could just make out the shadows of two figures face-to-face, and the moment after they moved so close they seemed but one together as if never to let go.

When she had returned after seeing Harriet Soames and Matthew, Charlotte was in a buoyant mood, full of elation that the matter had gone so well; but there were other visions to be dealt with, which she was much less certain even as to how to approach, let alone what their resolution might be. It had all begun with the death of Arthur Desmond. Susannah's murder was a tragedy she felt keenly, having known her; but Sir Arthur's death was the one which hurt Pitt, and his grief was interwoven through everything because it was part of his life and could never be set aside or forgotten. And she knew, even through his silences, that there was still guilt in it.

She had the framework of a plan in her mind, but it needed someone to help, someone with access to the Morton Club, who would not in any way be associated with the police but could go there as an innocent and curious member. That person would also, of course, have to be willing to conduct such an enquiry.

The only one she knew who fitted even part of that description was Eustace March, and she was very uncertain if he could ever be persuaded to satisfy the last requirement. Still, there was only one possible way to find out.

Accordingly she sat down and wrote a letter.

"Dear . . ."

She hesitated, confounded as to whether she should address

him as "Uncle Eustace" or "Mr. March." The first seemed too familiar, the second too stiff. Their relationship was unique, a mixture of distant kinship, acute guilt and embarrassment, and finally antagonism over the tragedies at Cardington Crescent. Now it was a sort of truce, nervous and extremely wary on his part.

She wanted his help, needed it. His own estimation of himself was such that he would always leap to assist a woman in distress; it fitted his conception of the respective roles of male and female, and his vision of a righteous and powerful Christian, as well as a beneficent gentleman.

"Dear Mr. March," she wrote.

"Forgive my approaching you so forthrightly, and without any preamble, but I need help with a matter of the utmost moral gravity." She smiled as she continued. "I can think of no one else to whom I could turn with the assurance both of their ability to help, and their willingness to do so with the courage it would require, and the supreme tact. Quick judgment may be called for, great perception of men, and their motives as well as their actual honesty, and possibly even a certain physical presence and authority."

If that did not appeal to him, nothing would! She hoped she had not overstated her case. Pitt would instantly be suspicious of a letter like that. But then Pitt had a sense of humor, and Eustace had not.

"If I may call upon you this evening," she continued, "I shall explain precisely what the trouble is, and how I believe we may solve it to the satisfaction of both honor and justice.

"I have a telephone, the number of which is at the top of the page. Perhaps you would be kind enough to let me know whether it would be convenient for me to call . . . that is if you are willing to come to my assistance?

"Yours with affection and hope, Charlotte Pitt."

She sealed it and stamped it and sent Gracie to put it in the post. It would be delivered that afternoon.

She received the answer by telephone. It was an enthusiastic affirmative, delivered with gravitas and considerable self-assurance, not to say satisfaction.

"Well, my dear lady," he said to her as she was shown into his withdrawing room at Cardington Crescent. "What may I do to be of assistance to you?" He stood in front of the fireplace, even though on such a balmy summer evening there was no fire lit. It was simply a matter of habit and the prerogative of the master of the house to warm himself there all winter, and he did it without thought. "Perhaps if you were to tell me the precise problem?"

She sat in the seat he had offered and tried not to think of the past associations of this place and all the memories of tragedy.

"It is to do with a terrible death," she said, meeting his gaze frankly and endeavoring to look as appealing as possible without any shred of flirtation. "But it is a matter which the police, by virtue of their social standing, or lack of it, are unable to solve. At least, Thomas knows a great deal about it, but the final answer is beyond him, because he has not access to the place where it happened, except as a policeman. So everyone will be on their guard, and observing them will be no good at all." She smiled very slightly. "Besides, some people need to see the authority and natural status of a gentleman before they will respond with the truth. Do you understand what I mean, Mr. March?"

"Of course I do, my dear lady," he said immediately. "It is one of the great drawbacks of being of the social . . ." Just in time he realized he was about to be offensive. His dilemma was plain in his face. "Occupation," he finished, with a flourish at his fortunate extrication. "People are forewarned," he added for good measure. "Where is it that you believe I have entrance?"

"To the Morton Club," she said sweetly. "I know you are a member, because I recall your saying so. Besides, it is the most distinguished gentleman's club, and I am sure you would find yourself welcome there, even as a visitor, were that necessary. No one would question your presence or think you out of place, and I know of no one else who could do that, and who would also have the . . .

forgive me, I do not know how to phrase this without sounding fulsome."

"Please, just be frank with me," he urged. "I shall not criticize either what you say or the way in which you say it. If this is a matter as serious as you intimate, then it would be an unfortunate time to find fault in so small a subject."

"Thank you, you are most understanding. It will take a love of justice and a courage which puts that love before comfort and convenience. Such people are not as common as one would wish."

"Just so," he said sadly. "It is a grim reflection of our times. What, precisely, is it you wish me to do?"

"To find out what happened to Sir Arthur Desmond the afternoon he died . . ."

"But surely that was either an accident, or a suicide." He pulled a very slight face. "To take one's own life was not the act of a Christian, or of a gentleman, unless he had debts he could not pay or had committed a grave dishonor. Or suicide," he finished.

"No, no, Mr. March! That is exactly the point, it was most certainly murder . . . for reasons I shall not go into now." She leaned forward, facing him with an intense look. "It is not unconnected with the death of Mrs. Chancellor." She ignored his look of amazement.

"And with members of the Colonial Office I am not free to name. Indeed, I only know the veriest fraction which I have overheard, but matters where England's interest, and those of the Empire, may have been jeopardized." Now his face was agog and his round eyes wide.

"Sir Arthur was murdered because he drew attention to matters which exposed certain people to suspicion and eventually ignominy," she finished.

"Good gracious! You don't say so!" He drew a deep breath. "Dear lady, are you perfectly sure you have this quite right? It seems . . ."

"Mrs. Chancellor is dead," she pointed out. "And now Mr. Chancellor also. Can you doubt the matter is profoundly serious?"

"No. No, of course not. But the connection . . . ?"

"Is to do with Africa. Will you help me?"

He hesitated only a moment. How could he refuse, and deny himself the opportunity for such gallantry, a noble part in such a matter, perhaps a small place in history?

"Of course," he said enthusiastically. "When shall we begin?"

"Tomorrow, about lunchtime?" she suggested. "Of course, I cannot come into the club. . . ."

"Good gracious no!" he agreed with a look of alarm. Such a thing would be tantamount to sacrilege.

"So I shall be obliged to wait outside in the street," she said with as little irritation as she could manage, although it called for more self-control than she thought she possessed. It was absurd. Why on earth should they all be so appalled at the idea of a woman coming into the club? Anyone would think that they were all sitting around naked! That idea was so amusing she contained her laughter only with difficulty.

He noticed her expression, and his face filled with alarm.

"I hope you are not considering . . ."

"No!" she said sharply. "No, of course not. I shall wait in the street, I assure you. If nothing else will convince you, remember that Thomas has been promoted. I have every interest in behaving with the most perfect decorum to see that I do not in any way embarrass him." That was a major stretching of the truth, but she felt Eustace would believe it.

"Of course, of course." He nodded sagely. "I apologize for having doubted you. Now tell me what information it is you wish?"

"To begin with, to know precisely who was there that afternoon, and where they were sitting, or standing, or whatever it is gentlemen do in their clubs."

"That sounds very simple. Surely Thomas would have learned that from the stewards," he said with satisfaction.

"No, apparently they are so terribly busy waiting on people they don't notice," she responded. "Anyway, people tend to avoid speaking to the police if they can, especially if they fear it might compromise their friends unjustly."

"I quite see the point. . . ." He was dubious.

"But you will not be talking to the police, you will simply be telling me," she pointed out.

She wondered whether she ought to mention Farnsworth's opposition to Thomas's working on the case at all, and decided it was too big a risk to take. Eustace was very impressed by authority. Apart from that, he might conceivably be in the same ring of the Inner Circle, and that would never do.

"Yes, that is certainly true," he agreed, apparently calmed by the thought. After all, who was she, that anyone should mind? "Right." He rubbed his hands together. "Then we shall begin tomorrow morning, shall we say outside the Morton Club at eleven o'clock?"

She rose to her feet. "I am enormously grateful to you, Mr. March. Thank you very much. I have taken the liberty of writing a short description of the principal suspects," she added hastily, passing him a piece of paper. "I am sure it will be helpful. Thank you so much."

"Not at all, dear lady, not at all," he assured her. "In fact I am quite looking forward to it!"

He was not nearly so certain that that was how he felt at ten minutes past eleven the following day when he was actually in the main sitting room of the Morton Club, looking for a place to sit down and wondering how on earth he was to begin such an extraordinary undertaking. To start with, in the cold light of a public place, he realized it was in the most appallingly bad taste. One did not question a fellow member about his acts, whatever they were. It simply was not done. The very essence of the purpose of having a club was in order to remain unquestioned, to have both company and privacy, to be among people of one's own thought, who knew how to behave.

He sat down where Charlotte had told him Sir Arthur had died, feeling a complete fool, and quite sure that his face was scarlet, even though no one took the slightest notice of him. But then people never did in a decent club. He should not have undertaken this, whatever Charlotte Pitt had said! He should have declined politely and kindly, pointing out the impossibility of it, and sent her on her way.

But it was too late now. He had given his word! He was not cut out to be a knight errant. For that matter, Charlotte was not really his choice of a damsel in distress. She was too clever to be satisfactory, much too sharp with her tongue.

"Good morning, sir. May I bring you something?" a discreet voice said at his elbow.

He started in surprise, then saw the steward.

"Oh, yes, er, a small whiskey would be excellent, er ..."

"Yes sir?"

"Sorry, I was trying to recall your name. Seems I know you."

"Guyler, sir."

"Yes, that's right. Guyler. I, er ..." He felt hopelessly self-conscious, a complete ass, but it had to be done. He could not possibly go back to Charlotte and tell her he had failed, that he had not even had the courage to try! No shame here could be worse than that. To confess such cowardice to any woman would be appalling; to her it would be intolerable.

"Yes sir?" Guyler said patiently.

Eustace took a deep breath. "Last time I was here, very end of April, I was talking to a most interesting chap, been all over the place, especially Africa. Knew the devil of a lot about settlement there, and so on. But can't remember his name. Don't think that he ever said. Sometimes one doesn't, you know?"

"Quite, sir," Guyler agreed. "And you were wishing to know who it was?"

"Exactly!" Eustace said with intense relief. "See you understand completely."

"Yes sir. Where were you sitting, sir? That might help. And perhaps if you could describe the gentleman a little. Was he elderly? Dark or fair? A large gentleman, or not, sir?"

"Er ..." Eustace racked his brains to think of how Charlotte had described the main suspects. Unfortunately they were quite unalike. Then a brilliant idea occurred to him. "Well, the gentleman in question was quite bald, with a powerful nose and very clear, pale blue eyes," he said with sudden conviction. "I remember his eyes especially. Most arresting ..."

"Africa, you said?" Guyler asked.

"That's right. You know who I mean?"

"Would you have been in the reading room, sir?"

"Yes, yes, possibly." Deliberately he looked uncertain.

"Then that was likely Mr. Hathaway, sir."

"He was here that day?"

"Yes sir. Not for very long though." Guyler's face clouded. "He was taken unwell, as I recall. He went to the cloakroom, and then I think he went home without coming back into the reading room, and was never in this room at all. Most unfortunate. So maybe it wasn't him, sir. Did you speak with him for long, this gentleman who knew so much about Africa?"

"Well, I rather thought it was a while." Eustace let his imagination loose. He had never lied about anything before. He had been brought up to tell the exact truth about everything, regardless of how unpleasant, or how completely tedious it might be. To invent, with a free conscience, had the sweet taste of forbidden fruit. It could be rather fun! "Actually I think there was another gentleman there with considerable knowledge. In fact he had only lately returned from his travels. Very sunburned, he was. Fair hair, don't you know, but weathered complexion. Tall, lean fellow, military type of bearing. German name, I think, or possibly Dutch, I suppose. Sounded foreign to me, anyway. But English fellow, naturally!"

"Would that be Mr. Kreisler, sir? It sounds uncommonly like him. He was here. I recall it especially because that was the day poor Sir Arthur Desmond died, right here in this very chair you are sitting in. Very sad, that was."

"Oh very," Eustace agreed with alarm. "And yes, you are right, that sounds like the name I recall. Did he know Sir Arthur?"

"Ah, no sir. Sir Arthur was only in this room, and as far as I know, Mr. Kreisler never came out of the reading room. Actually he was there quite a short while anyway. Came to see someone, and then left just after luncheon."

"Never came in here?" Eustace said. "Are you quite sure?"

"Absolutely, sir," Guyler replied with conviction. "Nor Mr. Hathaway either, so I suppose it must have been neither of those two gentlemen. It doesn't seem as if I can be of much assistance, sir. I'm very sorry."

"Oh, don't give up yet," Eustace said urgently. "There were one or two other fellows around who might know him. One was remarkably well read, as I recall, could quote anything, but as plain as you like, short, heavyset, face melted right into his neck." He was using Charlotte's words, and felt artificial doing it. It was not a description he would have chosen. "Round eyes, fat hands, excellent hair," he gabbled, feeling the heat burn up his cheeks. "Good voice."

Guyler looked at him curiously. "Sounds not unlike Mr. Aylmer, sir. And he certainly knows about Africa. He works in the Colonial Office."

"That'd be him!" Eustace said eagerly. "Yes, sounds exactly right!"

"Well he was here that day. . . ." Guyler said thoughtfully. "But seems to me he only came in and went right out again. . . ."

"Ah, but at what time?" Eustace demanded.

"About . . . about noon, sir. Could that not have been him?"

Eustace was warming to this. He was really rather good at it. The evidence was piling up. Come to think of it, it seemed he had something of a talent for it. Pity it was all negative, so far.

"Well, there was another fellow there," he said, looking at Guyler with wide eyes reflecting absolute candor. "Speaking to you reminds me of him. Tall fellow, dark wavy hair, distinguished looking. Gray a bit." He touched the sides of his own graying head. "Can't quite think of his name."

"I'm sorry, sir, that description fits rather a lot of our gentlemen," Guyler said regretfully.

"His name was . . ." Eustace furrowed his brow as if trying to remember. He did not want to lead Guyler too obviously. Lying, of course, was sinful, but invention was rather fun. "Something to do with feet, I think . . ."

"Feet, sir?" Guyler looked confused.

"Reminded me of feet," Eustace elaborated. "Not sounded like feet, you understand?"

Guyler looked utterly confounded.

"Understand . . ." Eustace repeated the word as if it were deeply significant in itself. "Understand . . . stand . . . stand . . ."

"Standish!" Guyler said excitedly, and so loudly that several of the somnolent gentlemen in nearby chairs turned and glared at him. He blushed.

"Astounding!" Eustace said with admiration. "By jove, that's exactly it. How clever of you." Flattery was also a sin, but it was a remarkably useful tool, and it was surprising how the ordinary chap responded to it. And women, of course, were slaves to it. Flatter a woman a trifle, and she could swallow it like cake and do anything for you. "That's absolutely right," he went on. "Standish was his name. Indubitably."

"Well, Mr. Standish was in and out that day, sir," Guyler said with a flush of pleasure at being praised so heartily. "Can't say that

I have seen him since then. But if you would care for me to find him, sir, I am sure Mr. Hathaway is in the club today. He does occasionally come in for luncheon."

"Ah . . ." Eustace was momentarily caught. "Well . . ." His brain raced. "Er, before you trouble Mr. Hathaway, was Mr. Standish in this room on that day, would you know?"

Guyler hesitated.

"Rather a difficult question, I know," Eustace apologized. "Long time ago now. Hate to press you. Asking rather a lot."

"Not at all, sir," Guyler denied it instantly. His memory for gentlemen's faces was part of his stock in trade. "Difficult day to forget, sir, with poor Sir Arthur being found dead, like. I was the one who found him, sir. Dreadful experience."

"It must have been," Eustace sympathized. "Most unnerving for you. Amazing you recovered yourself so rapidly."

"Thank you, sir." Guyler squared his shoulders.

"Er . . . was he? Standish, I mean?" Eustace pressed.

"No sir, I rather think he played a game of billiards with Mr. Rowntree, and then left and went home to dinner," Guyler said with concentration.

"But he was here in the late afternoon?" Eustace tried to keep the excitement out of his voice, and felt he failed.

"Yes sir, I remember that, because of poor Sir Arthur. Mr. Standish was here at the time. Saw him in the hall as he was leaving, just as the doctor arrived. I recall that plainly now you mention it."

"But he didn't come into this room?" Eustace was disappointed. For a moment it had looked as if he had the answer he was seeking.

"No sir," Guyler replied with increasing certainty. "No sir, he didn't. It must have been Mr. Hathaway you spoke to, sir, and you must have been mistaken about the place, if you will forgive me saying so. There is a corner of the green room not unlike this, the arrangement of the chairs and so on. Could it have been there that you had your discussion?"

"Well . . ." Eustace wanted to leave himself open for a rapid redeployment if necessary. "I daresay you could be right. I'll try to clarify my memory. Thank you so much for your help." He fished out a crown and offered it to a delighted Guyler.

"And the whiskey, sir? I'll fetch it immediately," Guyler said.

"Thank you ... yes, thank you." Eustace had no choice but to wait until the whiskey came, and then drink it without indecent haste. To do anything else would draw attention to himself as a man without taste or breeding, a man who did not belong. And that he could not bear. All the same, he was bursting to go and tell Charlotte what he had learned, and in such a remarkably short time. He felt very pleased with himself. It had been accomplished completely, and without raising the least suspicion.

He finished the whiskey, rose to his feet and sauntered out.

Charlotte was on the steps in the sun and quite a sharp breeze.

"Well?" she demanded as soon as he was out of the door and before he was halfway down to the street. "Did you learn anything?"

"I learned a great deal." He grasped her arm and linked it to his, then half dragged her to walk side by side with him up the pavement, so to a passerby they would look like a respectable couple taking a stroll. There was no point whatever in making a spectacle of oneself. After all, he was a member of the Morton Club and would wish to return one day.

"What?" Charlotte said urgently, threatening to stop.

"Keep walking, my dear lady," he insisted out of the corner of his mouth. "We do not wish to be observed as out of the ordinary."

To his surprise the argument seemed to sway her. She fell into step beside him.

"Well?" she whispered.

Glancing at the expression on her face, he decided to be brief.

"Mr. Standish was present that afternoon, and at the appropriate time, but the steward is positive he did not go into the room where Sir Arthur was seated."

"Are you sure it was Standish?"

"Beyond doubt. Kreisler was also there, but left too early, as did Aylmer." They were passed by a man in a pinstripe suit and carrying an umbrella, in spite of the pleasantness of the day.

"However," Eustace went on, "Hathaway was present, but also not in the same room. He was apparently taken ill, and went to the cloakroom, from where he sent for a cab and was helped into it. He never went anywhere near the room where Sir Arthur was either. I am afraid it appears that none of your suspects can be guilty. I'm sorry." Actually he was sorry, not for her, but because although it was a far more suitable answer, it was also an anticlimax.

"Well someone must be guilty," she protested, raising her voice against the noise of the traffic.

"Then it cannot be any of them. Who else might it be?" he asked.

"I don't know. Anyone." She stopped, and since she was still clinging to his arm, he was pulled to a sudden halt also. A middle-aged lady on the arm of an elderly man looked at them with suspicion and disapproval. From her expression it was obvious she had supposed some domestic quarrel which no dutiful wife would have allowed to happen in public.

"Stop it!" Eustace hissed. "This is most unseemly. You are causing people to look at us."

With a great effort Charlotte bit back the response that came to her lips.

"I'm sorry." She proceeded to walk again. "We shall just have to go back and try harder."

"Try harder to do what?" he said indignantly. "None of the people you mentioned could possibly have passed by Sir Arthur and put laudanum in his brandy. Not one of them was even in the same room."

"Well where did the brandy come from?" She did not even think of giving up. "Perhaps they passed it on the way."

"And poisoned it?" His eyes were round and full of disbelief.

"How? Passing by and slipping something into it while it was on the steward's tray? That would be ridiculous. No steward would permit it, and he would certainly remember it afterwards and testify to it. Besides, how would anyone know it was meant for Arthur Desmond?" He straightened his back and lifted his chin a little. "You are not very logical, my dear. It is a feminine weakness, I know. But your ideas are really not practical at all."

Charlotte was very pink in the face. It did cross his mind to wonder for a moment if it was suppressed temper. Not very attractive in a woman, but not as uncommon a trait as he would have wished.

"No," she agreed demurely, looking down at the pavement. "I cannot manage without your assistance. But if there is a flaw in the argument, I know you will find it, or a lie in anyone's testimony, perhaps? You will go back, won't you? We cannot allow injustice to triumph."

"I really cannot think what else I could learn," he protested.

"Exactly what happened, even more exactly than now. I shall be so very grateful." There was a slight quaver in her voice, as of some intense emotion.

He was not certain what it was, but she really was a very handsome woman. And it would be immensely satisfying to place her in his debt. Then he would be able to face her without the almost intolerable embarrassment he felt now. It would wash out the hideous memory of the scene under the bed!

"Very well," he conceded graciously. "If you are convinced it would be of service."

"Oh I am, I am!" she assured him, stopping and turning around, ready to return the way they had come. "I am so obliged to you."

"At your service, ma'am," he said with considerable complacency.

Once inside the Morton Club again he had profound misgivings. There was nothing to find out. He began to feel exceedingly foolish as once more he approached Guyler.

"Yes sir?" Guyler said helpfully.

"Forgive me," Eustace began, feeling the color flush up his cheeks. Really, this was too bad of Charlotte. And he was a fool to have agreed to it. "I fear I am being extremely tedious. . . ."

"Not at all, sir. What can I do for you?"

"Is it not possible that Mr. Standish could have come through here that afternoon, after all?"

"I can make enquiries for you, sir, if you wish, but I think it most unlikely. Gentlemen don't usually leave a game of billiards, sir. It is considered bad form to leave one's opponent standing waiting for one."

"Yes, yes of course. I know that!" Eustace said hastily. "Please don't trouble yourself. I should not like Mr. Standish to imagine I thought him discourteous."

"No sir."

"And, er . . ." He could have sworn under his breath and cursed Charlotte, only the steward would have heard him. He could not get out of it now. This was appalling. "Mr., er . . . Hathaway. You said he was taken ill. That is most unfortunate. When was that? What hour? I don't think I recall that happening."

"Oh it did, sir, I remember it quite plainly. Are you sure you have the right day yourself, sir, if you'll pardon me, sir? Perhaps you were here the day before, or the day after? That would account for a lot."

"No, no, I have the day right. I recall it because of Sir Arthur's death, just as you do," Eustace said hastily. "What was it you said happened to Mr. Hathaway?"

"He was took a bit queer, sir, and went to the cloakroom. Then he must have decided to go home. He'd been there a while, no doubt hoping he'd get to feel better, but seems he didn't, so he rang for assistance, poor gentleman, and one of the stewards went to him. And when he asked for a cab, the cloakroom attendant called him one, and helped him out into the hall and down the steps into it. He never came back into any of the club rooms at all, sir, that is for certain."

"I see. Yes, I see. That wasn't you, by any chance?"

"No sir. Tell you the truth, don't know who it was. Saw him go, but only out of the corner of my eye, so to speak, and I didn't recognize him. Might have been Jones; it looked a lot like him, sort of heavyset and with very little hair. Yes, I think it might have been Jones."

"Thank you, yes I expect it was. Thank you very much." Eustace wanted to end the pointless conversation. Charlotte would have to unravel the meaning of this, if there was any. There was no more for him to learn. He must escape. This was getting worse by the moment.

"Mr. Hathaway is here this afternoon, sir," the steward persisted. "If you like I can take you across to him, sir."

"No . . . no thank you," Eustace said vehemently. "I . . . I think I shall go to the cloakroom myself, if you will excuse me. Yes, yes indeed. Thank you."

"Not at all, sir." Guyler shrugged and went about his errands.

Eustace made his escape and fled to the cloakroom. It was really a very agreeable place, suitably masculine, set out with all the comforts: washbasins with plenty of hot water, clean towels, mirrors, spare razors and strops, shaving soap in two or three different brands, lotions, Macassar oil for the hair, fresh cloths for buffing one's boots, and polish, brushes for its application and removal, and overall a pleasant aroma like sandalwood.

He had no requirement for the water closet, and instead sat down on one of the wooden bench seats that were rather like well-shaped pews. He had had occasion to come here only twice before, but it still seemed pleasantly familiar. Hathaway must have sat here, feeling ill and wondering if he would be able to get home without assistance. Eustace glanced around. There was an ornate bell pull near the door. Nothing was written on it or under it, but its purpose was obvious. Without premeditation he stood up, crossed the couple of steps to it and pulled.

Almost immediately it was answered by an elderly man in a uniform which was less than livery but more than merely a steward.

"Yes sir?" he said quietly. "Is there something I can do for you?" Eustace was taken aback. There really was nothing at all. He thought of Hathaway.

"Are you a steward? You wear a different . . . uniform."

"Yes sir," the man agreed. "I'm the cloakroom attendant. If you wish for a steward I can send for one, but perhaps I can help you, sir. It would be more regular. Stewards attend to gentlemen in the drawing rooms and reading rooms, and so on."

Eustace was confused.

"Doesn't this bell ring on the steward's board in the pantry?"

"No sir, only in my room, which is quite separate, sir. Can't I be of assistance? Are you not feeling well, sir?"

"What? Oh, yes, yes I am perfectly well, thank you. Always well." Eustace's brain raced. Was it possible he was on the brink of discovery? "It is just that a friend of mine, more of an acquaintance, told me that he had been taken unwell here in the cloakroom and had summoned a steward from the drawing room who had called him a hansom." He waited, almost holding his breath.

"No sir," the attendant said patiently. "That is not possible, sir. The bell here doesn't ring in the steward's pantry. It only leads to my board, sir, nowhere else."

"Then he was lying!" Eustace said in triumph.

The attendant looked at him with as much amazement as his duty and position allowed, not at the conclusion—which was unavoidable—but at Eustace's delight in it.

"That seems a harsh judgment, sir. But he was certainly mistaken."

"It was Hathaway," Eustace said, plunging in where only moments before he would not have dared to be so blunt. "The day Sir Arthur Desmond died. Didn't you call him a hansom?"

"Yes sir. One of the temporary stewards told me he was unwell, but I don't know how he knew that."

"You mean one of the attendants? Someone junior to yourself," Eustace said.

"No sir, I mean a temporary steward, from one of the main rooms. Though, come to think of it, I don't know how he knew, if Mr. Hathaway was in here!" He shook his head in denial of the impossible.

"Thank you, thank you! I am most obliged to you!" Eustace fished in his pocket and brought out a shilling. It was excessive; still, it would look so paltry to put it back and hand over a three-penny bit instead, and he was feeling in a highly generous mood. He gave it unstintingly.

"Thank you, sir." The attendant masked his surprise and took it before Eustace could change his mind. "If I can be of any further assistance, please let me know."

"Yes, yes of course." Eustace only glanced at him, then strode out into the foyer and down the front steps to the street.

Charlotte was a few paces away; apparently she had been walking back and forth, maybe in her impatience, perhaps to make her waiting less obvious. She saw the expression of jubilation on his face and ran towards him.

"Yes? What have you found?" she demanded.

"Something quite extraordinary," he said, his excitement fighting his normal manner and the condescension he considered appropriate when speaking to women. "The cloakroom bell does not connect with the steward's pantry or any part of the rest of the club!"

She was confused. "Should it?"

"Don't you see?" He caught her by the arm and began walking. "Hathaway said he called the steward from the cloakroom to fetch him a cab when he was taken ill. The drawing room steward told me that. He saw the steward go. But he couldn't have, because the bell doesn't ring there." He was still gripping her arm firmly as he paced the pavement. "The cloakroom attendant said a steward from the drawing room told him that Hathaway was ill and wanted a cab. Hathaway lied!" Quite unconsciously he shook her gently. "Don't you see? He said he did not come back into the main rooms. At least the steward said he didn't ... but he must have, if he called one of the ordinary stewards to get his cab!" He stopped abruptly, the satisfaction fading a little in his eyes. "Although I'm not quite sure what that proves. . . ."

"What if . . ." Charlotte said, then stopped.

A lady with a parasol passed by, pretending not to look at them, a smile on her face.

"Yes?" Eustace urged.

"I don't know . . . let me think. And please don't grip me quite so hard. You're hurting my arm."

"Oh! Oh . . . I'm sorry." He blushed and let go of her.

"An extra steward . . ." she began thoughtfully.

"That's right. It seems they hire one or two now and then, I suppose if someone is ill or otherwise absent."

"And there was one that day? Are you sure?"

"Yes. The steward I spoke to said he saw one."

"What like?" She ignored two women carrying pretty boxes of millinery and chatting to each other.

"What like?" Eustace repeated.

"Yes! What did he look like?" Her voice was rising with urgency.

"Er . . . elderly, squarish, very little hair . . . why?"

"Hathaway!" she shouted.

"What?" He ignored the man passing by them who looked at Charlotte in alarm and disapproval, and increased his pace.

"Hathaway!" she said, grasping him in turn. "What if the extra steward was Hathaway? What a perfect way to murder someone. As a steward he would be practically invisible! As himself, he goes to the cloakroom saying he is not feeling well. Once in there he changes into a steward's jacket, then returns to the pantry, collects a tray and brandy into which he puts the laudanum, serves it to Sir Arthur, saying it is a gift from someone. Then he says that Mr. Hathaway has been taken unwell in the cloakroom and has rung for assistance, so he establishes that Hathaway was in the cloakroom all the time." Her voice was rising with excitement. "He goes out, changes back into himself, then further to establish that, he leaves directly from the cloakroom. He calls the attendant and has him fetch a hansom and assist him out into it. He has established his own whereabouts, with witnesses, and become invisible long enough to give Sir Arthur a fatal dose of laudanum, virtually unseen. Uncle Eustace, you are brilliant! You have solved it!"

"Thank you." Eustace blushed scarlet with pleasure and satisfaction. "Thank you, my dear." For once he was even oblivious of the giggles and words of a group of ladies in an open landau. Then the brilliance of his smile faded a little. "But why? Why should Mr. Hathaway, an eminent official of the Colonial Office, wish to poison Sir Arthur Desmond, an erstwhile eminent official of the Foreign Office?"

"Oh—" She caught her breath. "That is regrettably easy. By a process of deduction, he must be the executioner of the Inner Circle. . . ."

Eustace's expression froze. "The what? What on earth are you talking about, my dear lady?"

Her face changed. The victory fled out of it, leaving only anger and a terrible sense of loss. It alarmed him to see the fierceness of the emotion in her.

"The executioner of the Inner Circle," she repeated. "At least one of them. He was detailed to kill Sir Arthur, because—"

"What absolute nonsense!" He was appalled. "The Inner Circle, whose name you should not even know, is a group of gentlemen dedicated to the good of the community, the protection of the values of honor and wise and beneficent rule, and the well-being of everyone."

"Balderdash!" she retorted vehemently. "The junior new recruits are told that, and no doubt sincerely believe it. You do, Micah Drummond did, until he learned otherwise. But the inner core of it is to gain power and to use it to preserve their own interests."

"My dear Charlotte . . ." He attempted to interrupt, but she overrode him.

"Sir Arthur was speaking out against them before he died."

"But what did he know?" Eustace protested. "Only what he may have imagined."

"He was a member!"

"Was he? Er . . ." Eustace was confounded, a worm of doubt creeping into his mind.

"Yes. He found out about their intentions to use the Cecil Rhodes settlement of Africa to gain immense wealth for their own members, and he tried to make it public, but no one would listen to the little he could prove. And before he could say any more, they killed him. That's what they do to members who betray their covenants. Don't you know that?"

With a sudden sickening return of memory, Eustace thought of the covenants he had been obliged to make, the oaths of loyalty he had taken. At the time he had thought them rather fun, a great adventure, something like the vigil of Sir Galahad before receiving his spurs, the weaving of good and evil that belongs to high romance, the ordeals of those who dare the great adventures. But what if they had meant them truly? What if they really did mean that the Circle was to come before mother or father, wife or brother or child? What if he had pledged away the right to choose on pain of his life?

She must have seen the fear in his eyes. Suddenly there was gentleness, almost pity, mixed with her anger. Neither of them was even aware of the world around them, the pedestrians who passed within a yard of them on the pavement, or the carriages in the street.

"They count on your secrecy to protect them," she said more softly. "They count on your not breaking your promises, even when you gave them without being aware what they would lead to, or that you might compromise yourself, and betray what you most believe in, your own honor, in their keeping." Her expression hardened into contempt and the anger returned. "And of course they also count on fear. . . ."

"Well, I'm not afraid!" he said furiously, turning back towards the steps up into the club. He was too angry to be frightened. They had taken him for a fool, and even worse than that, they had betrayed his belief in them. They had pretended to espouse all the things in which he most dearly believed, honor and openness, candor, high-minded courage, valor to defend the weak, the true spirit of leadership which was the Englishman's heritage. They had shown him an Arthurian vision, made him believe something of himself, and then they had perverted it into a thing that was soiled, dangerous and ugly. It was an insupportable outrage, and he would not be party to it!

He strode up the steps, hardly aware of Charlotte behind him, swung the doors open and made his way across the foyer without a word to the doorman. He pushed his way through the drawing room doors and accosted the first steward he saw.

"Where is Mr. Hathaway? I know he is here today, so don't prevaricate with me. Where is he?"

"S-sir, I—I think . . ."

"Don't trifle with me, my good man," Eustace said between his teeth. "Tell me where he is!"

The steward looked at Eustace's gimlet eyes and rapidly purpling cheeks and decided discretion was definitely the better part of valor.

"In the blue room, sir."

"Thank you," Eustace acknowledged him, turning on his heel to march back into the foyer. Only then did he remember he was not sure which way the blue room was. "The blue room?" he demanded of a steward who appeared at the pantry door with a tray held up above his head in one hand.

"To your right, sir," the steward answered with surprise.

"Good." Eustace reached the door in half a dozen steps and threw it open. The blue room might once have lived up to its name, but now it was faded to a genteel gray, the heavy curtains blue only in the folds away from the sunlight which streamed in from four long, high windows looking onto the street. Through the decades the brilliance had bleached out of the carpet also, leaving it pink and gray and a green so soft as to be almost no color at all. Portraits of distinguished members from the past decorated the walls in discreet tones of sepia and umber, many of them from the seventeenth and eighteenth centuries. In some the whiteness of a powdered wig was the only distinguishable feature.

Eustace had not been in here before. It was a room reserved for senior members, one of which he only aspired to be.

Hathaway was sitting in a large leather armchair reading the *Times*.

Eustace was too enraged even to consider the impropriety of what he was doing. Greater decencies had been blasphemed against. No one was going to be permitted to hide behind the conventions of a gentleman's club. He stopped in front of Hathaway's chair, put his hands on the *Times* and tore it away, dropping it to one side in a heap of crackling paper.

Every head in the room looked up at the noise. A whiskered general snorted with offense. A banker cleared his throat ostentatiously. A member of the House of Lords (who actually attended now and then) put down his glass in amazement. A bishop dropped his cigar.

Hathaway looked up at Eustace with considerable surprise.

"I am making a citizen's arrest," Eustace announced grimly.

"I say, old chap . . ." the banker began.

"Somebody robbed you, old boy?" the bishop asked mildly. "Pickpocket, what? Cutpurse?"

"Bit high-handed, taking a fellow's newspaper," the earl said, regarding Eustace with disfavor.

Hathaway was perfectly composed. He sat quite still in the chair, ignoring the wreck of his paper.

"What is it that has disturbed you so much, my dear fellow?" he said very slowly. At another time Eustace might not have noticed the hard, unflinching quality of his eyes, but all his senses were sharpened by his outrage. Now he felt almost as if Hathaway might offer him physical violence, and he was poised, ready to react, even to welcome it.

"Yes I have been robbed," he said fiercely. "Of trust, of . . . of . . ." He did not know how to express the feeling he had of having been used, insulted, then suddenly it came to him in a rush of words fraught with pain. "I have been robbed of my belief in my fellows, of those I admired and honored, even aspired to be like! That's what you've taken. You've destroyed it, betrayed it."

"My dear fellow!" the banker protested, rising to his feet. "You are overemotional. Sit down and calm yourself. You are making a mistake. . . ."

"You are making a damned noise!" the general said angrily, his whiskers bristling. "I know that, sir!" He shook his newspaper with a snap and buried his head in it again.

"Come on, old chap." The banker took another step towards Eustace and put his hands forward as if to restrain him. "A good douse of cold water and you'll feel better. I—"

"I am as sober as a judge," Eustace said between his teeth. "And if you touch me, sir, if you put one hand on me, I swear by God I shall lay you flat. This man"—he was still looking at Hathaway—"has committed murder. I am not speaking figuratively but quite literally. He cold-bloodedly and intentionally took the life of another man by poison."

This time no one interrupted him. Hathaway sat smiling very slightly, composed, tolerant.

"Poisoned his brandy right here in the club. . . ."

"Really . . . Come now," the bishop spluttered. "That's . . ."

Eustace glared at him and he faded into silence.

"You are the executioner!" Eustace swung back to Hathaway. "And I know now how you did it! You went to the cloakroom and changed into a steward's jacket, then came back into the main room, gave poor Sir Arthur his poisoned drink, which you had prepared, then went back to the cloakroom. . . ." He stopped. He could see by the sudden whiteness of Hathaway's face that he was no longer sure of himself. He was shaken; for the first time he was afraid. The secret he had trusted to protect him was not secret anymore. Eustace saw the fear in his eyes, and now he saw also the violence. The mask was gone.

"I am arresting you for the poisoning to death of Arthur Desmond. . . ."

"Absolute nonsense," the earl said levelly. "You are drunk, sir. Arthur Desmond took his own life, poor devil. We shall forget this appalling behavior of yours, March, if you withdraw this on the spot and resign your membership."

Eustace turned to face him, recognizing another member of the Circle, by act if not by feature. "If that is what you wish, sir," he said without giving an inch, "then it must be that you are equally guilty with Hathaway. You have perverted your power, sir, and betrayed all that is best in England, the people who trusted you and whose labor and belief gave you the very position you now abuse."

Hathaway had risen to his feet and made to move past Eustace. The earl took Eustace's arm in a tight grip and pulled him sideways.

Eustace was outraged. He was of a robust physique, and a disciple of good health. He landed a powerful and well-placed punch on the jaw of the earl and sent him crashing backwards into one of the armchairs.

Hathaway lunged past to escape, swinging a hard kick at Eustace which landed on his shin with acute pain. Eustace swung around and dived after him, catching him in a tackle which would have been cheered to the echo in his rugby-playing days. They both went down onto the floor in a crash, kicking over a small table, splintering one of its legs, and sending a tray of cups and saucers flying to break in shards all over the carpet.

The door was thrust open and a horrified steward stared with utter dismay at the earl spread-eagled across the chair, and Eustace and Hathaway locked in desperate combat on the floor, thrashing around grunting and gasping, arms flailing and legs kicking. He had never witnessed a scene like it in all his life and he had no idea what to do. He stood in an agony of indecision.

The general was shouting out commands no one was obeying. The bishop was making noises of disapproval and muttering something about peace and wisdom, and was totally ignored.

Out in the hallway, a judge of the Queen's Bench demanded to know what was going on, but no one would tell him.

Someone sent for the manager. Someone else sent for a doctor, assuming that one of the members had taken a fit and was being restrained, with difficulty. An advocate of temperance was delivering a monologue, and one of the stewards was praying.

"Police!" Eustace shouted as loudly as his lungs would bear. "Send for the police, you fool! Bow Street . . . Inspector Pitt." And with that he hit Hathaway as hard as he could on the point of the jaw, and his left foot caught the table on the other side and sent it hurtling sideways into the trolley. There was a final crash as a decanter of brandy and half a dozen glasses smashed on the wooden floor at the edge of the carpet.

Hathaway subsided into unconsciousness, his body limp, his eyes closed.

Eustace did not entirely trust him. "Get the police," he ordered again, struggling upright to sit astride Hathaway's chest.

The steward in the doorway hastened to obey. That at least was an order he both understood and agreed with. Whatever was going on, the police were obviously needed, even if it was only to remove Eustace himself.

Then he was face-to-face with the impossible, the worst offense of all. There was a woman standing in the doorway staring into the blue room and watching the appalling scene, a young woman with chestnut-colored hair and a very handsome figure, and—although her eyes were wide with amazement—she was also on the verge of laughter.

"Madam!" the bishop said in horror. "This is a gentleman's

club! You are not permitted in here. Please, madam, observe the decencies and take your leave."

Charlotte looked at the debris of broken china and crystal, spilled coffee and brandy, the splintered furniture, the overturned chair, the earl with his collar askew and a bruise fast purpling on his cheek, and Eustace sitting astride the still senseless form of Hathaway on the floor.

"I always wondered what you did in here," she said mildly, but there was a lift in her voice, and a slight huskiness that threatened to erupt in giggles. She arched her eyebrows very high. "Extraordinary," she murmured.

The bishop said something completely unholy.

Eustace was beyond embarrassment. He was flushed with victory both moral and physical. "Has anyone sent for the police?" he asked, looking at each in turn.

"Yes sir," one of the stewards said immediately. "We have a telephone. Someone is on their way from Bow Street right now."

Charlotte was bundled out and persuaded to wait in the foyer, and that only on sufferance. The blue room was out of bounds. For goodness' sake, it was out of bounds even to junior members!

Eustace refused to leave Hathaway, especially when he regained consciousness (albeit with a profound headache), although he remained silent and made no protest or defense.

When Pitt arrived he found Charlotte first of all, who told him that Eustace had solved the case, adding modestly that she had given him some assistance and direction, and that he had the murderer under citizen's arrest.

"Indeed," Pitt said dubiously, but when she explained to him precisely how it had come about, he was generous in his praise, both of her and of Eustace.

Some fifteen minutes later Hathaway, under arrest and manacled, was put in a hansom cab to the Bow Street station, and Eustace emerged to receive the praise of his fellows. Charlotte was sent home, under protest, in a hansom.

On the journey towards Bow Street, Pitt sat in the cab beside Hathaway. Hathaway was manacled and unarmed, but still in his quiet face with its long nose and small, round eyes there was a sense of strength. He was afraid—he would be a fool not to be— but there was nothing of weakness in his expression, no suggestion that he would break the covenants by which he too was bound to the Inner Circle.

This was the man who had murdered Arthur Desmond. It was Hathaway who had slipped the laudanum into the brandy and passed it to him, and then discreetly left, knowing what would happen. But it was the whole senior hierarchy who was guilty of his death. Hathaway had carried out the sentence. But who had pronounced judgment, who had given the orders that Hathaway had obeyed?

That was the man Pitt wanted. That was the only justice which would be enough to take to Matthew, and more importantly still, to ease the ache of guilt within himself and allow him to rest with the memory of Sir Arthur.

He believed he knew who it was, but even certainty was futile without proof.

He glanced sideways at the silent, almost motionless figure of Hathaway. The small blue eyes looked back at him with biting intelligence and hard, ironic humor. Pitt knew in that moment that whatever fear Hathaway might have, whatever beliefs of death or what lay beyond it, loyalty to the Inner Circle would supersede them all, and would remain unbroken.

He shivered, cold with a new perception of the power of the oaths that bound the society, far more than a club or an association. It was mystic, almost religious, the vengeance for betrayal more than merely human. Hathaway would hang alone rather than speak even a word that would lead to another.

Or did he imagine that even now some other member, someone as high as a judge, would somehow contrive his escape from the rope?

Was even that possible?

He must not allow it, for Arthur Desmond's sake, if nothing else. Pitt looked at him again, meeting his eyes and holding them in a long, steady stare. Neither of them spoke. It was not words, arguments, he was seeking, it was emotion and beliefs.

Hathaway did not flinch or look away, and after several seconds the corners of his mouth turned upwards in a very tiny smile.

In that moment Pitt knew what he must do.

When they reached Bow Street they alighted. Pitt paid the cabby and with Hathaway still manacled, led him inside past the openmouthed desk sergeant who leapt to attention.

"Is Mr. Farnsworth there yet?" Pitt demanded.

"Yes sir! I sent the message to 'im like you told me, sir—that you was off to make an arrest for the murder of Sir Arthur Desmond. . . ."

"Yes?"

"And he came straightaway, sir. He's been here about ten minutes, maybe. And Mr. Tellman is here, sir, as you said, sir."

"Is Mr. Farnsworth in my office?"

"Yes sir. And Mr. Tellman's in his room too."

"Thank you." Pitt felt a sudden surge of excitement, and at the same time a hardening of fear inside him, as if a hand had closed into a fist in his chest. He turned and strode up the stairs, almost pushing Hathaway ahead of him. At the top he flung his office door open and Farnsworth swung around from where he had been standing at the window. He saw Hathaway and although his expression did not flicker, the blood drained from his skin, leaving it blotched, white around the eyes and mouth.

He parted his lips as if about to speak, then changed his mind.

"Good morning, sir," Pitt said calmly, as if he had noticed nothing. "We've got the man who murdered Sir Arthur Desmond." He smiled and nodded at Hathaway.

Farnsworth's eyebrows rose. "He did?" He allowed his surprise to border on incredulity. "Are you sure?"

"Absolutely," Pitt said calmly. "We know precisely how he did it, and have all the witnesses. It is just a matter of piecing it together. Very clever and very efficient."

"Are you," Farnsworth said coldly.

"No sir, I meant Hathaway's means and method." Pitt allowed himself to smile. "Only a chance observation of stewards' bells on a board caught him. But it's enough." He looked at Farnsworth guilelessly.

Farnsworth came forward and took Pitt by the arm, guiding him towards the door.

"Speak to you privately, Pitt," he said tersely. "Call a constable to wait in here and keep guard."

"Of course," Pitt agreed. "I'll get Tellman." It was what he had intended anyway, and would have contrived if Farnsworth had not.

"Yes sir?" he asked as soon as they were in an adjoining office with the door closed, and Tellman with Hathaway.

"Look, Pitt, are you sure you have the right man?" Farnsworth said seriously. "I mean, Hathaway's a respected official in the Colonial Office, a thoroughly decent man, father in the church . . . son too. Why on earth would he wish Desmond any harm? He didn't even know the man, except by sight as a fellow club member. Maybe you have the right means and method, but the wrong man?"

"No sir. It was not a personal motive. Knowing him by sight was all that was needed."

"What on earth . . ." He trailed off, staring at Pitt's face.

"Quite simple." Pitt met his eyes, keeping all subtlety out of his own. Not a thread of suspicion must enter Farnsworth's mind. "Sir Arthur was killed because he broke the oath of the Inner Circle and betrayed them."

Farnsworth's eyes widened almost imperceptibly.

"And Hathaway was the executioner deputed to deal with the matter," Pitt went on. "Which he did, with coldness and precision."

"Murder!" Farnsworth's voice rose with disbelief, a high, hard note in it. "The Inner Circle doesn't murder people! If Hathaway did indeed kill him, then there must have been some other reason."

"No sir, as you just pointed out, he did not even know him in any personal sense. It was an execution, and we can prove it." He hesitated only an instant. Please God he could trust Tellman. But if there were any man in the police force he would stake his life on as not being a member of the Inner Circle, it was Tellman. He took precisely that chance now, facing Farnsworth squarely. "But it will all come out in the trial."

"If the society were what you say, Pitt, then Hathaway would die without telling anyone what you charge," Farnsworth said with certainty and faint derision.

"Oh, I don't expect Hathaway to admit it," Pitt replied with the shadow of a smile. "I am sure you are right. He will go to the gallows without betraying his fellow members. We may never know who they are," he said slowly, meeting Farnsworth's eyes. "But every man and woman in London who can read a newspaper will know what they are! That we can prove, and we will do, in open court."

"I see." Farnsworth took a very deep breath and let it out. He looked at Pitt with something like surprise, as if he had done more than he had foreseen. "I would like to speak to him myself for a few moments, alone, if you don't mind." It was delivered with courtesy, but it was an order. "I find all this . . . distressing . . . hard to believe."

"Yes sir, of course. I've got to go back to the Morton Club anyway, and make sure of the steward's evidence, and see what happened to the other witnesses."

"Yes, by all means do that." And without waiting any further, Farnsworth went out of Tellman's room and back along the passage to Pitt's office. A moment later Tellman came out and looked questioningly at Pitt.

Pitt held his finger to his lips, walked noisily down the stairs half a dozen steps, then crept back up to stand motionless beside Tellman.

They waited for what seemed an endless five minutes, ears straining, hearts thumping so violently Pitt could feel his body shake.

Then the faint murmuring of voices ceased from behind the office door and there was a very soft thud.

Pitt flung the door open, Tellman barely a step behind him.

Farnsworth was on the floor almost astride the prone figure of Hathaway. The paper knife from Pitt's desk was protruding from Hathaway's chest and his manacled hands were just below it, but it was Farnsworth's fingers which were now clenched around it, and his body's weight behind the blow.

Tellman gasped.

Farnsworth looked up, his face slack with disbelief for an instant, then horror. He started to speak.

"He . . . he took the paper knife. . . ." he began. "I tried to stop him. . . ."

Pitt stepped a little aside.

"You murdered him!" Tellman said with amazement and fury. "I can see it!"

Farnsworth turned from Pitt to Tellman, and recognized the incorruptible outrage in his eyes. He looked back at Pitt.

"Giles Farnsworth," Pitt said with satisfaction he had seldom felt in the solution of any case, "I arrest you for the murder of Ian Hathaway. I must warn you that anything you say will be taken down, and may be given in evidence at your trial . . . which I will make very sure you live long enough to face, for Arthur Desmond's sake."